Exordium

Moarte's Maw (Devil's Maw)—Europea

'Blazing Wheels'

"Behind us!" Sentinel Askivar screamed over at Sentinel Octvaian Izbasa. Octvaian whipped his head around to see what had spooked his partner, his mouth dropping open in shock and horror. The darkness had spawned a dozen riders that were bearing down on them rapidly. He, like his fellow Sentinels, had been so fixated on entering the Devil's Maw that they had not been paying attention to their fields of vision — a potentially fatal mistake for all of them.

"It's the Spiriduş!" Octvaian screamed back. Their mission, which was now in jeopardy due to the Spiriduş, was to get the cargo safely to their destination, Hişoaraga.

Octvaian noticed Sentinel Beryx, the wagon driver, looking back at him with an equally grim look. "Time to see if that mad inventor's creation was worth all the time and effort to install it. You guys know what to do — rip it up. Let's show these fools just how foolish they really are!"

Octvaian shared the same opinion as the driver. They were lucky — Beryx was the best driver that the Sentinels had. If they had any chance to escape, the right man was driving the horses.

"How did they know? How do they always know?" lamented Askivar to him. Octvaian silently agreed. Had the Spiriduş infiltrated the Sentinels? But that couldn't be— could it? The two sides hated each other; they had been at each other's throats since before he had joined the Sentinels. That hate was quickly galloping towards them with a collective evil grin spread across its many faces.

"Weapon up" Octvaian yelled to Askivar, who nodded back. They set to work to prepare the wagon's defense.

Secretly the wagon had been heavily modified in preparation for the night's trip. No one had known except for a handful of people. It wasn't until Octvaian showed up at the Ironworks in the early morning that he had learned what had been done. They had drilled for hours, getting as proficient as possible in the short amount of time they had using the weapon. Something had been puzzling him the entire time. He was an outcast in the Sentinels, yet he had been tasked to partake in something so secretive. *Why?* Unless…they had expected the weapon to fail. Was he considered expendable? Were they a *suicide squad*? Perhaps all this was an elaborate decoy. The real wagons with their cargo were taking a secret route. Too many questions, no time for answers, he thought, unlatching the espringal from the wagon floor.

He glanced over at Askivar, who was unbolting the extra side boards which would become makeshift walls for protection. The wagon had picked up considerable speed. Was Beryx going to drive full speed into the Devil's Maw? If they made it, though, they would be free. Hişoaraga was located just on the other side of the mountain. The Spiriduş had never attacked close to any village or city. He did not suspect they would start now.

"Help!" Askivar called out to him. Octvaian helped him slide another side panel up and together they titled it up, and then bolted it. It was high enough to protect them up to their neck, so they still had an unobstructed view of their immediate area. He quickly inspected the panels, making sure they had done it right. He was grateful for the speed at which it had gone up as he heard thuds against the side of one of the walls.

They were being shot at.

Most of the moonlight was blocked out by the clouds, but it was still light enough to navigate and return fire. Octvaian steeled his nerves for what was to come. He had never been engaged in mortal combat before. Even though their assailant's intent was to kill them, he was still uneasy about killing another person.

Acknowledgments

To my family and friends who supported me along the way that were instrumental part of this book's creation, ***thank you.***

Special mention to those below who helped bring Soul Moon Draw to life.

Terry Bolinger; President of Zane Grey West Society who helped me on my path to gain permission to use the character Jim Lacy©

Grey Murphy; the great-great grandson of Zane Grey who gave me permission to use the character, Jim Lacy©

Adaptive Studios; who granted my continued use of the character

Jess Shulman; who was my chapter one editor who helped me understand structure

Katrina Tortorici; my book editor who worked magic bringing the book to what it become.

Clarissa Kezen; book cover designer who worked her magic to create the amazing cover.

To my readers, I hope you enjoyed reading this as much as I did to create this world.

To those that leave comments, whether they be good, bad and everything in-between, ***thank you.***

Soul Moon Draw

Ronald Hall

Several more cross-bolt arrows thudded against the wagon's walls. "Ready?" Askivar asked him. Nodding back grimly, Octvaian knew it was time for business. During testing earlier, he had been the best shot, hence the espringal was his to command. It had been modified to shoot "special" vireton bolts. Instead of the standard bolts, they were shooting ceramic-tipped bolts loaded with black powder that also had a fuse delay. They would explode with a spectacular *BOOM*. Attached to the sides of the cross-bolt shaft were seven small steel-shafted arrows.

Even if the vireton missed its target, the hope was that one of the smaller shafts would make up the difference by hitting something strategic from the resulting explosion. In theory, it sounded good to him. He had been able to fire five off for practice. The results had been most impressive.

The sides of the wagon walls were designed so the espringal could push through the wall. When unbolted from the wagon floor, the weapon could slide up and down and side to side. It could be rolled to the other side of the wagon if required by the unique wheel system built into the wagon walls. It was genius. Octvaian nodded to Askivar, who unlocked the wheels while he pushed the barrel through, making an opening in the wagon's walls. It had been designed so the shafts could feed through the bottom, as once the barrel was out, it would be impossible to reload from the top. "Load!" he bellowed. He watched Askivar hastily ram the vireton into place.

Octvaian double cranked it. He nodded to Askivar, who had lit a wooden rod and touched it to the small fuse on the ceramic jar to light it. He aimed it towards the nearest rider. He could see the look of confusion on the man's face wondering what was going on. He knew there was a decent blast radius, so he didn't have to be perfect. Closer, closer… "*Now!*" his mind screamed as he pressed the trigger.

The ceramic fuses had a short delay before they exploded. Unfortunately, they were not effective long range. The viretons were painted black, including the ceramic bowl. Octvaian had been told that it would make them harder to see. He had to admit they had been right, as he had hard time tracking it. "Come on," he whispered, and was almost instantly rewarded with a tremendous *boom*. He saw two of their would-be attackers propelled through the air headfirst.

"Yesssss!" he cried out in victory.

Beside him, Askivar exclaimed, "Damn, that was awesome! Keep doing that all night and I just may take back all those mean things I ever said about you to your face…and behind your back." Octvaian wondered if Askivar meant it or was just caught up in the heat of the moment.

If they didn't make it through the Devil's Maw alive, it wouldn't matter anyway.

"Reload. Damn all this trouble for some pots and pans!" He screamed to Askivar, who quickly got to work feeding the weapon. He was too old to be doing this anymore. Didn't being a Sentinel for over ten years mean he earned to be his own bed every night? It was almost his thirty-fourth birthday. His plan was to spend it with Deidra. He had been saving his atria for months. He had spoken to her more than once to make sure nothing had changed.

She had told him how special she felt that he had chosen to spend his birthday with her. She even had something extra special planned for him. There was something about her, behind those emerald eyes that dazzled when she smiled. He was bound to make her his wife. It didn't bother him that she was married before, or what she did. Everyone had to make a living, which was why he was still with the Sentinels. If he made it through this night, he would go to her, sweep her up and over his shoulders, and take her to a better life, with him.

"We need to get through the Devil's Maw, push the horses harder!" He heard Askivar yell to Beryx.

The Devil's Maw was an opening in the mountain which lead to Hişoaraga, their destination. Inside the opening was a massive cavern with a thick, naturally formed rock bridge, underneath which flowed hot, flesh melting lava. The lava glowed blood red through the Maw. Approaching the Maw in the dark, there looked to be two large demonic eyes watching him as he neared. The opening itself wasn't large. There was crystalized stalactite that hung downwards. It gave the Maw an illusion of vicious-looking teeth to match the fiery glowing eyes.

The cave was considered unnatural for good reason. Both sides of the mountain looked identical upon entering. No one believed either side formed naturally. Octvaian had heard stories from other Sentinels that they had seen large black, demonic creatures come out of the lava stream to chase their caravans. He had never seen such a creature. To go through it wasterrifying enough. He glanced over at Askivar, seeing the same terrified look on him that he knew he had too.

"Damnit. I hate this part." Beryx grumbled to him. He didn't know if he was more scared of the Spiriduş, which were trying to run them down and kill them, or of entering the Devil's Maw.

"It's getting exciting now!" Octvaian cried out, trying to rally his comrade's spirits.

But Askivar seemed in no mood. "Exciting? On second thought, even if we do live, I ain't taking anything back I ever said about you!"

Octvaian sighed heavily. Spying the next target, he yelled, "Light that bad boy up!" and watched as Askivar lowered the flame to the vireton.

Octvaian slid the espringal hard to the other side of the wagon. The movement caught the approaching rider off guard. Striking the hammer down, the vireton launched toward its target. The rider was startled, tried to swerve the best he could, but the momentary hesitation had already killed him. Octvaian watched the horse try to do what its master commanded, but it stumbled going down face first. Its rider flew forward and took the full blast to the face. *Booyah!* As a bonus, Octvaian saw the horse get up and run off. He was happy the horse was not seriously hurt. "Quicker on the espringal, our damn lives depend on it!" Beryx screamed at them.

Knowing the driver was right, he cursed himself for being so distracted. "How much longer until we're at the Devil's Maw?" Octvaian yelled back as he scanned for his next victim.

"Not quick enough for my liking." was Beryx's reply to him.

The riders were now keeping their distance, though still taking pot-shots at the wagon, no doubt hoping for a lucky shot. Rolling the espringal from side to side, Octvaian knew with any shot now the riders would have time to swerve out of the way at the distance they were at. What were they doing? If they had been scared off, why were the riders still pursuing from a distance?

"Something's wrong!" Octvaian yelled out to his partners.

"It's all wrong!" Askivar yelled back at him.

"That's not what I mean. Why aren't they attacking harder? What's the purpose other than to scare us?" he growled back.

Beryx jumped in. "Maybe that's just it—because they saw us and were bored out of their skulls, so figured, why the hell not. Though, they didn't know about our secret weapon. You could tell they were surprised as sudden mule kick. Serves them right, too."

Damn straight, Octvaian thought, looking at the riders. The Spiriduş were still weaving behind them but not getting any closer. They had taken up a large reverse arrowhead position behind them.

They were being herded into the Devil's Maw.

"It's a trap!" he yelled. "If we try to swerve away from the Maw, they got us. They are forcing us to go through the maw, which means they have something planned on the other side." Damned if they did, damned if they didn't. Octvaian banged his fist hard against the wagon wall.

"Settle down, boy! We are not finished yet!" Beryx yelled back at him. When we get to the other side, we will show them the same surprise that these fools got. Get the espringal prepared to shoot forward, we are about to go through. Let's break their formation just in case something else goes wrong. Get those flasks going and light up their life."

Nodding back, Octvaian noticed the eerie red glow coming up fast. *Crap!* There were two long ceramic flasks that ran the length of the wagon that had three spouts that pointed in different outward directions on each side. Both Askivar and him uncorked the flasks, and oil started to spew out from each opening. They looked over at each other and nodded.

Octvaian watched Askivar light the main spout, and the oil caught fire. He did the same on his side, his oil now fired up, too. He grinned seeing the riders' startled reactions to the streams of fire spewing from the wagon as the riders backed off, widening the gap between them and the wagon.

Octvaian positioned the espringal to the right of Beryx's head. "Lock it!" Octvaian yelled at Askivar. He heard the click.

Askivar tapped him on the shoulder, and he nodded back in return. Looking up at the "eyes" staring at them sent a cold shiver down his back—he swore they were staring back at him.

"Hang on," Beryx called out to them. Octvaian braced himself. Even though there was light glowing from the cave, the path ahead was pitch black. It was as if the path was sucking in all the light touching it. He had only gone through once before in the darkness. Even though nothing had happened, he had never been more terrified in his life.

"You got the path memorized right?" he asked Beryx.

"You know it. I can do this in my sleep." Beryx said back as he cracked the whip, driving the horses forward.

In a blink, the world went black. Every hair on his body stood on end.

"Yeah, Yeah! That's it, my beauties. It's only the darkness. Just listen to my soothing voice." Octvaian heard Beryx calmly reassure the horses.

Glancing over to where Askivar should have been, he couldn't see the man— only feel the fear emanating from him.

"That's right my beauties, almost there... When we get out of here, Daddy's going to get you a special treat." Beryx said in the darkness. The man had balls and was as batshit crazy as he had heard. If they got through this, he would buy Beryx all the Blood Cider he wanted as a thank you.

"Ahhhhh, frack, frack, frack!" Askivar cried out, terror in his voice which in turn freaked him out even more than he thought possible.

Glancing around trying to spot what was freaking out his partner, Octvaian saw glowing red eyes looking back at him. He recoiled in terror. They looked like they were bobbing up and down alongside the wagon.

They were unnatural.

"Ahhh!" he blurted, stumbling back into Askivar, who yelled back, startled.

"Get ready on the espringal, we should be out momentarily." Beryx called back to him.

Whew, Octvaian thought to himself as he pulled himself to his feet. He felt the shaft and double cranked it. His hands found the trigger next. He looked around and still couldn't see a damn thing. "See if you can find the lighting stick, then light it." he said to Askivar. The stick had been treated so when someone struck it, it would just light. "Looking!" was the frantic reply he got.

The lighting stick lit brightly for a second and then just as quickly went dark. It wasn't working. They were going to have to just get through to the other side, then deal with whatever trap was waiting for them. What kind of trap were they barreling into?

"I'm going to count it down as we leave the cave…get ready to fire…5…4…3…2…1…Now!" Beryx screamed at him.

Octvaian was able to make out shapes instantly. His worst fears had come true.

There were wagons spread out with eighteen Spiriduş men. It didn't matter which way they turned, there was no escape.

"Light the damn vireton. We are going to try to punch a hole. See those two wagons off to the left? Shoot there!" Beryx commanded him. "We are going through!" Octvaian took aim as Askivar lit the vireton.

Hammering down on the trigger, Octvaian watched it spring to life, past Beryx's head. His aim had been true. There was an opening between two wagons now. They cheered.

His excitement was interrupted as he found himself flying though the air. The wagon was lifted from the ground. The Sentinels launched into the air.

After what seemed like an eternity, he crashed to the ground. He tumbled across the ground. His body screamed in pain from the impact. He attempted to stand up but crumbled to his knees. The cave around him spun. His head felt woozy…what had happened to them? Trying to focus, he saw the destroyed wagon and two bodies limp on the ground.

"Askivar? Beryx? You guys okay?" he cried out as he stumbled towards them. Feeling his body for anything that might be sticking through it, he was thankful there was nothing protruding.

An unfamiliar voice answered his question. "Such concern for his fellow Sentinels, how touching." Octvaian heard loud laughter from at least a dozen voices. "Unfortunately, during your quick nap, your comrades in arms decided that death was preferable to being traitors. I applauded their bravery and laughed at their foolishness. Sentinels these days, I tell you boys", the unfamiliar voice added, and he heard more laughter ring out.

As he slowly got to his feet, a stocky bald man stared at him with an amused look on his face. And he knew who the man was. Preslav, the leader of the Spiriduş.

Preslav was physically impressive and quite the sight, as the man's face was heavily scarred. Octvaian had heard he had survived a physical confrontation with Victor Drăculeşti during a heated confrontation and had paid for it dearly.

"Traitor!" Octvaian spat at the man, who in turn chuckled at his outburst. He hadn't met Preslav before, but he had seen him from a distance. Preslav had been the leader of the Sentinels years ago. Anger swelled inside of him. Vengeance burning, he grinned, silently swearing that he would get it, if he could figure out how to survive this encounter.

"Your 'toy' was an unpleasant surprise for my men. Not to mention those trails of fire. I gotta admit, I was impressed as hell. Trust me, though, we are going to put those inventions to good use and make some minor…tweaks," Preslav said with a grin, then walked up to him and punched him straight in the face.

Octvaian's world spun. Why were there three Preslavs? He felt weak in the knees. "That was for the cost of my men's lives. I should kill you, but that would be too easy. I know who you are, Sentinel Octvaian Izbasa. I know that you are an outcast, yet you stay to serve. I don't know whether you're stupid or desperate, or perhaps both. In the end, it really isn't going to matter—you will return to the Sentinels and tell them that you somehow managed to survive another encounter with the Spiriduş.

"Tell me, how does it feel to be the most mocked man in Sentinel history? Do you wear it like some badge of honour?" Preslav spat at him.

"I have my honour." Octvaian snarled back. Preslav laughed, and everyone joined in, fueling Octvaian's rage. "Night night, sweetness," Preslav taunted, and winked blowing him a kiss along with a massive fist coming down on his face. Octvaian's last thought before darkness overtook him was of Deidra, imagining her soft arms wrapped around him.

***

"He is quite handsome, even in death," Chione said to her sister, Xifeng. The latter was of stark contrast to Chione, in every way: her flowing black hair mirrored the personality within. Even the hanfu Xifeng wore was as black as night with only a tinge of crimson highlights on the cuffs and belt, which kept the robe snug. Xifeng's eyes had once been a dazzling emerald green, but over time, the light in them had faded.

"Adequate," Xifeng commented back to her. *More than adequate,* Chione thought, but her sister had her own opinions. Chione golden eyes radiated like a hot sun in the sky: full of passion. Her galebiya styled dress was tan with a gold-trimmed neckline that highlighted her pale skinned complexion. Her gold mesh headpiece sat snuggly on her bald head. "There is just no pleasing you, is there, sister?"

"I know, I know…all work and no play." Xifeng said with a sigh. Chione was disappointed she was not able to get more of a response. Since her sister was slowly and painfully killing her good mood, it was best to get their task done. Looking down at the dead Sentinels, Chione knew they would serve their purpose well. The deception would be flawless.

Chione kneeled, leaned over the corpse, running her hand through the bloodied, blonde hair and gently stroked the cold, decaying face, smiling gently at its lifelessness.

"Askivar…time to wake up." Chione whispered. The man's eyes flared open in shock, and she put her finger to his lips. "Shhhhh. It's okay, Askivar. You…took a nap of sorts. What do you remember?" She waited patiently for the Sentinel's senses to return. The answers varied from the people that she had asked over the years. People had answered her question about death, from blackness to bright light to nothingness. Rarely, it was that the person woke up laying in a bed with a large, mangy cat resting on top of them. The Quintessence. She had tried many times to locate it, but to no avail.

"Who…who are you? I…remember being…killed?" Askivar stammered as he tried to get up, looking around. She could tell the man's mind was desperately trying to grasp what was happening.

"Get over it. There is work to be done." Xifeng said behind her.

"Askivar, what do you remember?" she prodded him.

"I saw…only…darkness," he told her. Chione sighed.

"Get on with it, Chione." Xifeng moaned impatiently. Now, it was her turn to roll her eyes.

"Why did you become a Sentinel, Askivar—truthfully." Chione asked him.

Shame came across the man's ashen face. "Women."

Chione was not surprised by this. The number of women that would have fallen for his looks would be legion. "How would you like a second chance? To become a true Sentinel. To vanquish an evil threat and earn women's adoration with your deeds, not just words?"

"How would I do that?"

She smiled. "There is a great threat coming. It threatens everyone that you know. You and Beryx together can stop it before it infects this land."

Askivar nodded slowly. "Yes, what is this threat? I shall defeat it myself." he said eagerly.

"The threat is Pharaoh Tutankhamen and his evil forces."

Askivar stared blankly at her. "What is a Pharaoh Tutan—?"

Chione put her finger to his lips. "Wake the other, sister. We have much to do." A wide grin spread across her face. Everything was going according to his plan.

Chapter 1

Cucurbăta Mare Mountain—Europea

'The Obsidian Trifecta'

"Are you sure you *want* to survive? Your father's gonna kill you if you do …"

Breaking out the craziest smile he could muster, Vladimir Drăculeşti brought a finger to his lips "Shhhh." winking at his friend Tomas for good measure. He was technically too young to enter the contest: the minimum age was seventeen, and he was only fifteen. He wanted to be the youngest winner ever. He had to enter "unofficially" to achieve that. Their friend Erik, who was trailing behind them, had signed up to enter the competition was part of the ruse. The master plan was for him to quickly take Erik's place once the race started.

As they trudged up Cucurbăta Mare's steep path towards the starting point, Vladimir's insides twisted with excitement. He hoped his size would help him—he was big for his age, also the largest among his friends. He, Tomas, and Erik were wearing their grey school shirts and matching black pants, the standard dress for the youth of the village.

"Of course, he does." Erik piped up from behind him. Vladimir turned and grinned. Erik was seventeen, and as tall as Vladimir, but frailer. Even though Erik had signed up, Vladimir knew his friend would never actually compete in the Trifecta himself—it took a certain amount of crazy or desperation. "Vladimir is about to become the youngest winner in history. If he doesn't get turned into lava charred human steak. Though he does have some chicken legs made for running…fast…away"

Vladimir shook his head. "Asshats." He chuckled along with his friends. As they reached the plateau, he glanced up at the clear blue sky. Almost clear. There was a single dark cloud. As he stared up at it a cold shiver went down his spine. *Weird.* He though. He looked around and there were many villagers had already gathered on the grassy area and were talking excitedly among themselves.

Everyone in the village either loved or hated The Obsidian Trifecta. The people who loved it had never lost a loved one to it, so they simply enjoyed its sheer madness. The people who hated it were those who had lost somebody. Vladimir was a Drăculeşti. It was expected that when he came of age, he would enter. But the thought of standing there with his entire family, the villagers all staring at him expectedly, terrified him. So, he was going to surprise everyone and do it when they were least expecting it. His brothers, Radu and Micrea, had told him that when they had competed, they'd been more afraid of coming in last and embarrassing their family than of dying. Both agreed that death would be preferable to losing and facing their father's disappointment.

He had an advantage: his father would not be watching the Trifecta today. Father was away, dealing with another kind of danger, the Spiriduş. The band of thieves had been extra aggressive lately. People were worried, so Vladimir's father had been travelling around Europea to quell their fears. He was due back tonight. Vladimir hoped his father would be too tired from the trip to give him too much hell for what he was about to do.

He walked over to the ledge overlooking the lava flowing below. As he got closer, the heat became almost unbearable, like sticking one's head in a foyer. Sweat started to roll down his face. He wiped it off, but it did nothing. When he had been here before to watch his brothers, he never got this close. The long, wide lava river ran over two hundred feet to the overhang, where it cascaded down another hundred and seventy-five into a massive lava pool below. *Whoever came up with the concept of The Obsidian Trifecta was truly mad,* he thought.

"What's wrong?" Erik asked him, coming up behind.

"I know what's wrong," Tomas teased Vladimir, gesturing with his chin at the prettiest girl in their school. Tomas put his hand on Vladimir's shoulder. "Kazia. Poor Vladimir is more afraid of looking like a buffoon in front of her than of being chewed out by his father, and that's saying something."

Vladimir shrugged Tomas's hand off his shoulder. They were right, of course, but he would never tell them so. Looking over the edge again, he spotted eight gliders dangling from a rope stretched over the lava flow. Each one had a name sewn into its sail. He picked out the deep purple one with Erik's name on it. He would need to grab Erik's glider while falling toward it. *Fun times,* he thought.

"I don't think I've ever seen Vladimir so silent." he heard Erik say.

"The poor lad looks like he's about to soil himself," Tomas said.

Vladimir looked at his friends and whipped out his crazy grin once more. "The only things that are gonna be soiled are *your* undergarments when you find me holding the extremely large bag of atria at the bottom…*asshats*." He strutted past them, trying to look like he didn't have a worry in the world. His friends kept teasing— "cluck cluck" —behind him; he grimaced inwardly at his failure to convince them.

A booming voice brought Vladimir's thoughts back to reality. "May I have your attention please? Would all contestants report to The Lip for instructions?"

It was almost time! The plan was that when the announcer yelled, "Start!" Erik would false start toward his board, but Vladimir would rush past him, grab the board himself, and enter the competition. They had worked together in secret to balance the board for him. Along with practicing his surfing too.

"Let's go." Tomas whispered to him. The three of them headed toward The Lip. All the Obsidian boards stood on end, guarded by three Sentinels, so no one could get close to try to tamper with them. With five thousand atria at stake, people were likely to seek any edge they could think of. Since the competition's conception, more than one family's fortunes had changed because of it. He and Tomas managed to get to the front of the staging area as Erik stepped into the semi-circle with the other contestants.

Vladimir stole a look at Kazia Hindrick. She was standing off to his far right wearing a grey silk top and black dress, her light blond hair hanging free to her waist. They locked eyes. She smiled, and he smiled back, until he realized Marku Frankesen had spotted him and was frowning deeply. Marku was to marry Kazia when she turned seventeen; it was all arranged. Vladimir's parents said it was a good match, but he was torn on.

Kazia was beautiful, yet also brilliant. Looking at her stirred his insides. There was something about her he. Marku, on the other hand was exotic with his black skin. Marku's *vistka* was from the southern city of Bucharest. It was the hottest part of the land. Over the centuries the sun had baked their skin black. Both Kazia and Marku excited him in different ways. With Kazia the attraction was mental and physical. Marku's attraction was more primal to him. It made him hunger in ways he didn't understand. Was it wrong to want them both differently?

"Welcome to the sixty-fifth Obsidian Trifecta!" Marshal Angelin's voice snapped Vladimir out of his reverie. *That man is different,* he thought, taking in the announcer's bright cyan shirt and violet pants. As Angelin spoke, Vladimir began to grow uneasy. "This is a contest of bravery and skill, plus it helps if you are…well, you know…" At this, Angelin twirled a finger in circles around his left ear and everyone laughed at his attempt at humour but Vladimir didn't.

"Ladies and gentlemen, may I present to you, the brave contestants that will be competing for five thousand atria, the richest prize to date." He held up a burlap bag marked with an *A* and the crowd, including Vladimir, gave a collective "Ohhhhh." The plan was for the three of them to split it equally. He didn't need the atria, but neither Erik nor Tomas were wealthy, and he knew they could each use their share. Vladimir listened as Angelin continued his speech, "This is also the *largest* field of contestants I believe we've ever had, which warms my heart.

"Now, to the business at hand. Every contestant has a custom-made Obsidian board and glider. As you can see, their names are engraved on them; names are also on their respective gliders. We can't have anyone grabbing someone else's property, that would be… bad. Starting at my far left, we have Hester, Lash, Erik, Menowin, Bartley, Django, Silvanus, and finally Patrin."

Cheers erupted from the villagers, including Vladimir, who called out, "You the man, Erik!" and was rewarded with a mischievous smile. His friend was playing his part like a superstar.

"The sequence of events is this," Angelin continued, and Vladimir listened intently. "First, everyone will run to their respective Obsidian board, grab it, and jump off The Lip, slipping their feet into the carved grooves in their board for balance. Using skill and poise, they will surf down the lava river until they get to Cascade Point, where they'll soar downward as gracefully as they can, grabbing onto their suspended gliders. From there, continue down, just skimming the surface of the lava flow, but remaining over the lava itself. Now, this part is important—there are Sentinels stationed throughout this part of the competition. If anyone deviates from the course through their own deliberate actions, they will be immediately disqualified and banned from competing ever again. Contestants, is that clear?"

The contestants nodded in unison, and Angelin continued. "Once contestants land at the staging area, they will extract themselves from their gliders. Sentinels will be there to hand them each a lasso rope. The contestants will then try to lasso themselves a tri-horned Bichon-Buffalo. Believe you me, the buffalo *will* protest. Once lassoed, the riders will hop on their respective conquests and ride them through Razorteeth Valley. We all know what awaits them there."

"Whoever survives the treacherous journey will continue to race into Sighișoara until they get to the finish, the Tree of Life. Vasilisa Drăculești will be there to greet the winner." Terror shot through Vladimir at the thought of facing his mother at the finish line.

"Crap!" whispered Tomas to him. "Your mother!" Suddenly, Vladimir didn't want to be there anymore. He had expected to face his parents' wrath, but not at the finish line itself, in front of everybody.

La naiba! Crap.

"Contestants…get ready!" Marshal Angelin yelled as Vladimir glanced at his friends. Tomas looked as scared as he felt, and Erik looked like was going to be ill. The buzzing of the crowd had stopped. He saw fathers praising their sons and mothers crying. If their children won, it would change their fortunes. If they lost, they would likely be dead. Vladimir flexed his legs and rubbed them nervously.

"Just breathe," whispered Tomas reassuringly to him. "You got this." Vladimir nodded absently in return. Closing his eyes, he tensed his whole body, waiting for the word that would bring him glory or death.

"GO!" screamed Angelin as Vladimir uncoiled himself and sprang forward. The world was moving in slow motion as he raced toward the Obsidian board named *Erik*. He vaguely registered Kazia yelling, "Vladimir!" Reaching out, Vladimir grabbed the Obsidian board and leaped over the ledge of The Lip. He brought the board underneath him, sliding his feet into the grooves. "Auugghh!" came a scream from his left. He recognized the voice of Patrin, but he didn't turn to look; he had to focus on the Trifecta. His board connected with the lava flow. He quickly raised his arms to steady himself. Two competitors surfed right alongside him: Django and Bartley. "Whoooo!" he heard Lash call from behind him. Charred, blackened rocks stuck out of the lava flow, and he swerved to avoid them. "Hey!" he heard Hester's panicked yell from the back, then "Auugghh!" and *silence*. Hester hadn't made it.

Cheating was not permitted, but certain allowances were made. Killing during the competition was one of them. Competitors couldn't use any weapons or methods that weren't available as part of the normal course of events, but they could make physical contact with the other contestants. When that happened, there were always cheers along with screams of terror if anyone fell into the river.

They were almost halfway to Cascade Point, quickly picking up speed. Vladimir heard Lash scream "Yeah, baby!" He glanced over as he deftly swerved around another rock; Lash was grinning insanely. Lash was twenty-one. His eyes were two different colours, one green and one yellow, which always freaked people out, including himself. They were neck and neck as they raced toward Cascade Point. "Hey, Vladimir, do your parents know how naughty their youngest son is?" teased Lash as he did his best to ignore him.

Suddenly, Vladimir felt himself pitch forward, almost tilting sideways, but he managed to steady himself. Teasing came from behind: "Oh, Vladimir, where art thou, my Vladimir?". It was Menowin. He was bumped again by Menowin, trying to make him lose his balance. Another bump from behind, but he managed to stay upright.

Then something brushed against his right arm; Lash was reaching for him, trying to pull him into the lava river. *La naiba!* Vladimir crouched low, trying to gain more speed and make himself less of a target. Menowin rammed his board again, and Vladimir knew he needed to do something quick. He swerved to his left and pulled up on his board, bearing hard toward a little lip of rock sticking out of the lava flow. Hitting the lip, he twisted his board, doing a three-hundred-and-sixty-degree spin in the air.

As he twirled, he saw terror in Menowin's eyes, who tried to swerve to avoid the bottom of Vladimir's board. Menowin crashed into Bartley—they tried to grab each other for support, but got tangled up, and down they went into the lava river. In a blink, they disappeared.

Vladimir landed directly behind Lash, who was slightly ahead of him. Django and Silvanus were alongside Lash. No one was jockeying for position anymore, being this close to Cascade Point. He braced himself for the jump. He tucked in lower to his board to get as much speed as he could. He watched Lash launch off and yell "Whooop!" followed by Django and Silvanus, who gave each other a high five in the air before disappearing from view. The moments before he reached the edge seemed to stretch for an eternity.

Until finally, Vladimir was propelled off the lava flow and into the air. Throwing up his hands as he crested, Vladimir screamed as loud as he could, "Freedooom!" He had never been so terrified and thrilled at the same time!

Vladimir twisted mid-air to line himself up with Erik's deep purple glider. To his horror, he realized he was off course. Normally, grabbing another contestant's glider would be an automatic disqualification. Since Hester had perished, its owner would not be needing it. He grabbed the base tube of the glider, as it easily detached from the rope. He adjusted his feet to make sure they were still secured to the board. Dipping down low to skim the surface of the lava flow, Vladimir quickly found himself gaining on the others. They were all close, and no one was taking extra chances. The three ahead were all friends. He wondered if they made a secret pact to split the atria.

"C'mon, c'mon." he muttered to himself. Suddenly, the lava belched outward at him, and he had to zig hard to the left to avoid getting a face full of it. He was right behind Django now, who did not seem to know Vladimir was there. Should he reach out and make Django crash? He didn't want to purposefully harm anyone, especially if they could die.

But they *had* tried to kill him, so fair was fair, wasn't it?

He was close enough to reach up and yank Django's legs, but as he reached out for the other glider, he found he couldn't do it. *Frack!* He re-focused, going as straight as he could, and slid right beside the other three competitors.

"It's Vladimir!" Lash shouted in surprise. He didn't pay attention as needed to go as fast as he could to the bottom. The lava flow was almost straight downward from here, and he was going faster than he ever thought possible. He needed to pull up within seconds or he would risk going head-first into the lava pool—but he also needed to put as much distance as he could between himself and the others.

"Whoohoo!" Someone shouted. He looked left to find Django beside him. "Whooo, Vladimir, whooo!" Django repeated with the most maniacal expression on his face that Vladimir had ever seen. Had his mind snapped? Scant seconds from the lava pool, Django blew Vladimir a kiss, and Django pulled up slightly. *Too soon,* Vladimir thought. A second later, he tilted his own glider back and started to slow down.

"Damn you!" Silvanus spat.

"Auugghh! Let go!" yelled Lash.

Vladimir couldn't look back, no matter how much he wanted to know what was happening. Moments later, he was over the lava pool and could see the corrals up ahead where the buffalo would be waiting.

"Auugghh!" Silvanus cried.

He glanced back just in time to see Django and Silvanus go headfirst into the lava pool.

Seconds behind him was Lash, an evil grin on his face. Vladimir saw the corral off to his right and angled for it. He reached up to pull the wooden flap that would slow his glider, but something was wrong—he was going too fast. Sentinels were waving at him, motioning for him to slow down, but his brake flaps wouldn't work. Spotting a pile of thorn bushes on the riverbank, Vladimir angled for them instead, hoping he knew what he was doing. He slipped his feet out of the board, letting it fall on the ground. Just as he was about to glide over the bushes, he let go, falling full force into them. He rolled, crashing through the thorns until he came to a painful stop.

He got to his feet. Thorns had pierced him all over, many of them still embedded in his skin as he stumbled out of the bushes. Lash was already there, trying, unsuccessfully, to lasso a Bichon-Buffalo. Vladimir grinned, feeling a sharp pain as he pulled a bloody thorn out of his cheek. Ignoring the dozens of other thorns in his body, he rushed to the wooden corral, trying to pick out which buffalo he wanted to try to lasso. Bichon-Buffalos were larger than normal buffalos, not to mention that they had three horns and had a much thicker hide which created a natural armour against predators. Scanning the herd, Vladimir picked out a lone buffalo off by itself. He approached one of the Sentinels and reached out for a lasso.

"Aren't you Vladimir Drăculești?" The Sentinel asked him. "You're too young for this! Your father will—"

"Yes, thank you." Vladimir replied, grabbing the rope from the stunned Sentinel's hand. Running to the corral, he heard a loud "Whoop!" from Lash. Lash had successfully lassoed one. *Damn!* Another Sentinel opened the gate and Lash galloped off toward Sighișoara. Vladimir needed to act quickly.

An insane idea popped into his head.

Bichon-Buffalo were tough to lasso, but once they were caught, they became instantly obedient. Vladimir climbed up to the top rail of the corral and ran atop it, twirling the lasso in the air. His timing needed to be perfect. He ran toward the buffalo and leaped, tossing the lasso at the same time. The lasso roped the buffalo around the neck just as Vladimir landed on its back. The animal reared up and Vladimir called out, as calmly as he could, "It's okay… I'm not going to hurt you. We have a race to win now. What's say we get us a prize and get some special oats for you?"

The buffalo bucked slightly, but seemed to be calming. *Success!* Lash had a lead, but it was not insurmountable. The buffalo bolted toward the entrance to the corral. The Sentinel opened the gate; his mouth fell open as he saw who it was, but he didn't do anything to stop him. Razorteeth Valley was not far off, and Vladimir kicked the sides of the buffalo to spur it on.

It was called Razorteeth Valley because all the creatures that dwelled in it had razor-sharp teeth which they used to rip the flesh off their prey. Bears, wolves, and lynx lived there, not to mention the many more unnatural creatures. Vladimir was riding toward hundreds of hungry, bloodthirsty teeth with his name on them. Part of him hoped that Lash would provide a distraction so he could race through the valley relatively unhindered. As he galloped, he scanned its grassy sides for any creatures.

Reaching the valley entrance at breakneck speed, he was confident that he could catch up to Lash. He looked around, scanning for any creatures that might be hiding in bushes or behind trees, but he didn't see any. He saw Lash weaving left in the distance with three large grey wolves hot on his trail. *Yesss!* He watched as Lash drove his buffalo up the side of the valley toward some rocks, understanding what Lash was trying to do. Lash was going to maneuver his buffalo through the rocks, hoping the wolves would be too focused on the buffalo and would crash into them. Vladimir had to admit it was smart. It was risky, too, but with three wolves hot on his trail, Lash had limited options.

He caught sight of something out of the corner of his eye: smoldering yellow eyes were staring at him through the bushes as he rode by them. The hairs on his arms tingled. Whatever it was, it was unnatural. Loud yelping drew his attention back to Lash; two wolves stumbled over themselves trying to avoid the rocks, and a third crashed headfirst into a big boulder. But the wolves had cost Lash his lead time. They were almost neck and neck. Vladimir locked eyes with Lash. He saw the same desire to win—the same desire he knew Lash would see in him. Sighişoara was approaching… they were in the home stretch.

"Yee-haw!" Lash called out, and Vladimir kicked at his buffalo even harder to try to pass Lash's. They were only several feet apart. Lash swerved his buffalo into his, which snorted in protest.

"What are you doing?" Vladimir asked, eyeing him. To his surprise, Lash reached over and punched him in the face. Stars spun wildly around his head as he desperately hung on for dear life.

"How d'you like that?" Lash sneered at him.

Vladimir veered his buffalo away to avoid being punched again.

"You can't escape me!" Lash steered towards him again.

La naiba! Just then, an animal roar rang out from behind them. There was a huge bear chasing after them gaining fast. Its eyes were glowing yellow—it was the same one he saw earlier in the race!

Vladimir locked eyes with Lash, the rage on the latter's face now replaced by fear. Whoever was the slowest was going to be eaten. Vladimir kicked his buffalo again, pleading, "If you slow down, we become supper. I don't want to become supper, do you?"

Vladimir's buffalo sped up, but the bear gained even more speed. He was slightly behind Lash. The bear was pulling in his direction, sensing Vladimir was the easier prey. What was he going to do? He looked at Lash and felt a stone in the pit of his stomach for what he was about to do. He kicked the buffalo one last time to catch up to Lash's. The bear was only a couple of feet behind them now. *It was now or never!* He needed to time it perfectly. He raised himself onto his buffalo, then leapt. He grabbed the back of Lash's shirt for support as he landed hard on Lash's buffalo.

"Damn you, Vladimir!" Lash didn't fall—he had the lasso rope wrapped around his wrist.

"You tried to kill me, *asshat*, remember that!"

A monstrous roar came from behind. The bear was getting closer.

Sighişoara was just up ahead, with people lined up and down the street to watch their approach. *So close!* Shots rang out—Sentinels were shooting at the bear. A yelp rang out from behind them, and Vladimir turned one last time to see the bear tumble face first into the ground, then stop moving.

"I'm going to beat the crap out of you for this!" Lash bellowed. The latter was sliding off the buffalo, barely hanging onto it.

Lash was tough, Vladimir had to admit. The guy did not know when to quit. As they entered the village, the streets were lined with people cheering, some gawking in disbelief at what they were witnessing. He spotted some familiar faces. His heart beat excitedly, seeing how close he was to the finish. He was going to be the youngest winner in history!

"Take my hand, Lash—I'll pull you up. We can win it together." Vladimir stretched out his hand. Lash stared up at him, an expression of uncertainty.

"Take it!" he screamed. Lash started to reach for Vladimir's hand, but they rounded a tight corner, and…

Lash disappeared. He had slammed into a wall. Vladimir stared at his empty hand, unable to process what just happened.

"Vladimir! Vladimir!" People were shouting his name. The spectators gasped in both excitement and shock.

Without warning, the buffalo tripped, and he found himself flying through the air. "Frackkk meee!" He tried to find something to grab onto, but all he felt was air. He hit the ground hard, then rolled and rolled until finally, he came to a stop.

Struggling to catch his breath, he reached to pull a sharp thorn from his butt. His body was in too much agony. He decided to lay still and close his eyes.

As he closed his eyes a shadow fell over him. He thought he saw the harried look of an extremely worried mother. Mustering a weak smile, he managed to stammer out a "Hello, Mother." before he passed out, the darkness taking all the pain away.

Chapter 2

Thebes—Egyptia

'Assassination Aftermath'

Pharaoh Tutankhamen sat on his massive golden throne, cushioned by the soft, cream fabric that had his image sewn into it—so that even when he was not there, his people could still worship his image. Looking down at the heavy, strange object in his hand, he turned it, trying to understand how it worked. He was completely baffled. A combination of hardened wood and a long metal tube with an opening at its end that shot small, deadly metallic round balls. What madman could have created something so insidious? It felt dirty to his touch, reeked of death. If his enemies had weapons such as this, what else did they have?

He felt the weight of the golden, gem-encrusted neme on his head, along with a heavy gold-laced shendyt around his waist. Both complimented his handsome features. Normally, he despised wearing them for their weight on his body, but today it felt different. They were no longer just ornamental to him. They symbolized his position of power.

His young eternal life had barely begun, yet it had almost ended. The attempt on his life had been carried out by two mysterious men dressed in strange uniforms. They had penetrated the Royal Pyramid without being detected and attempted to kill him using the weapon he was now studying. They had burst into his room expecting him to be alone and found him in the arms of several women. He had used them as human shields while he screamed for the guards. In the ensuing fight, he had managed to kill the first assassin by thrusting the long golden spear he kept above his bed through the back of one of the women and into one of the assassin's chest. Before he could pull it out though, the other assassin managed to get a shot off, striking his face. He caressed his cheek; his face had burned hotter than he could have ever imagined. Moments later, the Royal Guards stormed into the room, quickly striking down the last would-be assassin. Shortly after, he had ordered all the Royal Guards that had been on duty that night to be killed for failing their duties. His disfiguration was proof of that.

Trying to ignore the itchy heat under his bandages, he looked around his majestic throne room. Almost completely empty, save for the stone staircase leading up to his throne. The only other objects were large braziers, strategically placed at the bottom of the stairs. Their purpose was so that those that came before him would feel their heat. The more uncomfortable those before him were, the more comfortable he felt. The golden ceiling was retractable, so the sun could shine directly on him—a reminder to all his subjects that even the Sun God, Ra himself, worshipped him.

Today, however, there were only four people fortunate enough to be in his presence. At the bottom of the golden stairs stood the woman who had changed everything he thought he knew about his Kingdom *and beyond*. *He* was not the only ruler there was. The woman who had opened his eyes was standing in front of him. She was tall and slender with golden eyes and an intricate symbol of a hawk tattooed on her bald head. She wore a light purple gown that covered her from neck to toe, with golden ankh earrings and a matching belt. Her name was Chione. Was she a gift from the Gods to protect him? How was he to know?

His anger burned as hot as the wound on his face. It made him feel…*almost human.* "It is called an arquebus, my Pharaoh." Chione informed him.

"Where did it come from, how did they get it, and why have I not seen anything like this before?" Tutankhamen demanded of her.

General Pentu stepped forward stating. "There is nothing like this in the army. It is…truly remarkable. A piece of lethal workmanship. Nothing like it has even been conceived."

"How am I supposed to get revenge on the people who did this when they have weapons we have not even dreamed of yet?" Tutankhamen roared, viciously throwing down the foreign weapon and watching it bounce down the stairs. To his disappointment that the weapon did not break.

"My Pharaoh, we too have weapons that can kill from a distance, many such weapons." General Pentu added hastily to him. This did not please him.

A tall, thin man with white eyes stepped forward. Adorned with chains and multicolored gems, he wore a simple black shendyt. "I do not know about this weapon, but I do know about the Gods and Goddesses. Wadjet has done her duty in protecting you. You are worthy in the eyes of the Gods. As our Pharaoh, above reproach. You are a living God." High Priest Nakhte offered to him, bowing his head, and stepping back.

"Perhaps, if I may be so bold, my Pharaoh, I may make a humble suggestion." Sorcerer Haphestus requested. A heavily tattooed man in a yellow, square patterned shendyt stepped forward to address him. Long-haired with golden eyes, Haphestus was extremely tall and heavily muscled, rare for someone in his position. "With your permission, I will take it to my workshop. Perhaps my acolytes can determine how it works and replicate it, with improvements, so when the time comes, we can equip your army with the improved versions to exact your vengeance for their treacherous actions."

Tutankhamen nodded in agreement while rising to his full height. "Your idea has some merit. Proceed. But be warned—my patience is thin, and my thirst for vengeance insatiable, do not fail me. You must create something that will not just kill but make them suffer as well." The Sorcerer cringed at his warning, which pleased him greatly. He watched as Haphestus took the weapon and scurried out of the room, as though he had a prize in hand. The Sorcerer was indeed…different.

"Now, where did my would-be assassins come from, Chione?" he demanded. "Which one of the lands you mentioned when we first met?"

"The assassins come from a land called Europea." Chione stated to him. "In certain ways, their culture is like ours—they hunt, fish, and farm just as our people do. They too have cities and villages spread out through their lands. Families travel throughout, visiting relatives. They have established routes to move their goods and supplies quickly and efficiently. The land is generally peaceful, though there is one small group, The Spiriduş. Much like our raider's northeast of Thebes, they are a disruptive influence. Their leader is called Preslav.

"He is as smart and vicious as a jackal and will sacrifice everything and everyone to defeat their ruler. It is said that the current ruling family are...different, shall we say, from the other families. They possess unique abilities that make them virtually unstoppable. Almost impossible to kill. Whether it is true or not, I do not know, but I have heard that once they achieved these abilities, it made them become...unnatural."

"What are the unnatural abilities you speak of?" Tutankhamen inquired.

"I have only heard whispers of their abilities—superior strength, far sight, plus a resistance to damage of any sort. I have also heard that the original source of their power came from drinking human blood. Over the generations, their abilities have grown stronger, and their dependence on blood diminished. Although, should the need arise, drinking blood while in a time of crisis enhances their natural abilities into something more terrifying than any one of us could imagine. Not just any blood, living blood. Blood from dead people will not boost their abilities, just sustain them if required."

Tutankhamen knew she was overstating her case for dramatic effect. It was working. He leaned back on his throne. "What is their name?"

"*Drăculești,*" Chione said.

Tutankhamen glanced down at General Pentu, who was wearing a rapt expression. He could tell the man was enthralled by all this. "Excuse me, Chione. You mentioned fishing. I would think water vessels...do they have vessels of war, or an army that would pose a serious threat to our kingdom?"

The Pharaoh smiled. The General was ever the tactician, and dutiful soldier.

"There is a civilian army, of sorts." Chione stated. Tutankhamen hoped they were as defenceless as sheep, but the look in Chione's eyes told him otherwise. "They are called The Sentinels. They watch over the cities and villages and monitor the trade routes to ensure that goods and supplies move freely, as well as provide protection from the Spiriduș. They are not a traditional army, such as our Royal Army, more of a police force. They are strong and determined and will carry out their duty to the end, even if it means their death. They have no war vessels, just fishing trawlers on the lake that the village surrounds. There has never been a naval battle in their collective history."

General Pentu looked enthused. "Excellent, my Pharaoh. That will make retribution all that much easier. With your permission and blessing, I will lead your forces into battle to inflict whatever vengeance you wish on these vile would-be usurpers."

Tutankhamen ignored the General's plea, his focus on Chione. "That still does not tell me how you know any of this, or why they decided to kill me, or how they got to my kingdom. There is still much you need to explain." Tutankhamen demanded of Chione.

"My Sisterhood has existed long before there was a kingdom. Our duty is to keep the lands ignorant of each other's existence. Long ago, lost to the annals of time, the lands did interact with each other, to great disaster. The more advanced cultures decimated the weaker ones. The Sisterhood agreed that certain barriers would be implemented to make sure history did not repeat itself. Alas, it seems that is no longer the case. How the assassins got here... The Sisterhood I belong to has the ability to travel between the lands. One of my sisters must have helped the men come here to assassinate you and destabilize your kingdom, which would allow their people to subvert your lands, increase their own influence, and procure your resources and subjects for their own."

Anger blazed through him.

"Whatever these Drăculești are, they have incurred the wrath of our Gods." said High Priest Nakhte. "Even now, I can sense their anger. Horus demands retribution, my Pharaoh!"

General Pentu looked over at the High Priest with annoyed interest, and the same doubt as he had. "Chione, does this other land have the ability to conduct aerial warfare, like our Sphinx Squadron?" Tutankhamen wondered this, as well.

"No, General, they do not use creatures for fighting in the sky. We have the advantage there." Chione said.

High Priest Nakhte stepped forward and looked up at Tutankhamen before addressing Chione. "You said that the lands have interacted before in the past, ages ago, yet we have explored our land and found no indication of any foreign Gods or temples outside our culture. Other than the infernal Duat Pit that is truly...unnatural. How it came into existence defies even the Gods. How do you explain this lack of evidence?"

"The Sisterhood worked diligently to remove all traces. This was well before my time, so I do not know places or names, as there are no historical records of where they did all this, unfortunately."

Tutankhamen nodded slightly. His teaching never revealed anything close to the nature they were discussing. "How did the assassins get to my bedroom?" Tutankhamen growled, scowling down at Chione.

"I cannot say how they made it into your bedroom, as I was not there." She said, holding her own.

"Is it possible more assassins made it through?" The High Priest bellowed. "What if there is another team lying in wait to see if the first two men were not successful? Once they find out that they were not, is it not possible they shall move in to kill our glorious Pharaoh or his closest advisors? How do we know there is not already an army planted in our kingdom? Ready to invade even as we speak? How do we know other lands have not sent spies?" He looked around the room nervously.

Tutankhamen sighed. The High Priest was not as brave as the General.

"I would know." Chione said smoothly. "Whenever a curtain opens, those in the Sisterhood can feel the energies used. We do not know specifically where it opened, but we can sense what land opened it." She turned to face Tutankhamen. "I sensed the curtain, which made me rush to your Royal Pyramid to save your life. My Pharaoh, if more curtains had been opened, I would have been here when that happened, for it is my duty to watch over my homeland."

Tutankhamen shifted nervously on his throne. "Why now? Why is this happening? What has changed in this Sisterhood you speak of?"

"I have not talked to the other members of the Sisterhood since I became the Sister of your kingdom. I can open curtains to the other lands. Unfortunately, I have no way of knowing who the other sisters are, nor where they are in the other lands. All I can do, my Pharaoh, is inform you immediately if more curtains open."

There were forces beyond his control at play, forces more powerful than a living God. How was this possible? High Priest Nakhte had told him all this life that he was a living embodiment of the Gods, yet he had not received any gifts like the woman before him had, or these Drăculeşti. Had Nakhte deceived him? Was he not worthy of such gifts? If not, why bother with the Gods at all? What had they done for him?

Perhaps it was time for a change, one that did not involve any Gods.

"These curtains...just how large can they be?" General Pentu asked. "Is it possible to create one to accommodate a vessel, or perhaps several, so that an entire fleet could go through if required?" He did not even try to conceal the excitement in his voice. Yes, Tutankhamen knew nothing made the General happier than crushing his enemies.

"Yes," Chione replied, facing Tutankhamen and not the General. "I can open curtains any size. However, it does tax my abilities and sap my strength to do so. I have not opened one since I came into this land. Until I master it, there will be a limit to my capabilities."

Pentu's eyes gleamed in anticipation, mirroring his own.

"How?" Tutankhamen asked, curiosity in his tone.

"I think of the name of the place I want to go to, and the curtain will open in the general vicinity. If I know specifically where it is, it will open at that exact place." Chione responded.

"Do you know where the Drăculeşti live?" He asked expectedly.

"I know their chief village's location. It is called Sighişoara, and it resides against their largest lake, Sfanta Ana. And yes, General Pentu," Chione said, turning to address him. "If you wanted to, you could plant a fleet in their harbor and still have room to spare. I would open a curtain on the lake, and your vessels would head to the harbor to commence the attack."

Excellent, Tutankhamen thought. The Drăculeşti would pay for their treachery. Their land and people would become his. "You examined the bodies, Nakhte. Were they any different than we are? Is there anything that makes '*those*' people more special than us? Other than their Drăculeşti?" Tutankhamen demanded of his advisor, who shifted uncomfortably. "Tell me…now!"

"My Pharaoh, your attackers…I know this does not make any sense. I believe…were already dead before they were killed…again." Nakhte said as he kneeled in front of him.

Kai me ton kuna! Tutankhamen sat there speechless at his advisor's conclusion.

Pentu stepped forward, slamming his hand down on a stair. "What madness are you talking about, High Priest?" The General was clearly as stunned as he was at the news.

"My Pharaoh," Nakhte began. "I examined the bodies thoroughly. The bodies had additional wounds on them that would have been fatal. I believe somehow, they were brought back to life to kill you."

Tutankhamen sat wondering just how much Blood Cider his advisor drank before being summoned.

"My Pharaoh let me show you the truth." pleaded Nakhte as he turned and clapped his hands loudly. Moments later, two sets of Royal Guards entered the room carrying wooden stretchers. Each with a dead body on it.

He absently reached up to his cheek and touched the dressing on it. "What is the meaning of this, High Priest?" He demanded, shooting up from his throne and racing down the stairs toward his advisor.

Nakhte backed up in fear, which momentarily pleased him. "My Pharaoh, I beg of you— let me show you…"

But Tutankhamen didn't care. He raged, "You are grasping at camel hairs, High Priest. Those men were real enough when they tried to kill me. They are not Mummies!"

As Nakhte reached to take off the dead attacker's wrappings, Chione stepped forward. "My Pharaoh, no one can bring the dead back to life in this way. It is known. I believe the High Priest Nakhte is trying to deflect from the truth. That the Gods prefer the Drăculești."

Tutankhamen was stunned. He was not the chosen one! It was true—he had never received any gift like the Drăculești had received. "Explain why the Gods did not bestow their gifts on me?" he demanded, seething at the thought of others with abilities that should have been his birthright.

"My Pharaoh, Horus is greatly displeased with what has transpired. Knowing they were trying to kill you, the Gods' thirst for vengeance will not be sated until the Drăculești lie dead or kissing the ground beneath your feet. You have gifts bestowed upon you, a living God. You are wise beyond your years. You are more handsome than any other person alive. Your reign is eternal." High Priest Nakhte said, his voice starting to quiver in fear.

It was clear that the Gods did not favour him as much as they did the Drăculești. How did being handsome grant him special abilities? What was the purpose of worshipping these Gods if they did nothing for him? They had allowed these assassins through to his Royal Pyramid. They allowed him to be harmed. It was his quick thinking and bravery that had saved his own life. "I saved myself, the Gods have done nothing. It is time that I re-evaluate their worth."

High Priest Nakhte looked apprehensive. "My Pharaoh, surely you are not suggesting..."

"Why should we continue to worship these Gods when they clearly do not care about us? They have forsaken me!" Tutankhamen screamed, making the High Priest jump. "I have had enough of these so-called Gods. I am a living God, which is all my people need."

With a snap of his fingers, two heavily muscled Royal Guards appeared. "Remove the High Priest from my sight and round up the other priests. Take them to Luxor Prison for now. Then, they are to be taken to the Duat Pit, where we will see if their Gods come to their rescue. If not, it only proves I am the only true God. See to it that the statues of our false Gods be changed. To my image alone! My face is the only image my people need. I am a living God, and therefore the only God that deserves to be worshipped." He raised his fists as an exclamation point. The Royal Guards nodded to him and grabbed the High Priest's arms.

"My glorious Pharaoh, please. I have been loyal..." High Priest Nakhte pleaded as he was dragged out of the room to murmurs of nervous laughter.

He turned to Chione. "What about the Royal Fleets that were sent out over the ages to discover the new lands? If there are barriers separating these other lands, as you say, what happened to them?"

"All ships, regardless of their place of origin, wind up in the middle of the ocean, in a place called the Paroxysm. It is an additional safety mechanism to keep the lands separated. None of the Royal Fleets have been lost, my Pharaoh."

Kai me ton kuna! Excellent. He would become the ruler of this land, as well! He turned to face the General. "What is your plan, General Pentu? I want immediate retribution for their treachery. I will not accept any excuses."

Chione spoke before the General could respond. "My Pharaoh, may I remind you that Europea has Sentinels, and despite the confidence I see in General Pentu's eyes, it will still be a battle to conquer the land." Chione warned him, and continued, "Sighişoara is the capital, yes, but invading it will rally the land's two biggest forces against you. *Any* issues between them will be put aside until your forces are defeated. If it is your desire to do this, it will take great resources before you are successful."

He did not care about details, just results. Looking over at General Pentu, Tutankhamen said, "Yes, General, we have yet to hear your battle strategy. Tell me now."

General Pentu smiled confidently at him. "Attack the head, and the body will fall. The Drăculeşti are their leaders and mightiest warriors. Without them, the Spiriduş will more than likely become more aggressive. As for their Sentinels—when they stop getting wages, they may simply disband. Their leader sent assassins to kill you and leave our land in ruin, so I humbly suggest we return their kindness. We shall create chaos in their lands."

Hmm, interesting, Tutankhamen thought. The General turned to Chione. "When you open a curtain, can you provide any sort of cover for our vessels as they pass through?"

"A mist will form as the curtain parts on their side, which will shield our vessels from their view," she assured him. *Excellent,* Tutankhamen thought again.

"My Pharaoh, my plan requires two ships to attack the village." General Pentu stated with a veneer of calmness, which surprised Tutankhamen.

"Two ships only, General?" Chione scoffed. "That does not seem enough to carry out an invasion. The capital village is guarded by Sentinels, who presumably are skilled enough to be able to defend more than long enough to get reinforcements into the village. Never mind that their weapons are far more advanced than ours."

Was she trying to gain favour? Tutankhamen thought.

General Pentu nodded. "You are quite right, Chione. Their weapons are most effective against the living, as we have seen. I do not think they will do so well against the undead, or our Ushabti warriors. Their small metal balls would be an annoyance, at most." He faced Tutankhamen, explaining calmly. "My Pharaoh, against the might of the Ushabti warriors and Mummies, their weapons would mean nothing. When the ships are through the curtain protected by the mist, the oarsmen will become archers and launch fire arrows into the village. The chaos will force the Sentinels to split into smaller groups to deal with the fires. Once the village is burning, our ships will make land, allowing the Ushabti Warriors and Mummies to leave their respective ships and spread into the village, destroying everything in sight. We will let them remain in the village, causing havoc and killing anyone foolish enough to enter.

"The next phase in the plan is to let the land fall into disarray and ruin," he continued. "When we 'liberate' the village, you shall be hailed as a savior. The people, in their most desperate hour, will flock to you. Whatever possible resistance remaining between The Sentinels and The Spiriduș will be no match for a highly trained, well-organized army with the flying Sphinxes above as eyes in the sky. Any resistance will be crushed easily as your Royal Army moves inland to secure your new resources and people. You will be their greatest leader. You will be the sun in their sky. You will be loved."

Tutankhamen laughed, clapping his hands, then gestured to dismiss the General. "Use whatever forces you deem necessary, General, for this plan of yours." *Indeed, the General may have outdone himself on this plan,* thought Tutankhamen.

"Your bidding is my command, my Pharaoh."

"Excellent. I demand quick retribution for what they have done. The ships must be loaded and prepared for the attack as quickly as possible." he declared with vigour. He noticed General Pentu wilt a bit under the fury emanating from him, and it gave him momentary satisfaction.

"Your mighty forces do not require sleep nor food, so we can attack almost immediately." the General said to him. "We can plunder the city and bring you the glorious spoils of war—trinkets, and slaves, and prisoners for your amusement…"

"No prisoners. When we 'liberate' the villagers from our forces, they will be more than willing to tell us everything we want to know and give us everything we could ever need. If some resist…well, they will not be around for long. Though I do want a prize—bring me a Drăculești, *alive.*" he demanded, slowly walking to a tall, thin brazier. He stared into the flame. These Drăculești shall be wiped from their own history.

General Pentu beamed and bowed towards him. "That night shall be the greatest night in the history of your glorious kingdom. I shall make the necessary arrangements immediately." He hastily left the room, leaving him alone with Chione.

That it shall, General. That it shall.

* * *

Everything Chione expected to happen, had happened. And this was only the start of what was to come. She walked over to the dead Sentinels. She was not surprised that the two Sentinels had failed. Yet they had served their purpose. High Priest Nakhte proved to be exceptionally perceptive, which had surprised her. She had thought quickly on her feet and had outmaneuvered him. She would see him again soon.

Watching the Pharaoh leave the room, she went over to stroke Askivar's hair and thought about bringing him back again. Should she? If she did, he would be a mere shell of his former self.

No, she remembered the last time she got attached to someone, what it cost her. She reached down and kissed Askivar on the lips and whispered, "You would thank me if you were still alive."

Chione walked up the stairs to the Pharaoh's throne, and slowly walked around the majestic chair, letting her fingers glide over it. Chione knew what she was going to do next was punishable by death, but she was not worried. She sat down on the throne and leaned back. So, this was what it felt like. It felt good. She reached inside her dress and pulled out a thick cigarillo. Smelling it was like smelling victory itself. She brought it to her lips, and it lit instantly. She inhaled deeply.

Victory.

Chapter 3

Imperial Grandstand—Chang'an

'False Freedom'

Princess Pingyang Gaozu sat on the plush purple cushioned seats, bored. She looked over at the empty seat where her father, Emperor Gaozu of Tang, would take his place shortly. She wished her father had not forced her to come to watch the upcoming spectacle. At first, she had been excited at the prospect of escaping the Imperial Castle but sitting alone in the booth for some time had dampened her mood considerably.

Before leaving, her handmaidens had taken extra care in putting together her outfit. Her extremely tight seaweed green dress ran the length of her body. There were large clam shell halves sewn into her shoulders and metallic silver stripes on the skirt. Her waist-length hair had been intertwined with lime-green seashells, which stood out starkly against her black locks. Her cheeks had been painted moss green to complete the ensemble. Never had she felt so utterly humiliated. Why did her father hate her so?

She was informed by her father that her outfit was to show support for their Imperial Expedition Fleet. She knew the three previous fleets had not returned and was confident that the sailors departing today would have the same fate as those before. She had been told more than once that those who do not learn from the past are doomed to repeat the same mistakes. Yet her father was sending out another Expeditionary Fleet. Her father ruled the Empire, which consisted of all that there was already. Why did he feel the need to send more men to their deaths to search for new lands that did not exist?

As she sat there, she thought back to the journey to the Imperial Grandstand. It had been the highlight of this outing so far. The streets had been lined with people jumping and waving at them. It had been the first time in quite a while that she felt like a princess instead of a prisoner in a gilded cage. Many children had tried to run up to the carriage, squealing with excitement and offering her flowers, but had been stopped by the legion of Imperial Guards. At first, she revelled in the attention, but as the carriage moved further away from the Imperial Castle, she noticed people's appearance became filthier. The side streets were filled with excrement from all manner of beasts. She had asked her father why no one cleaned them. He had merely shrugged. "Those that are born poor are not at fault. Those that continue to live and die poor *are*," and he had left it at that. She understood what he was saying, but still wondered why he was not doing more to help.

The sound of girlish whispers brought her back to reality. A gaggle of girls sat down to her left in a huddle glancing up at her. She knew what they found so amusing—her outfit. She recognized them as her cousins, though she had not seen them in years. They were triplets. All wearing the same lavender-coloured dress, with matching sailor's cap, which were flat with a small wooden rim in front. She thought they looked as ridiculous as she did. Their hair was tied in ponytails, which made them look even sillier. Feeling a little better about how she looked, she threw them the most deliciously, wicked smile she could muster. They turned away, ignoring her, pretending to look over the Imperial Harbour.

The Imperial Grandstand was the tallest, largest building outside the Imperial Castle. It was built to commemorate the first Imperial Expedition Fleet departure. Since that time, it also served to witness military parades, highlighting the Empire's might. It was constructed with different wood brought in from all reaches of the Empire. In the centre of the facade was an emblem created from dark rosewood, shaped in a four-pointed star, and at each point was a carved, circular symbol representing an element. The top was the sun, with small rays stemming from the smaller interior circle, representing air; on the left point, a mighty oak tree stood for the earth; on the right, waves were for water; and the bottom point stood for unity, symbolized by the feng huang, the phoenix—the balance in all things in life. At the heart of the star was not a symbol but a single word: 死亡. Death. No matter the power one holds or what someone can achieve, it still comes.

The Imperial Grandstand had four seating tiers to it, each one corresponding to a different class. Half-walls had been erected between the tiers, so there were no "accidental" unpleasant encounters between the classes. Each tier had its own entrance. Section entrances were guarded in case someone was foolish enough to try to rise above their tier. The largest was the bottom tier that ran the length of the Grandstand, which was for the lower class. There was a three foot high wall that separated them from the wealthier working class, which sat above them; their section ran three-quarters of the length. Above them sat the aristocrats, the elite of society, a much smaller area that took up a mere quarter of the Grandstand. The top section was for the Imperial Family; the wall separating it was slanted downwards so they had an unobstructed view of the classes before them. When Princess Pingyang Gaozu was younger, she often wondered why everyone couldn't sit together. She was instructed that everyone had their tier.

There was a large dirt road that ran in front of the Imperial Grandstand. This is where the sailors would be marching today towards the Imperial Harbour, which it overlooked. The Imperial Harbour was the single largest structure in all the lands. She could see all four Expedition ships quite clearly as they dwarfed the other vessels in the harbour, but the workers were too far away to make out. It reminded her of an anthill of sorts. She saw the smaller trade vessels, which would depart all over the lands. They were half the size of the Expedition vessels, part of the Silk Fleet that transported goods all over the land.

A noise caught her attention. Her father was about to enter the Imperial Grandstand to take his seat. She stood up. Everyone else followed after her in standing. He, too, wore a seaweed-coloured ensemble. His silk tunic covered him down past his waist with matching trousers. Her father liked to dress simply, the only Imperial marking on him was a symbol of his title, being the gold dragon medallion that was placed over his heart. He was bald with a crow's nose.

As he walked toward her, she put on the best smile she could muster and bowed. A familiar scent hit her nose—it was opium perfume, a favourite among women at the castle. She raised an eyebrow at him, wondering how he smelled like that.

He sat down on his pillows, and she followed suit. Excitement rose inside of her as she heard the music from the reed flutes in the distance.

The Imperial Orchestra was made up of dozens of men and women, sharply dressed in their Imperial green tunics with matching brown pants. They began to march past, playing various musical instruments, from reed flutes to various drum sets. The air was filled with a symphony of music that she had never heard before. It was enthralling. As they marched past, she wished she could play that well. Part of her studies was music, though she failed at it. Her musical master had lectured her many times that music comes from the soul. If she could not play, her soul was lacking. She had not been truly happy since her mother, Duchess Dou, had fallen sick. It had been many years since it happened. She missed being in her mother's safe, warm arms. Father was not comforting when it happened. All he had said was, "Life is like a tree: Grow strong roots, and you will live your life healthy." and never spoke of her mother again.

The captains of each vessel walked along the Imperial Grandstand alongside their respective crews. *Brave*, she thought, as each man in the sea of red marched past. She was told sailors wear red because it stood out against the colour of water, so when someone fell overboard, they would be easier to spot.

Cheers came up from the lowest section of the Grandstand. Not from anywhere else. Odd. Why was no other section supporting their sailors?

A woman holding a child rushed toward the sailors. What was she doing? The woman grabbed a man and tried pulling him out of the parade, toward the Grandstand. Pingyang stood up to get a better view of the ruckus when a single word rang out: *"Sit."* She recognized her father's stern voice and sat, still immensely focused on what was happening. She wished she could hear what the woman was saying to the man, her husband?

Three Imperial Guards raced to the woman and pulled her away from the man. Pingyang could hear the woman screaming loudly, "Don't leave us!" The man pulled away from her and raced back to his place in line without looking back. How could he abandon his family like that?

"Foolish woman!"; "Dishonoured!"; "With a woman like that, he is better off leaving." She heard come from around her. How could people be so cruel? "Why do poor people have babies?" was another she overheard.

Her blood began to boil. Did no one have compassion?

She looked over at her father. "Can you not do something to help the family? You know that once those ship leave…."

But the anger in her father's eyes silenced her. She knew that he didn't care either. No one cared. She glanced around and saw that the aristocrats were all staring at her accusingly. She closed her eyes, hearing more hushed whispers. "How dare she raise her voice to her father!"; "A daughter should know her place."; "No wonder he never smiles."

She immediately regretted her actions. Looking back up, she watched the last of the sailors march downwards towards the harbour, to their deaths. Every time she cast a glance at the ocean, something strange swelled inside of her. Like she was being summoned by a distant voice.

A loud *roooooaaarrrrrr* pierced the air. Pingyang perked up. What the…?

Three large dragons swooped past the Grandstand. There were "ohhhhs" and "ahhhhs" from all around. Even she gave in as she watched two emerald dragons dive down and pull up at the last minute, rushing over the Grandstand. More cheers rang up from the spectators. Another *roooaaar* as a large black dragon landed in the grassy area in front of the Grandstand. Moments later, the two smaller ones swooped down and flanked it on either side.

Rooooaaar!

The cheers grew louder.

The riders looked tiny next to the beasts they mounted. All three dragons at once lifted their heads and opened their mouths, unleashing a blast of flames.

Everyone clapped at the spectacle. She had not been expecting the dragons to make an appearance. Judging by everyone's reaction, neither had they. People were glancing up at her direction, waiting for the Emperor to do something. Pingyang glanced over too, watching her father intently, but he sat there, expressionless. How was he not excited by what he had just witnessed?

A small smile appeared on his face. She had seen him smile like that before, fake. He slowly rose to his feet and gently clapped his hands in approval. A ruckus erupted all around her—everyone stood and clapped and hollered. They had permission now.

"Follow," her father said as he walked past her. Startled, Pingyang stood there momentarily and rushed to follow him.

They walked to the side exit of the Grandstand where four Imperial Guards were waiting for them. Dressed in Imperial Purple silk tunics with midnight black trousers, they were an imposing sight to behold. Tall, emotionless, highly trained killers. Each held their Qiang proudly out in front of them. Their lethal tips, polished to perfection, glistened in the sunlight.

As Pingyang walked past them, their cold, dead eyes were terrifying. She exited the Imperial Grandstand, with the Imperial Guards taking positions around her and her father as they walked to the dragons. With every step, she grew more and more excited. She was not afraid of the dragons—they made her eyes wide with wonder.

As she got closer, their scales reflected the sunlight. They were truly majestic beasts. The riders dismounted as they approached. How brave and strong they must be to be able to control the dragons. She stopped when her father did, several feet away from them still. The largest of the dragons was closest to her, and its eyes found hers. She returned its intense gaze.

"Daughter!" her father called. She rushed forward, almost bumping into him.

A dark look flashed across her father's face, and Pingyang stood there paralyzed. "To be aware, is to be present." he scolded.

Bowing her head in shame, she wished she could jump on one of the dragons and fly far, far away.

"Most impressive, how you handle these beasts," her father said, praising the three men before them, head-to-tow in black silk. The leader had gold trim added to his uniform, to signify his rank. Tall, with flowing dark hair, he was extremely handsome, she thought as he stepped forward to introduce himself to them.

"You are most generous, my Emperor. I am Duizhu Chao of the Imperial Dragon Squadron. May I also present Duifus' Biming and Cheng. Our powerful mounts respectively are Gang, which is Cheng's mount. Yun is Duifus Biming's mount. My magnificent dragon is Guang. She is unlike any other I have ever seen." Duizhu Chao said, beaming as he stroked his mount.

Pingyang admired the way he carried himself. Most impressive. Most people were terrified of being in her father's presence, but not Chao. If he could fly dragons, then nothing could intimidate him.

"Indeed," her father said nonchalantly. Did nothing impress her father? "May I present my daughter, Princess Pingyang. She quite thoroughly enjoyed the exhibition that you presented us," her father added as she stepped forward.

Chao gave a low bow of his head. "It is my greatest honour to meet you, Princess Pingyang."

Pingyang stepped back slightly, curtsying back. "Thank you." she said, hoping to conceal her excitement. Chao stared into her eyes. As she gazed into his, something flicked behind Chao's eyes that threw her off. Was it a flicker of darkness? She blinked and it was gone. Perhaps she had just imagined something.

"Perhaps you would like to join me, up in the air with Guang. I was going to fly overhead of the Imperial Expedition Fleet, to give them a glorious send-off. With your permission of course, Emperor." Chao offered as he extended his arm to her.

Inside of her screamed, "Yesss!". It would be the most thrilling experience of her life. Yet, the thought of being in such proximity to Chao made her slightly uncomfortable. She had never been in personal contact with a man before.

Her father's face indicated that he was contemplating it. She needed to say something now before it was too late. "That is most gracious, Duizhu Chao. I am ashamed to say that I am behind in my studies. Once we are done, I must spend the rest of the day doing such." Pingyang said meekly, hoping Chao would not press the issue.

A flash of disappointment came across Chao's face. Instantaneous as it was, Pingyang had still caught it. Chao was not told "no" often, she sensed.

"My daughter is too modest. She will join you. Bring her back to the Imperial Palace no more than one hour from now." her father stated to her absolute horror.

What?

"As you command," Chao said with a bow of his head, then reached a hand out to her. Reluctantly, she took it, letting Chao lead her toward Guang. She was resigned to her fate. *Tā mā de!*

As she approached the dragon, she felt simultaneously excited and nervous. She never dreamed to be so close to one. Guang reared her head up a bit as Pingyang got closer to her.

"Have no fear, Princess," Chao whispered. "She will not harm you. Show her that you are brave, worthy to ride her. Guang does not just let anyone ride her. The dragon choses the rider, Princess Pingyang. Let her choose you."

The dragon choses the rider? Pingyang thought that was odd—if she was a dragon, she would not want anyone riding her.

Chao led her straight to the front of Guang. Pingyang was in awe of the size of the dragon and its massive teeth, which she could have sworn were as long as her arms. Guang leaned her head down in front of her, and she locked eyes with the dragon. As she gazed into her large grey eyes, an overwhelming sense of sadness overtook Pingyang. The dragon was mourning. What had happened to her?

"Duizhu Chao, has something happened to Guang?"

Chao shot her a quizzical look. "Guang is the most powerful dragon there is, nothing can harm her."

Something did, Pingyang sensed, even if he was oblivious to it. *How could someone spend so much time with their partner and know nothing about them?*

Chao placed his leg into the leather stirrup, reached up to grab the reins, and pulled himself onto the dragon. Pingyang had been excited to ride, but after looking into Guang's eyes, it seemed bittersweet now.

Chao reached down, extending his hand for her to take it. She did not want to, but her father commanded her to. As she reached for his hand, something caught her attention. A long leather whip was curled up on the saddle, with six tails dangling down, each with a small metallic fist attached to the reins.

"What is that for?" Pingyang said angrily, pointing to the whip.

Chao, who looked to be taken aback by her tone, began to chuckle. "It's just a whip, Princess. Guang is a beast like any other. Sometimes she needs to be put back in line." Chao said lightly.

She wanted to grab the whip and put *him* back in line.

Looking over, Pingyang saw her father speaking with an unfamiliar woman. She was tall, with long black hair, wearing an olive hanfu that was decorated with golden trim. Was she a concubine? Pingyang couldn't remember concubines being let out of the Imperial Castle before, other than on long trips. Strange.

"Princess, we should go. Your father will wonder, if we do not take off soon, that something is wrong." Chao said impatiently.

She looked up at Chao and raised her voice. "Something is wrong. You whip Guang. You are the one that should be whipped."

Panic formed in Chao's eyes. *Good!* "Princess, people will hear! Take my hand, and together, we will go for a nice quiet ride, where we can get to know each other better." Chao said, flashing his best grin.

Tā mā de! She glanced back at her father. He and the woman were still talking. Her father rarely talked to a woman for any length time.

"Princess Pingyang, please. We need to go. We do not want to upset your father." Chao pleaded. She was not worried about upsetting her father too much. She was torn between the woman taking up so much of her father's time and flying on the dragon.

"I have decided to go see my father," Pingyang retorted and started to head toward him and the mystery woman.

"Princess, please. Flying is the most incredible experience in the world. I promise I won't use the whip. The Emperor is looking over this way."

Pingyang had no desire to ride with Chao, but was reluctant to defy her father in public. *Tā mā de!* "One quick ride. No whip." she demanded.

"Whatever you want, Princess." Chao said, looking relieved. Chao got up first and held his hand out to her. The thought of having to touch it repulsed her, but she knew she had to. She grabbed it and moments later was on the back of the dragon. Guang shifted under her, and Pingyang squealed, startled at the sudden movement.

"Loop your hands through the grips, Princess. They will keep you secure. Also, double loop your feet for added support." Chao instructed, and she complied, making sure there was no way for her to fall off.

"Yeahhhhhh!" Chao yelled out, and Guang responded by raising her head and letting out a loud *rooaaar,* which both thrilled and terrified Pingyang. Guang lurched forward and started running, flapping her massive wings at the same time, and within seconds, they were lifted into the air.

"Ahhhhhh!" Pingyang squealed and gripped on even tighter. She looked down and saw the people by the Grandstand getting smaller. She was breathless! She closed her eyes, feeling the cool breeze hit her face. *Amazing!* She had never imagined anything like this before. Throwing her head back, she laughed, longer and harder than she could ever remember. This was freedom!

She opened her eyes and looked down; they were going so fast that everything was a blur.

"What do you think, Princess?" Chao yelled back to her. Overwhelmed, she couldn't find any words. All she wanted to do was look at everything below. She noticed the Expedition Fleet in the distance and pointed towards it. Chao nodded, pulling on the reigns, so Guang turned in that direction. As they swerved, Guang went into a steep dive, which instantly brought her stomach into her mouth. She screamed in terror and thrill. They came up to the ships quickly, pulling up as they zoomed over the Imperial Harbour.

Chao had Guang skim so low over the water that Pingyang could reach down and dip her hand in it. Waving at her own reflection, she laughed again, and Chao joined in.

"Princess, we are approaching the vessels, I am going to go between two of them," he said, and she yelled back, "Woooooo!"

The salt smell in the air was almost overwhelming, but she relished it. It was invigorating. A horn blared from ahead, then two more followed out in succession. As they came up from behind the vessels, sailors waved up on them on the masts. Pingyang knew she wasn't supposed to, but she loosened her hands, lifted them up over her head and waved wildly at the ships.

"Princess, fasten your hands! It's not safe!"

She did not care. As they passed between two vessels, she continued to wave at the sailors, who waved back.

"Princess!" Chao screamed again. Grudgingly, she refastened her hands. They banked left and did a long turn back toward the Imperial Harbour. Pingyang had no desire to go back to the Grandstand, nor to land anywhere at all. All she wanted to do was be free. "I am taking us back," Chao informed her, darkening her mood.

There was only one place for her to go: home, which was the Imperial Castle. It was the largest single building in all the land. With its thirty-foot walls, it doubled as a fortress. Emperor Ju-Long of Clan Tang ordered its construction when he came to power. It served as a symbol of Clan Tang's power and how it could not be defeated. Her ancestor had been right—its walls had never been breached. There was a massive courtyard in the middle, which is where she spent most of her free time when she was not studying.

A sadness overcame her. She was flying back to her cage.

The Imperial Castle came into view, and a tear went down her cheek. Moments later, Guang landed in front of the massive wooden entrance gates. Pingyang unhooked herself, and as she let herself down, she took the whip with her.

"Hey!" Chao called out.

Pingyang looked up darkly at him. "Why so upset? You said you were not going to use it again. It's useless to you now. I am doing you a favour by disposing of it for you. Know your place and thank me, Duizhu Chao." The stunned look on Chao's face gave her immense satisfaction.

"My apologies if I overstepped, Princess Pingyang. I am honoured. I enjoyed our time immensely together. Your father permitting, I wish to see you again."

She needed to think up an excuse, quickly. "I am honoured, Duizhu Chao. Unfortunately, my father has extremely strict rules. I do not think we will meet each other again." she countered, hoping he would be discouraged by the news.

Chao smiled, bowing graciously to her. "It is a special day to meet a princess. I believe we were destined to meet, Princess Pingyang, and I cannot wait until the next time."

She placed her hand on Guang's head and whispered, "I don't like him either." For a moment, Pingyang thought a hint of a smile appeared across the dragon's face.

"Until next time, Princess Pingyang." Chao pulled on the reins, and Pingyang watched Guang run, beat her powerful wings and lift off. She waved up to the dragon. Chao waved down at her. Then it dawned on her: Chao thought she was waving to him.

Tā mā de!

Emperor Gaozu watched the dragon lift off and fly into the sky, hearing more cheers coming from the Imperial Grandstand. People were so easily amused.

Duizhu Chao was a most impressive young man. He was the youngest to ever lead the Dragon Squadron. How he achieved that position, however, had not been done honourably. Gaozu could overlook such things if that person could excel, which Chao had done. Perhaps his search for a husband for his daughter was ending. There were many suitors that had answered his summons for a potential mate. She was almost of age, fifteen. He had to be careful in his choice. Gaozu knew if he selected someone too ambitious, his place as Emperor would be in constant jeopardy. He planned to rule for many more sunrises. Especially with the knowledge he now possessed. How quickly everything had changed. There was no going back. Ignorance had not been bliss.

He turned to face the Imperial Harbour. The four massive vessels were starting their voyage across the ocean. He had never sought out to expand his Imperial influence beyond what it already was. There was nowhere else to conquer. Historically, the most progressive rulers had sent out Expeditions. He wished to be such. He thought he was the absolute ruler, until *she* showed up.

He had not been prepared for her; how could he have? When she had mysteriously entered the Imperial Castle and presented herself, he had been outraged at her nerve. How dare a mere woman think she could stroll into his throne room as if she owned it? His first instinct had been to have to her executed for her brashness, but when she showed him her abilities, he ordered his guards to stand down. What she presented to him was beyond his wildest dreams.

His Empire was not the only that existed.

There were new conquests to be had. Untold treasure for him to enjoy. The thought excited him immensely. His legacy as Emperor would be the greatest that ever was. He took one last look at the ships. He had given the Captain's their final orders earlier this morning: come back with treasures, or not at all. But now, their mission had become secondary. He would have many more talks with the woman, Xifeng. His legacy as Emperor was at stake. As well as his clan's very survival.

Interlude 0.1

The Quintessence

Ksenia stepped outside her diner onto the wooden porch and sat in her rocking chair under the wooden awning. She looked up at the peaceful moons, seeing it was almost time for the Soul Moon Convergence. She wondered how many souls would be drawn to it if any at all. Looking down at her scruffy cat that jumped up on her lap, she said, "What a wonderful night, Hunter." Hunter looked up at her and purred, lazily stretched out on her lap without a care in the world.

As she gazed over the lake, something dawned on her. This was not the same lake that she had grown accustomed to looking at. The diner had shifted locations without her feeling it. She sighed heavily; time was taking its toll on her.

"Getting old, Hunter. Just don't get old." She sighed. It was quiet and calm. Why had the diner brought her here? "Something is happening, Hunter; I feel it in my weary bones." He offered a concerned *purrrr* in return.

She studied the lake, trying to figure out which one it was. There had been so many over the centuries, it was becoming hard to keep track of them all. She noticed there was a village along its shores.

Then it came to her. They were beside Sighişoara. Were the Drăculeşti going on another murderous rampage?

An "Evening, ma'am" startled her, and she turned to see a figure in a black leather trench coat with a matching wide-brimmed hat, standing a few feet away. Ksenia investigated the man's handsome face. This was no ordinary guest. There was an aura about the man. Something familiar, yet something she could not place.

"What are you and why you are here?"

"Just here for a meal, ma'am. As for who I am, my name is Sam. Like you, I have my duty to fulfill," and said no more to her.

She did not like the answer, but part of her sensed her "guest" was telling the truth, as vague as it was. There was something familiar about him. "Have we met before?" she asked cautiously.

"Yes, ma'am. There have been rare occasions where your guests have found a way to escape our touch and were required to come to your diner."

She sat there, not entirely sure what the stranger meant. But something stirred inside of her. "I understand."

"Don't mind Sam, he loves being mysterious," teased a playful female voice from out of the shadows. "My name is Jessica."

Ksenia turned to her left, where a tall, blonde woman stood smoking a large cigarillo. She was dressed in a black leather dress with a large black sunhat.

Two of them! *Tchah!*

"It's been a long busy day. I don't suppose you have any hot meals on your grill, now, do you, ma'am?" Sam asked her.

"This is most peculiar, but I suppose," Ksenia said with uncertainty. "Everyone is welcome. Go inside, I will be inside in a minute to take your orders." The guests tilted their hats before entering.

What in the blue blazes was happening? Ksenia sighed and petted Hunter. "Well, I should go see what our 'guests' want. There is something odd about them, that's for sure. Business sure is about to pick up, I feel it in my bones, unfortunately. What do you recommend, chicken soup or sea bass?" Hunter licked his lips at the thought of both and then purred.

She smiled. "Good choice, chicken soup is good for the soul, they say. Best start preparing some before more customers arrive. Hunter, we may need more meat—would you go into that creepy forest that is in the area? Shoot…what's it called…the Dark Woods. Yes, that is what it is called. Go fetch something delicious."

He licked her face, jumped out of her arms and moment later, was out of sight. Ksenia went inside The Quintessence to learn more about her 'guests' and take their orders.

Hunter stopped running and looked back to the diner in the distance, filled with sadness. How could a mother forget her children? What would happen when Death forgot that she was supposed to be Death? Ksenia's abilities powered The Quintessence as a whole, and in turn, her children, as well. If Ksenia forgot to use her power, would the Reapers lose their abilities? Would people just stop dying? What would happen to her children? Would they cease to exist? The thought of unliving people wandering around made his fur shudder. Hunter wished he could help, but he had no idea how. What if Ksenia retired? If Sam took her place, was that possible? Was it possible to retire from being Death?

Hunter decided that if the 'guests' were still there when he returned from his hunting trip, he would talk to them about this.

Hunter sighed, then started sprinting toward the Dark Woods. Out of all the lands he had traversed, there were only two places that terrified him: this place and the Duat Pit.

The Duat Pit was an infernal pit of death and despair—nothing lasted long in its grasp. He feared no beast in the Dark Woods, it was the unnatural that terrified him.

A cold breeze wrapped around him, gently tickling him. "Enter," it whispered to him. As Hunter sat there, only one thought came to mind.

Crap!

Chapter 4

Drăculeşti Castle—Sighişoara

'Hide and Dream'

"Vladimir?" Vasilisa Drăculeşti called out as she entered her son's bedroom shaking her head. It was as messy as ever, and empty. She walked over to the bed sitting down, running her hands on the messy blanket.

Vladimir was probably hiding somewhere in the castle like he always did when it was time to get ready for dinner. At least he had recovered from his ordeal and was out of bed. She had been immensely worried about him.

She left the messy bedroom and walked down the hall lined with paintings of former Drăculeşti ancestors thinking about where he could be. Vladimir had been alternating between the roof of the castle and the cellars, so she decided to look on the roof first—she always did her best to avoid the cellars of the castle. Whenever she went down there, she sensed an unnatural presence.

She walked to the oak door and opened it to go up the creaky stairs to get to the roof of the castle. At the top of the stairs she pushed the lock back, opening the latch. As Vasilisa climbed onto the roof, a warm breeze hit her, and she smiled. She wondered if Vladimir chose the roof to see something specific or simply the view.

The roof was made of grey bricks, only broken up by the various red chimney stacks. There were seven chimney stacks in all, sticking out from the roof, yet there were only six fireplaces. The roof also had several hatches spread out, but when she opened them all, there was merely blackness. She could never figure out where they led to.

When she had first married Vlad and moved into the castle, she had spent days exploring every part of it, as it was to be her home for the rest of her life. She had marvelled at its beauty and structure. The Drăculești Castle was the only castle that existed in all the lands. It had been created as a symbol of their strength. Very few challenged that strength over the years. There were the Spiriduș to the north, but they never travelled too far south, nor along the coast or rivers. She often pressed Vlad to learn more about the history of the Drăculești and why the castle seemed...unnatural at times. Vlad assured her that the castle was fine repeatedly. When she would press him harder, he always gave the same answer—it was an old castle, and who knew what his ancestors were thinking when they built it. It was a flippant response.

Quietly along the roof she walked and peeked around the nearest chimney. He wasn't there. She tip-toed towards the next chimney and crouched down slightly; it was sunny with no clouds in the sky, so Vladimir would easily be able to spot her shadow. As she got closer to the chimney, she heard muffled breathes. She smiled, knowing that she had found the right chimney. She stopped and listened for a minute to see if the sound of Vladimir's breath was going to move or remain still. And still, he kept it. She counted to three in her head and lunged around the chimney, grabbing Vladimir laughed.

"What gave me away?" Vladimir asked her, joining in the laughter.

"Nothing much. Just your breathing."

"That's what usually gets me caught, I think." Her son was over a head taller than her now. How had he grown up so fast?

"Lately, you seem to come up here more and more, Vladimir. Are you longing for something beyond what you have or simply enjoying the view of the village?"

Overlooking the village and Lake Sfanta Ana, the view from the roof was magnificent. The lake stretched out beyond the village to the Ikornis River, which flowed into the ocean. On the water, they could see the larger fishing trawlers sailing, as well as other various small crafts. The lake was an important source of food for the village and trade, as well. The Drăculești family had decreed long ago that fishing could only be done at certain times of the year. Like the crops that the farmers grew, everything took time to grow back.

Sighișoara had become the capital when the Drăculești took control over the land. Since then, the population had grown exponentially. It had started off as humble village with a few small houses that were built when people first began to settle in the area. Now, it had a sprawling harbour for fishing and trading boats as well as smaller personal crafts. Facing the harbour was the trade district, which was a bustling area of activity, with delicious aromas emanating from it at all hours. From fresh baked bread, to the salty smell of fish and lobsters, to the comforting scent of coffee. Off to the left of the trade district was the craftsmen area, where the carpenters and metal workers had their shops that were instrumental to the growth and maintenance of the village and the land. To the right of the trade area was the living quarters, many buildings of all shapes and sizes that housed families. Surrounding the castle was the farmer's fields, where most of the crops were grown in the land. It was a fine capital that she was proud of.

Vladimir turned to her. "Do you think there are other places that we do not know about?"

She thought about it for a few seconds before replying, "I do not know for sure. No vessel has ever returned from the ocean, and the last expedition left over thirty years ago."

"I think there is." Vladimir said boldly to her. "One day, I am going to find it. And when I do, I will bring you a necklace from whatever place I find."

She smiled—she adored necklaces. "If there are strange lands far away, make sure you dress warm enough and have enough food and water with you to last."

"Yes, mother." Vladimir said with a sigh and looked back at the lake.

There was something in her son's sigh that worried her. "Vladimir, what's bothering you? I do not think it is faraway lands," she asked, touching his shoulder.

He stood there motionless, looking over the village for quite a while. Vladimir sighed again, heavily, and turned to her with his head down, tears pouring down his face. "Lash. When I woke up, I saw Lash's face. The look of happiness when I said we could split the winnings. We went from trying to kill each other to partners instantly. Then *poof!* In a blink of an eye, he was gone. I almost saved him, Mom, but I failed. I know deaths are part of the Obsidian Trifecta...but..." Vladimir lamented, and she took her son and held him tightly.

It pained her to know how much her son was suffering inside. Vladimir continued to sob. "It's my fault. I was reckless, thinking the rules shouldn't apply to me. Lash's *viskta* is going to hate me forever."

She knew that their *viskta*—family—needed the atria badly. Lash's father had three fishing vessels, but a storm had recently sunk their largest, newest vessel. Years of savings, gone.

She stroked her son's hair gently as she held him. "Actions have consequences, Vladimir. What you did changed the fate of that *viskta* forever. This was an incredibly painful lesson, and I am sorry you went through it. Deaths are commonplace in the Trifecta—it is expected. What is unexpected is an underage contestant. The village will not forget this for a long time, though not everyone is against you. Some applaud your bravery; others curse you for your foolishness."

Vladimir pulled away from her and looked into her eyes. "What about you?"

She had been dreading this question. Treading as lightly as she could, though as firmly as possible she stated, "You are the youngest Trifecta winner in history. I am immensely proud of you for that. But you disgraced our *viskta*, and your father will have to explain your action to the council. Because you were not officially entered, your winnings will be held over to the next Trifecta." Her son cringed.

"What should I do, Mother?"

She smiled as best as she could, stroking his arms. "Go into the village. Let people see you. What is done is done. Put on the biggest smile you can. Act normal. If you don't, then the whole village will know you are sulking. If you walk through the village sad, they will take it as weakness. As the ruling *viskta*, any sort of weakness is not an option. Your entering the Trifecta showed everyone you are man enough to do it. Also, man enough to take any consequences from it. Do you understand, Vladimir, that this is important?"

Vladimir was silent for a while before nodding his head.

Good. She beamed even more broadly. "It will be rough on you for a while, but it will pass—I promise."

A hint of a grin appeared on Vladimir's face. Time to change the subject.

"I am sure if there are strange lands far away that you would be the one to find them. Your curiosity knows no bounds," she said as cheerfully as she could, then looked up at the sky. The three moons shone nearly as bright as the sun.

Her son was gazing up, as well, asking her. "I have never seen them this close together before. Is it possible that they may touch each other?"

"It is said that when the moons do, they create the Soul Moon Convergence. No one has seen one since I can remember, and I'm old," she declared.

"You are not old mother. And besides, you cannot get old—I will always need you."

She glowed. "What do you think about the legend, Vladimir? Do you think there is a soulmate for you?" She could see the wheels spinning in his head, until he replied, "I don't know. I mean there are a couple of classmates that interest me."

"Don't worry, Vladimir. I am not going anywhere for an awfully long time."

"Good."

She was intrigued. Who else besides Kazia?. "You have some time before dinner, so head down to the village—but do not be late. Best to be home on time, as your father will be home tonight." She watched Vladimir's face crumble slightly as he turned to head back inside the castle, disappearing. It was not going to be a pleasant meal, but she was happy to have her family whole again.

Looking up at the moons again, she marvelled at the sight. The two moons in front she knew would touch one another. The red one on the left was Becalm, and the blue one on the right was Soever. The third and largest white moon that appeared to be coming down behind the front two was called Sopanis. Legend said when all three came together, the Soul Moon Convergence was set to occur.

The thought of the Soul Moon Convergence had fascinated her ever since she had heard about it in school as a young girl. Excitement filled her—she was going to be alive while it happened.

She looked down for Vladimir and caught sight of him walking along the path to the village and waved to him. She had been talking to the baker's wife, Anca, yesterday, who had mentioned that she had seen Vladimir hanging around the bakery more often—and it was not for the baked goods. Vladimir was smitten with the baker's daughter, Kazia.

She was happy Vladimir had a crush, but there was a problem. Kazia was arranged to be married to Marku, which spelled disaster for Vladimir. She knew if he persisted, this was going to be a hard lesson for him. *You do not always get what you desire in life.* Though who else interested her son?

Suddenly, an ice-cold blast hit her, chilling her core and climbing into her very soul. Where did the cold blast of air come from? It was a warm day, and the sun was shining brightly in the sky. It seemed... unnatural, she thought, the small hairs on the back of her neck standing on end.

She ran to the edge of the roof and leaned to look over the village. Nothing was out of the ordinary. She rubbed her arms absently, even though she was no longer cold. Had she imagined it? No, her very core had been chilled, even if it had been momentarily. Tonight, was a night for love. She decided to dismiss it. It was probably just a side-effect of the moons being so close together.

She looked out over the village again. All was peaceful. Smoke escaping dozens of chimneys, and various scents hit her nose, even from the rooftop, from baked sweets to steaming steel. When scents filled the air, she felt that was when the village was most alive. It meant it was humming with life. People were bustling about carrying out their duties, and life was progressing. That was the best part of living in Sighişoara, which was a far cry from being raised on a farm.

After she turned ten, her adopted father became ill and could not work on the farm anymore, so the responsibility fell on the three of them.

It was a struggle. She, her mother, and her brother had never done farm work before. They wouldn't cut the crops properly and would take much too long pulling them. A good part of the harvest was lost the first year, and they had all suffered through a long, cold winter with next to nothing. Tempers flared, as everyone was hungry, each blaming another family member for the harvest failure. Nothing was the same after that.

She saw a family walk along the outskirts of the village, the father playing with his son and daughter. A touching moment.

Vlad often warned her that she was being too soft on her sons, but she did not care. She wanted better for them, plus she could handle a little disobedience on their end. There were other ways of handling irresponsible behaviour than with a belt. She shook visibly, thinking of her adopted father menacingly holding his belt in his hands before he hit her with it.

"Most husbands come home and find their wives in the kitchen or having afternoon tea with a friend. I come home and find my wife daydreaming on the roof," a rough, teasing voice said from behind her.

She whirled around to see her husband standing there. She rushed towards him and jumped into his arms, and they kissed passionately. Gently, he settled her down, and she gazed into his piercing black eyes. They were tired and weary. She knew it had been a long, miserable trip for him, investigating the latest attack The Spiriduş had committed. She reached up and touched his scarred face. He was still the most handsome man in the world to her. Tall, powerfully built, with long black hair, Vlad towered over her. She often teased him about the lack of colour in her husband's choice of clothing over the years. Vlad was wearing his customary black shirt and pants, though he did have a red handkerchief around his neck. *An improvement.* Any colour that he wore was a small victory in her ongoing battle to add flavour to his image. She reached out and straightened it.

Vlad took her hand and they walked towards the edge of the roof. She put her arm around his waist, and he did the same. They stood there in silence, enjoying the quiet moment they so rarely got. "How is Vladimir?" he asked with a hint of concern in his voice.

She sighed; the moment had passed. "He is physically recovered for the most part. He is a Drăculeşti, tough as they come. Emotionally, he is shaken. Lash's death has hit him hard. He blames himself for the death. I talked to him not long ago. I told him to go into the village and act normal, but warned him that some of the villagers blame him for Lash's death, as well. Many wives have come to see me over the past couple of days about this. It has not been pleasant. Some of the village applauds Vladimir's actions as deaths are just part of the competition. None of the victors have ever been held responsible for the deaths during the competition. The village will be divided for quite some time."

Vlad stepped away from her and crossed his arms. She saw her husband's eyes go dark. She braced herself for whatever was to come.

To her surprise, he didn't yell. Instead he looked at her and growled quietly, "This is my fault."

She blinked. How was it her husband's fault? "At Vladimir's age, I never would have entered until I was of age, for fear of my father's wrath at breaking such a rule. I have been far too lenient with that boy, and because of that Lash has paid the price. We didn't see Radu or Micrea entering underage, now, did we? I have gone soft. Now look at what happened."

Perhaps he had a point. Their eldest sons waited until they were of age before entering. Vladimir had nearly died during childhood, and since then, she had spoiled him more than her other sons. "How did you find out?" she asked.

"Mr. Hindrick. When I entered the village, he was on a delivery. It's bad enough our boy has been seen hanging around with his daughter who is arranged to be married. Now this? He blasted me about Vladimir's action, how reckless he is. He made it quite clear that Vladimir needs to stay clear of Kazia from now on. I will talk to Vladimir tonight about this, among other things."

Vladimir *really* liked Kazia. She nodded. The Hindrick and Drăculeşti *viskta*s were civil to each other most times. There was bad blood between them going back many years, ever since a member of the Hindrick *viskta* had been sentenced to death. The only evidence was the word of a drunkard. "How about our other sons? Since no other fathers have yelled at me for their actions, I can assume they have been behaving?" Vlad asked. Micrea had taken his father's place at the City Council meetings. Radu disappeared most mornings, leaving Vasilisa clueless about his activities.

"Micrea hates the meetings," she said. "He understands why he has to go, but he hates the politics of it. Radu…well…he has "stuff" he does every day. I ask him for details, and that's all I get."

"Hmm." Vlad looked contemplative. That was it? "I believe Radu is going through 'stuff'. I will speak to him. He needs to be reminded that 'stuff' is not a valid excuse for all his actions. As for Micrea, I feel his pain, but it's a necessary pain."

Vasilisa was worried about Radu. Ever since his seventeenth birthday, he had changed. "What could Radu be going through? He is done school now, yet he still disappears. It has been like this for over a year now. I remember when the change happened. It was after the trip you took him on for his birthday that year. Radu came back…different somehow. He jokes more now about everything. Nothing is serious to him anymore," she said, looking up at Vlad. She knew her husband, and the look on his face told her that she was right.

Vlad smiled, kissed her on the forehead and looked down at her. "Radu had his first kill on the trip. It affects everyone differently. Micrea was freaked out on his birthday trip after his first kill, as well. There is a monumental difference between sitting down and cutting into a steak and going out into the bushes and hunting your meal. Seeing all that blood, I admit, can be…overwhelming. Radu is not a hunter. There is no requirement for him to go on a hunt again if he does not want to."

Vasilisa knew Vlad was right. Out of all their children, Radu was the gentlest. Yet she had heard idle gossip from other wives of Radu getting into fights at the harbour. Especially after he had consumed Blood Cider. It felt at times as though Radu was two different people trapped in one body. Radu had proved he could defend himself if needed. More than once, she had to break her boys up. When she told Vlad about their scuffles, he merely shrugged and asked who was winning. If killing had affected Radu so much, then it was best that he never went on any more hunting trips.

"Will you take Vladimir out hunting on his seventeenth birthday? Vladimir is sensitive, as well, though not as much as Radu. Perhaps seeing the aftereffects on Radu, you could find something different for Vladimir?"

"It is Drăculeşti tradition," Vlad stated matter-of-factly. "*Our most important.* I know you do not understand. It is a rite of passage, and it must happen."

Rite of Passage? What did that even mean? She had asked Vlad when he took Micrea out, and he did not go into any details. Vlad remained tight-lipped about it ever since they returned. "I don't want Vladimir to go through the same 'stuff' that Radu is going through," she said defiantly.

"I believe Vladimir's early entrance into the Trifecta shows he is made of sterner stuff than Radu, *and* Micrea." Vlad shot back at her with a half grin.

"You are proud of him, aren't you, my husband," Vasilisa said teasingly.

Her husband's expression lightened for a moment before becoming serious again. "Damn straight. Any father would be of their son competing in the Trifecta, especially winning. But I can't tell him that, now can I? It would only serve to justify what he did in his mind. As proud as I am of him surviving, let alone winning. A harsh example needs to be made of Vladimir. If I don't, other underage children will enter. No, I will have to set a punishment for Vladimir, one harsh enough to deter anyone else from thinking about entering before they are legally allowed."

She did not like the sound of that. She knew her husband was right, but she dreaded the outcome for her son. "What have you decided?"

He shook his head. "I do not know. I don't want to be overly cruel. I know far too well how that is." Vasilisa's adopted father was cruel, but he paled in comparison to Vlad's father.

Vasilisa was silent for a moment, then reached for her husband's hand. "I trust you," she said. Vlad gently squeezed her hand back.

She knew when Vladimir got home, it was not going to go well. So much going on, especially with The Spiriduș becoming more active—which is the one subject they had yet to broach. "How bad was it?" she said quietly.

Vlad let out a heavy sigh. "Preslav has become bolder. He has started attacking larger, heavily guarded caravans. In that, too, I have failed. I have let myself be convinced that attacking them head on would create more deaths, unnecessary deaths. Just like Vladimir, they do not fear my retribution. My failure is just about complete."

Failure? "*No*. You are the best father I could ask for my children. As for The Spiriduş, you will figure it out. I believe in you, my husband." Vlad was taking everything too hard, he burdened himself with everything.

"Thank you, my beautiful wife. I have lived in this castle all my life, yet never thought to come up here. Offers a unique perspective on things. Vladimir definitely has the right idea," he mused.

Vasilisa smiled. Of course, he knew. "What about the moons? Do you think the legend is true?"

Vlad looked up at them, and she did, too. Tonight was going to be special, she could feel it. After a few moments, Vlad replied, "It does seem like they will touch. Perhaps it is true."

Vasilisa embraced her husband. "Do you think if we were young and the Soul Moon Convergence happened, we would be soulmates?"

Vlad brought her close to him. They shared a tender kiss that left her breathless. "I have no doubt. No other woman has ever been your equal, nor will ever be. You are the absolute best wife I could have asked for." She beamed. "In fact, later tonight I will prove just how thankful I am," Vlad teased, sliding his hands below the small of her back and pulling her tight against him.

She grinned mischievously in return and returned the favour, locking her lips to his in a long embrace.

The moment was broken by Vlad's stomach rumbling. They giggled, and she pulled away. "My ears tell me you might need some energy for tonight's festivities. I am going to head down to the kitchen and start on dinner."

Vlad rubbed his gut. "Yummm to both." She laughed, turned on her heel and headed back down into the castle, leaving her husband on the roof by himself, imagining their 'dessert' later that night.

***

Vlad watched his wife head into the castle, his face still lit up. Truly, he was thankful for Vasilisa. No other woman would put up with him, he was sure of it.

He walked over to the edge of the roof and peered into the village. Where was his son? He scanned the village, his eyes finally spotting Vladimir talking to his friend Tomas. He felt sorry for the *viskta*'s lost fortune; with Tomas's father falling sick, he was forced to quit school and work in the mines.

A thought struck him. *Vladimir's punishment.* Vlad knew his wife would not be fond of it, but it would serve its purpose. Vladimir would work in the mines for five hundred hours. If that did not deter future underage contestants, nothing would.

As for the Spiriduș, a more direct approach was needed. His own father had been harsh, borderline cruel, but he had been effective in keeping the Spiriduș in check. *The predator does not listen to the baying of sheep*, his father had often told him. The sheep, in this case, being the council. How had he forgotten that? It was time for him to do the same. It was time to remind the land what the name *Drăculeşti* truly meant.

Chapter 5

Luxor Prison—Thebes

'Slide or Die'

High Priest Nakhte sat on the filthy floor, resting against the stone wall, still in shock from the unexpected events that occurred a few days ago. The cool night air blew through the window—a large opening on the outermost wall. Ever since he had arrived, the breeze sent chills up and down his bones. He had searched the entire level for something to wrap himself in for respite against it, but there had been nothing. The prison guards had laughed at him when he had brought this up, recommending that he end his life that very night. They believed he would not survive the harsh reality that was the Duat Pit. Or the long, horrific nights he had to spend here as he awaited transport.

Yet he was still here. He had heard the horror stories about the Duat Pit, but never paid much attention to the details, other than it was a living, twisted nightmare. He got up and looked out and down at the rocks and sand, wondering how long it would take for him to hit the ground below to his death.

The prison dwarfed all the buildings around it. It was a crimson, narrow obelisk that seemed to have no peak, as it went straight up into the sky itself. No one in the history of the prison had been able to successfully escape. Each floor held sixteen cells, four along each side of the outside wall. There was a small corridor that ran along the inside of the prison on each floor that linked the sixteen cells together so that the prisoners could interact with each other if they wanted. He was lucky, as the floor he was on was empty. In the middle of the cells was a shaft that opened when the food came up twice a day and when it was time to replace their pails. He never felt more truly alone than he did this night.

He stared up at the moons. Was this his punishment for his misspent life? Had he foolishly believed that he could have escaped this fate with his lifestyle? Had he truly ever believed in the Gods? He had seen rituals done successfully before. He had done them, as well. In his final ascension to High Priest, he had to perform a complex one, which he had done successfully. Where had that ability come from? He could not remember the last time he had even attempted a ritual. As the highest of the priests, he delegated those menial tasks so he could enjoy taking liberties from those asking for his help. Many a woman or man seeking help for a loved one paid his price willingly, no matter what it was. Over the years he had become more and more creative with his 'prices'. Had the Pharaoh been aware of these dealings, he would have been killed years ago, but everyone was sworn to secrecy. Plus, no one wanted to admit in which ways the Priest assisted them.

Perhaps it wasn't too late. If he threw himself at the Gods and Goddesses' mercy, they might grant him a way out. He walked over to the opening in his cell and fell to his knees, spreading his arms wide and yelling at the top of his lungs, "I have been lustful, laid with men and women. I have drunk until I could drink no more. I have done rituals in your names, yet still lost my faith and forsaken you. I am not worthy. I beg of you for your help…. Free me, and I will believe again and get vengeance in your names. Please, help me… Help me. Let me be your instrument of retribution, and together, we shall undo what this young, foolish Pharaoh has ordered."

He had no doubt that since the Pharaoh's massive army of workers had started smashing the faces of statues, it would not take long to begin reconstructing them with their ruler's figure. Crying out again, "Please. You once deemed me worthy of your gifts. I know I can be again if you let me." He looked up at the sky for any sort of sign, but there was still nothing.

Anger washed over him. How dare they ignore him now. They needed him just as much as he needed them. Once the statues' faces were destroyed, their followers would stop talking about them, and in time, they would be utterly forgotten. Is this what they wanted? No, they were testing him—he was sure of it. "Fine," Still on his knees, screamed once more up to the `Gods. "What must I do to prove I am worthy of your gifts?"

"Xara!" He spun around in shock at the sound of the familiar voice. General Pentu was standing in his cell with a look of exasperation on his face. The General walked up to Nakhte and held out his hand to help him up.

Nakhte took it and got to his feet, putting on his best face andattitude he could muster. "General Pentu. What a pleasant surprise. I apologize for not being a better host. Unfortunately, housekeeping is not up to our usual standards. Perhaps if you would be so kind as to talk to the Royal Warden on my behalf, I would be eternally grateful."

The General walked past him, gazed down at the distance to the ground, and gave a low whistle. Nakhte was puzzled as to why the General was in his cell.

He decided not to beat around the camel's ass and just ask why the General was here. "I appreciate the visit, General Pentu, though I am at a loss for the reason. I have no illusions that we were...*friends.* In fact, I know that you disliked me immensely…"

The General walked up to him, cutting him off. "Cut the dung pile, High Priest. I know all about you, your 'miracles'. The 'prices' you charge for them. You disgust me! Did you not think I knew what was happening in my army, to the people in my charge? That I was not informed of the problems so many of them had encountered over the years and how those problems were 'fixed' somehow?

"At first, I was grateful that you were able to help my people. Jealous even. But as the years passed, it became less about helping those that came to you and more about you helping yourself. Yet I said nothing. Those people that came to you were consenting adults and knew the price. Jealousy turned to disgust. But I digress—time is of the essence, as I have an attack to lead later tonight."

Nakhte was stunned at the revelation. How arrogant and deluded had he become over the years? His fall had been truly complete. He walked over to the window in his cell.

"Not yet," Pentu called out from behind him.

Nakhte stood there, dejected. "Why not?" Truthfully, he did not really care about the answer.

General Pentu inched closer, staring deeply at him. "I need information."

He was even more confused now. *What information?* He decided to play it cool. He was a master in the Art of the Deal. "Of course, General Pentu. How may I be of service?"

The hard stare never left the General's face. "The dead bodies in the Royal Pyramid. You stated they were already dead. Explain how you knew this."

It took a moment for Nakhte to realize what he was being asked. Then a small smile crept over his face. He had his advantage. Now, how to use it to his benefit? "Of course, General. I would be glad to help you, though I do have a small request in return. Something simple, well within your means," he added coyly.

All at once General Pentu rushed toward him, wrapped his hand around his throat, and lifted him to the window, suspending him in the air. "I don't have time for games, nor am I as young as I used to be. I may not be able to hold you very long."

Nakhte grasped desperately at the hand around his throat, but it was iron tight. He kicked as wildly as he could, punching at the hand that seized him, but to no avail. "Alright…I'll t-tell…y-you…" he managed to say, as he felt utter desperation at the situation.

The General unceremoniously dumped him onto the cell floor. His head hit hard. He touched his temple, and blood covered his fingers. Rage built inside of him. "I said I would tell you what you wanted to know!"

General Pentu looked down at him and kicked him in the stomach, making the Priest double over on the ground. "My patience grows thin, High Priest. Tell me what I want to know…. *now!*"

The Priest help up his hand and nodded. "The assassin's throats had been slit. It was barely noticeable, as there was paint covering up their necks. Their bodies were also heavily bruised, like they had been slammed hard against something. The Pharaoh killed one using a spear, rammed into one attacker's chest, and the Royal Guards killed the other with their swords. They had far more injuries than they should have. The fact that both their throats were slit is evidence enough that there was something off about the attack. Neither one had their throats cut during the attack on the Pharaoh."

The General stood there silent for some time. Nakhte could tell the General was deep in thought. "Chione knew," the General said at long last.

Chione had been the quickest to discredit him and the Gods...*why?* The kingdom would never accept a female ruler. Was she sponsoring someone else? If so...*who?* Nakhte grew hopeful as a thought popped into his head. "General Pentu, take me with you. Together, in front of the Pharaoh with the dead bodies as proof. All will be forgiven!"

General Pentu stared at him. *What was the General thinking?* "No. I can discover this treachery myself. The time of the High Priests is over. For too long you and your class of servants have gone on unchecked. It ends now. Enjoy the Duat Pit, former High Priest Nakhte," the General declared, turning to leave the cell.

"I will have my vengeance for this. You shall suffer at my hands, General. I promise you this!" he shouted.

The General stopped and turned, a cold smile forming on his face. "I look forward to it," he said, then he left him to his fate.

The High Priest began to sob, falling to his knees. His Gods had forsaken him, his Pharaoh—he was truly alone.

"No need to be so sad," a unfamiliar male voice said behind him.

Nakhte whipped his head around and saw a large, filthy bald man wearing a tattered green shendyt towering over him. He was instantly terrified of the man. He closed his eyes, hoping this was all a hallucination because of all this mental trauma he was suffering.

"The General wanted me to give you a token to remind you of your stay here, sweetness," the man continued.

Nakhte opened his eyes—he was still there.

"Oh, I'm real, alright. I am Rakne. Tonight, will be a very special night for you." He walked over and stood directly in front of him.

Looking at the smoking hot firebrand that the man was twirling in this hand, Nakhte knew he needed to do something quickly before he was branded like a common camel. The ember's firebrand had the initials 'LP', which he knew stood for Luxor Prison. He was not going to allow this monster to desecrate his flesh with it. He lunged towards the window; he was not quick enough. The man caught him.

Nakhte fought to free himself, but it was hopeless. He had to find another way. Even though he had risen to the rank of High Priest, he had spent many years exploring the human body as his main distraction. And while he was still scared of the man, he refused to be a victim. There were parts of the human body that didn't require a lot of strength to inflict punishment.

"Do you need a hug first?" the man taunted, approaching Nakhte with the smoldering firebrand.

Now was his chance.

Nakhte drove his left knee straight into the man's groin, simultaneously driving his thumb into his eye. Nakhte dropped to the floor as the man went down, groaning in pain. He bolted out of the cell and down the small corridor that led to the other cells, but there was nowhere to escape. The only exit was the window in each of the cells. Desperate, he searched the ground for a rock or something he could use as a weapon.

Nakhte had never killed a man in mortal combat before and knew he was probably going to die. But he would rather die fighting here than be dumped in the Duat Pit, where he would slowly descend into madness. He was quicker on his feet—his only hope was to outrun him around the middle shaft until he tired him out.

"You're going to pay dearly for that, sweet cheeks." The man had already caught up to him. The man was just a few feet away. "I was only going to brand you once. Now, every inch of you."

He had caught the man off-guard once, but he doubted he would allow it to happen again. Frantically, he searched through the cells, but there was nothing that resembled a weapon. *Doomed!* He needed to stall, think up something other than soaring out of a hole in a wall.

"General Pentu wanted a token for you to remember your stay. I am used to hamburgers, but tonight I have a special treat: steak…delicate steak, still fresh. Goddess Hathor has been extra kind to me tonight, and it would be a waste not to take advantage of her offerings…"

He backtracked and stayed close to the shaft, blinded by the darkness. He wished it was daylight. The moonlight helped, but it still was difficult to spot anything.

"Ohhh, sweetness, you've been naughty and made daddy upset. You need a branding, a good hard one to teach you a lesson. He he, I am good at brandings. Years of practice." The voice was moving closer now, it was only a matter of time before he was caught.

Nakhte heard the scraping of pebbles on the stone and moved around the shafts quietly as possible. He peeked around the corner—it was clear. As he made to turn, the man appeared out of an empty cell and sprung in front of him.

"Boooo!"

Nakhte tripped over his own feet and fell flat on his face.

"I hope you didn't bruise that pretty, smooth face of yours," The prisoner said in a mock-concerned tone.

Nakhte got up as quickly as he could and retreated in the direction he came from, the man in full pursuit behind him. The latter was catching up to him, as Nakhte's legs burned from the overexertion. He forced himself to keep running.

"Save some strength, my pretty, I don't want you to be completely tuckered out for tonight's festivities."

Nakhte was running out of breath. He could not fight or hide—there was only one option: climb down the side of the wall.

He did not have the strength to climb all the way down, but did he have a choice? "Please, Goddess Wadjet," he said under his breath. "I seek your protection on this night so I may live and get vengeance for you, your brothers, and your sisters. So that I may put the Pharaoh that has forsaken you, who seeks the destruction of your images, to justice. *Please...*" He was coming up to another turn, but he ran straight for a cell instead. He could feel the man's breath nearly on him now. The time for running was over.

Nakhte took one last deep breath and pushed himself further, gaining more speed than he imagined he was capable of. When he got near to the edge of the cell's opening, he threw himself on the floor, sliding legs first. He twisted his body as he slid, pebbles digging into him, but he didn't care. He was dangling off the edge of the cell, holding himself up with his arms.

The man stared down at him in disbelief. "Is death really so much better than being poked a few times? Come on up, sweetness, and let's talk about this. I have a job to do, one that pays very well. Now climb up, or I will pull you up. I can't promise how gentle I will be. What do you say, sweet cheeks?"

Nakhte knew he only had seconds before those gruff dirty hands would be all over him, and he would be violated with that firebrand in more ways than one.

"Keep dreaming." Nakhte let go and fell straight down alongside the wall. He felt with his body for something to stop his fall. His hand caught onto a small ledge which abruptly stopped his fall. He cried out in pain, his hand on fire from the jagged top of the ledge. carrying his weight. Knowing he could not hang forever and too afraid to look down, he whispered into the night air, "Goddess Wadjet...please," and let go.

He seemed to fall for an eternity, until he felt himself being stopped in mid-air. *Impossible!* He was thrown through the air and seconds later landed hard on the stone floor. *Owww...* He did not know how much more abuse his body could handle. Looking around, he saw he was in another cell, virtually identical to the one he had just been in.

"Your nails are such a mess, so bloody and bruised—what has happened to you, High Priest Nakhte?" said a concerned voice.

Nakhte opened his eyes. Chione was looking down at him. *What the...?* "How are you here? Did Wadjet send you to rescue me?" he asked hopefully. This woman's unexpected appearance might change his fortunes. She had saved him for a reason—he was sure of that. Who was this woman truly?

Chione gave a short laugh. "No, Wadjet did not send me. You don't even believe in the Gods—why would you ask that? Or are you a believer now and hoped they would save your sorry ass?" she said, an amused expression on her face.

What was going on? "Why are you here? If you want me dead, you could have just let me continue my fall down the side of the prison to my death. What are you, truly?"

Chione sighed. "All in good time, High Priest. I believe you still had quite a way down to your death. I have an offer. Just know it comes with a price that I will come to collect at the opportune time—and no, I am not going to tell you what it is," she added. "Accept my help blindly, or I toss you out of the cell, and you take your chances with falling again. Who knows, you may land on a soft shrub and only half your bones will break. What is your choice?"

He suspected the price would be one he was not going to like, but did he really have a choice? When he called out for help, did he mean it, or were they hollow words?

And then a thought occurred to him. This was their test...he was sure of it. "I choose my Gods. I believe. Keep your damn help...I already have it" he fired back, then turned to climb back to the edge and continue his voyage down.

"You are more foolish than I possibly imagined. Your Gods will let you fall to your death, you know, but if you choose death, so be it. I shall enjoy watching your body fall."

When he reached the ledge, he turned to face her. "Since I am going to die anyway, what's your plan? What's in this for you? You do not care about our Pharaoh or his glory. What is your game? What are you playing at, Chione? You knew about the assassins, that they were already dead before they attacked the Pharaoh." He hoped his imminent death will be enough for her to spill her secrets to him.

Chione simply smiled and winked at him.

"What's going on over there?" They were not alone on the prison level. He heard feet shuffling nearby, and they belonged to more than one man. *Crap.* Nakhte turned, but he was facing a solid wall—the window was gone.

He looked over at Chione, who was casually ignoring him. "Look, fresh meat," a man's voice yelled, and then another: "Come and get it boys, tonight we are going to party like a Pharaoh." There were hollers of joy. He was completely trapped.

"I agree!" Nakhte shouted, and he witnessed the evilest grin he had ever seen come across Chione's face. She blew him a kiss and walked out of the cell before disappearing out of sight.

A half dozen prisoners were making their way toward his cell. It was now or never. He spun round and sprinted for the window; he dropped to his legs as he neared, sliding to the ledge and swinging them over the gap where the window had reappeared. He was prepared to slide down.

"Wait, wait…we won't hurt you…" said one of the men, who looked almost identical to the one who was chasing him around with a firebrand. "We were just joshing…honest. You don't want to die; we will treat you nice. Your face is so pretty that we will let you wash it every day, won't we boys?" The men nodded in agreement.

He had no desire for their hospitality. He closed his eyes and let go of the ledge "*Nooooo!*" several men shouted above him, and then silence.

"Please, Goddess Wadjet!" he called out as his fingers desperately tried to get a hold of something to grip.

"Do you believe?" a strange feminine voice asked in his head, and Nakhte cried out, "Yes Wadjet, I do!" He thought this was it—that the Gods would save him. But he continued to fall. He started flailing his arms, trying to grab a hold of anything, but there was still nothing. "I believe Wadjet…I believe!" he screamed out, desperate for the mysterious female voice to return. Silence. Perhaps it had just been his imagination. Knowing he was almost at the ground, he spread out his arms, preparing for his death to be swift. He was going to die on his terms. He opened his eyes, feeling strangely at peace. The moons moved closer than they had ever been. It was the most beautiful thing he'd ever witnessed in his life. He smiled at their beauty, welcoming death.

Splash! Nakhte found himself being sucked around in circles in a large vortex of water. *He was sinking fast.* He struggled to swim to the surface, but the current was too strong. Was he dead and this was his afterlife? There was no water around the prison—he must be dead. The sensation felt real, though; he was instinctively holding his breath, and his eyes were burning… from the water? Had Wadjet saved his life after all? Was this part of her plan? Or had Chione intervened?

Panic hit him as he was engulfed in blackness. His lungs were on fire—he desperately needed to breathe. He convulsed and his mouth instinctively opened, water filling his throat. His body was still fighting, but his brain told him it was over.

Why had the Gods been so cruel as to tease him and still let him die? Nakhte felt something grab him, and he was being ripped out of the water. Moments later, he was on the ground, coughing violently. Desperately trying to get the water out of his body, he did not know how long he coughed for. When he finally stopped, he wiped his eyes. "Thank you," he whispered into the wind, then laid on the ground and started crying. *He was still alive.*

He felt drained and weak and could not move, but his senses slowly started coming back to him. How was he still alive? Who or what had rescued him? A strange odour filled his nostrils, and he thought he heard whisperings. Did he dare open his eyes? He heard a loud snort…animals? Slowly, he opened his eyes.

He stared in horror at the face of a filthy beast…that was wearing beads and earrings? And some sort of dress.

Clothed oxens?

The creature reached out to him with its hand, and he backed up as quickly as he could, smacking the back of his head onto a rock behind him. He groaned, cursing himself for putting his body in more pain.

Up ahead, there were dozens of clothed oxen standing around, staring him down. Where was he? Was this his punishment, after all? The one that had been closest to him stood up, and they locked eyes. "I am Kema Earthstone. Welcome to the Netherworld."

Nakhte was on the verge of passing out from exhaustion, and now shock. His last thought was of his fellow priests, still captive. He vowed to himself he would rescue them…somehow.

***

General Pentu stepped outside the Luxor Prison and looked up at it. Truly monstrous. He had heard that the original colour was supposed to be black. As the prison was being constructed, there were an obscenely high number of deaths that had happened. Workers falling to their death. Ropes snapping, dropping their heavy weight on unsuspecting victims. The prison was supposed to be completed in six years, but it took nearly twenty. The most ominous thing he found out about the prison was that when it was completed, it was painted completely black, as intended. But the next morning, it had turned blood red. No one could explain it.

He had his own theory—that the prison was painted by the spirits of the workers that died during its construction.

He shook his head and let go of any thoughts of it. He had more pressing concerns. The team of Medjays he had ordered to follow Chione were due to give their first report tonight, before he was to depart to command the attack. He did not trust her from the moment they met.

He knew he needed proof before he could say anything or move against her. Now, with this new information on the dead assassins, the General knew he would need to secure the bodies before confronting Chione and showing the Pharaoh her duplicity. *Something did not feel right.* After all the skirmishes he had fought over decades in the military, his ability to sense danger had been honed and never failed him once. Chione was more dangerous than any foe armed with the deadliest weapon. If he was going to survive this and not wind up with the same fate as the High Priest, he would need to be discreet and patient. First and foremost, there was a battle to be held tonight.

He heaved a heavy sigh. There were times he wished he were a poet or a farmer. Tonight was one of those nights.

Interlude 0.2

The Dark Woods – Europea

Hunter was about to enter the forest when he stopped. He was being watched. A dark cloud loomed overhead. It was the only cloud in the sky. He knew what it was— *The Nexus*. Someone was watching him from there. He hissed at it and lifted his paw, pretending to claw at it. Futile, he knew, but it made him feel better. He headed into the forest, glad he had excellent night vision. Even though it was still daylight, the forest was eerily dark.

He scurried through the trees. He did not want to stay any longer than necessary. So far, nothing was disturbing him. Perhaps whatever dwelled in here sensed he was like his brother, Neit. Peering through the lush green brushes, he spotted a large European Roe Deer grazing in the clearing. He licked his lips. It had four-point antlers, which were rare. This meant it was no ordinary deer—its meat would make an extra savory meal.

Its greyish-brown coat glistened in the small rays of sunlight that managed to pierce the tall trees. Slowly, he made his way closer, weaving through the bushes as quietly as he could so as not to spook the deer. He could hear the relaxed thumping of the deer's heart, strong and steady. It was not aware that it was about to wind up in a wood stove, seasoned and spiced and everything nice. Hunter inched away from the edge of the brush line. He licked his lips. He could not remember the last time The Quintessence had brought them to this land before. Normally, they wound up in Egyptia, which was nice, as it gave him a chance to stretch out and work on his tan.

He refocused on his unsuspecting prey and steeled himself to attack. The deer turned its head slightly away. He knew it was his moment.

Suddenly, the forest came alive. A dozen wooden doll-like creatures burst out of nowhere brandishing knives, dressed in tattered children's clothes. He could not believe his eyes.

Thinking back, he remembered what they were called. The Marionettes. They encircled the deer and made poking gestures at it. Remaining low and crouched, he was not sure what to do next. They were about to kill and eat his delicious supper. How was he going to explain to Ksenia that some oversized children's toys had stolen their meal?

They were about three feet tall, bald, with glowing crimson eyes. It was quite the bizarre sight: they continued to do some sort of intimidation dance as they moved around the deer. The scene before him would be inconceivable if it weren't for the fact that he was in the Dark Woods. Out of all the lands, this forest housed the largest number of unnatural creatures in one place.

An odd sensation came over him. He turned his head to the piercing gaze of one of the wooden dolls. It was wearing a tattered wooden five-pointed crown on its head—it was their leader. Their eyes met, and Hunter saw no fear in the doll's intense gaze back.

Regardless, he had no doubt he could take them all. But it would be a vicious fight. His brother had tangled with creatures in the forest before and had not come out unscathed. Hunter bowed his head in a sign of respect and moved back slightly in the bushes to show he did not want to fight. Their leader raised his dirty, blood-encrusted knife up in a sign of acknowledgment and turned to join in the odd intimidation dance.

Hunter watched the deer rear up in defence, but its attackers stood fast. The deer was surrounded by unnatural creatures that knew no fear. The deer didn't stand a chance. It must have recognized this, too, because it bolted, attempting to jump over its attackers. The Marionettes leaped onto its torso and started stabbing it repeatedly.

It was over in a matter of moments. The deer crumpled face first and was dead by the time its body hit the ground. Hunter was impressed by the speed of it all. The Marionettes jumped up and down in celebration but stopped abruptly as their leader approached the carcass. He raised his hands in the air, beat his chest twice, and placed his left hand on the deer's head. Hunter watched, astonished, at what happened next: the leader began to hum and was soon joined by the rest.

After several minutes of performing their ritual, they put away their bloody knives and rolled the deer over, slowly picking it up off the ground. He watched in amazement as they hoisted the deer above their heads and carried the much larger creature away, as if it weighed nothing. *Incredible.* Hunter stayed there for a few more moments and sniffed the air. No other large prey nearby. *Time to move*, he thought and left the bushes in search of his next target.

As Hunter got deeper into the forest, the buzzing of the forest lessened. He didn't even hear the rustling of leaves, and it was starting to freak him out. The forest was dead, or was it playing dead? Could a forest play dead?

He walked past more trees, then stopped in his tracks. He had reached the edge of the forest. Had he gone so deep that he had crossed it? Perplexed, he sat there alongside a dirt road.

Movement caught his eye. Hunter turned and saw a lone man jogging down the dirt road toward the village, at him. *What the…?* Hunter recognized the uniform as one Sentinels wore. The man looked injured, but determined not to give up. As he jogged past, Hunter raised his paw, giving him a wave. The man ignored him and kept jogging, muttering the same words repeatedly, "Birthday celebration. Deidra." Impressed by the Sentinel's determination, Hunter watched a little while longer, then headed back into the Dark Woods. He wondered what was so special about the birthday celebration with Deidra that was driving the Sentinel beyond the point of exhaustion.

Chapter 6

Imperial Palace—Chang'an

'Slithering Surprise'

Princess Pingyang sat in front of her large framed, cream coloured mirror, brushing her long black hair, thinking, *why did it have to be black?* Why couldn't it have been brown or red, something more vibrant? Something different to make it stand out instead of being the same boring colour that virtually everyone else had. She was a princess after all—she deserved better. Perhaps she should get one of the servant girls to paint her hair, make it special.

She dismissed the thought. Her father would never allow it. Her father never allowed her any freedom. Her days were spent at the library, listening to one master after another talk about military tactics and economics. Why her father wanted her to learn these things, she did not understand. Whenever she asked, the only response she got was that it was "important", and then he would urge her to finish her dinner and get ready for bed.

She was practically an adult, yet her father did not let her have the freedom of others her age. Ever since she was a little girl, all she was told was that she needed to grow up and be beautiful, get married, have lots of kids, and listen to her husband like a good wife. She would know nothing except happiness and joy. She would not want a better life, she was told.

Marriage and kids were not what she desired. Escaping the palace and exploring the land, embarking on incredible adventures—that was her desire. *Then*, perhaps, she would think about getting married. Deep down, she knew there was little chance of any of that coming true. Her father would immediately send the army after her, and she would be locked up until she was forced to get married. The mere thought made her miserable.

She was wearing the dark purple dress that was once her mother's favourite. She never got to wear what she wanted, she thought. When she got older, would it be whatever her husband wanted? Would she never have a choice in what she wanted to do or wear? Perhaps when she was thirty and had six kids, no one would care about what she wore.

She knew being born to status had its perks. She caught glimpses of those who did not have that. Sometimes while walking down the halls, she heard the women crying from the concubine's quarters on the way out to the stables. She always wondered why they cried so much, but she stopped herself from asking, as she did not really want to know the answer.

She was told that whoever she married was going to become the new Emperor, as women were not allowed to rule. She hoped her father would pick a man for her that was kind and gentle. Not like most men, who walked around the palace with their hard looks and battle scars. She feared most of them were neither gentle nor kind. She did not want to marry someone ugly, either. He had to be handsome, but most of all he had to be brave. As she put down the brush, her hand grazed something on her dresser—the whip Chao had used on Guang.

Duizhu Chao was certainly handsome, brave—she had to give him those traits. Not everyone was brave enough to get close to a dragon, let alone ride one. But if Chao used something so barbaric on a creature as majestic as a dragon, how would he treat her? Chao had made his intentions clear to her; he was bold, as well. The more she thought about it, the more she realized Chao had a lot of qualities she could admire.

Except for one. Perhaps in time, with a gentle hand, he might change. Putting the whip down, she thought of her mother. Had her mother similarly sensed the same of her father when they met? What had her father been like when he was younger? What did it matter? Her mother was told to marry her father. Perhaps that is why her mother wore a melancholic expression on her sleeping face when she snuck in to see her. Was sadness her own fate, too?

Her mother, Duchess Dou, was beautiful and vibrant until illness struck her when the princess was still a child. She vaguely remembered her father bringing in the best healers from all the clans. Each one had failed in diagnosing the mysterious illness that overtook her mother. They were all sent away after a time. Her father turned to the innovators, the brilliant minds of the lands, and they were brought in to study her, and to find a cure. Alas, they also failed. Her father gave up after that. After a time, he grew more distant, and their relationship changed from that point on.

The princess lifted out of her chair and walked to the window, staring out into the courtyard, where some concubines were having a stroll. She wondered why they looked like they were in pain all the time. Did they work that much harder than everyone else? If so, why were they not rewarded better, she thought, resting her forehead against the windowpane.

Her thoughts drifted to the dream she had last night. It was rare that she dreamt of snakes. The last time she remembered dreaming of snakes was the day after her mother fell ill. Did that mean that something bad was about to happen? The last thing she wanted was for her father to fall ill, too. That would mean that she would be forced to marry right away, and she did not like that thought at all.

The sun was high in the sky, and she felt the warmth on her face. She tried not to think of tomorrow—she was to visit the main army base as part of her lessons, seeing how it operated and how the units trained and worked together as a fighting force. Who wanted to see a bunch of sweaty, muscled men pretending to kill each other in drills? How filthy.

She loved history. She had read about the clan wars throughout the centuries. Perhaps if there was no military, their society would have advanced much farther than it had. Killing off the youngest and brightest did not seem like a good way to prosper.

Sighing, she made her way to the dragon decorated doors that led to the courtyard, which was adjacent to her bedroom. There was a large fountain in the middle—a carved grey dragon with water spewing out of its mouth.

She sat down on the edge of the basin and held out her hand, letting the cold-water drip over her fingers, then forming circles with her fingers in the water, which turned into random designs. She stopped when she looked up at the moons. Never had she seen the moons this close together before, she thought, awestruck. She tried to remember the tale she was told as a child...what was it again?

Her question was answered by a female voice emanating from behind her. "The Soul Moon Convergence." She turned to come face-to-face with a stranger: a tall, fair-skinned woman with black hair and striking red highlights at the ends. The crimson-eyed woman was staring intently at her with a smile spread across her lips, making Pingyang uneasy.

Looking more closely at her, she noticed something in her eyes: they were almost...dull. There was no radiance to them.

This was the same woman who was speaking with her father on the day the Royal Expedition Fleet left. There was something different about the woman in front of her. "Who are you?" Pingyang asked.

The woman's crimson eyes bore right through into her very soul, sending chills up her arms and legs.

"I am Xifeng. I am honoured to meet you, Princess," the woman replied with a slow bow.

"I have never seen you inside the castle before," Pingyang said defensively. The only time a woman arrived at the castle, it was as a concubine, which she sensed this woman was not.

Xifeng smiled at her question. "No, Princess. I have only just arrived. I believe you saw me not long ago speaking with the Emperor."

Pingyang decided that she liked this new addition to the castle. Xifeng smiled at her. Women didn't smile unless they were in private, which made Pingyang wonder why Xifeng wasn't afraid to show hers. "Do you remember hearing about the legend of the moons? What happens when they come together when they touch?"

Pingyang knew it had something to do with meeting your...soulmate. *Yes!* Did she have a soulmate? "It is the night you meet your soulmate."

"Very good, Princess. You remember your childhood stories. It is not just about meeting your soulmate, but believing that you have a soulmate, without any doubt. You must believe, Princess. Even if one does not believe or has not heard of the legend, soulmates will feel compelled to go to the Soul Rock. If one of you has faith, that is enough."

Pingyang was enthralled by what Xifeng was saying. She suspected if she had a soulmate, her father would not make her marry some stranger. He would send for her soulmate and bring him to her instantly. If she had one, she would be able to do as she pleased.

Beaming, she looked up at Xifeng. "Yes, I believe in the legend."

"You believe, just like that?" Xifeng asked skeptically. "Why do you believe? Because I said so? Or does the thought of having a soulmate mean more freedom to do as you please?"

Pingyang was stunned. Could she read her mind? She did want more freedom. Perhaps Xifeng knew something about her life in the castle, but how? She wondered if it had something to do with Xifeng's crimson eyes. They were so unusual. Perhaps they let her see inside of someone. She wanted to ask Xifeng about them, but she knew it would be extremely rude, so she restrained herself.

Why did she believe? It just felt...right. "I believe because it feels right. That I am meant to have one. Having someone that would listen to me, to go out and have adventures with. I know he would be brave and handsome, as well."

Xifeng smiled sadly. "I was once young like you, Princess, with hopes and dreams. Thinking of what my life would be like, what kind of man would I marry."

Pingyang wondered what had happened to Xifeng's hopes and dreams. Perhaps it was linked to why Xifeng's eyes did not have any sort of sparkle in them. "I do not wish to offend, but may I ask what happened?"

"You are young and curious, Princess, I understand. Life did not work out how I hoped it would. The man that I loved was taken from me, sent far away for the crime of loving me, and became a prisoner in a distant land. I spent many years searching for him, but to no avail."

Pingyang was stunned at the revelation… *Tā mā de!* "That's horrible Xifeng! I can talk to my father; I am sure he could help you."

With a weak grin, Xifeng shook her head. "That is most generous, Princess, but it is far too late for him to be rescued."

Pingyang was confused. Why wouldn't Xifeng take the help? "I do not understand…" Pingyang started to ask, but then realized what Xifeng meant—the man she loved had died. Her heart shattered into pieces at Xifeng's loss. She could not imagine the pain.

"What you *can* do, Princess, is to be with your soulmate. No matter how far away he is, no matter how hard it is. You don't stop until you are together, forever."

Pingyang beamed. "Do you really believe I have a soulmate?"

Xifeng moved toward her so she was inches away and placed her hands on Pingyang's shoulders. "Look at the moons. Something incredibly special is going to happen tonight: The Soul Moon Convergence. I believe you do, Princess. With all that I am."

Pingyang leaped forward and gave Xifeng an excited hug. This was going to be the best night of her life. She felt it inside that something amazing was going to happen. There was only one thing she did not quite understand. "How will I meet him?"

"Tonight, when the moons touch, a new moon will be created—the Soul Moon. The new moon will appear in the shape of a magenta heart. When the Soul Moon appears, come out into the courtyard, and you will find a grey stone in the shape of an hourglass. It will be raining during this time, so you need to stay at the Soul Rock. As the rain pours, if you have a soulmate, they will appear in the water that collects at the top of the Soul Rock, and you will be able to see him."

Her heart was pounding with excitement. She had to force herself to remain calm. She was overwhelmed with emotions. She was going to meet her soulmate! She was going to live a long and happy life…a life of what she wanted, whenever she wanted it. She would have all the adventures she dreamed of. She was sure of it.

Interrupting her daydream, Xifeng asked softly, "What are you willing to sacrifice to be with your soulmate?"

Startled at the question, Pingyang leaned back slightly. "Why would I have to sacrifice anything?" Nothing they had talked about had mentioning sacrificing anything.

"There is always a price, Princess, for everything. Nothing in life is truly ever free." Xifeng said gently.

A coldness gripped her heart. She felt it hard to breathe, but she wasn't sure why. The conversation had suddenly shifted in another direction. "What would you sacrifice for true love?"

Xifeng warmly smiled back. "Everything."

Pingyang believed her. She considered her sacrifice. Her father was Emperor, so she would always be protected. She and her soulmate would live here, of course, as it was a castle. Pingyang could not think of anything that she would have to sacrifice at all. "Everything for me, as well."

"Do you think it will be Duizhu Chao that you will see tonight?" Xifeng asked her. The question threw her. Chao? Why would it be him? Pingyang did not know what to say. "What's wrong, Princess?"

"It can't be Chao; he is cruel to Guang. He hits her with a whip," Pingyang said.

Xifeng looked down at her like one of her teaching masters would, "Do you act up? Are you always the perfect princess?"

She shook her head.

"Do you think a dragon is always perfect?"

She had never thought of that before. Perhaps Chao was justified in hitting Guang sometimes. Maybe he needed the whip to keep the dragon in check. "Perhaps Guang does get out of line. I never thought about it."

Xifeng's look lightened. "Do not judge until you know all the facts. I would think your masters would teach you something similar."

She nodded, knowing Xifeng was correct.

"Indeed, you are a very brave young princess, willing to risk it all for love and happiness. I believe your mother would be truly proud of you."

Surprised at the mention of her mother, Pingyang asked, "Did you know my mother?"

Xifeng shook her head. "No. I have heard she was a very special woman who had strength and beauty."

Saddened, Pingyang said, "I wish she had not fallen ill...I miss her so much. I visit her secretly."

"As you are so strong and brave, and to help with your loneliness, I have a present for you." Xifeng said.

Pingyang perked right up—she loved presents.

"The present I have for you may seem a little strange, but I believe in time, you will come to think of him as truly remarkable." Xifeng held out her arms with her palms up. After a few moments, Pingyang frowned. Nothing happened.

Xifeng's grin looked a touch mischievous. "He's still young and quite shy. Perhaps if you called his name, he would come out and introduce himself."

Pingyang stared blankly at her. The present was a 'he'? Unsure of what was going to happen, she asked cautiously, "What is his name?"

"Slithers."

What kind of name that? Curious, she inched closer to Xifeng's outstretched hands and called out, "Slithers!"

She stared intently at her hands, but at the corner of her eye she spotted something moving under Xifeng's sleeves, shifting toward her hands. There was a quiet hissing noise before it stopped moving altogether. She pulled the sleeve back slightly to reveal a baby King Cobra emerge from the sleeve and look up at her quizzically.

A snake! For some reason, Pingyang did not feel afraid, though part of her felt that she should have. Snakes were dangerous.

"It's okay, Princess, you can reach out and touch him. He may lick you to taste your skin, but do not be alarmed."

Pingyang slowly brought her hand forward to pet him, and he did stick his tongue out, licking her palm. She giggled at the touch.

"What did I tell you? Nothing to fear at all from Slithers—and I hope you think the name suits him." Xifeng said cheerfully.

"Yes. The name suits him quite well." Pingyang watched Slithers slither over and slide onto her hand, then hiss softly at her. Slithers was introducing himself, she thought, and she returned the favour. "I am Princess Pingyang." She bowed her head—Slithers bowed back.

She had a new friend! Pingyang lifted her chin up to Xifeng. "Thank you," she said, and then did something very unprincessly: she threw herself at Xifeng and pulled her into a one-armed hug.

"You're most welcome, Princess. Slithers is a special snake, as he can sense things. Trust his instincts. Also, you can not walk around the castle with a snake in your hand, your father would…" Xifeng made a slicing gesture at her throat, pointing to Slithers.

Pingyang nodded. "How do I hide him? Keep him in my room the entire time?" She hoped not, as she spent so little time in her room. She did not want Slithers to feel lonely and neglected; she knew the feeling only too well.

"No, Slithers is special, as I said. Do you know what a tattoo is, Princess?" Xifeng asked her, and she nodded back. "Slithers can become a tattoo on your body. Though, once he becomes one, he cannot change the location on your body. You must choose carefully. Remember, as Slithers grows, he will take up more room. As you need to keep him concealed, you must think of a place where he can grow yet remain invisible. Or you can carry Slithers around with you, not becoming a tattoo. He could stay in your room and such. Your choice."

Pingyang thought about it for a moment. Slithers becoming a tattoo was the best choice—so her father would never discover him—but where? She wanted Slithers to be able to see, as well as remain covered.

An idea struck her. What if he were placed underneath her hair, with his head coming up to the back of her neck. Not out too far, but out far enough so that if she pinned her hair up slightly, he could still see. "I know the spot!" Before she could say anything, Slithers slid up her arm to his designated placed at the back of her neck. Having Slithers slide over her felt weird, but not *bad* weird. Touching the last spot he settled on, Pingyang no longer felt him.

"When he is a tattoo, you will not feel him. But know that he is there," Xifeng added reassuringly. "He will come out when you call him or are in dire need of help."

Amazing.

"Remember, Princess: tonight when the Soul Moon Convergence begins, look for the Soul Rock. Let tonight be the night where your new life begins. One filled with adventures beyond your wildest dreams."

"Thank you for Slithers. I will look after him and make sure he is well-fed so he will grow up big and strong," Pingyang promised.

"You are most welcome, Princess. Remember what I said," Xifeng said, flashing one last smile before bowing and walking away, out of sight.

Pingyang was overwhelmed by everything that had just happened. She looked up at the moons. They were on the verge of touching each other. Was Chao her soulmate? She had treated him badly at the Imperial Grandstand. Had she been too caught up in the moment and been too harsh? He had done nothing bad to her. In fact, he had not lost his temper, nor been cross with her.

Guilt washed over her. The more she thought about it, the more she regretted her actions. She sighed heavily and headed towards her bedroom. Soon, it would be dinnertime, and she needed to be ready.

***

Xifeng was lying down on the grass, twirling a long green grass blade in her fingers. It had been awhile since she returned home to The Nexus. She was looking down at Sighişoara. The village was a hustle of activity, with smoke rising from chimneys, people scurrying like ants all over the place. A bright light came from behind her, and Chione appeared beside her on the grass.

Xifeng looked over at her sister, who looked back at her. She was closest to Chione, out of all their sisters. Her other sisters did their own thing. She knew they cared but were not close. It didn't matter to her; she was thankful that she had someone.

"Hey, Sis, how's tricks?" Chione asked playfully.

She smirked. "You know." They giggled. "They have no idea what's going to happen to them tonight. I almost feel bad for them."

"Almost," Chione said. Xifeng turned her head back down to watch the villagers, and fell silent again. She didn't know how long they people-watched before either one of them spoke.

"How long has it been?" Xifeng asked.

Chione considered this for a moment. "I don't remember anymore. You still miss him, don't you, Sister?"

Xifeng nodded. How many lifetimes had it been? It didn't matter. She could never forget him, even if she wanted to.

"For being characteristically dark and moody, Sister, that present you gave the Princess was very generous. I did not think you had that sort of kindness left inside of you."

Xifeng knew her sister was trying to change the subject. "Well, she could use a friend, like I did."

Chione reached over and clasped her hand. Xifeng squeezed back. "Is the attack ready to go for tonight?"

"Yes. The Pharaoh wanted quick retribution for the attack on his life. These people below will be the first of legions of deaths for this game that's about to begin."

Xifeng nodded and looked backwards, seeing the waterfall behind them, along with the large, black castle that was the home of the Specter. Now that he was once again free, disaster and chaos reigned supreme.

"Hey!" Chione shouted, pointing down toward the village.

"What?" Xifeng said, following her finger.

"I don't believe it. Look, over by the farmer's fields. Do you see him? It's Hunter!"

Xifeng scanned the fields in search for the cat. *There!* If Hunter was here that meant *she* was here, as well. "You don't think…" Xifeng started to say.

"The Quintessence must be around here somewhere," Chione finished. "Follow back the direction you think Hunter might have come from." Together they scanned the grounds…nothing.

Xifeng did another scan, peering around the area then back in Hunter's direction. The cat was out of sight…how was that possible? "I don't see Hunter anymore," Xifeng said.

"Bahhh, the cat went into the Dark Woods, we can't see into that place," Chione reasoned. "Though, admittedly…I don't want to."

The Dark Woods. Xifeng had only been inside that place once before, and she swore she would never allow herself to be swallowed up by its darkness again. There was one other place that truly terrified her: The Duat Pit. But still, this place…if visitors weren't eaten by creatures, then they would face other...unnatural creatures, who would surely want to have their fun—either way, entering the forest was a risk. She remembered she had inadvertently stepped on a trap and was swept up off the ground, hanging upside down by vines. She didn't know how long she had been hanging there before her capturers came: a pack of large, black rabbits. They gnawed through the vines, making her fall to the ground, then dragged her body all the way to their home. When she had arrived, Xifeng was stunned at the sight of huge black bears sitting around a large fire, a black cauldron suspended over it. The bears were slicing carrots and celery and tossing them into the pot. She was going to be their main course. She remembered pleading to the animals, but they merely laughed in return. If it hadn't been for Neit, she would not be here—Neit had come to her rescue, nearly dying in the fight. But even outnumbered, he had won. Xifeng shuddered at the thought of being cooked and eaten by forest creatures. Since then, she had not eaten any meat, nor liked the company of creatures that she couldn't control.

"It's that time, Sister. We both have a big night ahead," Chione said, and Xifeng nodded back. They got to their feet and hugged. "Be safe, Sister."

"Like they can hurt us," Xifeng said. "Besides, you are the one that will be in the most danger tonight. Don't let a Drăculești get too close to you. We know what they are capable of."

Chione pretended to yawn to her and walked to the edge of the floating island, then allowed her body to fall. A bright light appeared for a second, then disappeared.

Chione was so dramatic. Xifeng gave the village one last look, blowing it a kiss.

Chapter 7

Sighişoara—Europea

'Familiar Faces'

Vladimir Drăculeşti rushed down the large dirt path that led from the castle into the village. Glancing back, he spotted his mother still standing on the rooftop. He smiled and waved to her.

The dirt path split into three directions as it joined the village streets. Heading straight, Vladimir passed by large dirty black buildings, which he suspected had been white some time before all the black soot got baked on them. He arrived at one of the smaller weapon shops and stepped inside, then straight towards the shop's work area, where he saw Sasha Costache hammering a piece of long hot metal on a black stone. Sasha was a short, older balding man, sporting his usual black leather apron and protective gloves and working on his latest creation.

Sasha was the best weapon smith in the village. Vladimir remembered seeing a weapon being made for his father when he was just a child. It was so majestic, with intricate engravings; when he approached Sasha with his request, he knew the weapon smith could make it. Sasha was a friend to their *viskta* since he could remember. Plus, his father trusted the man, so he did, as well. His father seemed to understand people in a way Vladimir knew he never could.

He stopped a safe distance away from the sparks flying above Sasha's head and waited patiently for him to finish, even though Vladimir knew he had little time before dinner.

When Sasha stopped hammering, he picked up the hot metal object he was working on and placed it into a large black metal cauldron that sizzled when the object touched it.

Finally, Sasha turned to him. "Vladimir, what can I do for you today?"

They both knew why he was at the shop. "I came to see them, of course," Vladimir said with a grin. He waited excitedly as Sasha walked to a long wooden counter, reached for something below it, and came back up with a lavender cloth that was wrapped around something small. "You know it would have been easier for a jeweller to have made something so delicate, Vladimir," Sasha said, gently unwrapping the cloth.

Vladimir half-nodded as he looked down with wide eyes. His heart leapt with joy—they were just as he imagined: two small earrings in the shape of small golden daggers, with hearts for the tips, each handle adorned with a single, small round diamond. "*Magnificent,*" Vladimir whispered.

Sasha's face filled with pride. "Thank you, Vladimir."

Vladimir couldn't tear his eyes away. "Thank you, Sasha. They are...I am speechless." He watched as Sasha carefully wrapped up the earrings and held the cloth out to him. "Thank you, Sasha," he repeated. "What do I owe you for this?" Vladimir asked, reaching into his pocket hoping he had enough atria.

"Nothing, Vladimir. The expression on your face was payment enough."

Vladimir held out his hand to thank Sasha, but Sasha did not shake it. "It's a shame isn't it? Poor Lash. Their *viskta* really could have used the atria. Had I known about your foolish actions in entering the Trifecta beforehand, I never would have agreed to make them." Sasha's tone turning bitter.

Vladimir stood there, not knowing what to say as he watched Sasha go back to work. Guilt washed over him, his stomach starting to twist inside; he didn't know how to respond. The earrings felt heavy in his hands, just as his heart felt equally heavy at Lash's death. His mother had warned him this would happen. He hadn't taken her too seriously, which he was now regretting. He expected Lash's *viskta* to be upset with him. But not Sasha's *viskta*. Vladimir's guilt was quickly replaced by anger. What right did Sasha have to judge him? *Asshat!*

He turned on his heels and left the weapon shop, slipping the earrings into a pocket inside his shirt. As he left the shop, he spotted Tomas coming up the street—he was grateful at the sight of one of his best friends. Tomas was wearing the traditional black one-piece coverall that symbolized he worked in coal pit near the outskirts of the village. He noticed Tomas's face light up when he saw him. "Shouldn't you be polishing my boots?" Vladimir teased.

"Ha, ha, you wish, just you wait," they embraced each other, laughing, and continued down the road together.

"How was work today?" Vladimir asked as they passed the school for all ages. The school was not large and usually half empty during class time. Usually once children hit teenage years, they were forced to stop school to either work in the village or fulfill duties around their homes. Very few completed their education.

"Long and tiring." Tomas replied wearily to him. It was not often that they were able to hang out anymore. Vladimir felt lucky, as he did not have to work in the pit or out on the docks. Even though his *viskta* ruled, it came with its own set of hardships. Vladimir had seen father return from dealing with The Spiriduş and their raids on the trade routes looking extremely angered and tired.

"We should do something," Vladimir suggested with his let's-get-into-trouble-grin that his best friend knew only too well, but Tomas shook his head. "I have to head home. Father is getting worse, and stuff needs to be done around the house. But I will stop over this weekend and chug back a couple tall cold beverages if you know what I mean—Say, what's wrong, Vladimir. You look like someone whose grave got jumped all over!" He added, "You have a weird look about you."

Vladimir knew he must have looked grim. He sighed. "I just saw Sasha for the gift I asked him to make. He mentioned...Lash." Thinking about it grinded his stomach into knots.

Tomas nodded in understanding. "The village, it's…not pretty. Erik has lost customers over this. Many feel he was a coward for not competing and letting you take his place. He's afraid he might have to close his shop if he keeps losing more customers. I gotta go. Talk soon, I promise."

They said their good-byes, and Vladimir watched his friend head home. He wished he could help him—he missed Tomas a lot. The atria prize would have helped his friend a great deal, along with Erik, who was now paying the price.

Vladimir continued down the street, past the rows of the filthy, busy, and smoky trades building. He saw the exasperated, tired looks of the workers and was secretly glad he was not one of them. He wondered how many hated him now. The workers ranged from teenagers to old men. The biggest building was the ironworks, where the household items were made, from chandeliers to the big wood burning stoves for cooking. He decided to stop in to visit Erik. He opened the door a bit too quickly, almost making Igor Chitu drop the slab of iron he was carrying. "Sorry, Igor!"

Igor was a bald, middle-aged overweight man with a beak nose. "Watch it, *murderer,*" snapped Igor.

Murderer? Vladimir stood there, stunned. "Igor! Keep your opinions to yourself in here!" Erik yelled, and came up to stand alongside him.

"I quit," Igor said, his face red from rage, then walked past Vladimir, bumping hard into his shoulder.

"Damnit. Igor was a jerk, but a good-at-what-he-does jerk, so I tolerated him." Erik stated to him. "I'm sorry, Erik. I didn't know…" Vladimir didn't know what else to say. Erik replied, "It's okay. Ever since the Trifecta…Igor…well, has been bitter. He ran you down every chance he could. I think seeing you put him over the edge."

Vladimir felt horrible. How could he have been such an *asshat* and got his friends to go along with his crazy death-defying idea? "I'm sorry, Erik. For all of this. I ran into Tomas, he told me what's been happening here. Teach me, and I will come work in your shop for free—for as long as you need," he offered, hoping he could help in some way.

Erik shook his head. "Thank you, Vladimir. It would just take too long, and I can't spare the time to train you properly. I wanted to take today off, but the last shipment we sent out northeast never made it. The Spiriduş ambushed the delivery and took everything, killing the Sentinels that were with the shipment, from what I heard. I respect the Sentinels, don't ever want to be one, though, after hearing what they have to deal with. Anyway, it was only one wagon, but it was important. Now, we need to redo all the work and get it shipped out quickly, at a loss." Vladimir knew The Trifecta winnings would have helped make up some of the losses that were hurting Erik.

He had heard of attacks on larger wagon caravans, but hitting a single wagon was not common, as the risk was not generally worth the reward. "What was in the wagon?"

Erik's voice shook slightly in anger. "It was mainly kitchen supplies, pots and pans and stuff like that. No weapons or anything useful to a group of criminals like that. Weapons are usually what they go for. Maybe they just ran into the wagon accidently and they attacked, I don't know."

Frustration built inside of Vladimir's chest at the unfairness of his friend's situation. He needed to do something, somehow to make it better, "You sure you can't take some time off? Go down to the Squirmy Squid and let loose with me and Tomas for a night?"

"Sorry, Vladimir. I am stuck here. People are waiting for the replacements to be delivered to them. It will take a few days to get everything done, especially now that Igor quit. When we are caught up here, then perhaps I can take a few hours, and we can hang out." Erik said weakly.

Vladimir knew that it was wishful thinking, but he went along with it. Vladimir forced a smile, and clapped his friend on the shoulder. "Who knew about the lone wagon?" he asked.

Erik looked thoughtful. "Just me and the Sentinels. We tried to keep everything low key, as there are eyes and ears everywhere. The Sentinels and the Spiriduş have been fighting each other for so long that there is no chance they are working together. But it was more than just that; it was a test, as well, I was told. We will talk soon and discuss it." Vladimir's heart sank as his friend turned around abruptly and got back to work.

He knew there was nothing he could do to convince Erik to take a break. He wished he could help him, but he knew nothing about iron working. All his free time was taken up by studies or honing his fighting skills. He looked over and saw a spear laying against a wall. Growing up, he was forced to learn how to use a sword. Spears thrilled him. Having a spear in his hand felt like a natural extension of himself. Vladimir had surpassed his masters with the weapon. Everyone said he truly was gifted.

Looking up at the setting sun, Vladimir knew supper was quickly approaching, but he still had a little bit of time. He was close to the docks, so he took a small detour down to them. He always tried to make the most of his free time.

He tried to avoid talking to people. The streets were lined with merchants carrying or pushing their wares to customers. Every time he came down to this part of the village, it always felt so alive. A constant hum of activity, an unorganized dance that nobody knew the steps to, and yet everybody moved to its rhythm.

As he ducked and weaved around people on the street, like Iskra Milcu—a drunkard who was passed out on the side of the street holding a bottle of Blood Cider. Iskra was frail-looking, with salt and pepper hair, who never wore boots. He heard that Iskra was a great sailor in his youth, but during a storm while out on the lake, Iskra swore he encountered something unnatural. Whatever happened had broken the man, as all he did now was drink and beg for money.

Another familiar face greeted him; her floor-length red dress hard to miss. It was Deidra Voiculet. She was holding a small violet umbrella to protect her freckled face from the sun; her long golden hair went down to her lower back, matching the sun's bright rays. She was taller than most woman. Vladimir had to admit that she was quite striking. She was married only two years before her husband fell ill and died within a few weeks of marriage. There were no visible injuries, so people just assumed it was "one of those things that happened". He once met Deidra out in one of the fields, and while her face was hidden away even then, Vladimir could spot fresh bruises on her cheeks. Since then, his gut told him that it was not merely "one of those things".

Deidra had sold the farm and had moved into the village, down by the docks. He had heard that she spent time with the sailors, among many others—she charged considerable atria for anyone that wanted to spend time with her. Something must have happened during the short time she was married. As to what, he never asked.

"Hello, Vladimir," Deidra greeted him with a coy smile, knowing it would make him blush. It worked, as his face turned beet red, he was sure.

Vladimir sensed she liked him. He had not told anyone about her bruises, nor that he suspected she had something to do with her husband's death, so he gathered her teasing him was her way of thanking him. "Hello, Deidra, how are you doing on this fine day?" He hoped this was going to be a short conversation; if word got back to his mother that he was speaking to her, she would have something to say about it. And after everything that had happened, he would do anything to avoid another lecture.

"Very well, Vladimir, you are quite the young gentleman for asking. Most men do not care to stop and ask. Your parents must be quite proud of you." There was a hint of mischief in Deidra's eyes.

The slight panic on his face must have given him away because Deidra added, "Don't worry so much about your mother. You are becoming a fine young man...and I know what young men want. You have already proved you are more than most men by winning the Trifecta. Congratulations on your achievement. I know if we talk too much longer, your mother will come down here herself and express her disapproval. So, I will leave you with this final thought, young Vladimir: my door is always open to you, free of charge," and she raised her index finger to her lips, mouthing "Shhhh".

He was stunned at the invitation and didn't know how to respond. A part of him was happy she liked him, but mostly, he was puzzled. "You don't think of me as a 'murderer', like everyone else?"

Deidra smiled and shook her head. "Death is part of the Trifecta. If Lash were worried about dying, he would not have entered. Therefore, Lash is the only reason Lash is dead, not you."

Vladimir was ecstatic to learn at least one person didn't hate him besides his family and friends.

"It was genuinely nice to see you again, Vladimir. Thank you for taking the time to spend a few minutes with me. It is getting late, and I have a 'special' visitor tonight." Deidra said as she made to walk past Vladimir but stopped, her mouth an inch from his ear. "We all have our reasons to do what we do." She grazed his arm and continued up the street.

That was the one thing she had never done until now; acknowledged what she had done. Vladimir turned and watched her go, a warm glow inside of him. He smiled slightly and continued toward the docks. There was a myriad of scents that hung in the air as he got closer and strolled past one of the cafes. The Squirmy Squid was aptly named, for every time a plate of squid was placed in front of him, his stomach squirmed. The texture of squid was indeed an acquired taste, one that he had yet grown accustomed to.

He passed two more quaint cafes, and made a right at the large, bustling harbour, lined with various ships and men crawling around the area like working ants. Unless one was assigned to a ship's crew or was delivering supplies, most people did not go down to the docks for fear of being killed by a falling crate or getting yelled at for being in the way. Being at the docks was a rush. So much energy and movement. Vladimir tried to remain invisible though, as supply containers were being loaded onto the ships.

Vladimir marvelled at the organized chaos. When you just stood back and watched, it was memorizing.

A sudden yell coming from his right snapped his head around. There was a large skid loaded with supplies being lifted into the air, but it was tilting to one side. Several men were struggling, trying to hold it in place, some underneath the skid, motioning for them to bring it down. Vladimir approached the scene with caution as the sailors slowly started to lower the skid down. Vladimir was inching close enough to help if needed when he heard a loud snap up and to his left: the next ship over was loading supplies, too, and one of the ropes had snapped. It was dangling in the air above another worker, who was busy getting the next skid ready and wasn't paying attention to what was happening overhead.

Vladimir had to do something. "Hey, look up above you!" he warned, but the sailor was too engrossed in what he was doing. Vladimir shook his head and headed over to him, frustrated that he was not paying attention to his surroundings. When he was nearer to him, there was another louder snap, and he heard yelling. Vladimir looked up—the skid had started to fall. Without hesitating, he rushed to the worker and pushed him out of the way, the two falling to ground.

Not a moment later there was a loud *Boom,* as the skid hit the ground and broke apart.

The man got up, glancing at where he had just been, wiping his forehead in relief.

"Hey!" Vladimir yelled as he got to his feet. He grabbed the man and spun him around. "What's wrong with you? Why did you not listen to me? You could have been killed!"

The man stood there making gestures with his fingers. Dumbfounded, Vladimir wondered what was wrong with him. The man was in his early twenties, with short black hair.

"Thank you, son, we will take it from here," Vladimir heard a gruff voice behind him say. Turning, he saw a tall, older man approach him. Vladimir realized it was probably the Captain of the vessel, so he stepped back. He made to open his mouth to speak, but the Captain held up his hand to stop him. The Captain walked up to the younger man, and to Vladimir's surprise, started moving his fingers in such a way that it looked like he was trying to make letters. Vladimir stood there bewildered as to what was going on. The crewman responded by moving his fingers swiftly, as well. After a few minutes of this, the man who had almost been crushed saluted the Captain and ran onto the ship. The Captain motioned for some of his crew to clean up the mess, then turned to Vladimir, holding out his hand, which Vladimir shook. "Thank you, son, for saving my crewman, Heilm. I am Captain Henrick Mihaili of the fishing trawler Skrulm. Heilm is deaf, so that is why he did not hear the commotion going on around him."

Vladimir beamed. Someone else that didn't hate him. "You are welcome, Captain. If you don't mind me asking, what was going on with those movements with your fingers? It was like you two were talking with each other. I have never seen anything like that before."

Captain Henrick smiled slightly. "What we do with our hands is called sign language. It allows us to communicate with each other. Everyone on my ship knows it so they can communicate with Heilm. He usually works below deck in the kitchen, where you need your nose more than your ears. He is an excellent cook, so the crew does not complain. We found Heilm adrift out deep on the lake, hanging onto a piece of wood. If that wasn't strange enough, the wood he was clinging to was blood red. Damnest thing ever."

Vladimir nodded in understanding. He had heard various stories from his trips to the docks of cooks on boats getting beaten and thrown overboard for making bad meals. Out of all the jobs on a ship, cooking is one that never appealed to Vladimir. "Well, I'm glad I was here to help, Captain."

"Anytime you want to come aboard, feel free, and I will show you around. She may not look as big or as impressive of some of the other ships, but she has it where it counts. My crew would also love to hear how you won the Trifecta. Quite the achievement for anyone, let alone someone as young as yourself. Very impressive indeed. Tragic about the loss of life, but those that enter know the risks. Perhaps when we get back, as we are going out again tonight. With the moons being all crazy like this, who knows what may rise to the surface. Best to be prepared for…anything." Captain Mihaili said, staring up at the moons.

"Thank you, Captain Henrick. I would be honoured." Captain Henrick gave him another smile before walking away, leaving Vladimir standing alone, admiring the vessel.

The Skrulm was a medium-sized fishing vessel with two masts, its decks lined with harpoon guns, and other things he did not know the name of but assumed helped catch fish. Of all the ships in the harbour, this was the only one painted black. Just as Vladimir was going to catch up to the Captain and ask why, bells rang all over the village. He realized it was the evening bells, and if he did not get home right away, his ears would be ringing with his mother's yells instead.

On the way home, he thought about what the captain said to him. Blood red wood, that was strange indeed. Was there such a thing as unnatural wood? His thoughts drifted to the Dark Woods. Yes, anything was possible.

He ran up the busy streets, weaving through the masses. Rounding a corner, he narrowly avoided a large pushcart. It belonged to the village's best baker, Mr. Lulka Hindrick, who was pushing it.

"Let me guess, you lost track of time and are rushing home?" Mr. Hindrick asked, narrowing his silver eyes at him. The baker was a plump, middle-aged man, who Vladimir could tell was clearly annoyed. This might be a good opportunity to get in the man's good graces, he thought. "I…I am sorry, Mr. Hindrick," Vladimir managed to stammer, looking at his face glaring back at him.

"You going to stand there all night or move so people can get fed," Mr. Hindrick barked.

"Sorry, Mr. Hindrick, is there anything I can do to help you?" Vladimir asked, apologized again, and moved away from the cart.

"Help me? The only help I need from you is to stay away from my daughter outside of school. Marku has told me more than once about you looking at Kazia. It is done, Vladimir. The sooner you move on, the better it will be for everyone. Though, I suspect someone who doesn't follow the rules couldn't care less."

Asshat, Vladimir thought to himself. He had to be nice, he had to win Kazia's father approval. Somehow. "Yes, Mr. Hindrick. I understand. But—"

"Have you talked to your father recently?" Mr. Hindrick interrupted him.

Vladimir wrinkled his brow, wondering what his father had to do with their conversation. "No, Mr. Hindrick. I have not seen my father since he left to go north. Is something wrong?" Vladimir asked worriedly.

Mr. Hindrick nodded, looking enraged. "Damn straight. You are by my shop, and I know it's not by accident. Just like Lash's death. Don't think I didn't hear about that. Lash was the rightful winner of the Trifecta. Marku is torn up about his cousin dying in the Trifecta and squarely blames you. Your arrogance and recklessness have cost a *viskta* dearly. I understand death is part of the Trifecta, my brother died in it. It's needless death I have an issue with. Lash would still be alive if not for you."

Mr. Hindrick hastily pushed the cart past him with the freshly baked goods, their mouth-watering aroma making Vladimir's tummy rumble with hunger.

Now, Vladimir *really* had no chance with Kazia. Not that there was ever much of one, but he had never lost hope. He watched Mr. Hindrick leave, and part of him felt relieved that he didn't have to be nice to the *jerk* anymore.

He stopped dead as Kazia emerged from the shop. She stopped, too, when she saw him, and the two stood there, staring at one another in silence.

"Hi," Vladimir finally managed to say, feeling his face get warm. Even though Kazia was wearing the same flour-stained baker's outfit, she still took his breath away. At that moment he didn't know which part of him wanted her more, his heart, or stomach as Kazia smelled like baked biscuits, his favourite.

"Hello, Vladimir, what a pleasant surprise. I thought you would be at home, grounded for the rest of your life," she said teasingly.

"I was down by the docks and lost track of time. I just bumped into your father as he was heading down with his deliveries. He hates me."

Kazia gave a sympathetic smile. Something about that smile warmed his insides. "I never did congratulate you on winning the Trifecta, so congratulations. I must confess, I was dumbstruck when you took the board and jumped over The Lip. It must have been quite exhilarating for you," she said, and then added, "Of course, it's too bad about Lash. The entire village is in debate about it."

Vladimir seemed to have lost all ability to speak, as he opened his mouth, but no words came out.

Kazia looked down at her feet and then up at him, "Well then, you better rush home. I wouldn't want you to get into further trouble. It was pleasant seeing you again."

Vladimir smiled and nodded in agreement. "Yes. you are quite right, of course. I thank you for your concern, and for the congratulations," he said, feeling stupid for attempting to act mature. He was sure his face was even redder than he imagined.

As Kazia stood there, Vladimir could see in her eyes that she very well knew he did not want to go. As though in response, Kazia darted into the bakery and returned moments later with a small freshly baked bun. She handed it to him. "To give you strength for the journey home," and ran back inside before he could say a word.

He stood there and took a bite. It warmed his stomach, and he couldn't help but smile. Kazia was amazing. Too bad she was being forced to marry Marku.

Marku...picturing him excited him. What was he going to do?

Interlude 0.3

Royal Harbour – Thebes

Master Medjay Ahmose finished wrapping the supplies on their modified water raft. Everything was secure. He glanced up at the Tutankhamen I in awe of its size. Ahmose felt like a flea next to it. The water raft was tied off to it, so it would be pulled behind it when they went through the "curtain" to the other side. There, they would cut the rope and row to whatever secluded spot they could find and make their way into the village, where they would remain hidden after completing their secondary mission. Medjays Rewer and Jarha should be on their way back from their final evening of "relaxation", and each would soon regale him with tales of their night for quite some time.

Ahmose smiled to himself—to be young and wild again. He moved to the rope ladder hanging down from the dock and climbed up it, a pair of black boots on the dock slowly coming into view. He nearly lost his balance but managed to finish the climb and got to his feet.

And then he was staring into the black, grotesque plague mask of a member of the Brotherhood.

Ahmose stood on the spot, staring at the absurdly tall, black-robed figure with glowing eyes beneath a beaked-mask. He was lost for words. He had never seen one outside of their establishment before. What did the Brother want with him?

The Brother raised their right arm to reveal in its black-gloved hand a cream-coloured parchment. Ahmose reached out and slowly took it, unsure if it was the right thing to do, and looked down at it. It was blank on the outside. Ahmose glanced at the Brother, who remained silent. "Uhhhhh," was all that came out of his mouth.

It suddenly struck him. The Brotherhood learned of their mission somehow and they wanted him to deliver the letter through the curtain. Which meant they knew about the other side and had an establishment there, as well. The Brother was still silent, so Ahmose lifted the envelope and placed it inside his right vest pocket, nodding to show he understood.

The Brother brought his hand to his plague beak-mask, a indicating it should be kept a secret. Ahmose nodded back, and the Brother turned and left, walking down the pier in the direction of the dock, passing Rewer and Jarha, then disappearing into a haze of smoke.

Ahmose was rooted to the spot in utter disbelief at what just happened. Rewer and Jarha had stopped to gawk at the Brother as they passed. They were as stunned as he had been.

"Even the Brotherhood is involved?" Rewer said. "What do they want?"

The letter weighed heavily in Ahmose's pocket. "To deliver a message to another Brother on the other side of the 'curtain'."

Ahmose stared at their puzzled expressions. This night was getting even wilder than he could have imagined, and it had just begun.

Rewer stepped forward. "There are more of...*them...in other lands?*"

Ahmose, too, found it hard to believe that The Brotherhood had more establishments, especially in unknown lands. What else did The Brotherhood know that no one else did? He wanted to open the letter and read it...*should he?* If the Brotherhood knew of other lands, did that mean that they could be part of a larger conspiracy that no one knew about? *Was Egyptia in danger?* Ahmose's senses weren't tingling with danger. No—this was a personal request more than anything. That's what it felt like to him. Should he honour the fact that The Brotherhood chose him to deliver the message? This letter led to too many questions that he did not have the answers to. *Time would reveal all.*

Ahmose looked at his Medjays, their expressions filled with uncertainty. They needed confidence tonight. He decided to change the topic, lift the mood. "How were your adventures tonight?" He thought back to all his adventures when he was younger. *Those were good days.* Now, his days consisted of aches and pains, offset by copious amount of Blood Cider. His chance of happiness ended many years ago with High Carrier Nenet. Nenet was the only woman he had genuinely loved. A tale for another night. "Master Ahmose, are you listening?" Rewer asked him.

Ahmose's attention snapped back to reality. "Of course, you were talking about the beautiful brunette that you met at the 'Rusty Sarcophagus'. Though with an establishment name like that, it does make one wonder about what kind of people would frequent such a place," he said jokingly.

"The kind of people that were about to partake in crazy, potentially life-ending missions," Jarha added. Ahmose had to agree with the Medjay. What they were doing was unheard of.

Ahmose continued to listen to his Medjays' banter, their mood increasing with every moment—and his. He knew the mission they were tasked with would be next to impossible to complete. Yet, he had faith in himself and the Medjays he had hand selected. Plus, with a visit to the Royal Apothecary to get a special request, Ahmose would make sure they would all make it back...alive.

"Alight. It's time to go to the Royal Pyramid. General Pentu has ordered our presence in front of the Pharaoh. Remember, say as little as possible and don't make eye contact. We don't want to become dung beetle food for doing something wrong!" With that, Ahmose headed to their destination with the other two in tow.

Chapter 8

Royal Pyramid—Thebes

'Royal Flush'

"My Pharaoh. The night of your divine retribution is upon us at last," Chione declared, trying to rouse the conversation during the exceptionally dull dinner. They were all gathered on the high grand balcony overlooking Thebes at the Royal Pyramid. There were three layers of balconies that encircled the pyramid, and each level had a purpose. The one they were on was the highest, which provided the greatest vantage point overlooking Thebes. Pharaoh Tutankhamen's seat was more elevated than General Pentu's and her own. Tutankhamen was on a replica of his throne flanked by five bald, golden, scantily dressed female servants. Each one took food from a different plate to feed him so as not to get one dish's flavour intermixed with another.

A living God should never lower himself so much as to touch food, or bathe himself, or any other menial chore, Chione mused to herself. The table that she and the General were sharing was smaller, less elegant than the Pharaoh's, but she did not mind. They had eaten so far in relative silence, besides sporadic conversations of nothing, which never went beyond a couple of comments. She suspected the General's mind was preoccupied with the attack. Tutankhamen was too busy ogling the women surrounding him to pay attention to much else.

She took another bite of catfish, and her mind drifted to Niet. She wondered how he was doing, how bored he was with his task. He would have enjoyed the meal, she knew. Then her thoughts turned to Hunter, who she knew would have been licking his lips at the delicious sight in front of her.

"On the eve of your glorious victory, the moons are coming together in celebration. They are showing their approval and their loyalty. You are a living God, and your people worship you, just as the moons do. There is nothing that you cannot accomplish," she said, knowing how important it was to stroke his ego and make him believe he was truly infallible. Tutankhamen had already ordered the re-facing of the statues of the Gods in his image, and he had imprisoned all the priests in the lands. Tutankhamen's fall would indeed be something to behold when the time came.

"There is an ancient story that I don't quite remember. I believe it's something about the moons coming together on a special night," General Pentu mused to her. The old General was no one's fool, Chione thought, therefore he needed to be handled delicately. He was loyal to Tutankhamen. She had heard through the Royal Court that he was a devoted family man who never strayed from his wife. She respected that about the man. Unfortunately, it made it harder for her to bend him into whatever way she needed him bent. It was a good thing she loved challenges. One old devoted General was no threat to the greater plan, so she was not overly concerned.

Tutankhamen gawked up at the moons. Men were nothing more than grown children, just with bigger egos and shorter attention spans. Chione smiled at both the Pharaoh and General and made a "Psshhh" sound, bringing their attention back to her.

"Stories are for young children to fill their minds with wonder and amusement. Something for them to dream about when they go to sleep," she stated plainly. "Tonight, is so much more than that, General. It is the night where you are the instrument of our Pharaoh's righteous vengeance on the Drăculești."

Chione noticed Tutankhamen was back to gazing upwards wearing the same dumbstruck look. If no one disturbed him, she wondered whether he would sit there all night clueless, which was really a good look for him. Tutankhamen lived a sheltered life and had virtually no experience outside of the Royal Pyramid's walls. Unfortunately for Tutankhamen, this meant any change was a huge event in his life that he treated rather immaturely. At least the servant girls were getting a brief break from him.

Though, there was one area in his life that Tutankhamen had lots of experience with—women. The Pharaoh had slept with virtually every female that toiled in the Royal Pyramid, regardless of age or looks. Tutankhamen had ordered her once to take off her clothes, but she told him that if he "graced" her with his physical prowess, she would lose the ability to carry out his vengeance. Chione reminded him that there was a whole new land of women for him to "grace". Why should the Pharaoh limit himself when there were so many more options? Tutankhamen immediately dismissed her. Chione knew she had saved herself from two minutes of utter boredom.

"How go the final preparations for the upcoming attack, General Pentu?" Tutankhamen said.

"The ships will be loaded on time, my Pharaoh, with an equal amount of Ushabti Warriors and Mummies," the General responded proudly. "Due to the nature of the attack, we need very few provisions, which has made the preparations go much more quickly and smoothly. We are loading two weeks of supplies for our Medjay team. Chione has reassured me that she can open a curtain to the village at any time, though I believe it best not to open any curtains until the sand settles, as they say. The Medjay team will be towed on their watercraft behind Tutankhamen I as they pass through the curtain. It has been painted midnight blue, so it will be camouflaged. Once through, they will make their way to shore and capture a Drăculeşti. Their riverboat has been mystically imprinted so that on command it will make its way back out to the Tutankhamen I. There, we will hook it, bring it aboard and head back through the curtain home.

"The Master Medjay in charge is a veteran. I have confidence in his ability to capture your prize. Then the Medjays will find someplace discreet for observation afterwards. While waiting for more supplies, they will note everything they see and report back when Chione opens the re-supply curtain. This will be a short trip there and back via the curtain," he said, took a sip of Blood cider, and then continued. "The oarsmen have been assigned heavier stringed bows, which will triple their effective shooting range. The arrows are also not standard issue, so nothing can be traced back to us in the future, and the ships have been loaded with large quantities of oil for our fire arrows. For a more destructive element, firepots have been loaded, as well, and have been pre-filled as ammunition for the catapults. Sorcerer Haphestus has assured me that his enhancements on the oil have made it even deadlier, and the fire arrows will survive water being doused on them. The heavy, thicker, smoke will deter them from making any sort of organized defensive posture, if that is remotely possible to begin with. Fire is an excellent deterrent, as well. As for the mist, it will provide cover for our vessels, so our sailors will be hidden from shore. I have taken the added precaution that they wear non-military clothing, as the unexpected can happen in battle."

As he sipped his Blood Cider, Chione could tell the General was incredibly pleased with himself. She decided to chime in. "The added bonus is that the 'mist' will not affect the oarsmen's sight." She saw doubt creep into the General's eyes, but he remained silent. Tonight, would prove everything she had been saying. Tonight, her promises would be kept. She had learned in the short time that she had been at the Royal Pyramid that the number of executions in the throne room were of those that made promises but failed to live up to them. Though she was in no danger, she had fun pretending she was fearful of the Pharaoh's wrath.

General Pentu leaned forward, glancing in her direction as he spoke. "My Pharaoh, as a bonus, with your permission, of course, I want to take the dead bodies of your would-be assassins and load them onto our vessels. The purpose would be to load them onto the catapult and return them to their home. Seeing dead bodies flying across their village would also lower the Sentinels' morale. Especially if it is of their own."

She was stunned at the request. *What was the General playing at?*

Tutankhamen leaned in, too, a wicked grin across his face, and Chione knew he was about to agree with the General's request.

"I am sorry, General, but your request is not possible," she hastily added before the Pharaoh could speak. "I had the bodies disposed of. I did not want their corpses around as a reminder of that horrendous night. If I overstepped, my Pharaoh, I apologize. I thought it best that the whole incident was behind us. Besides, General, I have no doubt that capturing our prize will send a much stronger message. That their Drăculești are no match against that which destroys their village."

The General's expression hardened, and Tutankhamen was distracted, yet again, by his golden servant girls, who began to serve him grapes, and no more was said on the topics. The look the General shot her was more than just annoyance. Did he know something? If the Pharaoh did not object, the General was powerless to do anything. "How unfortunate," General Pentu replied to her, visibly upset.

As though out of thin air, a woman approached the group whose appearance resembled nothing like the usual servants. The woman had dark black hair with whispers of white strands that partly covered a tattered, brown leather eye patch over her left eye, secured by string wrapped around the woman's head. The left side of the woman's face was heavily scarred. Chione eyed the markings, wondering who she was and why she was here. Her eyes dropped to her clothing: a simple black top and black leggings, with a hideous leopard buckle that adorned her belt. As the woman approached the group, she lowered her head in respect to her Pharaoh. *How curious,* Chione thought. The woman had the look of a warrior, but Chione knew there were no female warriors in the Royal Army. "High Carrier Nenet," the General greeted, rising to his feet. "I am glad you made it on the eve of our righteous fury that is about to be unleashed against those that sought the destruction of our Pharaoh. How was your trip?"

'High Carrier'? What did she carry, Chione wondered?

"It was uneventful, thankfully," Nenet said. "I was not too far off inside the Carrier Network when I received word. What may I do for the glory of our Kingdom?" Chione cast suspicious glances between her and the General.

"My Pharaoh, I have summoned the High Carrier here to send word to our garrisons to start intensifying training sessions and increase recruitment. There may be unexpected consequences to what we do here tonight. I want to make sure they are ready to handle anything unexpected that may come their way."

Chione watched the Pharaoh nod and dismiss the woman with a flick of his wrist. Nenet bowed to the Pharaoh, then the General, and to Chione, before leaving with her orders.

"Excellent! They will first feel my wrath, and in time, they will worship me. They will come to realize that I was the reason for their plight to begin with," Tutankhamen said, throwing his hands into the air in triumph.

For a split-second, Chione wondered if he cared in the slightest about the lives that would be destroyed.

Of course, not—why would you when you thought yourself a living God?

"My vengeance will be complete, will it not, General?" the Pharaoh asked, a twinge of impatience in his voice.

"Yes, my Pharaoh. When the rain starts and the moons are converged, that is when it is best to attack; those awake will be inside taking shelter no doubt from the rain, which in turn will make them slow to react," the General said, and Chione had to agree with his assessment. "It will only take moments to open the curtain," she added, "then the ships will sail through to the other side, and the curtain will remain open the entire time." Chione could tell the General was anxious to leave. Especially with the attack happening later that night.

"When I step foot into my new, extended kingdom," Tutankhamen began, leaning back on his seat, his gaze fixed past them as though peering into another world, "and I see their thankful faces reaping praise on me, I will be merciful, as they are ignorant of their former foolish leader's action. But know this: Should there be any sort of thanklessness…well, they will see my rage is equal to my mercy." Chione could tell he was lost in his own small world once again.

Moments later, the balcony turned silent. Chione looked over at the men, and they were both lost in thought. This was it, the calm before the storm.

Finally, the Pharaoh broke the silence. "I only want one prisoner, which for now is a Drăculeşti. Any Drăculeşti. General, do not fail me—nor you, Chione." Chione bowed her head as he stood up and motioned for his servants to follow him into the Royal Pyramid, leaving her and the General alone.

"How do you plan on capturing your prisoner, General?" Chione asked curiously.

The General sighed and said quietly, "If they are as special as you say they are, I have no doubt they will find their way to us. My only concern is how many of my men will die before we can subdue one of theirs."

The General was right, of course. The bloodbath was going to be beyond anyone will have ever experienced in their lives. The thought of the carnage the Drăculeşti could inflict excited her. "Yes General, any precaution you think you should take, I would strongly recommend," she said, suspecting that no amount of precaution would save his precious men.

Chione watched the General rise from the table and walk over to the balcony's edge. She joined his side and followed his gaze down at the harbour. Thank the Gods she was not one of them. There were two large ships that dwarfed all others in the harbour—the newest vessels in the Royal Fleet named after the current Pharaoh, of course, the Tutankhamen I and II, respectively. "Your vessels are very impressive, General," she said. "It is like they were designed for such an event."

An odd expression came over his face. He nodded, then proceeded to explain. "I had a dream, many, many moons ago, and in it I saw those very vessels we are looking upon now. I cannot explain it; it was like I was being foretold what was to come. I know there are those that claim to have visions of the future. I am not one of them, yet as I look down at them now, I am in shock that they exist."

Chione smiled. "Even in your dreams, you serve the Kingdom. Our Pharaoh is most fortunate to have you to serve him."

Pentu grinned. "Thank you for the kind words, Chione. I know the truth. As long as I am useful, I will serve. So, I strive to, always. Besides, if I died from incompetence on my part, my wife would bring me back from the dead just to send me back into the sand."

So, that was the secret to his success, a vengeful wife. She sensed she would get along with the woman quite nicely and decided that she would find her and meet her. "She sounds lovely, perhaps one day you will bring her by so I can meet her," she suggested and got a look of utter horror in return. "Don't worry, General, I have no doubt we would spend a lovely afternoon talking about…women stuff," she teased, but his expression did not change. "Perhaps you are right, we would have nothing in common anyway," she added, seeing the General's face relaxed a bit. Chione still fully intended to seek the woman out, anyway; any woman that can keep a man loyal and faithful to her was worth meeting. Plus, the fact that the General believed she could perform an act such as bringing him back from the dead interested her greatly.

"General Pentu," a male voice he had never heard before called out, and they turned to find three men standing by the dinner table. She had known that more guests would arrive at the Royal Pyramid. They all had the look of soldiers, but she sensed if they indeed were, they were not ordinary ones.

"Master Medjay Ahmose, Medjays Rewer, Jarha," the General said, giving each man a curt nod. "Is everything in order for you and your men for your extended stay in Sighişoara?""Yes, General. Our vessel has been laden with supplies until such time that we are resupplied," the Master Medjay replied, nodding toward Chione.

"I suspect we will find local food available once everything is settled to help supplement what we bring, as well," Master Medjay added.

The General nodded in agreement. "What about clothing? Have you packed according to the potential weather difference? I would not think that their lands would be as warm as ours." The General was quite brilliant.

"Yes, General, we shall be more than adequately equipped," Master Medjay said, which puzzled her. She glanced from one man to the other. "Why not just use the clothing from the dead villagers? There should be more than enough, and plenty of different sizes for you and your men, Master Medjay."

Chione could not justify the looks of horror on the men's faces.

"Clothing is personal, Chione," the General said, his tone sincere. "An owner's spirit resides within the clothing. Should the person be vengeful or angry at the time of their death, whoever wears their clothing would be constantly tormented. Even in war there are…standards!"

Chione was taken aback by his outburst, then quickly feigned horror. "My apologies, General. I was unaware of this this."

The General's face eased. *Men!* Chione thought.

"What is your plan to capture a Drăculeşti, as our Pharoah commands, Master Medjay?" the General asked. Chione was curious, as well; the Drăculeşti were devastating in battle. She did not think the Medjays stood a chance against even one of them.

The Master Medjay retrieved a large dart from inside his shirt. "Inside is mystically enhanced poison that will paralyze our target. Once that is completed, we will take our prize back to the watercraft, and it will head back to the Tutankhamen I. Then, we start our secondary mission, General."

The General nodded in approval. The Master Medjay had made it sound so simple, so *easy.* She knew it would be neither. Chione suspected she would never see any of the Medjays again after this night.

"Any other final commands, General, before we depart to make our final preparations?" Master Medjay Ahmose asked.

The General turned away and began pacing, a thoughtful expression on his face. What was he thinking? Chione was thankful he had not pressed her on the missing assassin's bodies, though she knew it was still on his mind. She hoped the General would finish thinking about whatever it was he was thinking about, quickly. She watched as the General continued to pace around the balcony, stopped to pick up his Blood Cider—gulping down the rest—then turned toward her and the Medjays. "Stay discreet. Stay safe. You are the tip of the spear. We are only as sharp as you are. Medjays, you have your orders."

The General stepped forward and shook each of the men's hands. The Medjays then turned and left them alone on the balcony. She walked over to the balcony and looked up at the moons, smiling at what was to come.

***

General Pentu stared at Chione as she stood beside on him on the balcony's edge, and a thought came to his mind. *What if he pushed her over?* Every bone in his body knew that woman could not be trusted. After his talk with the High Priest Nakhte at Luxor Prison, it had all but confirmed his original suspicions. With the bodies gone, there was no longer proof of any deception. He knew if he went to the Pharaoh with this tale, he would be the one sent out to the Duat Pit. No, what Chione was offering the Pharaoh was a prize greater than anyone could have imagined. Or was she leading to their greatest ruination in history? All he knew was Chione having an "accident" would halt everything, and the status quo would remain. He was fine with that.

As the days went on and he continued to oversee the preparations, a thought gnawed and twisted inside of him. It was not a pure military target they were going to unleash their vengeance upon tonight—it was a village full of people that he suspected had no idea what their leaders had done. Pentu was all for glorious bloodshed, not *innocent* bloodshed. Throughout his military career, he served to protect the innocent. Now he was commanding an attack to slaughter the innocent. There was a time when that wouldn't have bothered him much. In his youth, he called to war, regardless of the consequences. Had time changed him that much? Or was it something else, something more recent.

When he held his newborn granddaughter, Hatshepsut, two nights prior, for the first time he knew something had changed inside of him. How many granddaughters were the Ushabti Warriors and Mummies going to kill this night once they were unleashed? The thought was not a pleasant one. It made his stomach churn even more. He had been proud of his service, his dedication to his Kingdom, and all else he had accomplished. He had done his due diligence, making sure everything was prepared for tonight. He was duty bound to do so and took pride in it.

The true threat were the leaders, not the population. He needed a new strategy. The Drăculeşti still needed to be brought to justice for what they had done. *But how?* Pentu knew he couldn't send another Medjay team in secret to return the assassination attempt. Why hadn't they done that? The only conclusion he could come to was to eliminate Chione to prevent the upcoming attack.

Then what? The Pharaoh would need vengeance for the assassination attempt on his life. Then a smile crept on his face. He had his answer, if what he knew to be true were true. The Drăculeşti had their own Sister, as well. Pentu suspected they were organizing another assassination team to murder the Pharaoh. It is what he would do. If he set a trap for the team and was able to capture them, they would get the information required. It all depended on whether Chione was telling the truth about the assassins from the other land.

Pentu looked at Chione standing there, who was, of course, oblivious to his thoughts. How to end her life by making it seem like an accident? Glancing over at the dinner table, there were still goblets of Blood Cider, so if Chione...

Yes! Striding over, he grabbed his goblet and filled it with liquid courage. Taking a sip, he walked over and stood beside Chione once again. She smiled at him and said, "I wondered if you were going to join me." He was startled by the smile. It was like she knew something that he knew, but he didn't know what that something was.

"Lots of thinking tonight," he said, trying to remain neutral.

"Indeed, General. Our Pharaoh has placed his trust in you tonight. I know you will do what is right for your Kingdom." Her answer rattled him slightly. She did not say "Pharaoh" but "Kingdom". Was she a mind reader, as well?

"I understand you have a new addition to your family. A granddaughter, if I heard correctly?"

Why was he not surprised that she knew? He suspected she knew a great deal about many things that she did not let on that she knew about. "Yes, that is correct. The Gods have..."

Chione shot him a dark look at the mention of "Gods". "Remember our Pharaoh has forsaken them; they no longer exist to us. I believe the correct response should have been, 'Our Pharaoh was gracious enough to bless our family with a precious gift.'"

He stood there stunned at the dressing down he just received. *The nerve of this woman!* Any remorse he felt for what he was going to do was gone. He smiled as best he could and remained silent. *It was now or never.*

He took another small sip of Blood Cider and closed his eyes, taking a deep breath. Upon opening them, he threw the remaining contents of his goblet at Chione's face. The look of utter shock on her was momentarily satisfying; he grabbed her and lifted her off the ground, ready to toss her over the balcony.

She did not budge. *How is this…?*

A grip around his throat brought him back to reality, and he was hoisted up into the air and, moments later, he found himself dangling several feet above the ground, held up by a single hand. *Chione's hand. Not possible!*

"General Pentu. If I didn't know better, I would think you might have tried to throw me off the edge of the balcony. But we are such good friends, that's just a silly thought, right?"

He needed to do something quickly, or he would be the one falling to his death. Chione settled him down in front of her—*they were eye to eye.* Chione continued to smile. "Let me tell you a story. A true story. Would you like to hear a true story?"

Pentu nodded frantically.

"Excellent!" Chione said, her hands still around his throat. "The story is about Hatshepsut."

His eyes grew wide in anger. How dare she mention his granddaughter? "The story is about her tragic life, cut short because of the bad choices her elders made. Or do you want to hear a long, happy story? One where she grows up to be a mighty ruler of Egyptia?" Pentu's eyes grew wider. *Ruler of Egyptia?* He was starting to see stars and lose consciousness from the force of Chione's grip around his neck. "Excellent. Tell no one of what has transpired, and Hatshepsut shall have the long, happy story," Chione whispered. Without warning, he felt himself being tossed through the air, until he landed hard against the Pharaoh's secondary throne. He rolled over and watched Chione leave the balcony, motioning for him to follow. She didn't even look at him.

What had he done? He hoisted himself to his feet and brushed himself off. He still had a battle to win, but for now he followed her, like a dog after its master. Until such a time presented when he would sink his teeth into Chione's flesh and tear her apart…metaphorically, he thought to himself.

Chapter 9

Drăculeşti Castle—Sighişoara

'Dinner Time'

Vlad Drăculeşti sat at the head of the large, black locust table, enjoying his meaty soup that his wife prepared. Of course, they had servants that came to the castle everyday, but his wife was determined to be as active in the castle as much as possible. As proud as he was of her, he often warned her about carrying the weight of everything on her poor shoulders, and in turn, she would remind him that he was not getting wrinkled with age but scarred with age instead, and he had to admit she was not wrong. He played the part of the wounded husband, as it was a fun part to play. But it was true that the battles with the Spiriduş along with other unnatural creatures had taken its toll on his body. Even with his self-healing abilities.

Beside Vlad to his right sat his eldest son Micrea. Twenty-two and as powerfully built as Vlad was, Micrea had blackish hair and blue eyes that burned right into your soul. Vlad had already started grooming Micrea to take his place when it was his time to step down as the Ruler of Europea. It would be decades before that time came to pass, but his father had taught him at an early age, so he carried on the tradition. Even though he prided himself on being notoriously difficult to kill, life still had ways of throwing obstacles in his path with near-dire consequences. He learned that when his own father had died unexpectedly; he was thrust into being a leader at an early age, soo much of what he learned was through trial and error.

The Spiriduş had exploited many of his mistakes. He did not want Micrea to experience the same hardships as he did. Vlad had begun putting out feelers to several *viskta* about potential mates for his son. There was one promising match from the Northern Region, but he had yet to meet her for a final determination. He was planning on going north in the next week or so along with Micrea, but the latest Spiriduş attack had caused delay. More than once, Vlad had tempted to use the full force of the Sentinels, but had held back, as the Spiriduş had family members in Sighişoara and in other villages. Vlad did not want to generate any sympathy for them. Because of their bold action, he saw no other course of action. For too long he had not done enough. No longer.

To his left was Radu, who was nineteen and had a slender build, with dark brown hair and eyes to match. While Radu was not as big as Micrea, he could always hold his own during a scrap with his brothers. As the middle child, Vlad could see that he had always struggled to find his place. In the past couple of months, Radu was spending less time at home; there were rumours flying of his spending it with a blacksmith's daughter. Vlad was not opposed to his son enjoying the spoils of youth, if he was careful. Radu's only change since the hunt, was a newfound sense of humour which Vlad found refreshing. Life was taxing enough—what harm was there in a bit of humour?

Beside Micrea sat Vladimir, his youngest son. He was also the most curious and adventurous one of his three boys, which got him into more trouble than not—the latest being, of course, entering The Trifecta. When he had received word of what had happened, he found himself both extremely proud of his youngest son's achievement and enraged that he was capable of something so reckless. Vladimir had not even gone through his transition yet. It was remarkable. He had yet to speak to Vladimir alone since he had returned, but he would after dinner. Lately, Vladimir's attention had been directed toward Kazia, which was a point of concern for him due to the dynamic of their respective *visktas'* histories. Even over the decades, the damage had not been repaired between the two *visktas*; he hoped it was just an infatuation and that Vladimir would soon move onto another girl. Earlier today when he was in the village, Kazia's father had confronted him, expressing anger toward Vladimir for hanging around with his daughter, and for entering the Trifecta. Vlad did, however, have the authority to overrule Kazia's arranged marriage. As the ruling *viskta*, he was to officiate the wedding, which he could refuse, as it was his right. But it was not something that he desired to do. It was a good marriage, as both *visktas* would benefit. He had met Marku as well. Marku had the makings of a good man, given more time and experience. If he honestly thought it would be a sour marriage, then he would have not approved it.

Regardless of each of his sons' actions and behaviours, he was proud of them, as they were all growing up to be fine young men in their own way, at their own pace. He knew there would be bumps along the road, but that came with growing up.

Dinner was the only time they could all be together, so the time was precious to him. Everyone was busy living their lives, and soon, one by one, the boys would be leaving to start their own families.

Where did the time go? Vlad thought to himself sadly. Even though their lifespan was much greater than the average villager, there would come a time when he would have to step down and go into self-imposed banishment. Throughout the centuries, members of the Drăculeşti "died" at the appropriate age and were "buried" in empty coffins. The truth was they headed off into the desolate northern reaches, where they would live out their lives either in solitude or with others of their *viskta* in secret. The thought of leaving his family pained Vlad greatly. He knew he would need to have the talk soon with his boys, to prepare them for what was to come—what was expected of them in the future after his departure. How to explain this to his wife… He was still at a loss for words, as he did not expect her to follow him. His children would need their mother…always. He could not just leave her. She was his heart. It gutted him, the thought of her anguish over his "death".

"I have never seen the moons this close before, Father. Perhaps the old legend we learned about in school is true," Micrea said, and he smiled back, glad to be rid of the dark thoughts plaguing his mind.

Vlad looked over at his son. "We all know the legend. Not even our elders have seen this Soul Moon Convergence. I believe Ilga Kranicki is in her sixties, and she has never seen one before. Looking at the moons earlier, I will concede that it is a first for me to see them this close together, so I will not rule out any possibility. I believe your mother would love it if it were true and all three of you boys found your soulmates. You would all be off married before any of you could blink." He chuckled, looking over at his wife. Vasilisa gave a roll of her eyes and flashed him a knowing smile.

"I think since tonight is so special that if Vladimir went out, he would find his fabled hellsteed," Radu said, grinning evilly as he looked at his younger brother.

Vlad shook his head at his son's nonsense. "A hellsteed! No one has seen one of those in who knows how long. Indeed, tonight's conversation seems to be about myths and legends. Perhaps the moons are having some effect on all your brains, as well," he teased as his sons responded with false expressions of hurt.

"Indeed," chimed in his wife, who was gazing at him. He could tell she was glad tonight's conversation wasn't about the Spiriduş, so she was enjoying it more than usual. Lately, that seemed to be on everyone's mind. The attacks, the loss of equipment…and lives.

"I think that the legends could be true," Vasilisa said, a dreamy look in her eyes. "Just look at the moons tonight, as they are almost touching. Who would have thought that was possible?"

"All legends and myths are based on some sort of fact, no matter how ridiculous it may seem," Vlad said. "Ever the diplomat, my sweet, that's what I love about you."

She beamed at him. *How had he been so lucky to marry her?*

"Father, do you think there are lands beyond the oceans?" Vladimir asked, his eyes squinting the way they did when he was deeply curious. "I know no expeditions have ever returned, but do you think that there is more?"

His wife had told him about their conversation earlier, so the question came as no surprise. He thought back to his family's long history. No one had ever left and came back. Every vessel that left the harbour never returned. It wasn't that it wasn't possible, just highly improbable.

He added, "I do not discount the possibility, though. It does seem that if there were other lands, at least one of the vessels would have returned. I have thought on it and have no explanation other than they must have run into something terrible. Whatever it was, whether natural or unnatural, prevented them from ever returning. Thinking about taking a vessel out and seeing for yourself, Vladimir?" he asked, hoping the answer was no. Vlad had no desire to lose any of his sons. The chances of Vladimir leaving and coming back alive was next to none, and he did not want to live through the grief, nor did he want that for his beloved.

Vlad watched Micrea ham it up. "Vladimir has thoughts in his head, alright. All for Kazia," Micrea said, leaned his head back, as though gazing up at the stars, held out his arm and called out tenderly, "Ohh, Kazia, my sweet!"—but was quickly interrupted by Vladimir, who reached over and punched his brother in the arm.

Vlad shook his head. *Well, it had been a peaceful meal up to his point,* he thought. Pounding his fist on the table, he roared, "Enough!", and both his sons straightened up.

"Kazia is spoken for. We all know this, including you, Vladimir. Talk to her at school if you must, but no more. There is enough bad blood between our *visktas*. We do not need to add more. Is that understood, Vladimir?"

His son withered under his stern gaze. Vlad hated laying down the law like that, but he had no choice. He hoped to do it in private, but it was done. He would still talk to Vladimir afterwards, though. There was still the matter of The Trifecta.

There were other pretty girls in the village for Vladimir to choose from. With the Masquerade Dance coming up, Vlad was hoping that there would be a girl that might catch Vladimir's eye. Which would end the talk of Kazia once and for all. He needed to change the subject. "I think that with the moons coming together, which is something that no one alive today has witnessed in their lifetime, might mean that the impossible might be possible." But his words did nothing to help Vladimir's spirits.

The mood of the conversation had been killed by his proclamation, which made him hate himself for what he was about to say next. But alas, it had to be said. Taking a sip of Blood Cider, he took a moment to find the right words.

"As for the hellsteed, that will have to wait for another night. I am sure you have all heard there has been another attack by the Spiriduș on the latest supply wagon that was sent out, and it was only one wagon. They should have left it alone but didn't. I have decided that it is time to end their threat once and for all." He took a deep breath. "I went to the scene of the attack. The Sentinels' bodies are missing. They should have been left there for proper burial. That is unforgivable. For too long they have had sympathizers on the Council, and I have allowed them to persuade me to let the Sentinels handle them, going against my better judgment. I have only engaged them in skirmishes, nothing on a scale to wipe them out completely. I was wrong. More lives have paid the price for my willingness to be persuaded by others. I had assurances that the last shipment would make it through. It did not. They failed. *For the last time!*" He banged his fist on the table, startling his sons and wife. "The Sentinels and the Spiriduș have been at each other's throats for ages with neither side gaining an edge. I have sat back and thought about it carefully and come to an unfortunate conclusion."

"What's that, Father?" Micrea asked him. He could tell everyone was on edge with what he was about to say.

"I have no proof...yet. But the only logical conclusion is that the Sentinels and the Spiriduş have come to some sort of arrangement that benefits both. Look at history. Sentinels defeat some attacks, and the Spiriduş capture some wagons. It does not appear as though either side is pressing the issue overly hard. Even my father had suspicions before his end, but there was never any proof. The Council, as well, convinced my father that the lands would revolt against our *viskta*. We would be overthrown, so he stayed his hand. He thought it best to not throw the lands into turmoil once again, and to continue ruling. A few Spiriduş attacks here and there seemed like a small price to pay for relative harmony throughout the lands. Yes, people are upset, yet no one is banging down our door demanding heads be cut off and displayed in the public square. The Spiriduş have a lot of support, and I have heard whispers of there being tent villages in the mountain regions. If this is true, then we have a much larger issue. Settlements of groups that need to be dealt with...harshly. I have often wondered to where the Spiriduş ran off to. Now I know."

"How, Father? If it's true, who can we trust with this information that would not warn the Spiriduş and not turn the rest of the Sentinels against us?" Micrea asked. Vlad could tell everyone was nervous, worried about what was going to come. Vladimir was not of age yet, so the burden was going to fall on him to take his place on the Council, while he left with his eldest sons to eradicate the Spiriduş once and for all. "We leave tomorrow to hunt for a trail that will lead us to where one of their camps are," he said grimly, seeing the look of uncertainty on their faces. Though, there was no hint of fear, which made him proud.

"We?" his wife's concerned voice spoke. Vlad knew she would not want to hear the answer, but he needed his sons' help for the undertaking. The Spiriduş were too spread out and too large for him to take out alone. He needed more eyes and ears, as well as strength for what was to come. The only people he could trust was his family, his sons.

"Yes, we. Micrea and Radu will leave with me in the morning, along with the Sentinel guards who only thinks this is a fact-finding mission, not one of annihilation. I cannot guarantee anything that may come to pass but know this: we will all make it back alive." His eldest sons responded with determined nods, but Vladimir's face turned worried. He was wondering what his role was going to be in all this, Vlad knew.

"Vladimir. You will need to stay here and help your mother with whatever she needs. People will have concerns or questions regarding our absence, and you will need to answer them as best you can. You will take my seat at the head of the Council." Vladimir's eyes grew wide at what he said. Vlad knew his son had no experience with the Council, but it couldn't be helped. His son would have to manage. "If you're not certain how to respond, simply say you need to think on it, and come to your mother for direction, as I do not know who is to be trusted. If you feel you are being rushed for an answer, dissolve the Council for the day and delay until the following day. This is important, Vladimir," he added sharply, hoping it would drive his point home.

He could see the concern on his wife's face. The Spiriduş were becoming bolder with the Sentinel's help, and it was up to him to end their raiding once and for all. He knew his wife thought that it wasn't fair that every time there was trouble, her husband had to run off. Vlad craved more than just being a leader, and she was aware of this innate desire. It ran in his blood—not even being a father could change that. Vlad had a thirst for battle. The excitement, the rush of adrenaline that cursed through his veins… It made him feel truly alive.

"How many Sentinels will be joining us, Father?" Radu asked anxiously. Vlad could tell he was troubled at the news, as well as having to leave the castle. His sons were old enough and capable, but he had been protecting them at their mother's request. No longer.

"Must they go with you?" his wife asked. He could feel her uncertainty. But in order to appear that everything was normal, as well as to hide his true intentions, they needed to come.

"There will be a dozen of them with us. I don't suspect there will be trouble on the way there. Once we get close, you never know. I have selected Sentinel Captain Ivisk, as he knows the area where we will be going. Do not trust them blindly," he said, and stopped talking at the sound of footsteps approaching. He held up his hand for silence and turned to look at whoever was interrupting their meal.

Sentinel Commander Alexandar Yonescu entered the dining room. The Sentinel Commander was an older man with silver hair and a salt and pepper beard, heavy set, likely from all the drinking. A thought crossed Vlad's mind. Perhaps the man was a Spiriduş in disguise.

He looked down to see Sentinel Lacey, an overly friendly rottweiler, trailing behind him. Lacey trotted over to Vasilisa, who bent down to pet him. All sorts of creatures took a natural liking to Vasilisa.

"Good evening, sir. I hear that you have agreed to allow the Sentinels to accompany you. I will feel better knowing you will have their protection," Alexandar said.

Of course, you will. "Thank you for your concern, Sentinel Commander. What brings you here at this late hour? Has there been another attack?" Vlad prayed there had not been.

"No, thankfully, but there are other matters at hand. With the Masquerade Ball next week, we will have travellers coming in, and the roads will need to be protected. Chief Sentinel Balázs thinks it would be boost in morale if your sons were to be out there, as well. They would be in support roles, of course, and not required to take action, should any trouble arise. It would be strictly escort duty, and they would have a team of Sentinels by their side. Each would be sent to a different region to greet the oncoming travellers."

Divide and kill. It was clear, now, where the Chief Sentinel's loyalty ran. It wasn't with him.

"I understand. It would provide a sense of security and re-assurance, but I'm afraid that is not possible," Vlad responded icily, using all his willpower to stifle the rage swelling inside of him. Perhaps he should kill all the Sentinels, as well.

"But, sir…" Alexandar started to protest, but Vlad cut the man short. "You will be here tomorrow morning, along with Sentinel Captain Ivisk and his forces. Tell the Chief Sentinel this news. Thank you for coming and enjoy the rest of your evening." He made sure his gaze bore into the man's skull as his guest nodded and left the dining area without another word, with Lacey in tow.

Vlad held up his hand again until the Commander's footsteps faded, then picked up his glass of Blood Cider and chugged the rest. "The good Chief Sentinel is not to be trusted by any of you. What you heard tonight was his plan to divide and kill us. If he were loyal, he never would have devised a plan to separate us, therefore making us each individual targets. Vladimir, you are to stick close to your mother. To Council and back—that's it. Do you understand?" Vlad hoped his son appreciated the direness of the situation they were facing.

"Yes, Father," Vladimir said swiftly, nodding nervously. Vlad looked over at his wife. He could tell she had many questions but was holding off until they were alone.

The evening's mood went from fantasy to reality much too quickly for Vlad's liking, considering it was going to be the last night they would all be together for quite some time. "We cannot fight two enemies at once. Two united enemies are what we have. We need to kill the Spiriduş first. With them removed from the situation, the Sentinels cannot argue keeping such a large force, and we can reduce their numbers. Then I remove the Leader of the Sentinels, and I will place Radu in charge. I know, son," he said, turning to him, "this is not what you want, but this isn't about what's right or fair—it's about survival. Do you understand?"

Radu opened his mouth, but closed it again, merely nodding his dejected head. "For them to walk into our home, unveiling a plan to pick us off one by one, shows that they are not afraid of us. That is their second mistake," Vlad said.

"What was their first mistake, Father?" Vladimir asked.

Vlad frowned. "Getting in bed with the Spiriduş. For that, the Sentinel leadership will suffer. We do not know who is involved in the duplicity, so we cannot risk trusting the wrong person. Therefore *no one* can be trusted. No matter how nice they appear to be. Is that understood?" he asked again, and his family nodded.

Vlad turned to gaze at his wife, who had been silent. She had a strange look on her face. "What is it?" he asked as they locked eyes, and he saw something in them that he had never seen before, which rattled him slightly. She took a sip of her Blood Cider, slowly placed it down on the table, and stood up, staring at each of them. After a few more minutes of silence, she finally spoke, a fire burning in her eyes and determination in her voice. "They are threatening my family. I have one thing to ask of you, my husband."

Vlad could hear the anger rising with every word. "What is your command, my wife?"

It was as though a dark shadow had loomed over her. Vlad watched as she absently played with the crystal pendant around her neck. She took another sip of Blood Cider before saying quietly, "Kill them all. Kill all that would threaten my family."

Vlad stood up, his gaze hard. "As you command. It will be done." Vlad turned to Vladimir. "Vladimir, come with me." And he left the dining room, knowing his son would follow.

***

Vladimir watched his father leave the table and cast a glance at his mother, who nodded and motioned for him to follow. Radu and Micrea wore worried looks on their faces. Vladimir quickly got up and followed his father. *This is what he had been dreading.* He walked into his father's study. It was rather humble, with a small wooden desk and behind it, books lined on wall-to-wall shelves. Vlad stood in the doorway, waiting for his father to speak.

"Sit," his father ordered, and he jolted slightly and sat in the chair, wilting under his father's intense gaze. His father did not look pleased with him. Without a word, he continued to stare at Vladimir.

"When I was your age…" his father started to say.

Vladimir grimaced. *Here it comes!*

"…I would have waited patiently to enter The Trifecta until I was of age, do you know why, Vladimir?"

"No, Father," Vladimir replied meekly.

"Your grandfather was not…a kind man. I have strived to be better than him. But in doing so, I have failed in certain ways. You entered The Trifecta underage, and you have consorted with Kazia, who is arranged to be married. The Trifecta prize will be going to Lash's family as compensation for their loss instead of being held over for the next one as originally planned. I cannot stress enough how important it is that you stay away from Kazia. As punishment for your actions, you will work five hundred hours in the mines. This is not a debate."

Vladimir nodded.

"Now, let me ask you a question, my son."

Question? "Yes, Father," Vlad said, afraid of what it might be. His punishment was already beyond anything he imagined.

His father stood up. *"How am I supposed to expect the village to follow my rules when my own son doesn't?"*

Vladimir's hands shook on his knees, and his legs felt like they might give out. He shifted uncomfortably. His father had never been this cross with him before, and he didn't know how to handle it. He merely sat in silence, biting his bottom lip and trying his best to avoid his father's eyes as the latter continued to stare at him down. Vladimir didn't know how long the silence lasted.

"Do you have nothing to say for yourself, Vladimir?" his father finally said. Vladimir thought apologies were not adequate. He truly didn't know what to say, so he just blurted out the first thing that came to mind, "I'm sorry. I…I…just wanted to…"

His father's expression remained unchanged. "You wanted to what? Impress Kazia? I have no doubt it did. It also impressed her father, so much so that when I got back today, he let me know just how much. I have no doubt Marku also noticed how much it impressed her. They are going to be married—you know this, why, Vladimir…just explain what this is about…please," his father pleaded.

Vladimir didn't know how to explain it other than he *really* liked her. "I like her, Father, a lot. I never used to, but in this past year…something changed. I don't know how to explain it."

His father sat down in his chair and nodded. "I understand, son, I truly do. But I can't help you with this. You need to work this out, inside of you. Both Kazia and Marku deserve a chance. I know this is hard, my son. Can you honour their arrangement and give them that chance?"

Vladimir knew his father was right, but it didn't make it easy. "Yes, Father," he said, defeated.

"Be warned, Vladimir, you are my son and I love you with all my heart, but if you continue down this path, there will be consequences." Vladimir didn't know exactly what he meant by this but decided this was not the time to press the issue.

"I remember what it's like to be young and naive, Vladimir. There is the dance coming up. I highly recommend you set your sights on one of the girls there."

He nodded his head in agreement.

"I understand," his father repeated. "The heart wants what it wants. I felt the same way about your mother. I just knew she was the one. I have no doubt you feel the same way right now about Kazia. But you will get over it, I promise…in time." His father was trying to console him, but it didn't work, so he simply replied with another, "Yes, father" and hoped his words didn't sound as hollow as they felt.

His father's tone softened a bit. "How are you doing with The Trifecta and Lash's death?" He sensed that his parents had talked before dinner, and they discussed the conversation he had with his mother.

"It's been hard" was all he said. He really didn't feel much like talking.

"You know, I, too, went through the damned competition. I wanted to ban it when I became leader, but everyone begged me not to. It's a waste of young lives, full of potential. As I look back, I fear I have not become the leader I had hoped to be. I have let the baying of sheep influence me for far too long. We are the lions, Vladimir. Soon we will be having a different conversation, one about your future. There is something you *need* to know, but that is for another time. Is there anything else you have to say to me?" his father added, leaning forward slightly.

He shook his head in silence.

"You are free to go. Remember what I said at dinner when it comes to dealing with the council: remain in the castle tonight. I want you to be up bright and early when your brothers and I leave. Your mother will need all the support you can give her while we are gone."

Vladimir made to leave the room, but stopped at the door frame and turned to face his father. "I am sorry I disappointed you, Father."

He held Vladimir's gaze. "As a father, I have learned that children lead to many emotions. Disappointment is not one of them," he said, and smiled. Vladimir smiled back and left his father's study. He had weathered the storm.

Chapter 10

Royal Harbour—Thebes

'Curtain Time'

General Pentu heard the loud clanging of bells coming from both massive transport vessels beside him. They were of an entirely new class of vessel, born from his dreams. Never had wood been used in the construction of such large ships. Papyrus vessels would not have been up to the task he had been given. These new vessels were over two hundred feet long and sixty feet high: monstrous compared to anything in the Royal Docks. He had them ordered to be painted midnight blue for camouflage, with no ceremonial adornments painted. Should anything unexpected occur, there would be nothing to link to the Pharaoh or this land. There were no sails either. It was manpowered only. There were over one hundred fifty oarsmen per boat. Only the *Sky Tram* required more men to power it.

The loading ramps were being hauled up, with only the walking planks left lowered, touching the docks. Both vessels were sitting low in the water, due to the enormous weight of the cargo. He had no doubt the Oars Captains would be up to the task of motivating their charges using thick whips, or any other means they deemed necessary to get results.

The oarsmen were dredges of society. Their motivation was knowing that they could be freed by proving themselves worthy of a better life. Little did the freed ones know that their freedom was being walked to the Royal Apothecary to be experimented on.

He was standing on top of a large cargo pile in the middle of the massive pier that both ships were tied off to, bows first. The hustle of the pier was slowly ebbing away as he watched, satisfied that all his commands had been carried out to perfection. Tonight, would change everything.

He glanced up at the moons. They had started to overlap each other. It was an amazing sight to behold. Many of the workers were whispering among themselves. Excitement permeated through the air. He glanced past the pier out to the water and closed his eyes momentarily, then hopped off the cargo pile. He walked past the dock workers, who were finishing off their duties, and ignored all that was going on around him. Stopping at the end of the pier, he picked up the small wooden bucket and tossed it into the water. Scooping it back up, rope attached, and brought it up and onto the pier, then lowered himself to one knee and cupped his hands, scooping the water up to his nose. It smelled different tonight, and he knew the cause: the moons. He took out a small black dagger, making a small slice above his wrist, and let his blood drip into the ocean. "Accept my blood as a sacrifice to protect my men from whatever may lie on the other side," he whispered into the wind, "and return them home safely to their families." No matter the battle ahead, he always repeated this ritual for his men.

He had seen this done many years ago by one of his former Captains. He had thought him mad to not pray directly to Montu, the War-God. When he questioned him, he was stunned at what he was asked in return: "Why pray to the same War-God as our enemy?" During his time under the Captain, they had never lost a single battle. Ever since then, he performed the same ritual before every battle—to whatever or whoever was still listening.

He remained undefeated.

"If you keep leaking like that, you will be even more shriveled looking than you are now," his wife said, hitting him playfully in the back, "if that's even possible."

Grinning, he turned to face Massika, whose lips were smiling, but whose eyes remained solemn. She was as beautiful to him as when they first met all those decades ago. He had not spent a moment of his life regretting the decision to ask her to marry him. He gazed into Massika's moonstone-coloured eyes and tucked a grey hair behind her ear. For his departure, she was wearing her best dress, full-length and shimmering gold, that showed off some of her curves and simultaneously covered her "imperfections", as she called them, that had grown over the years—which to him were merely signs of a long, happy life.

As they stood staring at once another in silence, he knew they must have looked awkward to bystanders, but no such awkwardness existed, because no words were needed to express their sentiments. Her eyes spoke volumes. Looking into them, he knew she would be there waiting for him, as she had for the past forty years.

"Well, this must be the lovely Mrs. Pentu," Chione said, appearing beside them and breaking their silent exchange. Pentu turned to face her, most displeased. He fought the urge to tell Chione her showy outfit was not appropriate for the occasion: a crimson dress with gold highlights, surely meant to turn heads, would be a distraction to the mission at hand. "Oh, were you two lovebirds having a moment? My most sincere apologies."

He was about say something when Chione grabbed his wife by her right arm and feigned whispered, "One of these days we will go for Blood Cider and biscuits, and you can tell me all about that crazy husband of yours." Chione released her, a wicked smiled spread across her face, and then she left them alone once again.

"Well, she is most unpleasant!" his wife said.

He whole heartedly agreed. "Yes. I wonder where she really came from and what her true motives are." His neck was still tender from being held up in mid-air earlier that day. He knew the only reason why he was still alive was because Chione did not want him dead. That could change at any moment. Going forward, he knew he needed to be on his guard around her—and also find a way to end her if required. From her display of incredible strength, he knew that Chione was much more then what she appeared. *How many more latent talents does she have?*

"Do not trust her, my husband. When she touched me, a chill ran through me. Not a good omen."

He nodded in agreement, then thought it time to veer away from the subject to something more pleasant. "How is our precious granddaughter?" He smiled at the memory of holding her for the first time.

Massika beamed. "I held her today. When it was time for feeding, I did not want to give her back. I could hold her forever," she said, gushing. "Every time I hold her, it brings me back memories of our children. Why does it seem like yesterday and yet a lifetime ago, my love?"

He nodded again, taking his wife's hands, and lowering his lips to them. Her smile lit up his world. How had he been so lucky? He glanced over and saw Chione standing off in the distance, pretending to ignore them. His mood darkened.

"What is wrong, my husband? I see darkness in your eyes," she said, her eyebrows wrinkled with worry. "Something troubled you just now, what has happened?"

Pentu half-smiled. There was nothing he could keep from this woman. Nevertheless, he could not tell her what happened with Chione earlier. His pride demanded it remain with him.

"Nothing to concern you with, my sweetness. You know us old, decrepit Generals. The closer we are to battle, the more anxious we get," he said, trying to sound as reassuring as he could. The look on Massika's face told him that she did not believe him, but to his relief, she did not press further. His wife knew that there was a part of his life that he kept separate from her, a dark part that she had never dared to question, which he was immensely grateful for.

"War is a young man's game. We should be on the balcony of our home watching this, holding hands, and drinking blood cider," she said lightly.

Whenever he had to go off to a military exercise or battle in the Kingdom, she would bring up his age. He knew she was correct, but as long as his blood flowed, the call of war would reel him in. Secretly, he would not have it any other way. As much as he would want nothing more than to die next to his wife, there was a part of him that wanted to die in a glorious battle. Soon, that latter part may get its way, he mused to himself.

"Any last commands for me, my lady?" he asked.

"Only one. Come home to me whole or not at all."

"Yes, ma'am," he said, and gave her one final embrace before striding past her. As he did, his hand instinctively reached out, and their fingers touched one last time before they would reunite once again.

As he walked toward Chione, her lips were contorted mischievously, which worried him. *What did go through that woman's mind,* he wondered.

"Tonight, is going to be a turning point in history. How do you feel about this tremendous honour bestowed upon you by our great Pharaoh?" Chione asked, a sly smile on her face.

"I am but a humble servant," he replied, bowing his head slightly. He decided it best to play subservient to her, for now. Once they returned, he would take a secret trip to the Royal Apothecary. In its twisted walls he hoped there would be something to neutralize Chione. *If required.*

Chione smiled in return. "As are we all to our Pharaoh. I've never wished for anything more than his success and have gone to great lengths to help achieve it, in secret. It is a breath of fresh air, General, that I can do it out in the open."

He merely smiled and nodded, hoping his eyes didn't portray distrust. As they approached the ramp for the Tutankhamen I, he spotted Captain Khaemweset conversing with Captain Hekaib of the Tutankhamen II, looking stouter than usual next to Captain Khaemweset's lanky body. *Though, their bald heads did complement one another,* Pentu thought as they turned their attention toward him and Chione. He had met them both earlier that day during the final battle preparations, though he suspected they might have been a bit distracted by a certain someone in red.

"Good evening, Captains." He nodded respectively as they approached, as did Chione, even though it looked like it pained her to do something so…*demeaning.*

"General Pentu, it has been too long since we had a proper conversation," Captain Khaemweset said cheerfully. "How are you, old friend?"

At the strategy session, there had been little time for idle chatter, as everyone was focused on the upcoming attack—and Chione, unfortunately. "Indeed. Quite well. I must admit, I am excited about tonight's *festivities."* He turned to Chione. "Are you ready to proceed?"

Her smile made the General cringe slightly. "Yes, General."

Captain Khaemweset stepped forward, a note of caution in his voice. "With the weight of the Ushabti Warriors, we are low in the water. We will not be very maneuverable until we are unloaded. Sharp turning and abrupt stops are not permitted. Frankly speaking, General, if any damage is inflicted to either vessel fully weighted, it could be hazardous." He could detect the nervousness in the Captain's voice, but Pentu was not worried about the vessels sinking. He had devised a brilliant battle strategy. Every scenario in his mind resulted in success.

"Thank you for your concerns, Captain Khaemweset. They are most appreciated. I understand the lack of maneuverability for escape, if required. We have invisibility and the element of initial destruction," he responded, and continued. "Our strategy is sound, as long as your sailors execute it to perfection, which I expect. I trust your Oars Captains will be up to motivating their charges, *for any task at any time.*

"It is almost time for Chione to open the curtain to the other side for us to commence our Pharaoh's divine retribution." Both Captains nodded in return, though there was still uncertainty in their eyes. It was not entirely unexpected; they were about to do something monumental that would change the course of the Kingdom's future. They also knew if something happened and they failed, their Pharaoh's anger would be lethal to them.

"We are honoured that our vessels were chosen as the instrument of our enemy's destruction," Captain Khaemweset humbly stated, and Pentu knew that the Captain was speaking the truth. He had personally selected each of them for these assignments. So far, his choices had been correct.

"To our unbridled success!" Captain Hekaib shouted, and Pentu added on, "To our Pharaoh!" High morale was required for this night of death, destruction, and not least of all...*uncertainty.*

Chione cleared her throat. "We should board now, General. It is going to rain shortly. Most of the villagers will be keeping warm inside."

He agreed with her assessment. It would be best to strike when everyone was inside, unprepared. He hoped that many died in their sleep tonight. Innocent civilians should not have to face the horrors that were being unleashed upon their village. "Agreed," he said, adding, "Let us board and get these ships moving. A glorious adventure waits for us." Pentu could see the excitement building inside of the captains.

Pentu saw Captain Hekaib reach behind the pier post revealing a large bottle of blood cider and placed it on top of the post. Captain Hekaib also grabbed empty, rust-coloured goblets, one for each of them. Pentu knew that Hekaib had quite the taste for the beverage. "To a successful mission. We finish off the bottle when we return," Captain Hekaib cheered. *Nothing wrong with a little help taking the edge off.* Though he doubted Chione needed it. She was always cool.

Captain Khaemweset handed the four of them a goblet and filled them up to the brim.

"Any last words, General, before we embark?" Chione asked.

Pentu stood there for a moment, pondering. Raising his goblet, he declared, "Let history never forget the name…Tutankhamen."

Pentu drank along with everyone else. It was an excellent vintage. He made a mental note to talk to Captain Hekaib about who his supplier was. He felt the liquid warm up his insides, a feeling of euphoria overwhelming him. He savoured the moment.

After placing the empty goblet down, Pentu extended his arm out to Chione. "After you."

"How gracious," she said, walking up the plank and onto the Tutankhamen I with him in tow. From the bow to the middle of the deck were lined two rows of fifteen enormous Ushabti Warriors, ready to receive their first commands. Pentu marveled at their strength. They were truly monstrous. As he looked around the deck, he saw the excited faces of the crew. They were about to sail into the unknown, yet he saw no fear in any eye he came into contact with. He was proud of all of them. They stood at nine feet tall, made of dark brown clay and vacant, purple eyes. Their right hand had six fingers—easier for grabbing things, or people—and the other hand was formed in a fist, used for smashing whatever was in their path. They were queued up behind the two massive off-ramps that would drop once they reached the shore of the village, on the other side of the curtain. Pentu touched one as he walked by. Cold and soulless. He had only seen them in action once before, years ago. It had been…*impressive.* He strode over to the side of the boat and looked down at the small watercraft bobbing in the water below. He met Master Medjay Ahmose's eyes and waved at him; he waved back.

They were tied off to the vessel and ready to go. If the Drăculeşti were as formidable as Chione had promised, the Medjays would have their hands full trying to capture one…alive, as per the Pharaoh's orders.

He knew the Mummies were on the level below the deck, ready, as well—the same number of them to match the Ushabti Warriors. There were secondary off-ramps in the front of the vessels, each with a quick release that extended as they dropped. The Mummies would engage and destroy any enemy that threatened the vessels, while the slower Ushabti Warriors lumbered off the ship. Unlike the near-mindless Ushabti Warriors, the Mummies had the remnants of deceased warriors' souls inside of them via the Soul Crystals. The crystals contained the knowledge, cunningness, and memories of the soul, but none of the humanity. He hoped he would be spared after he passed, as he had no desire to spend the afterlife as one of those unnatural abominations.

He made his way to the side of the boat that overlooked the pier. It was empty except for one person, Massika. She never left until he was out of sight, and she would be there when he returned. He heard excited voices behind him, but he did not care. He gazed into his wife's eyes, and the world stopped. She reached up to touch his face, and he pulled her nearer to him, his lips finding hers over the whooshing of the gentle waves beneath them. She leaned closer and whispered in his ear, "If that is not enough incentive for you to come home to me, nothing is." He blinked, and she was already where she had been standing moments before on the dock. Stepping back, he turned to face the commotion behind him, and a drop of warm rain hit his scalp.

It had begun.

He lifted his gaze at the three moons. What was it exactly that would occur when the moons came together? They would create something…*majestic.* He wracked his brain, trying to remember... The only other thing that came to mind is that it would create a new moon…? Was that what it was called? He tried to remember the earlier conversation that he had. It had been so long since he heard anything about this.

As he continued to gaze up at the night sky, it came to him—the Soul Moon Convergence. It was happening. He was in awe at what he was witnessing. The three moons had come together to form a magenta heart-shaped moon, which lit up the night's sky so bright he had to shield his eyes.

Magnificent.

The rain started to pour onto his face, but it did not bother him. He had to shake himself back to reality. *It's time.* Wiping his wet face, he called out, "Captain Khaemweset, signal the Tutankhamen II. It's time to cast off!"

Many years ago, he had created a flag system to be used as a form of communication between two vessels. When he had first joined to serve and was posted on a vessel, he had found that trying to yell out commands was ineffective, costing precious time, along with lives. It had taken him many years and *considerable* convincing of his superiors to adopt his communication system. It had finally been implemented—with great success. He watched the Captain point to the flagman, who picked up a green flag and start twirling it. He looked over and saw the return signal on the other ship acknowledging the command.

Screams of "Stroke!" rang out through both vessels by the Oars Captains, along with the cracking of many whips to accompany them. Moments later, the vessel slowly started to crawl forward. *There had to be a better system to move vessels than this,* Pentu thought. He looked over at the Tutankhamen II and saw it had started to inch forward, as well.

He wiped more rainwater off his face. Engaging in a battle was hard enough, doing so in such conditions made it even more challenging. Though, he had to admit—regardless of the rain, the moons in the sky were magnificent. There were no clouds hiding them from view…

And then something dawned on him. It was raining, but there were no clouds in the sky. *How is this possible?*

Looking down at his hands, they were covered in rainbow-coloured water. He cupped his hands and watched the water pool into them, then lifted them to his lips. Instantly, it warmed his insides. There was no distinct taste, but it comforted him, nonetheless. In fact, he felt…*good!*

He looked back towards the pier and swore to himself, *"I will make it home to you, my wife… You are my heart and soul."* He was finding it hard to concentrate, though he didn't know why. Was it because of the Soul Moon Convergence? As much as the story intrigued him, he knew he had to put those thoughts out of his head. He had a mission to lead and complete. And lives depended on it.

Both vessels were still in the midst of picking up speed. Soon they would be travelling at just the right pace. Pentu walked to the back of the vessel and looked back toward the pier. Massika was still there, watching her husband leave yet again. He wondered what went through her mind whenever she was forced to stay behind while he left. He had wanted to ask her on one more than one occasion, but the truth was he was not entirely sure he wanted to know the answer.

The Oars Captains were up to their tasks tonight. *Excellent.* They were far enough out from the pier and were approaching at a good, steady rhythm in the water. The vessels did not need to reach flank speed, as when they reached the other side, they would need to glide to the shore. If they were to crash, the potential to do serious damage to the vessel was amplified due to the weight on board. If they were not able to make it back through the curtain to the Royal Harbour, it would be disastrous.

"Chione, I believe we are far enough from the harbour to start whatever process is required to open the curtain," he called over to her, trying to appear calm.

Meeting his gaze, she said, "Agreed." As Chione slowly walked from the stern of the ship to the bow, his curiosity intensified. He decided to move closer to her so he may observe the process of opening the curtain. He watched her take the Nexus Crystal from around her neck and marvelled how something so small and beautiful could also be the instrument of destruction and death. Lifting the Nexus Crystal high above her head, she closed her eyes and shouted the word that would change everything for so many beings, including himself: *"Sighişoara!"*

The moment the word met the mist, a beam of light emerged from the Nexus Crystal, slicing a red straight line through the air, illuminating its path with a prism of rainbow colours. Thunder sounded, and lightning danced in the air above the streak of red. An intense screeching sound then pierced the air. Everyone's hands flew to cover their ears, including himself. It was as though the air itself had been wounded, and it was shrieking in pain. The waters were beginning to churn around the two vessels, rocking them violently as they tried to keep to their course straight ahead.

The lightning began to dance more violently now, and the ocean grew more turbulent. It was starting to unsettle him. He hoped whatever was happening would end quickly. Moments later, the red streak from the Nexus Crystal started to glow brighter, and there was a loud *crack*.

It was done. He looked over at Chione, who was resting against the bow of the vessel, clearly drained from the exertion. If she could tire out, that meant she had limits, and limits meant that she could be killed. He smiled at that thought. He could see through to the curtain, the village that they were going to lay waste to. The buildings were strange looking. It looked very peaceful from a distance. All that was going to change. He felt a twinge of pain inside of him, but he dismissed it quickly. He had a duty to carry out.

***

Massika watched the lightening over the water in the distance. She was in awe. Normally when her husband left to go on a mission, she had no doubt he would return, but not tonight. Not with what she saw before her. This was different. She had watched the monstrous Ushabti Warriors being loaded onboard the vessels. All of Thebes had. They had marched down the streets to their respective vessels. It was very rare they were ever used. Seeing them tonight magnified her fear of what was to come.

Pentu had not told her anything about the mission, other than it would be short, though highly dangerous. She held her hand to her heart, as she lost her breath for a moment. *What was wrong with her?* She took several deep breaths and walked over to a post and held onto it for support, then began to understand what had caused it. It had been so long since she had astral projected that it consumed most of her strength. She was also getting older. Things that once came easy to her no longer did. She tried her best to hide most of her pain from her husband.

Her husband never asked her about how they were able to touch and kiss when he was about to leave for duty. She was thankful for that. She would not know how to explain how she did what she did, as she did not entirely understand it herself. She was just grateful that she could. Whenever he left, she spent some time at the pier recouping her strength. She was glad tonight that the pier was empty. She did not want anyone to see her this way.

Ahead in the distance, the pier had a magenta glow to it. She looked up at the newly formed moon. *It was stunning!* Wiping the warm rain off her face, she noticed it was not clear...*but coloured!* What did it mean? She cupped her hands together and watched them fill up with rainbow-coloured water. Unable to resist, she took a sip, and a rush of warmth and happiness filled her. She laughed with utter joy.

The legend of the Soul Moon Convergence is real.

She remembered hearing it as a small girl and wondered if it would ever come true. Throughout her adult life, she always wondered whether she married the right man. She loved Pentu and knew that he loved her. They had a good marriage. Was there someone else, though? Someone better suited for her? For years she had listened to her friends and family complain about their respective husbands. They had all told her they were jealous, some even threatening to snatch Pentu from her grasp. She had laughed off the idle threats. How could so many women be miserable with their spouses? As much as she loved him, a part of her always wondered if she had she settled for Pentu without truly knowing if they were destined to be together.

Tonight, her burning question was answered. She felt like the luckiest woman alive. She was linked to her husband in a way she never imagined. She could feel his heart, and it truly belonged to her.

She had found her answer after all.

Chapter 11

Drăculeşti Castle/Dark Woods

'Breaking Bad'

Vladimir Drăculeşti looked out his bedroom window into the night's sky, wondering what the moons would look like when they finally touched. He could feel it inside of him—tonight was going to be extraordinary. He thought back to what his father said about keeping within the castle walls. He knew he would get into trouble, yet something was compelling him to leave to find a hellsteed and bring it back to the village, like a conquering hero. He dreaded facing his parents if he returned without one. How could something that feels so right be so wrong? He just needed to do it quickly. Part of him questioned his confidence—if it could be done why had no one captured one yet?

Sliding his window open he climbed through it, slowly and stealthily shimmying down the side of the castle toward the ground. Once he reached the bottom, his eyes darted around, there were no Sentinel guards in sight. Beside the castle was a large hedge maze that stood there since the castle had been built by his ancestors. The Drăculeşti that had united the lands had constructed the maze for the villagers and visitors to explore once a year. At first, it had been a huge hit, but over the years many people had disappeared inside of it, so the villagers demanded it be destroyed. A compromise was reached—no one would be allowed into it, and a Masquerade Ball would take its place as the main attraction for the annual festivities.

At the back of the maze was an exit that led to the Dark Woods. He had been in the maze many times and knew his way around it; fearlessly, he ran full tilt into it and navigated his way through until he made it out the back. He had heard the legends of people screaming at the horrors they had encountered, things that some considered unnatural. Somehow, nothing bad ever happened to him. He was immensely proud of himself for being able to escape the castle without being detected, proving, in his eyes, that he was doing the right thing.

It was rumoured that hellsteeds dwelled in the deepest part of the Dark Woods called the Darkest Depths. He heard stories about the groups of people that had gone deep into the forest, with few members returning. And the ones that did were never the same again. There were also other dangers in the forest, such as wolves and bears, and small, wooden live dolls called Marionettes. The Marionettes never killed anyone, but had beaten them senseless, terrorizing them until they took their victim's sanity. He had never met anyone that had encountered one of these creatures, but there were enough stories floating around to know that they had to be true.

He had no desire to meet any creatures in the forest, especially any such as those. He just needed to find a hellsteed, capture it, and bring it back to the castle before sunrise before his family woke up. As he plowed through the cornfield bordering the Dark Woods, he looked up at the tall trees before him. Their presence was more ominous than he imagined. A few feet past the trees was total blackness, even with the glow of the moons and clear sky. Perhaps something unnatural was preventing the light of the moons from piercing through the trees. He turned back to look at the castle in the distance, and his eyes lingered on it for a few moments before steeling himself away toward whatever awaited him in the forest. As he took his first step beyond the trees, he murmured to himself, "I got a bad feeling about this."

Carefully, he stepped forward, keeping his footsteps as light as possible, but a loud *snap* beneath his feet broke the silence. He froze. A sudden cold blast hit his face, and for a split second he thought the forest whispered to him, "*Drăculești*". The hairs on the back of his neck stood, and he could not remember being more terrified in his life than at this very moment. The Obsidian Trifecta hadn't been this terrifying.

Another cold blast hit him. "*Welcome,*" it hissed. He looked around to see if he could find where the voice was coming from. And then another strong wind hit him square in the back, hard enough to propel him forward. He stumbled but managed to stay on his feet. He was walking through the forest yetit was as though his legs were moving of their own accord. His entire body vibrated from fear. Willing himself to stop, he leaned up against a tree and wiped his brow; his hand was drenched in sweat. He hadn't even realized he had been sweating. Closing his eyes, he took deep breathes until he physically relaxed. "Nothing can hurt you; nothing can hurt you," he chanted to himself as he put one leg in front of the other to continue his search.

As he moved deeper into the forest, his mind jumped to his brothers. They had never dared to venture deep into the Dark Woods, though they joked that they had. He could tell when they were showing off. Terrified though he was this very moment, it would be worth it when he saw the looks on their faces after he showed up with his prize. *Positive thoughts need more positive thoughts,* he kept repeating.

He stopped walking. He was completely lost. From which way had he entered? From all around him were rustling sounds and movement. Was that the giggling of children? No, it wasn't possible. It was merely his fear and overactive imagination.

The more time he spent in the forest, the longer it would take to get back to the castle. He saw bushes rustling and he anxiously looked around. He had the distinct feeling he was being watched from every direction; he decided to stop and listen.

Nothing. He continued forward, doubting with each step whether he was ever going to make it home, let alone on time. *Why wasn't he turning around and leaving?*

He was feeling more and more tired with every step, fear and anxiety sapping his strength away. He stumbled over a large tree root, falling hard on the dirt ground. Deciding to lay there for a minute, he closed his eyes and covered his ears, trying to block out the strange voices filling the forest, but "*Drăculeşti*" still rang out clearly in his head.

He knew he could not lay on the ground forever, so he slowly got to his feet and looked around. Relief washed over him, as only trees and bushes surrounded him. At least nothing was rushing out to kill him. But panic struck again when he realized nothing around him looked familiar. It was like the trees moved around and changed position. *Was he losing his mind?* Is this what happened to anyone that entered the Dark Woods? He was starting to question whether he would be the same person as he had entered—if he made it out of here. The terrified voice inside of him—his own voice, this time—told him that nothing was ever going to be the same again.

Squinting in the darkness, he saw a small clearing to his right. As he moved through the trees to the clearing, an oddly shaped rock came into view. He approached it; smooth and grey, it was shaped like an hourglass, with a deep groove on top. He knew that there was no way it was natural. It did not belong here.

He kept on guard, glancing around and over his shoulder, making sure he was alone.

He wasn't.

His jaw dropped—a large black bear had entered the clearing and was staring directly at him. *Frack me!* He frantically looked around for something to use as a weapon, and nothing.

The bear was slowly approaching him, a very hungry look in its eyes. Now what? He moved to keep the rock between them, hoping he could lose the bear in the trees if he bolted through them. He had been taught bears had bad eyesight, and his was excellent. He started backing up from the rock to get closer to the trees, keeping the rock as a shield as the bear moved closer. Knowing the rock could not be a buffer for much longer, he readied himself to turn and run when something else caught his eye.

A hellsteed.

It was standing across the clearing, grazing the grass, completely unfazed by the scene it had stepped into. *Magnificent!* The hellsteed was blacker than the night, with glowing bloodshot eyes, a kind of red smoke gently flowing from them, and its mane the same fiery red. He was in awe of it.

Something caught his eye, and he remembered that the bear was still in the clearing. The bear was now focused on the greater threat which meant he got a temporary reprieve from being a late-night snack. What he was searching for was right in front of him, but he couldn't do a fracking thing until the bear was gone or dead. He decided to step closer—he may never this opportunity again.

Another *snap*. He hadn't noticed the small branch laying on the ground he had just stepped on. Both the hellsteed and bear turned their heads toward him. He took a step back warily, whimpering, "Sorry." The bear's low growl was directed towards him. *Frack!*

He was frozen on the spot without an inkling as to what to do. He didn't want to move forward or backward and anger the bear even more, nor scare off the hellsteed. He was in an utterly impossible situation. One that he couldn't see a way out of that didn't end in either losing his prize or being eaten. He needed to do something quickly, but what? *Think.* What would his brothers do in this situation? He realized that neither brother would ever be in this situation, so he switched to think of what his father would do and groaned at the thought. His father would pick up the rock, run over, and bash the bear in the head until it was dead. His father had no fear of any person or creature, nor was he afraid to risk everything. He was not as brave as his father…*yet.*

He decided to take small, slow steps toward the stone, keeping it between him and the bear but remaining closer to the hellsteed, and started to speak to the latter in a gentle tone. "It's okay. I'm not going to hurt you," he said, doubting he could hurt it even if he tried. From the corner of his eye, he could see the bear's gaze still rested on him. As he neared the stone, he stopped and wondered what to do next. The bear and hellsteed had not moved. It seemed like the two animals were deciding their next move, too, though the bear seemed to be the most agitated between the two beasts. *"Please don't eat me,"* he pleaded. The bear lunged but not at him—at the hellsteed.

He watched in awe as the bear leaped at the hellsteed but was a sliver too slow. The hellsteed dodged out of the way, twirling, and kicking the bear with its hind legs, which sent the bear flying back hard against a tree. The bear got up and reared onto its hind legs, roaring at the hellsteed, and charged toward it again. It stopped short, rearing up again and swatting the hellsteed's head, making it almost fall backwards onto the ground.

The bear was going to kill the hellsteed. He needed to do something quickly.

He wished he had brought his sword. There were twigs around and some branches, but nothing he could harm the bear with.

Unless...

He picked up a large branch and snapped it in half with his knee.

It didn't break clean across, but at an angle. Perhaps he could use it as a spear, he thought. He watched the creatures rear up to attack and defend; it was almost a stalemate, as neither could get the upper hand. Only the weak die in the Dark Woods. The two beasts in front of him were tough survivors. He still held the makeshift spear, waiting to pounce when the opportunity presented itself. The bear attacked again, this time jumping instead of swiping, and managed to get a hold of the hellsteed's neck and hang onto it. The hellsteed reared, but the bear clung on and growled, then bit into the hellsteed's neck. It neighed loudly. The bear let go of its grasp, letting the hellsteed roll onto the ground, writhing in pain.

Yes! The bear's mouth was on fire from biting the hellsteed, which was dripping liquid fire from the wound inflicted by the bear's vicious bite. He looked back at the bear, and its entire face was now on fire. It rubbed its face in the dirt, trying to smother the flames, but its face was already horribly disfigured. He could see its blackened teeth, as most of its jaw had been melted off.

He backed up—it was glaring at him. *Frack!* Twirling the branch in his hand, he steeled himself for what was to come. His father had once told him the best defence is an even better offence. He charged at the bear as it reared on its hind legs to face him. Vladimir leapt up and drove the point of the branch into the bear's chest with all his strength. Almost simultaneously, the bear struck him hard on his side, and he was flung into the air across the clearing. He hit the ground hard, pain shooting through his body. He rolled up, half expecting the bear to be charging him, but it was laying on the ground unmoving with the branch sticking out of it.

Whewww…

He turned his attention back to the hellsteed. It was now on its side, bleeding liquid fire. The wound looked deep—he had to do something quickly. He couldn't touch the fire, but he needed to stop it somehow; he looked around, and then it struck him. He took a couple of steps forward, slowly, his arms up to show he didn't mean it any harm. It looked back at him, probably wondering what he was doing. He gained more confidence with every step he took toward it. Perhaps he could actually get close enough to try to save it.

He reached down and started ripping out grass, scooping dirt from the ground below it until he had a handful, then threw it on the open wound. He took a deep breath, hoping it worked like real fire—without air, it would put out the flames, and in this case, maybe even stop the bleeding. He knew it was a long shot, but he did not know what else to do other than to watch the animal die in front of him.

The dirt sizzled as soon as it touched the bleeding fire. To his amazement, it appeared to be working, as the blood flow began to cease. He reached back down and started chucking dirt as fast as he could, without paying attention to where it landed—he got *huffed* at for getting some on its face. "Sorry," he said meekly. At least the hellsteed was no longer bleeding, which was a good sign, though the wound looked clumpy and awful.

"It's okay, you're going to be fine," he whispered, putting down the rest of the dirt. As he reached out with his hand to touch it, it sprang to its feet, trotting backwards, nodding its head up and down. What was it trying to tell him? He glanced up—and all the stars were gone from the sky, and just the moons remained. They were almost touching, nearly ready to merge into one. *Amazing.* That's likely what was causing the hellsteed to act up. He noticed that the colour of the moonlight was slowly changing, as were that of the two moons and the third moon, which moved behind the first two, turning from white to golden yellow. Even the moons were unnatural! Moons do not change colours…ever.

Tonight, had been more terrifyingly wonderful than he could have possibly imagined. He wondered what was next for him. The hellsteed was staring at the moons, as well, as transfixed at what was happening as he was.

It happened. The two moons finally joined to make one heart-shaped moon, with the third moon behind it glowing its glorious golden hue, as if to complete the picture. A sound from around him pulled his attention back to his surroundings; the hellsteed had lowered one of its legs and lowered its head. Was it bowing to the moons? He decided to bow, as well, just in case—he did not want to offend the hellsteed or the moons.

Moments after the Soul Moon Convergence, it began to rain. He held out his hands. The water was warm, and the raindrops he held in his hands were not clear but a rainbow of colours, like the stars had been. How was this possible?

He glanced back at the hellsteed's wound. It was gone, as were the clumps of burnt dirt washed from its side. *Amazing*. Their eyes locked, and it nodded its head at him, like it had approved his actions. He smiled, feeling a sort of confident he hadn't felt in a while. He began to laugh a tired laugh, replaying everything that had just happened in his mind. *It was a crazy night indeed*. He threw his arms out into the air and continued to laugh hysterically. When he was done, the hellsteed was looking at him like he was nuts. He decided he was going to try to approach the hellsteed when he started to feel a strange sensation: his body started to boil as he started to sweat profusely. He collapsed to his knees and pain overtook him. Every inch of him felt like it was going to burst into flames. He screamed in agony from whatever was causing him to be in pain. His skin started to turn magenta from the rain, and suddenly his hands caught fire, along with the rest of his body. He fell to the ground wriggling in pain. What was happening to him?

After what seemed like forever, the flames dissipated along with the pain, and he laid there breathless. *How could rain turn to fire? What had happened to him? And how could he have not been burnt?*

"Hello," a woman's voice uttered from behind him. He snapped his head around, but all he saw was the strangely shaped rock. Even the hellsteed seemed taken aback by the voice. They held each other's gaze, and he could tell the animal was just as confused as he was.

"Hellooooo!" the voice yelled again. He could detect an accent, though couldn't place it. Where was the voice coming from? He narrowed his eyes at the stone on the ground; was it possible it was coming from there? At this point, not even a talking rock could surprise him.

He ambled toward it and saw that some water had pooled on the top—the same rainbow water that he had cupped in his hands.

He was at a loss for what to do, until all at once, he was no longer worried. His eyes darted toward the hellsteed—its tail disappeared into the trees, and he knew he had lost his chance to capture it. He wiped his forehead, utterly devastated at the loss. Part of him wanted to go after it, but his feet refused to move away from the rock. He turned to face it. "Hello," he murmured into the rainbow water and waited, but nothing happened. He felt like slapping the water out of the rock from the frustration, but something told him to take a drink from it. He lowered his mouth to the surface and took a drink.

It was the sweetest water he had ever tasted. He closed his eyes, wanting to savour it. He cupped more in his hands and continued drinking, no longer caring that he was getting drenched from the rain. When he felt like he had enough, he opened his eyes and took one last look at the rainbow water.

And the face staring back at him was not his own.

***

The Marionette King stood there watching as the young Drăculeşti leapt and speared the bear. It was most impressed with the bravery and strength of the young man. The Drăculeşti had been transformed by the Soul Moon Convergence. It did not know where the Drăculeşti's soulmate was, but sensed it was not in this land. She was far away. It would be a great challenge for them to meet. Especially with what was to come.

The Drăculeşti's abilities were legendary in the Dark Woods. That is why they served them, though it had been quite some time. It had been many generations since a Drăculeşti had come requesting their service. He could barely remember the last time it had happened, but when it did, the land shook in battle against those monstrous creatures. Many had died fighting them in the Dark Woods. Even the Brotherhood had joined in the fight.

The world had risen to defeat the Specter and put him back into his cage. Now he was free once again to wreak havoc. Did the Sisterhood release him somehow? It could feel the energies of The Nexus gathering—something was going to happen very soon. It needed to gather the forces of the Dark Woods together. There was a war coming, and they needed to be ready when it hit.

It stepped back and mounted the small howler. Its howler was furless but had tough skin, with spikes running along its back.

A deafening crack shattered its thoughts as he rode. The howler stopped in its tracks. It climbed off its back and ran to the tallest tree and merged with it. Blackness overtook it but he could sense the tree's life essence and used it to glide to the very top of it. Once it got to its peak, The Marionette King emerged from the tree and looked off in the distance, where it saw lightening strike over the lake. A curtain had been opened! Things were far worse than It could have imagined. It was already happening. It looked up over the lightening, and Its eyes opened wide. How had It not sensed it before—the Nexus. Even though It only saw large, dark clouds, the power from it was unmistakable. This was the start of a terrible thing that was going to tear the land apart.

A scent caught Its attention. Death. It looked over at the village and caught glimpse of a small orange glow. The village was catching fire.

It thought of the young Drăculeşti. His great adventure was off to a horrific start. It was bad enough that he would have to travel far to meet his soulmate. Now this. Staring off into the distance, The Marionette King saw the Drăculeşti castle, along with its attackers. Not even the Drăculeşti could repel such an attack. What madness had the Nexus started? The Specter needed to be stopped once again. How much death and destruction before that happened?

Chapter 12

Sighişoara—Europea

'Night Patrol'

Night Patrolman Sentinel Olaf Busca looked up at the clear night sky, marvelling at the sight of the moons being so close together. Fingering one of his gold buttons, he thought of his wife at home, Rika. How she would run her fingers through his dark hair and comment on how his broad shoulders fit the Sentinel uniform so well. He secretly thought that's why she had married him. He missed her immensely along with their newborn baby, Henik. His firstborn son was named after his father, who died years ago in a mining accident.

Olaf had heard stories of women marrying other Sentinels for their status, but he did not dwell on it…much. There was a derogatory term for women that sought out Sentinels; they were called "mice". Being a Sentinel paid well and was a lifelong job—even in old age, Sentinels were still employed to train the next generation. Being married to a Sentinel meant security. Part of him couldn't entirely blame women who sought out Sentinel husbands. Who wouldn't want security? Especially with The Spiriduş being extremely aggressive. Besides trade shipments being hijacked, there were rumours that people were mysteriously disappearing in the northern villages. There was no direct proof that it was The Spiriduş, but what else would cause people to disappear? There were wild creatures that roamed the land, but an attack was rare indeed, especially with people in groups travelling together. There used to be safety in numbers. *Not anymore.* The land was becoming more dangerous every day, it seemed.

Olaf's uniform was complemented with a small hat, the same golden 'S' stitched on it as on his jacket buttons. His outfit was completed with black knee-high leather boots that he swore were a size too small and hurt with every step. He often saw Sentinels rub their feet and wondered if they were issued smaller boots on purpose, so the pain might keep them awake. Even his partner, Sentinel Night Patrolman Sven Goian, frequently complained about how sore his feet were after being out on patrol. Sven was slightly younger than he was and unmarried. Thinking back, Olaf couldn't remember if Sven had ever had a girlfriend since he had met him. The man never mentioned girls. Sven was not a bad-looking man, his wife had told him once; he had dirty blonde hair and blue eyes and was short and stout but was no push-over. They had known each other since they had gotten into a drunken brawl, funnily enough, against each other. In the end it had been a draw, and they wound up respecting each other. Over the years, they had grown to be close friends. They joined the Sentinels together and graduated near the top of their class. Luckily, they had been assigned the night patrol route together, as neither had mixed all that well with the other recruits. Olaf could not imagine doing this job with someone he did not like. They generally walked in silence the entire night, other than the odd comment here and there. They were both naturally quiet, so it worked out well for them. "I wish I was at home with Rika, looking up at this with her in my arms. I might get some love." He sighed longingly.

Sven looked at him and laughed. "What's wrong? You two have not been married that long. Or is it true that once you are married, the chains get clamped to your manhood and it's locked away other than for special occasions?"

This made Olaf chuckle. His friend was not entirely wrong. *"Pfft…*at least I know what it's like to be with a woman," he retorted. Feeling something press against his leg, he looked down at the rottweiler accompanying them on their patrol. With her black and brown coat, Lacey was almost invisible at nighttime. She had an official "S" too, shimmering gold and looped around a clear crystal, which hung from her black leather collar. Olaf found having her there made the nights seem less ominous, especially when the moons were hiding behind the clouds and it was darker than usual. She lived with Sven, who she had taken an instant liking to, more so than to him. Sven had adopted her as his pet, though she was not technically his. Having Lacey around helped boost morale, and of course, was an added sense of security. They were never without their weapons, but there were occurrences of patrolmen stepping out of the village perimeter, never to return.

"I think Lacey has a special friend. Sometimes when I wake up, she is not by my bed, and I don't see her come in until I am about ready for the day," Sven said lightheartedly, and adding, "How sad is it that the dog gets more action than its master?"

"You, my friend, need to get the courage to go and talk to a woman, perhaps at the dance next week," Olaf suggested. Next week was the annual Masquerade Dance. People from neighbouring villages and cities flocked to Sighişoara for the event.

He looked forward to the celebration, as he enjoyed meeting new people, even though he was generally a loner. This was the highlight of the year, as well, for the village. His wife dedicated hours and hours creating both their outfits. He hoped that Sven was going to go and meet someone. Perhaps wearing a mask might break him out of his shell.

"Sure," Sven said, "but then what happens when I take my mask off? I will have to talk to a woman face to face. They scare me."

It was like his friend had read his mind. Olaf smiled. "You are hopeless, but since you are a good friend, I will speak to Rika and see if she has a friend. You know, just so you can practice talking to a woman. Who knows, she may be cute." He winked, and Sven half grinned, half grimaced. Chuckling, they continued their route.

There were many more people out tonight than usual, Olaf observed. With the moons being so close together, the buzz around the village was that the legendary Soul Moon Convergence was going to happen tonight. He walked past groups of young girls gathering about, looking at the sky and giggling, excited wives with their semi-interested spouses, who just wanted to sleep after a long, hard day at work. It was going to be one of those nights.

They continued walking down the darkened streets, past various buildings and toward the docks, which were mainly empty. Most vessels were out in the lake due to an event that took place once every five years, the Emberfin's lustrum migration. The fish swam down from the top of the mountains to the lake before heading out into the ocean to grow, and years later they returned to lay their eggs and await their deaths, for when their eggs spawned, they were eaten by their offspring. Olaf had learned in school that the fry does this to gain the knowledge and experiences of their parents. He had asked if there was any proof, and his teacher had told him it was written in the books—therefore, it was true. The younger Emberfish were considered a delicacy, as their meat was still young and tender. Their fire red fins were used for medicinal purposes; many an ill person had recovered from eating the fins, as the sickness was burned out of them.

As they continued their patrol path, Olaf wondered if Rika was outside watching the moons. He smiled to himself, as he knew she probably was, and wished he were standing beside her. He looked over at Sven, who was also immersed in the moons, as they entered the outskirts of the massive dock area. Their patrol route took them through every part of the village, designed so that every part was patrolled three times throughout the night. There were also outer patrols to protect the village from attack, whether from a savage beast or The Spiriduş, so they could switch it up occasionally, which Olaf liked to do to keep things less predictable. *Predictability got you dead.* That's what one of his former instructors had told him during training. He knew the instructor was not wrong, and he had lived by those words. So far, they held true.

"Wait up, if you please!"

Olaf turned to find Mrs. Stoica Cristea, an older lady with kind green eyes, run up behind them carrying a small basket, from which a delicious aroma was escaping. Lacey began to wag her small stub.

"Mrs. Cristea, you should be resting, it's extremely late and chilly out. We wouldn't want you to catch a cold," Sven said to her, and Olaf had to agree. Mrs. Cristea was an avid supporter of the Sentinels since they had rescued her husband, Rienrich, from The Spiriduş years ago. This was not the first time she had stopped by during his patrols. While Olaf appreciated her treats, she was quite elderly and had recently fallen ill.

"How can one sleep on this night? Just look up to the night's sky. It's a rare and special night. I can sleep tomorrow," she said smiling at them both. He couldn't argue with her on that.

"What's in the basket?" Sven asked with an innocence that always made Olaf smile—that, and the fact that his partner was always thinking with his stomach.

"No fooling the Sentinels, is there?" She pulled back the covering on the basket to reveal two fresh baked sweet loaves, one for each of them. Sven reached into the basket and grabbed one for himself, splitting off a small piece for Lacey. Olaf took the other, nodding in thanks. His taste buds exploded with the sweetness of Mrs. Cristea's homemade roll. *All is right with the world.* Mrs. Cristea beamed at the blissful expressions on their faces.

A loud *bark* rang out. Olaf looked down, and Lacey was rubbing her head against Mrs. Cristea leg, looking up at her with eyes that said, "thank you", as only a rottweiler could do.

"What would the Sentinels do without your delicious sweets…" Olaf started to say, but then felt a warm raindrop hit his cheek, then another. He looked up at the falling rain, but there was not a cloud in the sky. How was this possible?

Of course, the Soul Moon Convergence. He watched, mesmerized, as the moons joined. As the three moons overlapped one another, their halves began to glow a bright magenta, and the heart-shaped Soul Moon was formed.

"Oh my…" Sven uttered.

"It's spectacular," Mrs. Cristea whispered excitedly. Stunned, all he could do was nod. It was more radiant than Olaf could have ever imagined—a heart-shaped moon the colour of magenta had taken shape, replacing the two other moons that once grazed one another. The Soul Moon lit up the entire sky with its radiant glow, casting over the entire village.

He looked around at all the crowds of villagers pointing up, huddled with their friends and families, some jumping up and down, some simply staring, mouths agape, lost for words like he was. Among them, gaggles of giggling girls, and he could just imagine what they were gossiping about.

"It was worth coming out on this night, boys," said Mrs. Cristea, pulling Olaf out of his trance. "Now if you excuse me, I feel the need to be with my husband."

"Of course, give him our best," Sven said. "Thank you for the rolls, they are truly appreciated." Olaf took another bite to finish off the roll before it was soaked.

What a night, he thought, shaking his head at the moons. Though, he did not care for the rain—he was soaked. He wished he were home with his wife. "Well, I suppose we should continue our patrol before we get in trouble," he said dully, looking over at his equally soaked partner.

"Yeah, you are right, unfortunately," his partner said. "I could just stare at the moons all night; they are truly spectacular."

"Agreed. However, we are on patrol, so let's continue our route. We can still enjoy it."

As they started walking, Lacey growled, then stopped abruptly, her eyes on the dock. She began barking in the direction of the lake. Olaf and Sven stopped in their tracks.

"Lacey, what are you barking at, girl?" Sven said. "There is nothing out there other than the fishing trawlers."

He was right. Scanning the water, Olaf saw no movement whatsoever. Was the Soul Moon Convergence causing Lacey to act up? Suddenly Lacey bolted, running toward the dock until she reached the end of one of the piers. He and Sven chased after her. She looked about ready to attack…whatever she was sensing. Olaf was beginning to feel on edge.

"What do you think, partner?" Sven asked him nervously. He scanned the lake—there were only boats out in the distance, and the waters were still. "Something has her spooked badly, is it possible there is a creature in the lake?"

"You mean something…unnatural?" Sven's voice shook.

Olaf remembered hearing stories of creatures attacking fishing boats, but there had been no attacks in years. The last attack was told by Iskra, the deranged village drunk. No one believed him, but no one could deny that he came back...changed. "I don't know, Sven." The night was quiet. Tonight, was supposed to be a night for *love*, not danger.

He waited a few more moments, but still, nothing changed. "Let's go, I don't know what's got her spooked, but there is nothing," Olaf said. "If there is, it's under the water and can't harm us, anyway. It's possible the Soul Moon Convergence is throwing her off."

"That's possible, we were standing there like statues, so who knows how it affects animals. Yeah, let's just go."

Olaf clapped his hands together for Lacey to follow, but she didn't move from the edge of the pier.

They exchanged glances. Sven shrugged and grabbed Lacey around the collar, who fought to release herself from Sven's grasp. "Lacey, that's enough!" Sven yelled.

And then something hovering over the lake caught Olaf's eye. He couldn't make out what it was, but it was…shimmering.

"Sven…did you see that in the air?" he asked Sven, who nodded. Olaf scanned the lake again, but nothing. Was it possible they both had the same hallucination? Maybe the rainwater was affecting their vision?

It happened again. Like an iridescent light dancing over the lake. *What the…*

An ear-splitting crack pierced the air. He covered his ears, which were ringing in pain. What was happening? Olaf looked back at the lake and couldn't believe what he saw: the very air was splitting apart in front of them. A massive red line appeared in the ether, growing larger and larger, until it pulled apart like a curtain. As it opened, it revealed what Olaf thought was an enormous golden, triangle-shaped structure, and then almost instantly, a greyish mist formed in front of it.

"What's happening?" Sven yelled. "What was that loud crack, and where is the mist coming from?"

Wait...the mist was growing, moving towards them. Lacey's barks brought him back to his senses. Something was very wrong. This is what she had been trying to warn them about.

"Olaf...what?" Sven started to ask, clearly at a loss for what to do.

"Let's go—we need to sound the Horn of Warning!" Olaf shouted. Sven released Lacey, who started running alongside him down the dock, and the three of them sprinted back to where they began their route. "Come on, Sven, faster!" His partner was struggling to keep up with him. "I'm here, I'm here," Sven replied, panting heavily at him.

As he darted past Mrs. Cristea, she pleaded anxiously, "What's happening?" He could tell she was scared. Her hand was pressed to her chest, and she wore a panicked expression. He paused for a moment and placed a hand on her shoulder. "Go back home to your husband, like you said you would. Don't worry about some silly mist," Olaf said, hoping she wouldn't detect the worry in his voice.

"Olaf, the mist is coming this way, faster than any I have witnessed before. There is something unnatural about it," Sven said. Olaf looked over the lake, and the mist was moving quickly. It looked like it was turning toward the beach area, which was where the nearest horn was. *Crap!*

Running down the street, Olaf noticed that villagers were no longer admiring the Soul Moon, but staring and pointing at the lightening above the lake and toward the mist. "Don't stand there, go back to your homes and don't come out until you're told!" he bellowed, but no one seemed to hear him—they were transfixed at the light show, unphased by the rain or the potential danger. *Crap!* How to get everyone to leave?

"Are those ships?" Someone called out, making Olaf stop. The mist was dissipating.

Ships. Two monstrous midnight blue ships.

Olaf didn't know how long he stood there, dumbstruck. A scream rang out, and a volley of fire arrows flew from the vessels. His worst fears were realized—it was an attack. The arrows arced high through the air. He watched in horror as they screamed downwards, hitting people that were too stunned to move. Moments later, people were dropping to the ground—*dead.* He heard a loud crash behind him.

Sven had two fire arrows in his chest. Olaf watched in disbelief as his best friend's body burned to ash. These were no ordinary fire arrows!

Olaf was stunned. He had been talking to Sven mere seconds ago. His mind was struggling to comprehend what was happening, immobilizing his body. He was finding it hard to breathe as he clutched his chest, forcing himself to breathe.

"*Olaf!*" Mrs. Cristea screamed in horror. *Crap!* "Go home!" he yelled, pushing her away from Sven. Her face was filled with sadness and fear, but he couldn't comfort her right now. "Go!" He pointed opposite the docks, and she nodded, wiping her face as she ran into the village.

He heard a squeal below him. There on the ground was a fire arrow pierced into Lacey's ribs. She lay there, dying in front of him. *Nooo!*

"Aghhhh!" More screams. People everywhere were kneeling over their dead friends and family members. His eyes began to tear, but an arrow shooting past his eyes shook him from his sorrow. He bolted toward the horn, an arrow missing him by inches— the only one he had seen so far that wasn't on fire. Whoever the enemy was, they had a variety of lethal arrows.

Running as fast as he could, he tried not to let the carnage and death around him slow him down. He needed to sound the alarm and get to Rika and his son. The thought of them made him run faster than he thought possible.

A sudden sharp, burning pain hit his right leg, and he stumbled, falling to the ground. A fire arrow had punctured his thigh. *Oh shit!* Without thinking, he pulled it out, screaming in agony.

Another arrow hit the ground in front of him. Then another. They were targeting him!

He forced himself up and began hobbling-running as quickly as he could toward the horn. Another arrow whistled by him. *Damnit.* The smell of smoke was widespread now. He looked back. Buildings were engulfed in flames, burning brightly, somehow, in the heavy rain. How? Was there something unnatural about the fire arrows, as well? It was a massacre!

He halted just as two gigantic green fireballs arced high in the air, one from each ship. His jaw dropped at the sight of them. He watched silently as they fell downwards towards the trade district. Several buildings were obliterated under the impact, colossal green flames lighting up the night's sky.

He had to warn the rest of the villagers. More arrows flew past him as he forced himself to continue toward the horn, which felt like it was miles away. He grabbed onto his right leg, using his arm to alleviate some of the pressure he was putting on it.

The horn was painstakingly becoming closer. *One step at a time, one step at a time. Your wife and child are counting on you, don't die.* He was about twenty feet away when he felt another sharp pain in his leg. Then another in his side.

He didn't stop. He couldn't. Too many lives depended on it, including his family. He forced himself to go on, even though he was moving much more slowly. He smelled his skin starting to burn. He pulled the arrow out of his leg and he screamed out in agony, his legs nearly giving out. "Ten feet!" he screamed out to no one and pulled the arrow out of his side. He glanced down and saw the tip was still on fire—he used the arrowhead to cauterize the wound, making him scream again as he fell to one knee.

The world was spinning. He could barely see. He stretched out his arm toward the horn, but he was too far away, still. An arrow appeared in front of him. It was protruding through his forearm. The head of the arrow was on fire and red with his blood. Olaf screamed out in horror at the sight, on the verge of passing out from the pain.

He knew he was not going to see Rika nor his son again, but he couldn't stop. He fell to his stomach and crawled along the dirt street, crying out every time he moved his arm, the arrow jabbed deep within. *Almost there, almost there,* he repeated to himself, until finally, he made it to the stand.

Taking his last breaths of life, he grasped the edge of the horn's wood base and managed to pull himself up to his knees. Another arrow pierced his thigh. He let out another agonizing yelp. Fueled by adrenaline and by sheer willpower, he was able to lift himself to his feet. He was already dead, but his actual death would have to wait. He had his duty to fulfill. With one final effort, he inhaled as deeply he could, knowing it was going to be the last deep breath of his shortened life. He grabbed onto the massive Capra Ibex twin horns, unclipping the large mouthpiece. He blew into the Horn of Warning with all his remaining strength.

A thunderous horn blast shattered his ears. He continued to blow until he had no more air left to expel. When he was finished, he staggered away from the horn, his ears still ringing in pain. Three more arrows pierced his body, and he finally collapsed onto the ground.

He had done his duty. His last thought was of his wife. He hoped Rika had heard the horn and had escaped with their son.

Chapter 13

Imperial Palace—Chang'an

'Moonlight Desires'

Princess Pingyang gazed out at the moons from her large open bedroom window as she leaned against the side of it. She was exhausted from the excitement of the day. Perhaps she should close her eyes for a minute and rested her head on her arms. Her mind started to wander toward Slithers. She was now a proud owner of a special snake, one who had moved to the very spot she had pictured in her mind. Receiving Slithers was the most wonderful surprise she had ever got, much better than the other "surprise" that she had received at dinnertime, when her father had informed her that Chao had requested her presence for an evening..

She had no real desire to go out with Chao, though after her talk with Xifeng, perhaps she had been too harsh on his treatment of the dragon. It did not matter what she thought, anyway—her father had agreed, so she had no choice. Her father had also informed her that a dozen Imperial Guards would be joining them. Chao would be taking her to the Imperial Playhouse to see the latest chorus dance. She did welcome the chance to get out of the Imperial Castle, but wished it was to go somewhere *she* wanted to go. Perhaps when she was married, that would change. Though deep down, part of her suspected nothing would change.

As her eyelids grew heavy, the familiar darkness of sleep washed over her.

Warm drops hit her face. Absently, she wiped them off, but more drops fell.

When she opened her eyes, the sun had gone, and what took its place was the most magnificent sight she had ever laid her eyes on: it was the Soul Moon Convergence. She stared in awe, utterly enraptured by the magenta heart-shaped moon.

"Slithers," she whispered, and felt the snake slide up to her neck, hissing lightly. "Isn't it wonderful?" She got a longer *hiss* in return. Her face wet from the rain, she wiped it again and drew back from the window. *How odd,* she thought, looking down at her hands. They were coloured from the rainwater. Cupping them together, she watched as the rainwater hit her palms—this was not normal rain. It was rainbow coloured. *Truly remarkable!* She jumped excitedly, as this was the day she was going to meet her soulmate.

"You need to go back to your spot, Slithers. I don't want you to catch a cold," she whispered and felt him return to the back of her neck. Moments later, she couldn't feel him anymore. She did not know if snakes could get a cold, but he was just a baby, so it was best to be safe than sorry. She could not imagine explaining to her father that her living snake tattoo had caught a cold and needed medicine..

She closed her windows so her room would not get completely soaked. She thought about Chao again. Was he her way out of her cage? Whoever it was, after tonight she would no longer be trapped and alone. She was going to meet her soulmate, and he was going to change her life for the better. What if it *was* Chao?

Either way, she will be looked upon with infinite admiration by every girl in the city. She smiled at the thought, as she opened the door to the inner courtyard, peeking around to make sure the guards didn't catch sight of her. She wasn't too sure what time it was but figured that most people would be asleep or staying inside to avoid the rain, which was surprisingly warm.

She took a step outside of her room, still half scared that a guard was going to appear out of thin air and take her to her father. Deciding to play it safe, she crouched down a little, closing the door as quietly as she could, and slowly walked up to the fountain, wondering where this mysterious rock would be. If she were a Soul Rock, where would she appear? Somewhere out in the open, easy to find. It was hourglass shaped, which would make it stand out.

She scurried to the dragon fountain, scanning the area, but did not see any rocks that had magically shown up. She wished she had paid more attention to the layout of the inner courtyard. Her father had ordered many changes over the years, and she had not paid much attention to them. As she made to investigate the shrubs, she heard male voices speaking. She quickly ducked back by the fountain, snuggling up to it as closely as she could.

"So, this is real...I wonder who will be pulled by the Soul Moon's Draw tonight?" one of the voices said in the darkness. She co knew they had to be Imperial Palace guards, as they would be the only ones out this late.

"Indeed. Whoever does will have a life unlike any other, one that I do not envy, I think. Yeah, don't get me wrong. It sounds cool and all, but only being with one woman just seems so...limiting." They laughed.

What was wrong with only being with one woman? How many women does a man need? She was confused by what she had heard, as it sounded perfect to her.

"Don't tell your wife that, she will kick your ass. And I don't want to have to break in a new partner," the first guard said, chuckling.

"Me? Look who is talking. Every time I see you in the market with your wife, it's obvious who is in charge, and it's not you. Most of the time, you look like you are going to pass out from exhaustion from all the parcels you are carrying," the second guard shot back.

"Hey, it's cheaper than getting one of the local kids to walk around and carry things for her. I don't know about you, but it's not like I make a load of money doing this, I got bills…and kids. You don't have kids yet, it's insane how much they cost. Wiau told me last week she thinks she is pregnant again," the first guard replied.

She felt bad for the guards. Maybe if she talked to her father, he would increase their pay. Yes! She decided she would talk to her father in the morning when she saw him.

"What? How many times have I told you, four kids is enough…more than enough!" the second guard said. "If you keep this up, you are going to wind up at The Brotherhood, gambling your limbs. Very few make it out whole."

The Brotherhood? She had heard that name in passing once, but she did not know anything about it other than people went there to gamble, and most lost pieces of their body. She could not imagine living without a finger or toe, let alone an entire limb. How desperate were people in the Empire to do such a thing?

She waited for a minute of silence, then she slowly started to move around the fountain again. Looking around first, she crept her way to the shrubs—nothing out of the ordinary. She frowned. She was getting drenched, and even though the water was warm, if she caught a cold, she would have to take the awful medicine called Ruklys. Every time she had been forced to take some, it felt like the vilest thing imaginable. She did not know what it was made of, but whoever invented it was truly distasteful. Every time she took it, she wondered if it worked or whether it was a secret punishment for getting sick.

She wiped the rainwater from her eyes. She needed to keep looking.

She nearly collapsed to the ground as a searing heat enveloped her entire body. She had never felt so hot before in her life. She fought back tears as the heat turned to unfathomable pain. What was happening? Was it the rain? She tried to wipe the rain off, but what was the point? She was drenched. And her hands…they felt like they were being cooked from inside. They grew hotter, and hotter still, until they burst into magenta flames. She was on fire!

She dropped to the ground and rolled around to put out the fire, but to no avail. She was on the verge of unconsciousness, but she refused to black out, instead fighting through the pain. At last, the dirt on the ground was enough put out the flames, and her body temperature lowered, as though it had not been on fire a moment ago.

What had just happened to her? She looked down at her frock—it was not burnt at all! Part of her wanted to run back into her bedroom, as she was more terrified than she had ever been. Her heart told her no; she needed to find the Soul Rock.

The Soul Rock could be anywhere. When she found it, she had no idea what she was expected to do. Did she simply have to just touch it? She hoped it would be that simple.

Her chest tightened, and she stopped in her tracks. What was happening to her? She took a deep breath and stood still for a couple of moments before continuing around the shrubs, staying low. Peering between the shrubs, she saw nothing. She quickly sprinted across the walkway to the other end of the shrubs, then paused for a minute to make sure no one had heard her. She continued to search in desperation. She came face-to-face with a tall hedge and slowly circled around it. She caught her breath.

Before her was the hourglass shaped rock, about five feet high and grey in color. She knew instantly that this was the Soul Rock. She would meet her soulmate!

Excitement washed over her, and moments later, so did terror. What happened if he was poor? She was a princess, so it did not matter to her. But what about her father? If he was poor, her father might forbid the marriage. Or could he? If they were soulmates, her father would have no choice but to accept him…she hoped. She stood there, not sure what to do. She touched her locks, dripping with rain, and felt panic inside of her. What if he thought she was ugly? Looking down at herself, her clothes were drenched, and she could only imagine how hideous she looked. Despite her fears, a voice inside of her screamed to move toward the Soul Rock.

As she moved toward it, footsteps sounded nearby. She crouched back down, but her insides were screaming for her to keep going. The footsteps grew closer, and she spotted a black-hooded figure emerge from the surrounding trees and stride toward the Soul Rock. Someone else had a soulmate, too? She waited as they inspected the stone. What was going on? The figure then took out a flask and dipped it into basin at the top of the rock. With every passing second, she felt the urge to rush to it.

They stopped and turned in her direction. Had she been seen? No, for they turned back around, now pouring something over the Soul Rock. Why?

Her stomach felt uneasy. But she was so close, she could not turn back. She had to do something, now. Feeling the ground around her feet, she felt a rock the size of a guard's fist and picked it up, just in case. It had only been a couple of minutes since it had started raining, but it seemed like an eternity. As the figure moved in her direction, she raised herself, clutching the rock in her hand.

Her body ached. She needed to get to the Soul Rock. When the figure was a mere few feet away, she charged forward, hitting them square in the face, knocking them down to the ground.

Whew. She did not stop to lift their hood and rushed to the Soul Rock.

Rainbow water had filled up in a small, concave crevasse, and all at once a weird smell hit her nose. A nausea overtook her, and her mind started spinning with doubts and uncertainty. What if he was ugly? She would be the ridicule of the Empire. What if he was poor? Or a criminal? She shook her head hard. *NO!* She needed to be positive. Her soulmate needed to be worthy!

She took a deep breath and investigated the water, waiting for a face to appear, the face of her soulmate. As she gazed downwards, calmness washed over her. Her heart was no longer pounding in her chest. She was able to breath once again. The smell was gone, and she began to feel normal again. What had just happened?

She grew more and more nervous, but mostly excited, as she waited. Her heart warmed at the thought of her future: what her new love might look like, how she was going to be the envy of the Empire. She would indeed have the grandest wedding in the history of the Empire, with all the girls eyeing her with jealousy. She smiled to herself. She was going to be the most beautiful bride that ever inhabited the city. She would have everything she ever wanted—including a man who worshipped her and did whatever she wanted him to do. It was obvious from the guards' conversation that a woman controlled the relationship, as they should. There was nothing more important than a woman's happiness.

She realized after some time that still, nothing had happened. Her excitement was starting to turn to annoyance. *Where was he? Did he not know there was someone waiting for him?* She was getting more and more soaked by the minute. How long would she have to wait? Why hadn't she asked Xifeng to explain what was supposed to happen? She found herself full of questions, with no answers.

"Ughhh," she grunted, though she kept her voice low. If she got caught, she would be in a lot of trouble. "Come on...please," she pleaded, hoping her soulmate heard it somehow.

And then something dawned on her. What if he was having the same issues as she was? If he were there, but was not able to see her, just as she couldn't see him? She wiped her eyes again and bent down, starting to feel the rock for something to press or move. Was there a secret compartment that needed to be opened? What if her soulmate had found out what he was supposed to do and was waiting for her somewhere she had not discovered yet? Her mind became more frantic at the thought, and she patted and felt down the Soul Rock, but the edges were smooth. She stood up, disheartened at her failure. Now what?

She put her fingers in the water and formed circles, half expecting something to happen. The water felt warm to the touch, which made her grin slightly. Looking up at the Soul Moon Convergence, she knew that the moon was meant for her and her soulmate. She closed her eyes and welcomed the warm rain, letting it soothe her mind. She no longer minded getting wet.

She opened them, taking a long, deep breath, and then another. Perhaps she was missing something, something simple. She scooped the water up with her hands and brought it to her lips.

It tasted unlike anything she had ever drunk before in her life. It was a cross between drinking liquid sugar and an imported bottle of Umeboshi Sour Plum. She wasn't revolted, nor was she satisfied with the off-putting taste. Deciding it was better to be safe than sorry, she took another sip. Instantaneously, her cheeks and belly began to feel warmer, almost to the point of becoming hot. *Not again,* she thought as she clutched her stomach and breathed in, praying the fresh air would cool her insides. What was happening to her? she drank too much too quickly…

No, her intuition told her she had done the right thing. She tossed her hair back and returned her gaze, peering downwards. Her eyes widened, for what she saw was not her own reflection.

She saw nothing.

What? Stunned, she merely stood there, then swatted the water and waited for it to settle. Still nothing. How was this possible? Now what?

Was it possible that she did not have a soulmate? No, she already had the wedding all planned in her mind.

She looked down again, but only the prism glinted back. "Hello," she said rather loudly, and instinctively clasped her mouth, afraid that one of the guards may have heard. She waited and listened.

"Hello…" she repeated, as loudly as she dared, getting more frustrated each time. Her mind started to race, filling up with even more doubts and fears. Suppose he was killed trying to get to the Soul Rock. Maybe he did not believe in the legend. Maybe he was a criminal and in prison somewhere. The thought of a soulmate that was a hardened criminal revolted her. Maybe he was old, and still trying to make it there. *Old,* she thought, *gross!* Yet she had faith that perhaps he would be a silver fox.

She looked up at the Soul Moon, realizing that she was standing at a rock that was not there earlier today, being rained on. Yet she was willing to stand in it, even though she hated rain. And Slithers—such a precious gift. Yes, she thought, anything was possible. She closed her eyes in an effort to clear her head, trying to push aside everything that had happened to her today.

She felt a tingle in her stomach, like butterflies fluttering. And she knew to open her eyes. This time, staring up at her, reflected in the mysterious water, was the face of a strange boy.

***

Xifeng crouched low on the Imperial Castle roof overlooking the inner courtyard. It was almost time. She knew by how close the moons were to one another. Soon it would be time for the Soul Moon Convergence.

She noticed something else in the night's sky—a massive dark cloud: The Nexus. She wondered how her sister was doing. Right now, Chione would be readying for the attack on the Europea village. It had been many years since this kind of excitement had filled her. Not since she had been with *him*. It had been a forbidden love, and one that she did not regret pursuing, even though she had paid a terrible price for it.

As she continued to gaze up at the clouds, she hoped one day that she would get her vengeance for what the Specter had done to her beloved. Though she had her doubts. The Specter was far too powerful. Last time, it had taken a concentrated effort to subdue him and put him in his cage. The Specter was too powerful to be contained forever, so when the Sisters were summoned, she knew that the cage had failed.

Cold rain hit her face. Just as she lifted her gaze, the moons converged. The two moons in the foreground merged, and before her eyes they transformed into one magenta, heart-shaped moon. It caught her breath. She had forgotten how beautiful the Soul Moon was. It had the power to link two souls destined to be together for an eternity. Few had experienced a love like that.

Her hands came together, and she waited for the rainwater to fill up. How she longed to taste its sweetness again…

She spat it out. It was bitter. Not as sweet as she had first tasted it lifetimes ago. Her link to the magic of the Soul Moon Convergence had been cut forever. The Specter had seen to that. She would have her vengeance on him one day. But until she could find a way, she was forced to do his bidding.

She heard movement and glanced down at the ground. The Princess looked to be searching for the Soul Rock. The Princess was very smart for her age—she had to give her that. It was amusing, watching her scurry around like a mouse sniffing for cheese. *You are almost there, Princess…*

But someone else was in the inner courtyard—the Black Witch. What was she doing here? She watched as the Black Witch went up to the Soul Rock and inspected it. How was this possible? Only those connected via the power of the Soul Moon Convergence should be able to see the rock. Unless…the Black Witch had unnatural abilities. In all her years, she had never encountered the Black Witch before. There was more to the woman that meets the eye. Xifeng watched as she scooped up some rain into a flask.

Should she intervene? The Princess was hiding, waiting to get to the Soul Rock. She knew that the Princess could not hold out much longer. Something needed to be done quickly. As she moved to the edge of the roof to jump down, the Black Witch poured something into the water basin at the top of the Soul Rock. Xifeng halted. *What the…?* This needed to be stopped. She placed a foot on the ledge, readying herself to leap, when the witch rounded on the Princess's hiding spot.

Come on, Princess…run, do something. To her amazement, the Princess bashed the Black Witch in the face, and the woman went down in a heap.

Yessssss, you go, Princess! She watched as the Princess made her way to the Soul Rock, and she knew that everything would turn out okay.

Now, she just needed to do something about the witch. Silently, she leapt off the roof and landed softly onto the grass, stealthily creeping toward the woman's unconscious body. As though a small child, Xifeng scooped her up in her arms, sprung back up to the rooftop, and scanned the grounds on the north side. Spotting the witch's hut beyond the large pond in the back of the Imperial Castle, she made one last leap before sprinting to the witch's home and laying her down beside the pond.

She placed her palm on the woman's forehead, whispering, "You went for a late-night walk, got tired, laid down and slept." As she made to leave, she remembered the flask of rainwater that the witch had gathered. She reached down in her robe pockets and snatched it.

Whatever dark magic the Black Witch intended to do with this rainwater, it could not be tolerated. Satisfied, she sauntered off, though one thing still troubled her.

What did the Black Witch put in the rainwater?

Chapter 14

Sfanta Ana Lake—Sighişoara

'Inferno'

General Pentu stood on the deck of Tutankhamen I, staring at the lightening in the distance over the vessels. The crew was struggling to comprehend what was happening, as the air was splitting apart before their eyes. It was like a curtain was pulling back, revealing a wondrous world.

Glancing over at the Tutankhamen II, he saw similar reactions from the crew. It was very impressive, though he wished they had been warned before everyone's ears shattered. Both vessels were approaching the curtain at the same pace. In mere moments, they were going to go through the curtain. He had no idea what to expect, so he steeled himself for whatever might be waiting. If the mission failed, he would be the sole person responsible, which meant his head would be removed from his body. Failure was not an option. However, if it happened, he would make sure he would die on the other side, as he had no desire to face Tutankhamen's wrath on this one.

He noticed that the water beyond the curtain was darker. Silhouettes of buildings lined the shore and docks in the distance. As the vessels entered the curtain, a light mist formed around both ships, just like Chione said. *Good.* They would be attacking from a position of concealment, which would protect them from any direct counterattack, if it were possible for the defenders to mount one. He felt the rain still hitting his skin, it was colder than before.

"Captain Khaemweset, keep course and speed for now. Light the pipes up, prepare all even numbered oarsmen to notch arrows, alternating either kind. Prepare the catapults for launch. When we hit shore, all archers go back to oars until we are free and sailing back to the curtain. Pass this along to the other vessel," he commanded.

They were approaching the shoreline quicker than he liked, but there was no immediate threat. He could see the village under the magenta moon in the night's sky, and people pointing in their direction. Could they see through the mist, as well? He noticed the mist was rapidly dissipating.

"Chione!" he bellowed, pointing to the village. "They can see us. What happened to the concealment you promised?"

Chione rushed over; her eyes wide in astonishment. "It's the rain. It's cutting through the concealment of the mist, like hot steel through flesh. I could never have anticipated the effects of the moons on this. Truly remarkable."

So, she was just as shocked as he was. There was no time to lose. "Captain Khaemweset, fire NOW!" he screamed. The element of surprise was gone now. He watched as fire arrows flew out from both vessels and saw more than one villager go down. He did not enjoy killing civilians. He looked past the bow—the docks were almost empty. *Where were the vessels?* He strode over on the port side, and there were none in sight.

"Captain Khaemweset!" he shouted again. "Instruct the helm to turn four degrees right. We are going to hit the beach to unload at the widest part. The harbour is nearly empty, signal the lookouts to look for those missing vessels. We do not want to be rammed in any possible counterattack." The docks were too small for ships of this size. He did not want to cause any unnecessary damage to them, as when the time the Pharaoh arrived in this land he would require them. The beach was the best bet. The Ushabti Warriors could push the vessels out more easily into the water with the wide-open space while the Mummies caused chaos. Pentu heard Captain Khaemweset yell out from the bridge horn, "Bridge crew, a full scan of outside the ship—find those missing vessels that should be tied up at the harbour! Signal the Tutankhamen II to do the same!" Pentu looked over and saw a member of the bridge crew signalling the flags to relay the message to the other vessel. At a glance, he could tell Captain Hekaib was barking out orders. He took a moment to scan his surroundings, to take it all in. A part of him still couldn't believe he was in a new land.

He was aware that Chione was eyeing him with an amused look on her face. "Enjoying our reactions?" he asked.

"General Pentu, there are multiple ships behind us, farther out on the lake!" Captain Khaemweset called out to him, pointing to the stern.

The Captain was right. He wiped his face to get a clearer view.

There were lights on the vessels and activity as well. What were they doing? The vessels were not moving, were they…*fishing at this hour?*

"What should we do about them, General?" Captain Khaemweset asked.

They were gliding to shore to unload the cargo, so he could not order either vessel to turn around. "Leave them for now. Delegate some archers to be ready if they are foolish enough to investigate, then light them up if that happens. Relay that to the Tutankhamen II, as well." It irked him that they were not tied up at the docks. He could have taken them out systematically. He did not want to leave any ships floating, but he was on a time limit.

"I believe you have a village to keep destroying, General. The curtain will not stay open indefinitely," Chione said flatly to him.

He noticed sweat dripping on her pale forehead. The effort was taking a toll on her.

Once they finished unloading their cargo, the vessels could then begin rowing through the curtain and back to Thebes, hopefully sinking some vessels along the way. He went over to the starboard side and looked down. The Medjays had made it through, as well. He gestured for them to cut themselves loose and head to shore. The Master Medjay acknowledged his command and within seconds headed toward the shore to carry out their respective missions. He silently wished them good hunting—they were going to need it. Their prey was unlike any they had ever tried to capture before. Even though he would not see them again for quite some time, he would know if they were successful: The High Sorcerer had imprinted a return spell into their vessel. Once their prey was captured, any one of the Medjays needed to utter the incantation, and their watercraft would return to the Tutankhamen I with their captured prize.

Turning to Captain Khaemweset, Pentu pointed at the archers. "Keep the destruction going! Set fire to everything, Captain, except to the docks themselves. Those need to be preserved for when our glorious Pharaoh liberates them from the abominations we unleashed upon them."

The Captain nodded and waved his arms, signalling his message be relayed to the Tutankhamen II. In the village, screams of suffering continued to ring out. The oarsmen were given two quivers to use, one for standard arrows and one for the fire arrows. They had been trained to use both very effectively. The oarsmen were exceptionally strong, so they could shoot at great distances.

General Pentu watched the oarsmen turned archers fire their arrows. His order of battle was to target Sentinels, then civilians until they were all neutralized. Building being destroyed would automatically come with wayward shot of fire arrows and the catapults. They were executing his plan to astounding effect. He strolled down the deck and saw the long wooden beams open along the side of the ship for the oarsmen to shoot accurately. The sides of the ship were designed to be taken down and raised quickly by a lever system. The men could not shoot from the holes where the oars dipped into the water; this had been another invention of his in his youth. With the side of the ship open, they could shoot at a greater range and with much more accuracy. It did leave each vessel vulnerable to ramming, but considering the only vessels out were fishing, he saw no immediate risk.

Even though both ships were primarily transport vessels, their decks had been respectively modified to hold improvised swivel catapults. They were crude but highly efficient. The catapult was a new weapon of war that was recently developed. There had been few trials, but this was to be the first practical battle test. He had to admit, the destruction they were able to cause during training was…*impressive*. He watched as the crew members loaded the catapult with its lethal cargo. It had a large scoop that would launch a mystically enhanced fireball into the village. He turned once more toward the village and hoped most people were not awake to experience such pain.

A dog barked loudly in the distance. He signalled to two oarsmen, pointing at the incessant noise. He watched as they nocked their bows and fired, and the barking stopped. He nodded at their respective marksmanship.

"Look!" Someone yelled. He turned, and another oarsman had spotted a lone Sentinel running toward something. He motioned for his oarsmen to aim and fire. After several shots, one hit him in the leg, and Pentu watched the man fall. He smiled, but it soon faltered when the Sentinel got up and kept running.

"KILL THAT MAN NOW!" Pentu shouted, pointing at the Sentinel running to what appeared to be a large horn. As they approached the shore, the distance between them grew. Arrow after arrow flew, missing their target.

"General Pentu—the catapults are ready to be fired!" said Captain Khaemweset to him.

"Keep firing at that man—*kill him!*" Pentu roared. He turned his attention toward the catapult, where the large, green ooze-covered bales of death sat in the catapult. This would be a sight to behold. "Fire!" Pentu screamed and watched a crewman light the sphere. Green fire erupted all around it. It was spectacular! He watched it arch high into the night sky, along with Tutankhamen II's green fiery inferno. It seemed to arch forever, until it finally started downwards. The crew fell silent, watching it soar. Pentu could swear the ground shook at their respective impacts: green fire lit up the village. Several buildings had been decimated upon the fireball's impacts.

Pentu turned his attention to the Sentinel. He saw the Sentinel had paused to view the destruction…*foolish!* He screamed, "Keep firing– kill that Sentinel now!" Arrows struck home again, making the Sentinel falter. *The man was done,* Pentu thought, relieved at the fact that no horn would be blown.

And then he watched in simultaneous amazement and horror as the Sentinel hoisted himself up to blow the horn. *Impossible!* The next volley of arrows was well shot. They were seconds away from their target when the Sentinel blew the horn. At last, the arrows pierced his body, and he stumbled backwards, his body now on the ground, surely dead— Pentu hoped.

Several horns sounded throughout the village. They were reverberating from all directions, yet he didn't see anyone alive to blow them. *What sorcery was this?* What other tricks did they have yet to be revealed? Were there any traps hidden, waiting to be inadvertently sprung once they hit the shore? *Only one way to find out,* he thought as he braced himself for the impending beaching.

Chione had come up beside him. Unsure what to say, he came up with something innocuous. "What do you think of the carnage so far?" he asked idly.

Chione smiled. "Our Pharaoh would be enormously proud if he was here now. Everything is going as I knew it would. Though, I am curious. What are you going to do now that the horn has been sounded?"

"It changes nothing. Look around. Do you see any threat?"

Chione gave a curt nod and left him. One thing did trouble him…*where were the Drăculeşti?*

Soon they would reach the shore, so they could unleash the next wave of death and destruction onto the village. Pentu looked at Captain Khaemweset. "Carry on with the plan, the horn blaring changes nothing." He pointed to the Ushabti Warriors, letting the Captain know it was time to awaken them. Motioning to the Tutankhamen II, he got the wave of acknowledgement from the Captain. He looked out past the bow. Shore was upon them. It was almost time for stage two.

He felt the ship shudder as it grounded itself to a halt on the beach. He was almost thrown forward but managed to maintain his balance. Looking back at the cargo, he saw the motionless statues of death. *Soon to be motionless no longer.*

The Ushabti Warriors had no spark in their eyes. No emotions coursed through their being. They were semi-intelligent, though more instinctive in their reasoning. Their primary mission was to destroy everything in their path. The magic that created these unnatural abominations also had safeguards for those commanding them. For this attack, Pentu's own blood was used in mystical rituals that bound the creatures to him though the *Ritual of Submission*. The Ushabti Warriors' limited intelligence and magical enhancements enabled them to recognize structures, as well as to see the difference between the dead and those still breathing. They did not need to eat or sleep once they had been activated, nor did they feel emotions or pain. Most importantly, they obeyed those who commanded them, namely him.

The Mummies, however, were not alive nor dead in the truest sense, as they were a re-animated corpse bound to the living world. This was done by the combination of mystical bandages that held them together, and the Soul Gems which held memories of their previous life. Pentu believe that Mummies lived a tortured, twisted existence. They had more intelligence than the Ushabti Warriors. It really depended if their brains were damaged before death, and if the re-animation process worked correctly. Sometimes it didn't, and what emerged was no more than a re-animated corpse with the intelligence of a child. Those were placed in the front lines to do as much damage as they could before their impending death. In this attack, they were to protect the Ushabti Warriors from being destroyed before completing their destructive missions, as well as protect the vessels until the Ushabti Warriors were unloaded, and their primary mission was underway. When they started to destroy something, they couldn't stop, even if they were being attacked. That made the Mummies essential for the Ushabti Warriors' survival.

Pentu pointed to two of the crewmen yelling, "Release!" He watched them hit the release levers so the ropes that were holding the ramps down sprang up. Both sets of ramps extended, from the ship down to the shore and crashed down on the sand. Walking over to one of the two ramps, he went partway down to make sure that it was stable so their cargo would not fall off. Pentu nodded to the Captain to give the signal to the other ship. There, the ramps were down, too. Captain Hekaib tested them successfully, then headed back to his ship to release his cargo of death. Pentu hoisted himself onto the bow so all eyes were on him, human and otherwise. *It is time!*

Pentu glanced to Captain Hekaib and saw he was in the designated spot, and nodded. Raising both his hands high, Pentu held them in place for a moment. Pausing briefly for effect, he shouted into the night, "Go forth for the glory of our Kingdom!"

The Ushabti Warriors started to lumber towards the ramp. They were taking the first steps in the Pharaoh's grand plan of vengeance.

He watched, as one by one, the Ushabti Warriors disembarked. An explosion of noise emanated from below deck—the Mummies rushed off the ships, with no enthusiasm or fanfare from the crew. He knew most of the crewmembers had never seen them in action, so they were merely watched in silence, and most certainly in awe. He watched the Mummies lumber on the beach, slowly creating a half-circle perimeter around the vessels.

Pentu watched the last of the Ushabti Warriors leave the ship, turn to face the ships, and waited, as they had been instructed. He raised his hands to the crew members to raise the ramps, then yelled to the Warriors, "Push!" They surrounded the bows of both vessels and started pushing, and he felt the ship slowly move back into the water. "Oars in water, hard rowing back, swing us around!" the Oars Captains yelled to the oarsmen. In moments, with the combined efforts they were off the beach; they needed to make their way back through the curtain before it closed, as Chione had warned. But he couldn't just yet—the Medjays had to complete their mission first, in less than an hour. He decided to get as close to the curtain as possible. "Captain Khaemweset. Once we are turned around, we drift back. The oarsmen will fire arrows only—no rowing. We need to give the Medjays as much time as possible to complete their mission. Signal the other vessel to do the same."

"Yes, General!" Captain Khaemweset shouted. "It will be done."

The Ushabti Warriors marched into the village. Pentu watched as they began to demolish some merchant shops. The Mummies had already started to fan out and enter the village, starting their own respective path of destruction while seeking out any threats there may be to the Ushabti Warriors. He had no doubt they were also killing the villagers that had woken up to the sounds of the horns. The entire village was screaming. *All those innocent people!* How many children were dying tonight? After this night, he knew in his heart he would not be worthy of being a grandparent.

"General Pentu, the fishing trawlers are heading towards the curtain or the shore, too far away to properly tell!" Captain Khaemweset called out. Pentu hurried to the stern and saw that they had indeed started moving.

"General," Chione said urgently, appearing at his side. "We need to get through the curtain more quickly than anticipated, or we will be trapped here for a while."

"Why? You said we would have about an hour. We timed this attack at the start of the Convergence as cover. What has changed?" He did not have time for a proper engagement if the defenders were able to mount a counterattack. His vessels were considerably larger, but if their escape route were cut off, things could take a turn for the worse. There were archers at the ready, lined up to let their arrows loose. But even if one of the fishing trawlers struck one of his transport vessels with their sides down, it could be disastrous.

"General, the strain was much greater than anticipated. It is taking all my strength to keep it open. A small one would not be any concern, but for two large vessels, it's taxing me...considerably."

Pentu saw the sides were still lowered and a thought came to him—an outlandish one, and those were usually the best. "Captain Khaemweset, increase to flank speed!" he roared. "On my command, hard-turn the rudder left, have the left oarsmen cease rowing, and take bows. As we swing around hard, launch fire volleys at the approaching vessels. The right oarsmen will do quick, hard rows to help spin the ship. The left oarsmen will continue to rotate between hard rowing and releasing fire arrows. We will not remain stationary to provide them with a target to be rammed. Relay orders to Captain Hekaib and get ready to commence on my command."

The Captain nodded. Pentu had never tried this before and hoped it would work. With the hard turns, his biggest worry was that either vessel may strain, cracking in half, then sink to the bottom. He may as well drown himself than go back and face the Pharaoh's rage.

With both ships carrying lighter loads, the oarsmen were able to pick up speed quite nicely. Standing at the aft, he saw the motley crew of fishing trawlers headed in their general direction. He didn't think fishermen were suicidal by nature, but the destruction of their village had undoubtedly replaced common sense with a lust for revenge.

As they picked up speed, the hairs on his neck stood. Something was wrong. Pentu glanced over at the fishing trawlers, and saw they were picking up speed. None of them, however, matched either size of the Tutankhamen transports. *Still...* "Captain Khaemweset, load the swivel catapult now! Short range volley!" He was on edge, though he didn't know why. His battle sense had never failed him before. The curtain was approaching. As much as he wanted to order the ships through it, he couldn't.

The gap was closing between the opposing ships, rapidly. He knew it was time. Raising his hand up so that flag commanders would see it, he commanded, "Captain Khaemweset. Hard turn *now!* Archers, prepare to lose your fire arrows!" He brought his arm down hard and fast. In harmony, both ships began their hard turn. Vessels this size were not designed to do maneuvers such as this. Cracking noises filled the air. *Shit!* Pentu ran to the side rails and looked down, expecting them to be cracked. To his relief, they were held together.

As fire arrows shot through the air, he watched them arc towards their targets. Several struck home and loud, boisterous cheers went up from the crew. *They were well trained indeed,* he thought, smiling to himself. He made a mental note to give the Oars Captains special military accolades for their hard work and dedication in training those beneath them. Even though they were the dredges of society, they were more than proving their worth tonight.

The uneasiness still hadn't left him. During the long, slow turns, the ships approaching were now scattering, no longer coming directly for his vessels. Some looked like they were turning around to flee from their unexpected maneuver. *Not suicidal after all.* He was extremely grateful for that. He watched another set of fire arrows soar. They were more spread out now, which would it make it harder to hit a single target. With the fishing trawlers grouped together, the chances of hitting one of them had greatly increased. Now, it was the opposite. Just as he was about to give the order to resume rowing straight ahead, he was interrupted by Captain Khaemweset, who screamed and pointed past him. "General Pentu, Look! *Look!*"

He turned around and saw blackness and smoke coming from the emblazoned village. Then something else emerged: a lone black ship, and it was barrelling toward them. This was what his "battle sense" had been warning him about.

Pentu yelled his command. "Stop turning—flank speed ahead! We are going to loop around the curtain. Once completed, let loose with fire arrows at the approaching vessel. Catapult at the ready!" Pentu didn't see any oars on the fishing trawler barrelling toward them, yet it seemed to be going much quicker than it should have been capable of. Another thought came to mind—he had never seen a black fishing trawler before. *Something is different about this one.* He ran to the port side and peered out to the shoreline. *No Medjays yet. Shit!* He noticed that they were going straight again, heading toward the curtain, but still unable to go through it. They took a wide turn around the curtain, heading back toward the direction of the black fishing trawler.

But it had disappeared.

***

Captain Henrick Mihaili watched the destruction of his village in utter disbelief. He had never been at a lost for words before, but this time there were none to describe what he was witnessing before him.

"Captain…what do we do?" his crew repeatedly asked. He had no answer. *How quickly the night had turned!* He wiped the cold rain from his face. Not even the rain seemed to be slowing down the fires that raged throughout the village. Henrick spied…*green fire?* There was no such thing as green fire, yet part of the village was being destroyed by it. *How? Why?* He had no way of justifying this to anyone, least of all himself. As they got closer, his attention caught hold of…lightening? *Had everything truly gone mad tonight?*

They had been out to the edge of the lake and were now homebound, but there were no more homes to get back to. Henrick saw the other fishing trawlers scatter. What was happening? Were those *fire arrows?* As the Skrulm approached, at the shore he saw the source of all the destruction—two large vessels. They were behemoth...and spinning around in the water. They dwarfed any vessel he had ever seen before, even from this distance. It didn't matter, they needed to be stopped. *But how?* There were no weapons on his vessels, other than the large whaling spears.

That was it! Henrick faced his crew and began to shout orders. "Hard port left! We need to get behind the lightening! All whaling spears need to be brought on deck. We need to wrap them in cloth and douse them in oil. We are going to light them and launch them at those behemoths responsible for the destruction of our village. Use your damn shirts if you need to wrap them with something. We need fire weapons. Put out all visible lights. We need to be as invisible as possible. Yeah it sucks...*deal with it,*" Henrick added, spitting in the direction of the destructive vessels. "Two can play at that game *you sons of...*"

The Skrulm needed more speed. Henrick commanded, "All sails up! We need full speed—blow on them if you must! *We need to get more speed.*" The Skrulm was more manoeuvrable, and undoubtedly quicker. He needed to use those to his advantage. Henrick didn't know if the attacking ships had seen his yet. Even if they had, the Skrulm had been painted black for a reason: to blend into the night. He had ordered for it to be painted black as soon as he had taken command of it. Everyone thought he had been a 'nutbar' for doing it, but he didn't care. To this day, nothing unnatural had ever attacked this ship. Henrick had gotten the last laugh.

The attacking vessels stopped spinning. The vessels were on course to steer around the lightening that shimmered above it. *What is causing this?*

They were picking up considerable speed, which pleased him greatly. His plan was to sneak up and attack from behind, then peel away and get his ship and crew to safety, if that was even possible. Even if they could sink one vessel, it would be a victory, albeit a small one in comparison to what he witnessed.

Henrick rounded on his crew. "Change course to come up behind the closest vessel! When we come up from the aft, throw the fire spears into their hull. Don't skimp on the damn oil on the spears either. I want to see one of those monstrosities sinking to the bottom of the lake within minutes." He watched as they raced behind one of the two behemoths. It wouldn't be long now. Did those vessels not have some sort of lookout, he wondered? Neither one was changing course. He was not complaining, though, as the element of surprise meant they might survive to fish another day. Henrick noticed one of the ships had stopped rowing—the massive oars were no longer moving. *Why?*

It began to glow green. *By Davy Jones*! He watched stunned as the massive, green fireball arched towards him, accompanied by dozens of fire arrows. "Hard right rudder…turn, turn, turn!" he shouted, but he knew it was already too late. He lifted his arms instinctively, but seconds later the green ball of death crashed into the Skrulm, directly into the bow, exploding on impact.

The last thought Henrick had before being consumed by the ivy flames was that he wouldn't be spending his special birthday night with Deidra, like she had promised.

Chapter 15

Drăculești Castle—Sighișoara

'Waking Nightmare'

Vasilisa Drăculești had been sleeping soundly when she suddenly awoke with an odd sensation inside of her. It wasn't quite panic but something else, something foreboding. In her sleepy state, she couldn't put her finger on it.

An image, reflected in her large stand-up mirror, caught her eye: a magenta heart surrounded by a golden glow. Pulling her silky, cream gown tightly around her, she went to the window. The Soul Moon Convergence took her breath away. The old legends were true. She held her hand out the window and felt the warm drops of rain. Even as she smiled, her apprehension intensified, which was puzzling. According to the legend, this was a night for love and romance, not for untold dangers. She looked lovingly over at Vlad, who was sleeping soundly, and wondered if the Soul Moon would have brought them together if they had been younger. She had no doubt it would have.

Perhaps the feeling was coming from another direction: the Spiriduș attacks. Vlad planned to take the fight into his own hands, taking their sons with him. She was more worried about her family's safety than ever before. She looked back at her sleeping husband. It had taken many years for him to find peace in slumber, as he'd led a hard and troubled life. At times, she felt there was a darkness inside of him that she would never see. She marvelled at his strength, not just his physical strength, but his strength of character, his will. When Vlad set his mind to something, he could accomplish anything he wanted. She loved him completely and considered herself the luckiest woman alive to be with him.

Looking back at the moon, she decided not to wake him. He and her older boys had to leave early in the morning. She hated the constant danger they were facing. She could not remember a time that there wasn't some threat from that bands of thieves and murderers; she would be glad once all of it was finally over.

She wondered if the boys were awake and looking out their own windows—would they even care about the moon? *Vladimir might, but not Radu or Micrea.* The older two would be too busy worrying; she doubted they were asleep. They had never been on a hunting party like this before. Their father had taught them how to hunt at an early age, and they had brought back kills as trophies before, but this was different. This time they would be hunting hardened killers, not animals grazing unknowingly in the fields. Killers fought back—*viciously.* Vlad had also taught his sons mortal combat, so she knew they could handle themselves one on one. She had seen them wrestle each other many times, she knew how rough it could get. She had berated them more than once for going too hard at each other, but their father had never discouraged it. Fighting was ingrained in them. Her two oldest boys were intense in ways that made her proud. They took their responsibilities and duties seriously, at least most of the time. They knew that when their father passed, they would have to step in and fill his shoes—and they understood just how big those shoes were.

Vladimir was different. He knew his duties, but he felt the call of something far removed from such duties, and he was conflicted because of it. It had been a constant source of friction between him and his father. She knew he would never grow out of it. Vlad scolded his son harshly about missing chores or being in places he was not allowed to be. She couldn't quite put her finger on it, but there was a wanderlust to Vladimir. It was as though he was being pulled in a direction that even he did not understand, and that he was lost trying to figure it out. Although she knew Vlad had been impressed with Vladimir's performance in the Trifecta, she knew he could not understand his youngest son; he had always believed that duty came first and everything else, second. Vladimir's duty seemed to be looking out at the ocean and wondering what was out there, past the horizon. She and Vlad had spent many hours talking about Vladimir, but they'd never come to an easy solution. No punishment was enough to deter her youngest son from his impromptu adventures. She hoped he grew out of it for his own sake, as the older he became, the more duties would be placed upon him, which meant Vladimir would find himself in more trouble.

She went back to the bed and kissed Vlad gently, which got a slight stir out of him. Smiling, she rested her head on the pillow and closed her eyes. She lay there for a while, thinking of her family. An overwhelming wave of sadness washed over her, a sense that everything she loved was about to be ripped away from her. She lay frozen in terror at the thought, barely able to breathe. Was she having a panic attack? She did not know how much time had passed as she lay there with the crushing sensations that were overwhelming her. Forcing herself to sit up, she took a deep breath to calm herself.

Outside, the Horns of Warning began to blare from the village. She knew instantly that the danger she feared had arrived. Whatever this threat was, she would not let the dread in her heart cripple her. She would face whatever it was and overcome it.

Vlad leapt out of bed beside her and ran to the large bay window she was staring out of moments ago. She joined his side. Fires raged through the shorefront, the largest illuminated a poisonous green. *Green fire? That must be unnatural.* She took her husband's arm and pointed out at the lake. "Are those...vessels?" She could not see all that clearly, but what else could it be?

Vlad nodded back; his expression grim. "Those are two large black vessels in the harbour, shooting fire arrows into the village. Fire arrows mean there are men on those vessels. Men that can be slaughtered." The humanity in his eyes was gone. All that was left was the darkness; something she had suspected in her husband. Yet now visible, she was not frightened. It would be their salvation.

The darkness that he had always kept hidden from her was now freed. To her surprise, she was not terrified, but hopeful. Whatever darkness lay inside of him might be her family's only hope of survival.

"Get dressed, get Vladimir, and head into the shelter in the bottom of the castle," Vlad commanded her. "That boy can sleep through anything. Make sure he has his armour and sword—they might be needed. Wait there until one of us returns."

Vasilisa nodded and rushed to leave, but she stopped at the door. She watched as he hastily got dressed and put on his black armoured breastplate. "And if you or the boys don't return?" she asked quietly, afraid of the answer.

"Then Vladimir oversees what's left. If nothing is left, you will make for the nearest village, tell them what has happened, rally them for a counterattack. Get the word passed out to all the villages and cities, our people will need to unite. In the meantime, you will need to remain there. A Drăculeşti presence will need to lead, *to inspire*, while the people and Sentinels group together and form a cohesive fighting force. You will send Vladimir north—to Varful Petrosul. It is far north, but he has no choice. Help will be there for him. This is important—he needs to go alone," Vlad stressed to her.

"What's there—why does Vladimir need to go there? What help is possibly there that the Sentinels can't provide?"

She had never seen Vlad look so adamant about something. "Drăculești help."

"I don't understand, my husband."

Vlad's face softened. "I know but trust me."

She nodded. "I do, with all that I am."

Vlad walked over to the doorway, grabbed her by the waist, and kissed her long and vigorously. A kiss to last a lifetime. "Whoever is doing this," he said through short breaths, "will not see dawn's early light, I promise you that." She put her forehead to his, nodding.

Micrea burst into the room, his armour on weapon sheathed. The sight made her proud. "Who could be attacking us?" Micrea asked, a look of determination on his face.

"We will find out before we rip their beating hearts out of their chests," Vlad said icily. She knew he could do it. She knew Vlad was the strongest fighter in the land. A great many would fall before him tonight, this she was sure of. She hoped her premonition was wrong. "Yes, Father," Micrea replied as Radu entered the room. He was dressed and was prepared for battle as well, though he looked nervous.

She gave Radu a tight hug. "I love you." He nodded, smiling weakly. She let go, then took two long strides toward Micrea, and pulled him against her. "I love you, too." He nodded, as well, but a smile never reached his lips.

Vladimir. She had to bring him to the hiding place at the bottom of the castle. If her husband and sons died, he would be the last of the Drăculești lineage. Though, she was still puzzled about the "Drăculești help" that her husband spoke of earlier.

She felt a strong hand on her shoulder. Turning around, she hugged her husband tightly, afraid she was never going to see him again. She beamed at her sons with pride; she knew they were nervous, but they had passed the Drăculești Rite of Manhood, whatever that was. Vlad had not specified when she pushed for an answer; he simply said he was proud of them when each of their respective times had come. Perhaps it was something that Vladimir needed to go through before he was ready to fight, as well.

"Your armour is on tight?" she asked her sons, and they both responded, "Yes, Mother."

Vlad went to the window and motioned for them to stand with him. They obliged. "You see the black vessels? Look at the fire arrows. Arrows are shot by men. That gives us the edge."

"Father," Radu said, pointing to an area of the town, "What are those creatures?" She leaned in closer, her eyes searching for what her son was gawking at. But everything was fire and smoke in the harbour. "What do they look like?"

"Those are something unnatural," her husband said darkly. "Unnatural things that need to be destroyed. Though I have never seen their kind before, I have no doubt they will fall before us this night. Do not go in and try to kill them as you would a normal creature. Even with your heightened abilities, fight and learn first, then kill when the opportunity presents itself. Rushing in against unnatural abilities could be fatal, even for us." The boys nodded in understanding.

She didn't know of these 'heightened abilities' her husband spoke of, but suspected that they were part of the reason the Drăculeşti rose to power over the land. When they survived the attack, she would have many questions, and this time, she would demand that all of them be answered. She watched as Vlad finished putting his armour on, going over to check his sons' before nodding in approval, which filled her with both pride and nervousness. Vlad pointed back out the window and said to her and the boys, "The village around the lake is in ruins, they will be making their way west now. That's where we will be for our counterattack and start to push them back. You two fight as a single unit. We are stronger united. Make sure both your backs are always covered. I will also be there, commanding the Sentinels as well, so stay together—I cannot stress that enough. Fight our fight and not theirs." Vlad gave each of them one last proud look before turning to his wife. He grasped her shoulders. "It's time."

She followed them out of the room and down the stairs. *Where was Vladimir? Was he still sleeping through all of this?* Ever since the Trifecta, it had been harder for her to wake him in the mornings. Something else besides Lash's death was deeply troubling him. She was his mother; she knew these things like a sixth sense.

Sentinel Commander Alexandar Yonescu was waiting at the bottom of the stairs. He gave a curt bow, then got to the matter at hand. "Two foreign black vessels entered our harbour area almost at the same time as the Soul Moon Convergence. They have released fire arrows and have burned the surrounding buildings. They are also killing everyone within their archery range. From what we can gather, the Sentinels on patrol in the immediate vicinity have been killed, as well. The harbour area itself has been strangely untouched."

Vasilisa could tell the Sentinel Commander was suffering on the inside. The Sentinels were his family. "The creatures have disembarked—one species of which is enormous and clay-like, with brute strength that can easily push down walls. The others are wrapped in what appears to be medical dressings, and who are proving to be extremely capable fighters; they are as good as any Sentinel I have seen. They are making short work of our village and defenders. I do not think this is a battle we can win, Vlad." Vasilisa was shocked to hear that the Sentinels sounded defeated even before the battle had truly started. Her worst fears were coming true.

"Take all the Sentinels you have left and set up a defensive position on the East side of the village. We will attack from the West and drive them to your position to finish them off. Whatever these unnatural abominations are, they will not live through this night. That I promise each of you." Vlad vowed to each of them.

Vlad led them all outside to the castle doors, and she followed, bearing witness to the horror that was continuing to unfold in her village. Vlad looked at Sentinel Commander, who said, "Good hunting." She echoed the statement. They would all need that tonight.

"Good hunting," Sentinel Commander Alexandar Yonescu replied, then nodded respectfully to her. She watched him as he went off with the other Sentinels to plan their counterattack. With there still being some Sentinels remaining, it increased their chances in destroying the attacking forces.

Vlad looked at his boys. "Regardless of what happens tonight, I am very proud of both of you and love you both." He hugged them both tightly, then met her eyes. No words were spoken. None were needed.

Vlad turned to face his village. "Let history never forget the name Drăculeşti!" he roared, and she watched her family race downwards toward the West side of the village to set up their counterattack.

Just as she started to turn back toward the castle, she stopped in her tracks. Her husband and sons were leaping high in the air, jumping from rooftop to rooftop. *Astonishing.* Now she had proof that the stories she had heard in whispers about the Drăculeşti were true! She had known Vlad had kept secrets from her, which had infuriated her on many an occasion. This, and with what Vlad had said upstairs, she had more hope now than ever that they were going to survive.

She had been so focused on her husband and sons that she hadn't even gotten properly dressed. She pulled the lever, which lowered the beam down to secure the door. Still, not a peep from Vladimir. How was it possible he slept through the Horns of Warning?

She pounded up the stairs to her bedroom. There was no fighting around the castle yet, so she was safe, but she still needed to be quick. She stripped off her gown and slipped on the black trousers she normally wore around the castle for gardening, with its matching shirt. She caught a glimpse of herself in the mirror: a brave and terrified woman stared back at her. She would not fail.

Out the window, orange sparks caught her eye, and her eyes opened wide. A building collapsed, and she recognized it as the bakery that Kazia's father owned. She thought of Vladimir. Their *viskta*'s lodging was right next to the bakery. She hoped the family made it out in time. She was transfixed by the scene below, but noticed something in the distance— creatures moving faster than humanly possible, rushing up the streets towards the castle.

Whatever attacked the village was now quickly rushing to her doorsteps. She needed to be ready. Pulling herself away from the window, she put her hair up in a quick bun, then reached inside the cabinet and pulled out a sheathed sword. It was a wedding present from Vlad, who joked that sometimes their marriage might get a little dull, but like a sword to a whetstone, it could be sharpened once more. She had thought him crazy, but over the years she spent some time with it, wearing it ceremoniously once or twice, and she knew he was proud of her when she had. It was slender and thin, but razor sharp. He had shown her how to properly sharpen it and was stern about ensuring the blade never dulled. It was not as heavy as it looked, as she could wield it with either one or two hands, which was due to the type of metal it was crafted with—it contained trace amounts of adamantizine. She did now know what that meant, though she hoped now it would give her some edge. He had asked her to name the sword, as all great swords had a name, but she had never been able to come up with one. However, now as she grasped the golden handle, encrusted with jewels, at long last a name did come to mind: "Mother's Malice". Malice is all she had toward those who threatened to kill her family. She tied it around her waist and gave herself one last quick look and nodded at her reflection. Now, it was time to get Vladimir ready. She bounded down the stairs to Vladimir's room. How quickly had her life just changed forever.

As she approached Vladimir's door, she noticed it was closed. Odd—he always slept with the door slightly ajar. All the boys did. She had gotten them used to it since they were small boys, this way, she could check on them without disturbing them. He probably closed it because he was upset at what his father had told him during dinner.

Why were they under attack? This made no sense to her. An enemy emerges the same night as the Soul Moon Convergence. What were the odds of that? They had to be connected somehow. She opened the door to his room and called out, "Vladimir!" but to her horror the bed was empty.

***

Radu watched his father leap easily into the air, Micrea following him. He hesitated at first but followed suit. They were leaping to their deaths, he felt it. No matter how much bravado his father had, something about tonight was horribly wrong.

As he leapt from a rooftop, he glanced up at the moon. The magenta, heart-shaped Soul Moon Convergence was breathtaking. It didn't even bother him that he was getting drenched in rain. It was warm, almost soothing to him. As it rolled off his body, it was taking his fears with him. He felt peaceful, even though he was heading into battle against unnatural foes.

As he continued to jump from rooftop to rooftop, he surveyed the destruction. It was...*unreal*. It was like he was in surreal surroundings, and the village he was in was not his own. He had only felt like this once before: when he went through the Ritual of Drăculeşti to become a true Drăculeşti.

When he tasted the warm, sweet human blood for the first time, it had consumed and repulsed him simultaneously. The day his father had taken him out hunting, he had no idea that they would be hunting people. It was the rite of passage for a Drăculeşti. He had been excited at first when his father took him out. It was rare that they did anything together without one of his other brothers involved, so he had cherished it. They had skirted along the eastern trade route that led to the village Bârlad. The Spiriduş had been hitting trade wagons and disrupting deliveries to the remote village. After three days of travelling, they had come across a small Spiriduş camp.

There were six Spiriduş members enjoying the fruits of their looting, and they were not aware they were being watched. His father told him to attack hard and quick, but not to kill everyone. When they were within a few feet of the camp, they struck. He had never felt more alive as he rushed into the camp, seeing their shocked faces. His fists had been armoured with metal, so they knocked people out cold and fast. Within minutes, they had subdued The Spiriduş. They had recognized his father and pleaded for their lives, stating they had been forced to carry out these actions. His father never believed them, nor did he. Their lies sang out to him like a song. All lies did. He was proud that they were going to bring these criminals to justice. Only they didn't. He watched as his father grabbed one by the hair and forced their head back, then bit into The Spiriduş neck and started drinking their blood. Radu had been shocked and horrified at the sight. He rushed over and tried to stop his father, but when he got close, he could smell the blood oozing down the side of the man's neck.

An overwhelming urge took hold of his senses, something *primordial*. "This was the secret to the power of the Drăculeşti's reign," his father had told him. He remembered looking at the terrified faces of the captured Spiriduş, who started pleading for their lives. Their pleas fell on deaf ears. He grabbed one of the larger Spiriduş members, and he stopped viewing the man as a man. The man had become a large steak that he wanted to bite into and eat. When he brought the man's neck to his mouth, he could physically feel his teeth change shape. It was extremely painful, yet it pleasured him. He was about to "eat" for the first time in his life. As his teeth pierced the soft flesh of the man, Radu felt his full body shake uncontrollably as he gave into the blood's intoxicating sweetness. *Paradise*. He didn't know how long he drank, but by the time he was done, he felt more satisfied then he had ever felt before. It wasn't enough. He wanted more.

He wanted the man itself.

He wanted to taste the flesh of his supper, so he took a bite out of the man's neck and ate it. It was more succulent then any steak he had tasted before. Before he knew it, he was chomping down on the man's throat, completely devouring it. He had lost track of all his surroundings. He had been totally consumed with eating his steak. When he was full, he had screamed at the top of lungs in pure pleasure. In that moment in time, all was right in his world. The power that coursed through his veins was intoxicating. His senses were heighted beyond anything he could have imagined. He could smell everything around him, including the scent of a brown bear. Radu rushed in the direction of the creature. Running faster than humanly possible, his steps becoming short leaps as he bounded towards it. When he landed near it, they locked eyes. The bear then reared up on his hind legs and roared at him. Radu roared back and leapt at the creature, punching it once in range. The bear went down, and he saw the look of death in its eyes. He had killed it in one punch! Radu screamed in triumph. He saw its blood trickle down its jaw, and as he got closer, the smell repulsed him. It didn't have the sweet smell of human blood.

"Once you have sirloin, going back to flank just isn't that appealing anymore," his father had told him. He was right. They spent many hours afterwards talking about the Drăculeşti way of life and history. It was rare, but he was known as an "eater": one who enjoyed the taste of both blood and flesh. His father warned him that he would need to be careful not to leave bodies lying around that looked like they had been chomped on. Also, the act of drinking the blood activated their abilities, and once activated they would always remain. Should a dire situation arise, and a boost was needed, drinking human blood would create a surge of strength and intensify the senses. It was not necessary to continue drinking blood, but he must be mindful of his choices if he does. The thought of taking that first bite into someone else's neck excited him greatly. His father had told him he was proud of him, that he didn't hesitate or reject his heritage. His father also told him these abilities were unnatural, and anything unnatural had consequences.

But there were unforeseen consequences for his actions: torment. On the way back home, he found himself waking up in cold sweats. He had eaten another person and enjoyed it. It felt so very right.

"Radu, snap out of it!" his father yelled at him, and he blinked. Radu was standing on a rooftop overlooking the annihilation of his village.

"You okay, Brother?" Micrea asked him worriedly. Radu nodded and looked around. Devastation was all that there was.

"There," his father pointed out where six bandaged creatures were charging up the street toward them. "Attack as one. Watch each other's backs." Radu nodded, and watched his father and brother leap down and run toward the attackers. He made to follow, but something caught his eye off in the distance: three men talking to someone outside of the Brotherhood's establishment. *Who would try to gamble when an entire village was being decimated? Maybe they were from out of town and seeking shelter?*

A secondary thought came to his mind as he leapt off the building, the air whipping past him. He wondered whether there was flesh under those wrappings. What would it taste like?

Interlude 0.4

Sighişoara - Europea

Master Medjay Ahmose raised his hand, signalling for his team to stop. It was hard to see through the thick smoke they surrounded themselves with as cover. They had stealthily made their way from the shore, skirting around the various bushes and buildings as the raging inferno engulfed the village. Staying out of sight as much as they could was challenging with survivors fleeing in all directions. He had not been told which building was the Brotherhood's, though he doubted he would have any trouble finding it. It would be the only one left untouched. He doubted that the abominations that they unleashed tonight would get past the Brotherhood. There was an aura that surrounded the Brotherhood—*invincibility*.

As they slipped between tall bushes, Ahmose took a moment to survey the damage. It was beyond anything that he could have imagined. "Aggghhhh!" Ahmose heard nearby, and an elderly man emerged from a sea of smoke, hobbling in their general direction. *Crap!* He had no desire to kill a defenseless old man.

Suddenly, a Mummy leaped down from the top of a burning building, taking the man's head off in one bloody slice with its sword. "Master Medjay, we need to go," urged Jarha, and he knew the man was right. They still had to drop off the letter and capture a Drăculeşti.

Ahmose brought up his hand, motioning his squad to move forward. He scanned the buildings, trying to spot one that was undamaged. The wind caught the smoke and cleared his sightline, and he saw it. It had no markings, signifying it was one of their establishments, but the tall, black-robed figure standing in front of it with its arms crossed gave it away. "There," Ahmose said, pointing. He glanced around one last time for any survivors. Not seeing any, he sprinted toward the Brother just as a lone Ushabti warrior came into view. Ahmose halted and watched it swing its massive battering fist at the Brother, who calmly caught the large battering ram hand coming toward him with his own hand. Twisting the arm clean off effortlessly, the Brother then proceeded to smash it into the Ushabti warrior's chest, instantly shattering it into a thousand pieces. "*Damnnnn,*" Rewer said behind him. He had heard the Brotherhood had unnatural abilities, but this had just blown his mind.

"Come on, the sooner we start our actual mission, the better," Ahmose stated, feeling the weight of the letter inside his vest getting heavier. He took one last look around, confident that no one would see them, and closed the distance between him and the building. It was a black wooden structure with two large doors, with a single window that stretched all the way from one end to the other.

As Ahmose approached the Brother, he became increasingly uneasy. There was something about being in their presence that always got under his skin. He studied the mask—it was identical to the one back in Thebes, with its strange eyes and beak-like nose.

"I am Master Medjay…" Ahmose started saying but stopped cold when the Brother held out his black leathered palm. *He was expecting us! How?* Reaching inside his vest, Ahmose took out the sealed parchment and handed it to the Brother, who accepted it. The man placed it inside the right inside pocket of his black jacket, then reached into his left one and pulled out another. He handed it to him.

What the…? He flipped it over; its seal was three small blue circles. A memory flashed in his mind—the parchment he had just handed him had a different seal. Each symbol represented a different place! "I…we have to stay, we…" Ahmose started to protest, but stopped when the Brother raised its hand. *Now what? Can't these people talk behind their bizarre plague mask? How was it that the Brotherhood dressed identical here as they did back home?*

The Brother reached up and pried open its golden, metallic beak, offering a view inside of it. Ahmose recoiled in shock—the Brother's mouth was sewn shut. *How do they…?* Reaching inside the mask, the Brother removed an object, holding it out to him. Ahmose had no desire to touch it. The Brother continued holding his hand out to him to take the object. Reluctantly, he did. It was wrapped in black, dried leaves. *What a strange offering.* Ahmose had heard whispers that the Brotherhood handed out special "presents" when a task was completed for them. Whatever it was, he wanted no part of it. "Thank you, but this is too generous…" he stammered, hoping not to offend. The Brother simply turned, walked back into his establishment, and closed the door behind him.

Ahmose stood there holding his present when a pungent smell mixed with a tinge of sickening sweetness caught his attention. He knew that smell. It was the smell of death. Steeling himself for what might be under the leaves, he cracked them open: a single preserved finger, with a ring on it. Ahmose stared at the gold ring in disbelief. It was pure gold. A fisherman casting a net while sitting in a vessel with the words CLEMENT-IV. He could feel power emanating from the ring. It scared him. *Why, God Shai, why?* A cold gust rammed into his body, freezing him to his core.

"Master Ahmose, what is it?" Rewer asked behind him. Ahmose held up the parchment.

"Another?" Jarha asked.

"Yes." Silence hung between them.

"Now what?" Jarha said after some time. Ahmose looked around him, the streets deserted, buildings in flames. "We do our mission, and we capture our prize. The Drăculești, if they are as fierce as we are told, will be engaging our forces directly. Be mindful of their Sentinel forces. We do not engage them in any way, unless to defend ourselves. We operate as a family now. Look around, Medjays, all we have is each other." Ahmose took their silence as agreement.

Ahmose figured that the fighting would be strongest near the centre of the village, which had access points to any direction. That's where he would set up a defence. First, there was something he needed to do to confirm his theory. There was no place safer than where they were now. "Medjays, climb," Ahmose ordered as he jumped and climbed the side of the Brotherhood's building. Their equipment had been mystically enhanced by the Royal Apothecary. Ahmose had chosen not to question Sorcerer Haphestus, who presented him his equipment for this mission. All of them were able to easily scale the wall. When they reached the top, he glanced around the area around the building. They were alone.

Ahmose sat down on the roof and took off his headdress. Closing his eyes, he took long, deep breathes. He started to clear his mind until it was empty of thought, trying to tune into his surroundings. He was now in harmony with his environment. He opened his third eye, the secret to the Medjay's successes as scouts. The nearest Ushabti Warrior entered his mind, and he was able to see what the Warrior was seeing. But no Drăculești.

Ahmose left the Warrior's mind, searching for the next one to penetrate. A scene caught his attention. Two men leaping from building to building. He smiled. His target had been sighted. It was time to go capture their prize.

Chapter 16

Sentinel Defensive Position—Sighişoara

'Sentinel's Fall'

Sentinel Commander Alexandar Yonescu mounted his white horse, spurring it as he raced off with two Sentinels in tow, heading toward the east side of the village. He looked to the lake as he wiped the cold rain off his face with the back of his palm. The black vessels were still in the lake, but were now moving backwards, away from the shore. He knew the vessels held the secret behind the village's destruction. He wished he could get aboard one and capture it to get answers to questions that desperately needed answering. He wasn't sure if he was going to survive this night, but if he did, he would find answers.

What purpose did the lightening serve? All he knew was that it was unnatural and that it was tied to the vessels somehow. The opening above the lake was massive underneath the lightening above it. He had not seen either of the creatures. Though, he suspected it was only a matter of time before he faced the attackers in battle. He hoped he was up to whatever challenges they brought with them.

He noticed the cold rain was not helping to slow the spread of the fire. The sheer amount of destruction was overwhelming. He looked around, but his view was skewed by the smoke, which was blocking out the light of the moons. People did live near the beach, and he suspected most of them did not make it out. The swiftness of the attack had left little chance of escape, and the Horns of Warning had been too late to save those caught in the initial volleys of arrows. The Sentinels needed to be ready—if that was even possible.

He arrived at the hastily made defensive perimeter, which consisted of wagons toppled on their side, along with a motley of crates stacked one above the other. The Sentinels were blocking off a major intersection of the village. The Horns of Warning were still blaring away. He knew the noise would make it hard to hear their enemies approaching. The horns had served their purpose. If not for them, many more lives would have been lost.

Some of the Sentinels were armed with the newly created Arquebus. As the weapons were new, most of the Sentinels gathered only had their traditional crossbows. All bore swords as well. He knew the Sentinels were hoping their ranged weapons would do most of the damage before the close quarters battle, which was inevitable. Mortal combat was something they had all been trained in, and he knew the men had been trained well. Those creatures approaching were not men, and he did not know if it was possible to kill them. He hoped they could…though hoping did not make it so.

He commanded several of the Sentinels to keep watch on the rooftops and call out the direction the creatures were coming from. With the smoke and noise coupled with the darkness, he feared that they would not get much of a warning. He didn't have a lot of troops at his command. Most of the patrols were outside of the village and surrounding area. He hoped they were helping people to safety as they fled. He suspected he was severely outnumbered, and most of the remaining Sentinels in the village were dead. He continued to walk around the defensive position like a caged animal, hoping they would be successful when the time came.

"Sentinel Commander Alexandar." It was Sentinel Captain Ivisk Norkdrem, hastily approaching. The color from the man's face had been drained from fear. He knew the man was terrified. Truth be told, so was he, but he did his best to hide it. "What do we do? This enemy…it's unlike anything we have faced. We need to escape now and regroup, or we will all die." Ivisk pleaded. The man's logic was not wrong, but it was not right either.

"Yes, escape would be the smart thing to do, but we are Sentinels; we do not run or hide, it is our duty to fight and die, if necessary. Tonight will be a glorious night to die, under the majestic Soul Moon Convergence. If it is our time, it shall be one worthy of song and drink."

He could tell Ivisk was not reassured, but he still nodded in agreement.

Villagers were being led through the barricade, weeping, and trying to carry whatever they could in their escape. Alexandar knew everyone was heading to Hişoaraga, and he hoped the Spiriduş would not do anything to stop them. Over the years, the group had become more active. He suspected they had ties to the Sentinels, but he never found any proof of collusion.

Sentinel Lieutenant Ionache Reickman rushed up to him, out of breath. "Sir, most of the villagers are gone now—there are undoubtedly some stranglers in the village, thinking they will be safe hiding in their homes, but I do not think they will last long," he reported grimly.

"How many Sentinels do we have left? I suspect most were lost in the opening attack," Alexandar asked. Lieutenant Reickman had been stationed near the harbour area— he was surprised the man was still alive.

"We have about a half dozen scattered throughout the village at last count. The bulk of the remaining Sentinels from the outer patrols have left with the civilians. They're headed toward Hişoaraga," Reickman replied. They did not have anywhere near enough to stop the attack, but Alexandar already knew that. Even two dozen more Sentinels was not going to make much difference. But if they could slow down the attackers, it would give the villagers more lead time to escape. That was worth dying for.

There was a loud *crack*. He and his fellow Sentinels turned around to witness a building collapse. Moments later, strange, dressing-wrapped creatures were climbing over it, closing in on their position. Alexandar went to the edge of the barricade and tried to focus in on what the creatures might be. They had no visible armour, nor clothes—they were just wrapped in…medical dressings?

"What the…?" Reickman started to utter. Alexander couldn't believe what was coming towards them. He had expected something unnatural, but nothing like this—these were truly bizarre. They did not look strong enough to push down buildings, though. *Where were the other creatures that were accompanying them?* He took out his sword and looked at it expectantly. It had never failed him before. He hoped it would not fail him tonight.

Could those creatures even be killed? "Make every shot count. If you don't think you have time to reload, then don't. You all have swords, and if necessary, use your Arquebus or crossbows as clubs. Your lives are on the line, see fit to defend them *as you will*—just remember your training and watch out for each other. We're all we have. We will survive or die as one. I have a wife, I want to go home to her, so dying is not an option— regardless of how unnatural the enemy is. Speak with your weapons, and they will know the *fatal fury* of the Sentinels. Should we win this night, think of the glory…Take it. It's already yours! Let history never forget the name Sentinel!" Alexandar screamed out, raising his sword high into the air. Cheers erupted all around him.

Lieutenant Reickman walked up to him and offered him a flask. "Blood Cider, for added courage." He winked. Alexandar nodded and brought it to his lips, taking a massive gulp. Normally, it was a little too sweet for his liking, but tonight it tasted different. It tasted like…*victory.*

He handed the flask back and patted Reickman on the shoulder in thanks. It burned his throat slightly, but he did not care. It would also help dull the pain a bit, which was always useful in battle.

He looked back up at the Soul Moon Convergence, feeling the warm rain continuing to hit his face. For a moment, he was transported to a distant happy place in his mind, but a shout brought him back to reality instantly. "Here they come," Alexandar heard Sentinel Captain Ivisk yell out.

He was ready.

Suddenly, there was another loud crack, and the building to the right in front of the barricade fell on its side with a piece of wall crushing part of the carriage blockade. *What manner of creature could create so much devastation?* He heard movement behind the partly demolished building and anxiously waited for whatever caused its ruin to make itself known. The last standing part of the wall collapsed. It revealed the instrument of its destruction.

There was an enormous clay-looking creature lumbering over the partly destroyed barricade. No wonder the buildings fell over so easily. Whatever it touched, it simply destroyed.

It lumbered slowly towards them with no speed, nor urgency. *Was it intelligent or simply instinctive*? It was a walking battering ram. *Was it possible to injure it? Did it even bleed?* Moments later, he got his answer: several Arquebus spewed their deadly bolt. The only damage was small chunks of clay, crumbling to the ground. Not one ounce of blood oozed.

"Ahhh!" Alexandar heard and turned to watch a Sentinel run up and swing his sword at the creature. The blade shattered on impact.

The creature turned and swatted the Sentinel, who flew back several feet in the air and bounced against an overturned carriage falling limp to the ground. They were unkillable! To his right, Ivisk emerged, running toward one of the creatures chopping down hard, shattering his sword on a massive clay leg. A large chunk fell off.

That was it—it was the same principle as chopping down a tree: *chop it at an angle*. Still, they desperately needed something that caused much more damage than what they had on hand. He looked around and saw small kegs of black powder, and a crazy thought popped into his head. He went over and uncorked it, then stuffed some cloth into it. "Get back from the creature!" he yelled, pulling out a flint. It struck a spark, which ignited the cloth, and he lightly blew on it until a flame lit.

He charged at the creature, diving off to the side as he threw the small keg at its feet. Nothing happened—yet. The cloth continued to burn as it rolled forward by its legs, until the cloth burned all the way through. A large explosion rocked the barricade, forcing him to shield his eyes from the blast.

There was loud *crash*. He opened his eyes, and the creature was on the ground. His ears still ringing from the explosion, he managed to get on his feet. He staggered forward, toward the creature lying on the ground, unmoving. *Was it dead?*

He cautiously moved around it, thankful that it was immobile. He noticed the other Sentinels were not moving but staring transfixed at the creature. Parts of its legs were blown off, but that didn't mean it was dead. *Was it stunned or wounded?*

Ivisk went up to it, poking it hard with his sword. Nothing. "It's dead!" he yelled.

Cheers erupted from the surrounding Sentinels. There was hope after all, Alexandar thought. There were four more small black powder kegs in sight, so they still had a chance.

Let them come.

"Look!" a Sentinel called out. All heads turned—it was the same medically-wrapped type of creature that they had seen before.

He thought at one time they might have been human. The destroyers of the buildings were tough to kill, but they were slow, so they could be avoided. But these creatures were the real threat. Fearsome looking, about seven of them were approaching fast, some wielding swords and others makeshift blunt wooden weapons. They were charging toward their defensive position. He held out his sword, pointing towards the group, and screamed, "Fire!" The village exploded with the sound of gunpowder and whistling of crossbow bolts as they streaked toward their respective targets.

The gunshots hit their marks, forcing the creatures back, but the latter kept to their course as the holes and shafts appeared in their bodies. *What the…? They didn't bleed?* Maybe not, though there was some sort of dark, thick ooze flowing from their wounds. But they kept coming.

"Reload, reload!" Alexandar screamed as the creatures picked up speed. He knew they would have time for one more round before they came face to face with them, and it would devolve into mortal combat. "Fire when ready!" was his next command, and the air filled again with the sound of gunfire and whizzing bolts.

They struck home, and yet creatures weren't slowing down. They were almost upon them.

Alexandar held up his sword. "Prepare to defend yourselves! Let them know what it means to fight against the Sentinels. Let them know we do not fear them!" The Sentinels responded with loud roars.

Another loud crack got his attention. Behind him, another building was collapsing. Sentinels who were keeping watch were now jumping off the roof for dear life.

"Everyone *move!*" he screamed. Spotting another keg, he picked up the gunpowder, then darted toward a clay monster, standing beside the tumbling building.

A scream of anguish hit his ears. Scanning the ground, a Sentinel lay trapped under some rubble. "Hold on!" he called out and ran over by his side. He seized his arms—

"Ahhhhh!" the man screamed as Alexandar pulled, again and again, but the Sentinel didn't budge.

Damnit! Reaching down again for the man's arms, he pulled with all his strength. Elrick screamed out in pain. "One last time! I can feel you budging…I swear," Alexandar promised, and poised himself for one last pull.

"Wait! I will help!" a familiar voice called out.

Alexandar stood there stunned. *It's not possible!*

The voice belonged to Sentinel Octvaian Izbasa, who was rushing toward him. "I thought you were dead, Octvaian! Glad you are here, I need your help." They were not friends, but he was still glad to find the Sentinel alive.

Panting heavily, Octvaian looked near-dead. He wondered just what happened to the man since leaving the village on wagon duty.

"I should be dead! The Spiriduş ambushed us and took the wagon. Preslav was there, taunting me—showed me the dead bodies of Askivar and Beryx. Then he took one of his massive fists and punched my lights out. Next thing I know, I am awake and alone. They took the dead bodies. I don't understand why—they never have before."

Alexandar didn't know what to think. He would need more time for his being alive to sink in. He had more pressing issues now—survival. "On the count of three, we pull. One…two…three—*pull!*" With Octvaian's added strength, they were able to free the trapped Sentinel.

"I can't feel my legs, sir…I can't feel them!" the man cried.

"You are going to be okay," Alexandar said, trying not to let on that the man's legs were indeed crushed.

Ahead, three clay creatures lumbered over the collapsed wall toward him and the remaining Sentinels. Alexandar was proud. The Sentinels were fighting bravely, not giving an inch to the creatures. He watched as one Sentinel jump on a bandaged creature. Repeatedly punching it in the face until it no longer moved. Well done! To Alexandar's horror, nine more creatures came into view.

They were trapped. There was only one thing left to do. Alexandar screamed as loud as he could, "Run! Get to safety, get to Hişoaraga and avenge us! Today is not the last day of the Sentinels! Goooo!"

With that, the remaining Sentinels disengaged and ran as fast as they could. Alexandar watched them escape, but he stayed put. As the creatures turned to approach him instead, he reached down and picked up a small gunpowder keg.

"What are you doing, Commander?" Octvaian asked, looking bewildered.

"We are going to kill those sons of bitches!" Alexandar screamed. Seeing Octvaian's confused face, he continued: "What, you're a Sentinel! Or aren't you? Go help the Sentinel we just pulled out from…" Alexandar trailed off as his eyes fell on the Sentinel they had just rescued. The light in the man's eyes was gone.

Octvaian shook his head, backing away from him. "I'm sorry, I have to go find Deidra. It's my birthday, see? I am going to ask her to marry me."

Birthday? Marriage? Octvaian didn't care about him or the other Sentinels. Only about Deidra and his damn birthday. Octvaian was selfish. "I am ordering you to stay, Sentinel Octvaian Izbasa, and do your duty." He kept his voice firm and his gaze fierce.

"No," was all Octvaian said before he bolted toward the harbour.

Alexandar screamed at the top of his lungs. "When we meet again, Octvaian Izbasa, *I will kill you!*" He didn't bother calling the man a Sentinel—the man wasn't. Perhaps Octvaian never truly was.

He noticed a lone Sentinel remaining, Captain Ivisk, who was in a staring contest with the closest bandaged creature. Suddenly Ivisk charged forward, ramming his sword right through it. In turn the creature raised its own sword and brought it down for the kill, but the Captain was too quick—he had pulled his sword out of the creature's torso and parried the blow. The man had guts, Alexandar thought, just as another one of their kind joined in the fight.

"Run, man, damnit!" he shouted at the Captain. "Get to safety—live to fight another day!"

The Captain did not cease. "If today is my day, so be it. I will not run in the face of these creatures. We are Sentinels, and we shall die as Sentinels."

Alexandar never felt prouder to be a Sentinel. This was their purpose.

He took out another cloth and popped the lid off the keg, stuffing it in, then removed the flint. He worked fast, but the creatures weren't yet near. *Probably thinks I'm no threat. Their foolish mistake*, he thought to himself, smiling.

There was nothing to bind the small kegs together, but he had a thought: he ripped off his uniform and wrapped it around the kegs to hold them together. He would take out as many as he could. The less that remained meant fewer innocents hurt.

A scream pierced the air, and he turned to watch Captain Ivisk fall to his death.

"No!" Alexandar screamed, his guts twisting in anguish at seeing his friend die. All the enemy's eyes were now on him. His time was coming to a quick end. As they approached him, his thoughts jumped to his wife. He still had no idea whether she made it out safely. "I'm sorry I wasn't there to protect you, please forgive me," he said under his breath, his head bent in prayer.

"What are you?" he screamed, demanding an answer he knew would never come. "What does it take to kill you?" As the bandaged things approached, he knelt and struck the flint. When the cloth caught, he blew until the flame spread; in seconds, he was going to be dead. He placed the barrel down.

Alexandar wielded his sword, likely for the last time, and swung wildly, hacking off the arm of the nearest bandaged creature. He was not going to die waiting for an explosion to go off in his face. He was going to die doing his duty.

Something sharp dug into his back. He looked down to see a sword's tip sticking out of his stomach. "Ohhhhhh," he said, and then the world disappeared from his eyes. He felt no pain; he merely felt himself fall for what seemed like an eternity, until he was no longer falling.

He woke in a field of grass, the rays hitting his face, radiating a pleasant warmth. He took a deep breath—that smell, so familiar…lilacs. Turning his head in the direction of the fragrance, his eyes fell on the face of the most beautiful woman, standing on a rock that was protruding from the water off the shore. Without thinking, he got up and walked toward her. As he closed the distance between them, another rock appeared beside the one she stood on. He jumped to it easily, a gentle breeze brushing his face. He couldn't remember feeling so at peace before.

Warm fingers interlaced with his, and he smiled at his wife, who beamed back at him. In death, they had found each other. They were at their eternal home, away from the horrors of the living.

"Please…" he started to plead, but his wife held her hand to his lips saying, "There is nothing to forgive." He reached for her and held her tightly…*for all of eternity.*

***

Octvaian bolted from the Sentinel barricade, ignoring what Alexandar was screaming at him. He did not travel all the way from the north to die in some "heroic" last stand. *No way!* He needed to get to Deidra! He knew their special evening had become a night fighting for survival, but if he could find her and show her how much she meant to him, then there was still a chance they could be together. Witnessing the devastation around him, the chances of her still being alive were…*slim.*

He ran down the street full tilt, hoping not to run into those things. There was no time for fighting, just rescuing. As he rounded a corner, one of the massive clay creatures charged toward him. He decided to do the same.

As he neared it, the monstrosity swung back its arm; its hand was shaped like a big round…ball? He knew he would need to time this perfectly. Just as the ball was going to connect with his face, he slid down to the ground, between the creature's legs. *Yes!* The roads were all mush now due to the rain, allowing him to slide more easily than expected.

He got back up to his feet and continued running down the street. He was near the harbour, which had been untouched so far. Why was that? He didn't know, nor did he really care—he was just grateful. Deidra lived in the harbor area. Most of her customers were sailors.

Octvaian didn't see anyone moving in the streets. They must have fled—he would have. He made it to the piers, stopping to watch lightning dance in the dark sky. It was mesmerizing. He was completely drenched, but he didn't care. Running to the Squirmy Squid, where Deidra lived in a spacious unit on the floor above it, he ran up the stairs and banged on her door.

"Deidra…Deidra! It's Octvaian. I have come to rescue you!" he yelled out. Waiting anxiously for a reply. "Deidra!" he screamed, but no sound came from the other side. He looked around at the inferno that was now their village. Was he too late? Summoning all his strength, he kicked the door hard, but it didn't budge. Pain shot up through his leg. He hammered on it with his fists, screaming Deidra's name repeatedly, but still nothing.

Devasted, he did not know what to do next. He leaned his forehead against the door and pounded on it with his fists, with no strength left in them. How quickly everything had changed.

A creaking sound brought him back to his senses. There, down the stairs, Deidra was looking back up at him, a look of utter disbelief on her face. "Deidra!" He bounded to the bottom of the stairs.

"What are you doing?" she said, anger rising in her voice.

Octvaian was taken aback by her hostility. "I am here to rescue you!"

Deidra was rooted to the spot, a confused look on her face. "Why?"

"Why what?"

"Why do you want to rescue me?"

"Because I love you!" he said, holding back tears, and held out his arms to hug her. She put up her hand to stop him.

"What are you doing?"

"Stopping you."

"But…I…" Octvaian started to say.

"Do you see those vessels out there?" Deidra asked. He looked out over the lake and nodded. "Once all this is over, more ships will come, with new customers, which means I'll be making more atria than I could ever imagine. When all this is over, I will be the richest woman that ever lived."

"What about me? What about my feelings for you? Don't you want a life filled with love and happiness?"

"No," she said coldly.

Where did all this come from? "I don't believe you. Something happened to you, something horrible, I know, but together, we can overcome it. You can find happiness again if you truly believe. I have survived an ambush, travelled all this way back to you. Tonight was supposed to be special—you said it would be."

Deidra said nothing, her eyes missing the sparkle they once had.

"Say something!" he yelled, unable to contain himself.

Finally, Deidra's mouth spread into a small smile. *There you go*, he thought. "You are absolutely right, Octvaian. Tonight is special. Tonight, is the day of your birth— and your death," she said, taking steps toward him.

He didn't know whether he was more confused or hurt. "I don't understand." And then a horrible sensation overtook him, and he could no longer breathe easy. He lowered his head—his chest had turned bright red, and an object was sticking through it. Was it a…*knife?*

"Deidra…why…?" He gasped as he took a slow, excruciating step toward her. To his horror, she stepped back.

"Deidra…" he called out again as he fell to his knees, gasping for air.

"Good-bye, Octvaian. Truth be told, I did have something special planned for tonight. Oh well." She turned on her heel, leaving him alone and bleeding. In desperation, he dove to grab the hem of her dress, but she sidestepped him.

Laying on his side, he watched her climb the stairs back home. This wasn't how his story was supposed to end. What did he do wrong? He had a life planned out for them. And she was using him…the entire time.

He knew he was on his last breaths. With all the strength he had left, he screamed, "*Damn you!*"

Eternal darkness swallowed him.

Chapter 17

Drăculeşti Counterattack—Sighişoara

'Drăculeşti Vengance'

With his sons in tow, Vlad Drăculeşti leapt from rooftop to rooftop to avoid the mass exodus of people fleeing to get to safety. He knew with every jump that what was happening around them was becoming more real to his sons. There was only one thing on his mind: vengeance.

As they made their way to the top of one of the damaged bakeries, Vlad held up his hand for his sons to stop. He had to decide on the best course of action. He stood there, quietly seething at the terror around him, contemplating the best counterattack.

"Father, how is all this possible?" Micrea asked. Vlad looked through the fire and smoke billowing from the shore. Movement. The creatures had spread out throughout the area and beyond now. Vlad saw another volley of fire arrows being unleashed from the enormous black vessels. His son Vladimir had been right all along with his suspicions that something lay beyond the horizon. And what was causing the lightening over the lake? It had to be tied to the attackers somehow.

He looked to the east. Instead of a Sentinel counterattack, the Commander Alexandar was at a hastily constructed barricade and appeared to be yelling out orders. There were not enough Sentinels there to mount an effective counterattack. That was disheartening. He hoped they would take a few creatures with them, but with what he witnessed coming toward them, he did not think their weapons would be remarkably effective.

The creatures advancing toward the barricade were methodical in their approach. They were not taking prisoners, nor were they leaving any buildings standing in their path. Their mission was the total annihilation of their village. But why?

More fire arrows rained from the black vessels, and he noticed the air behind the lightening was a slightly different hue than the surrounding air in front. Did this have to do with how the attackers got to the village? Where did they come from? He needed to get to the vessels and kill whoever was behind all of this. A small part of him wanted to send his boys away, to go and get their mother and brother, and leave the village to organize a counterattack with the full strength of the remaining Sentinels. But what would it be teaching them? That it was okay to run away and come back when it was safe? They would spend the rest of their lives regretting they had left their father, but at least they would be alive.

He knew it was their duty to stay and fight and die if necessary. Being the ruling *viskta* demanded no less. Should they fall, Vladimir would carry on the Drăculești name, knowing his father and brothers died protecting the village.

Vlad looked over at the horizon and thought of Vasilisa, and the day that he had met her. How they had saved each other's lives in the water, and how when they had gotten to safety, he had immediately asked her to marry him, and she had simply smiled and said yes. He had asked her over the years why she had said yes that night, and all he ever got as an answer was a kiss. In the end, that was all that really mattered to him—that she had said yes. He had not regretted a single moment of married life with her and had hated keeping the family secret from her, but history had taught him that spouses of their *viskta*'s clan did not react well to the news of what they had married into. It had been determined that the spouses would remain in the dark, and only the children would know what their true heritage was at the appropriate age to prepare them for their ritual. Vasilisa was strong, and he suspected she could handle it, but he still had not said anything to her. He glanced up at the wondrous beauty of the Soul Moon Convergence, wishing he was spending it in his wife's arms.

"Father?" Micrea asked him, breaking him from his thoughts. He looked at his sons and the danger coming toward them. Glancing up at the Soul Moon Convergence and feeling the warm rain on his face one last time, he decided it was enough thinking. It was time for action. "It looks like a large portion of the attackers moved to the edge of the town and have started to swing in a large arc, destroying everything since they decimated the area around the harbour, yet they had left the harbour itself intact…" he thought aloud. "We are looking at the destruction of our village, but the reason remains a mystery. The black vessels are where the attack started from. As you can see, they are slowly backing up to the shimmering in the air," he continued, pointing at the ships. "Once they go through, they will be gone, but their attackers are remaining behind, from the looks of it. Look at the shoreline—there are no transport vessels to take prisoners, nor return them to the ships."

There was one building still standing. It was the Brotherhood building. There were no Brothers standing out front. He wondered if they were watching it from inside or at all. He had not spent much time in their establishment, but he had heard enough stories to know they knew how to take care of themselves. Vlad was confident that if the Brotherhood fought, they would have taken out quite a few by themselves. But it seemed they were content to stay out of it. Perhaps the attackers sensed the Brotherhood's unnatural abilities and were cautious to attack. Or perhaps were told not to.

Too many questions, not enough answers.

"There, the Tree of Life—we head there. Watch each other's backs," Vlad commanded, pointing to where a group of creatures were headed. "When you attack, don't strike blindly. Engage and learn. We do not know what they are fully capable of," he added, and both sons nodded intently. "There doesn't appear to be anyone in that area left, so just focus on the battle in front of you. If you hear any screams, don't get distracted. We will let the remaining Sentinels handle the rescuing. We focus strictly on the creatures."

"There are so many, Father," Radu said, his voice hesitant. "They are spread out over the village. What happened to the Sentinels, and why are there not more of these creatures dead? I don't see one of their bodies on the ground."

Micrea, too, starting to look around, scanning for the bodies of the attackers. His face turned worried.

"The Sentinels are doing what they can. They are excellent fighters against human foes. This is beyond them. I am sure they did their best to escort as many villagers to safety. I suspect other than the section over there, the rest are dead. We can only rely on each other," Vlad said grimly.

"But Father, can we beat all them? We don't even know if they can be killed," Micrea asked.

Vlad placed his hand on his son's shoulders and looked him directly in the eyes. "This is our duty." They had never witnessed horrors like this before. Vlad had hoped to spare them the terror he had endured in his battles. Though, that was going to change due to his recent decision to eliminate the Spiriduș once and for all. But this…this was beyond anything even he had witnessed. He had never been given a choice in his life, and even though he had told them it was their duty to die if necessary, he wanted to give them the choice he never had. Vlad hoped they answered in a way that made him proud.

"Our duty is to defend this village and its people. I am ready to die to do so. You both are at the start of your lives, but you know what your duty is. So, I will give you the choice to join me or leave with the villagers and continue living, starting your life anew if I should fall here. You both will need to look within yourselves to make the right one." Vlad pointed down toward their course. "Death is knocking, and I am going to answer the door." With that, he let out a loud roar and leaped off the roof toward the destruction, and possibly his imminent death. He sensed his sons would not be far behind him, for as nervous as they were, their duty had been ingrained into them since childhood.

Vlad heard noises coming from behind him. He smiled, as he knew both his sons were following behind. As he jumped from rooftop to rooftop, he paid closer attention to what the invaders were doing. The larger, clay looking ones were pushing down the buildings. The smaller ones were killing any stranglers and protecting their larger companions. Why would the mightier ones need protecting? They moved slowly, yes, but he could tell they were immensely powerful. Were they vulnerable to certain attacks? Too many questions and no answers, he thought again as he landed beside the Tree of Life. Even in daylight the tree was ominous to behold. Its long black branches were a stark contrast to its white trunk that ran higher than most buildings in the village. Its crown was covered in emerald, hexagon leaves. It was…unnatural.

No one knew where the tree came from, as it had mysteriously materialized one night. The tree had a natural basin at the bottom of its trunk that collected rainwater when it rained. No leaves that dropped from the tree ever touched the ground—they all landed in the basin. The water that collected in the basin is what helped lead the tree to getting its name. Vlad vaguely remembered the story he heard as a child of a mother that brought her dead, unborn daughter to the fountain. She dipped her daughter in the water and miraculously it restored her daughter's life. A few years ago, a father had brought his dead son to the fountain but was unsuccessful in bringing the boy back to life. He had thought about investigating the Tree of Life more closely, but the few times he got close to it, he felt an eerie presence emanating from it and had decided to leave it alone.

Even for his abilities, there were certain things best left untouched. A loud crashing sound brought him back to reality. Another building collapsed. His two sons were behind him, waiting for instructions. Three bandaged creatures quickly approached them. He had always been taught that the best defense was an even better offence. "Radu left, Micrea right…*attack!*"

Vlad lunged full force at the middle creature. With a vicious punch, he laid into one of the bandaged creatures sending it backwards with its face smashed in. *"Yesss!"* He roared in victory. It crumbled to the ground, unmoving. *That's it?* Vlad watched Radu lunge and punch the closest creature in the face, expecting it to go down from the force of the blow, but it brought its head back up with a fist-sized indent in the front of its face. Other than that, it didn't appear to be hurt or crippled. A sound came from behind Vlad and he spun around as his mouth dropped open from shock. The creature had taken the full force of his blow and was back on its feet. His hairs stood on the back of his neck. He was rattled at the unexpected turn of events.

He yelled to his sons, "Punching them in the head doesn't work. We need a new strategy!" Nodding, his boys dodged attacks, sizing up their opponents. Vlad heard Radu roar and leap on the nearest attacker, biting it viciously in its bandaged neck. Vlad screamed out to his son, "Nooo! We don't know what they are!" He rushed and pulled Radu off the creature. His son had brown ooze dripping from his fangs and was starting to convulse violently. His son's body was rejecting the creature's...ooze, for lack of a better word. "Father. I don't feel so good." Micrea rushed over and asked him, "Father, what's wrong with Radu?" Vlad knew his son needed a boost to counteract what was going through his veins. "Radu needs blood, fresh blood." Vlad scanned around and saw many corpses with lakes of blood everywhere.

Vlad picked up his convulsing son and rushed over and started scooping up handfuls of blood, forcing it down his son's throat. "Father! We are being surrounded!" Micrea screamed out to him. Vlad looked down at Radu. The blood helped stop the convulsing, but his son was still deathly ill and weak. Looking around, he saw five creatures moving to attack. They needed more time for Radu to heal. "Watch your brother!" Vlad yelled to his son. He gathered his strength and rushed to the closest attacker, battering it which propelled it backwards into a wall twenty feet back. Not staying still to watch, he proceeded to toss the next one into the air, sending it into a building where it slumped, unmoving. The other two backed up, not willing to engage such a powerful foe. Vlad had bought them a few minutes. They needed a new plan, quickly. The creatures were not overly powerful, but they were incredibly resistant to physical damage. The ones he had bounced off walls were getting back on their feet!

He glanced over at Micrea, who was so busy dancing around, avoiding the sword swings coming at him, that he didn't notice the large clay behemoth come up behind him. "Micrea, move left!" he screamed, and dashed over. Leaping, Vlad punched the large clay attacker straight in the head, which recoiled. These clay abominations were something different altogether. He had hit it hard enough that he had punched a large chip off its face. Vlad stared in horror as the creature's face rippled and within seconds repaired its own face. *What the…?* No amount of punching was going to take these down. He stared into its lifeless eyes, wondering what would possess someone to create something so destructive.

"What do we do, Father?" Radu asked, slowly getting on his feet. That was a good sign, Vlad thought.

His sons were keeping their distance. Vlad scanned the creature. It had a form of kneecap, but its legs were so thick that he suspected hitting them would have no effect, either. "You are quicker—stay ahead of them for now. We will find their weakness." He looked back at the creatures facing him. Bandaged fighters and indestructible creatures. *What a lethal combination,* he thought as he rolled to dodge a swing from one of them. He got back up and dodged another slow swing when he heard a loud scream that chilled him to the core.

Vlad spun around: three bandaged creatures were standing over Micrea's dead body. Vlad let out a primordial scream of rage and pain. His son's lifeless face was frozen in shock, with two swords and a large shaft of wood sticking out of his chest.

"Micrea…nooooooo!" Radu scream out. Vlad looked down at his dead son being cradled by Radu. He choked back tears. Mourning would have to come later. He knew how to kill them. He was going to avenge his son.

He pulled Radu off Micrea and held him close, whispering into his ears, "There will be time for grieving…I promise you. There are many others we need to kill first. The living still need us. We must keep it together. Do you understand, Radu?" His son nodded, and he nodded back. "Use what you are feeling, let it consume you. Let it fuel your vengeance."

He let out an animalistic cry, and Radu joined in, and then he knew his son was one with the darkness within.

"Help us!" a man whimpered. It was Mr. Hendrik carrying his injured, bleeding daughter, Kazia in his arms.

"Why are you still here?" Vlad demanded angrily. "You should have fled with the others!"

"I couldn't leave my wife…she's dead. A wall fell on top of her, and we tried to get her out, but we couldn't. Kazia and I left, and we've been avoiding those creatures..." Mr. Hendrik said, sobbing uncontrollably. *Damn!* He looked down at his dead son, his heart breaking in half at the sight. Radu was leaning against the wall, still in agony from ingesting whatever the bandaged creatures were made of. The blood from the pools of blood was dirty blood. It didn't have the essence of the living in it anymore. When someone died, their blood became soulless, dirty blood. For a vampire to heal or reach super-vampire abilities, they needed living blood.

They were not going to win this fight. Punching simply wasn't enough. One dead son, another son that was still weakened. He looked around his surroundings at the dead bodies.

Too much death too quickly. More were going to die. Screams rang out through the village, screams of people dying. He started trembling uncontrollably. Not from pain or fear. Desperation to save the ones he loved. Vlad looked from the baker to his injured, frightened daughter. Both were huddled together again a broken wall, scared beyond belief. Kazia had a vicious stomach wound—her brown nightgown was drenched in blood. Mr. Hendrik was as white as a sheet. He was not much longer of this world. Vlad couldn't save them. He couldn't save anyone. He had failed his duty as a protector and as a father.

But Kazia and her father's death didn't have to be meaningless. Their deaths could serve a higher purpose.

Vlad knew what he had to do; he hoped that one day Vladimir might be able to forgive him. He had lost one son, and he was not going to lose another.

"I am sorry for your loss, Mr. Hendrik, and for what needs to be done," Vlad said, choking back his rising emotions. He glanced at Radu. "In order to win this, and for you to be fully healed, we need to enhance our abilities. I can tell from your pale face you are still too weak to fight. Do you understand?" For a moment, Radu's expression was blank, but with a slight tilt of his head, Vlad saw his son's eyes light up with understanding, and sadness.

"Father…Vladimir…" his son stammered while looking at Kazia.

Vlad knew he would need to take the first step for Radu to follow. "Mr. Hendrik, we will defeat the rest of the creatures and save what's left of the village, but it will come at a steep price."

"Price?" Mr. Hendrick asked, and Vlad nodded. "The needs of the many are more important than the few, or in this case…two." Confusion lingered for half a second on the man's face until Vlad's teeth were in his neck.

"Noooo!" Kazia screamed and began to strike him hard. But he did not stop feeding.

All at once, Kazia's screams stopped, and he knew his son was doing the same. To defeat these creatures, they would need to extend their abilities beyond their capabilities. *This is the only way to save my family.*

When Vlad was done feeding, he looked over at Kazia's lifeless eyes as Radu consumed her flesh, her blood running down his chin. There was no shame in his son's eyes. *Good.* Shame was for the weak. "We are doing what we need to," Vlad growled. "Put her body down. Just like with Micrea, there will be a time for grieving, but it is not now. We need to find a way to end this and get answers. We can try to kill these creatures again, but they are not the true cause. We need to get to those black vessels."

The look in his son's eyes told Vlad the girl's blood was taking over his senses. Soon he would be a raging, killing machine, which is exactly what he needed. Radu's complexion was back to normal again. The living blood had restored his son's strength and health.

He spun around at the sound of movement. Five bandaged creatures appeared—he leapt between them, snapped off one of their heads, and Radu joined. In seconds, all five had been rendered headless. The creatures had never stood a chance against them. He gave Mr. Hendrick and Kazia one last look. Vlad deeply regretted the actions they took, but the lives of the few paled in comparison to the population of the village. He only hoped *Vladimir could forgive me when all this was over.* He noticed that Kazia's dead hand was in the Tree of Life's basin at the bottom. It troubled him for an inexplicable reason, but he pushed past it. He made a mental note that after this was over, he would check to make sure her body was still there.

Vlad stared out at the lake. He had never jumped that far before. He would need added height to make the jump, he thought, hoping not all the buildings were destroyed. If there were some support beams or posts still standing near the harbour, he and Radu might have a chance.

He looked at the Soul Moon Convergence and cursed it before making a run for it, soaring from destroyed building to destroyed building, gaining speed with each jump, until finally he spotted the tall post that the harbour bell was attached to—it was still intact. With all his strength, he leaped onto the top of the post, and hurtled himself toward the vessels on the lake.

There were men manning the ships. He hoped he would land near the bow, as there weren't many crew members there, further back were the archers. He would deal with them when the time came.

A man with a whip stood above the archers. As Vlad landed on the deck, he grabbed the man by the head and bit into his neck, tasting the sweet blood on his lips, and then viciously snapped it. Radu should be close behind him.

The slaughter began aboard the Tutankhamen II.

*** >>

Master Medjay Ahmose sat in hiding behind a broken wall, revolted by what he was witnessing. *By the Gods...they eat their victims, even women!* How young do they start? The youngest one of the two men was chomping down on the poor young girl's neck. Goddess Hathor would strike them both down if she witnessed the abomination he did!

He held his hand up for Rewer and Jarha to remain silent as he continued to watch the scene unfold from behind the wall. How to take their targets down? He and his Medjays didn't stand a chance against those that would delight in eating them! Ahmose knew their only hope was their mystically enhanced darts. He had ordered the stopping power of the darts to be enhanced. Once he was informed of their strength, and how hard it was to kill a Drăculești, he had talked to the High Sorcerer about getting the darts' potency amplified. His foresight had served him well. He looked back and gestured to Rewer to load up his dart into his blow gun and for Jarha to get his ready too, just in case. He then proceeded to remove the long bamboo tube from his belt, took a dart from a pouch and slid it inside the tube. This was their opportunity, if they could capture both men instead of one—double the reward and glory.

He pointed to Rewer to target the elder Drăculești. He brought the tube to his lips to shoot the younger Drăculești when he saw the older one leap away. Seizing the opportunity, he shot his dart, and it struck its target in the neck. *Yes!* Ahmose watched his target remove the dart and looked back directly at him. *Oh snap!*

Ahmose blinked and felt himself being picked up off the ground and slammed hard into a wall. *Owwww.* He looked directly into the crazed eyes of the Drăculești and knew he was going to die. Two more darts appeared in the Drăculești's neck, and he felt the latter's grip loosen. "Again!" he managed to scream as he gripped his assailant's arms and tried to gain the upper hand. Even with the help of three darts, he could barely wiggle out of the Drăculești's grip. Even a fraction of their strength was more than enough to overpower a mere mortal like him.

Two more in the Drăculești's neck. He finally staggered back, nearly dropping to one knee. Ahmose struck quick and hard, driving his knee hard into the Drăculești's face, who finally dropped to the ground unconscious. Five darts...*five!* "By the Gods..." he exclaimed, grabbing his throat, tender from the Drăculești's grasp.

"Master. Are you seriously hurt?" Rewer asked him, and he shook his head. Talking would be a chore for the time being, so he opted for hand. He reached for the rope, wrapped it around his waist, and motioned for Jarha to do the same. He wanted to make sure if the Drăculești woke up, he would be able to finish the job he had started before being incapacitated. He grabbed a piece of broken lumber and slid it under the Drăculești, then wrapped his rope around both the man's arms and body, securing it tightly. Finally, it was done. Their prisoner was bound to the wood, which would make it easier to carry him. Ahmose wiped the rainwater off his face and looked around, noticing the strange looking tree. He had never seen a white tree with black branches. *Was nothing normal in this land?* Now they needed to get to their vessel as quickly as possible. He had been told they had less than an hour to complete their mission, as long as it was raining. They still had time.

He motioned for Jarha and Rewer to lift up and carry the Drăculești. Ahmose climbed a half-wall to find their best course to their ship and spotted both vessels slowly backing up to the curtain—good!

He scanned for signs for Sentinels or other villagers. There were none in sight. That didn't mean there weren't any—they needed an escort. Ahmose spied a handful of Mummies not too far off. Excellent, he could command them to escort them. Jumping down, he motioned for Rewer and Jarha to pick up their prize and carry the unconscious man. They hurried down the streets, burning buildings on either side of them. It was surreal.

Several Mummies walked toward them. Ahmose whistled the tune he was called to control them—they responded immediately, rushing up to them. "Guard," Ahmose ordered. Three Mummies took up positions behind them to cover their flank and one on each side of their prize.

He continued to stay ahead of Rewer and Jarha to make sure the way was clear. So much destruction. He was finding it hard not to be overwhelmed by what he saw. He nearly tripped on something but managed to catch himself. He looked down at what had cause it and gasped: the burnt corpse of a mother holding her child. Or that's what it looked like to him; he couldn't be sure.

"Master…are you okay?" Jarha asked. Ahmose gave a curt nod. He had to be okay, the mission demanded it. He turned away from the sight and continued to the shoreline, where their vessel was concealed. They sped toward it, rushing through the fire and debris, trying their best to ignore the horror around them.

Finally, they made it down to the shore. Ahmose grabbed the branches and threw them off, revealing their watercraft that was hidden under them. Within minutes, their watercraft was cleared off and he motioned for them to put their prisoner onboard. Luckily, the Drăculeşti was still unconscious, or this would have been a lot more difficult.

He closed his eyes, rapped the watercraft three times with his knuckle, whispering, "return" and opened his eyes, watching as their watercraft magically moved forward toward the Tutankhamen I. He had completed his mission.

There were sparks of orange and red on the Tutankhamen II… *What was happening?*

"Master…Could it be the Drăculeşti?" Rewer asked. Fire arrows flew from the Tutankhamen I to the Tutankhamen II. They were destroying their own vessel. Was the elder Drăculeşti unkillable? Surely one man, no matter how unnatural, didn't stand a chance against the might of the crew of both vessels.

"Impossible," he uttered, instantly regretting speaking as he rubbed his tender neck to try to soothe it. There was one last thing to do. He took out another mystically enhanced dart and aimed high. It soared, a light green glow sparkling in the night sky, signalling to the vessels that their "prize" would be on their way.

Ahmose hoped someone was paying attention. General Pentu was brilliant—he would dedicate someone to keep an eye out for their signal. Now, their primary mission would need to commence. He moved more branches aside, seeing their supplies were still intact. They were on their own now for two weeks.

"How are you both?" Ahmose asked, his voice still hoarse. He needed to know how his men were holding up against all this. He was proud of Jarha and Rewer immensely; they had proved their mettle once again.

"Fine," they said simultaneously. *Good.* "We will find a place to camp in the harbour area to keep watch over the remains of the village. Sink any vessel that comes into the harbour and wait until we get re-supplied. We will leave the supplies here until we find a suitable spot. Do either of you have any questions?"

The Medjays shook their heads. Ahmose wiped his face. It was still raining. It had to be ending soon. He made a motion to move out, and they skirted the shoreline to the dock area. Once they got to the piers, Ahmose decided to take refuge in a place called the Squirmy Squid. He pushed open the door and walked in, followed closely by the other Medjays.

And then Ahmose's eyes found the most beautiful, exotic-looking woman he had ever seen, with long blond hair that reached her waist and skin that had a honey glow.

"Welcome, gentleman. My name is Deidra, and my services can be yours for the right atria," she said in her sultry voice.

Ahmose seemed to have lost all ability to speak. He didn't know if it was her crimson dress or luscious lips, but he couldn't tear himself away. The sparkle in her eyes told him what services she offered. And he wanted very much to try them.

Chapter 18

Drăculești Castle—Sighișoara

'Mother's Defiance'

Vasilisa Drăculești stared in horror at Vladimir's empty bed. It was still made, which meant it had not been slept in. Her mind started to race in panic. Where could he be? He had answered when she had called for him to go to bed, so he must have left after that. She was terrified for her son's safety. His father had told him not to leave the castle tonight, as he had responsibilities tomorrow while his father and brothers were away, but he left anyway.

She started to think of all the other places he might be. Not in the village. Vladimir would not risk getting Kazia in trouble with her father, not after the talk his father gave him. She did not think Kazia would dishonour her *viskta* by being caught with Vladimir late at night, either. The only other place near the castle was the Dark Woods, and Vladimir had never ventured there at night. Those that went too far in the forest never came out quite right in the head. Or at all.

She was about to dismiss the Dark Woods altogether when she thought back to dinnertime and Vladimir's interest in finding a hellsteed. That was the only logical place that Vladimir could have gone. If he had found a hellsteed, he was safe from any attackers, but in danger from the things that dwelled in that damned forest. She should be cross, but his disobeying might just have saved his life. She needed to get to him, then flee to Hișoaraga to gather reinforcements.

There was an orange and green glow coming from the window. She went over to it and gasped at the sight. It seemed the whole shoreline of the village was on fire except for the harbour area.

She heard screams in the distance. No…this isn't supposed to be happening. This was some sort of cruel nightmare. She stared at the Soul Moon Convergence in disbelief. Something so beautiful was not meant to create so much destruction. Had the legend been a lie?

She shook her head. She didn't have time to stand there and wonder. She had to go rescue her son. Her happy bubble that was her family and home was shattered, forever. *Focus.* She had to go to the Dark Woods and get Vladimir. His safety was all that mattered. She would not fail her son, she thought as she steeled herself for the journey into the Dark Woods.

And then something else out the window caught her attention. There was a blur of movement heading fast toward the castle. It didn't appear to be Sentinels or villagers. Something else…something unnatural. A cold chill that went up her spine gave her the answer.

She watched as they approached the castle. She noticed they didn't have any armour that she could tell, just some sort of medical dressings wrapped around them. She spotted movement to her left and saw that there were four more of them, and they were carrying wooden sticks, the tips caught in flames. She absently clutched the crystal around her neck as they started lighting the gardens around the castle on fire. She needed to get out of the castle immediately.

She locked eyes with one of them. They now knew the castle was not empty.

She ran out of the room and down the stone steps until she got to the main floor of the castle and sprinted to the back of it. There was a back door that she hoped they hadn't made it to yet; she could escape undetected through the maze into the Dark Woods.

When she got to the back door, she yanked it open. The maze entrance was at the back of the castle's rear courtyard where they dined outside at times or held parties. The entrance was on fire already. *What to do? Run through it and hopefully make it, or stay and try to find another way somehow?*

There was a water fountain in the maze. If she could drench herself, then maybe there was a chance not to be burned alive. Something caught the corner of her eyes, and she turned and saw one of the creatures closing in. It was wrapped in long, yellowish medical bandages. The kind you would wrap around an injury. And it held a sword—the same the Sentinels used. *Who had it killed to wield it?* It was covered in dried blood. *How many innocents had it killed?*

She dismissed the thought, as she needed to remain focused. Her eyes met the creature's red glowing eyes, and she couldn't help but notice there was some intelligence behind them. *Could it be reasoned with?* Perhaps it had been a parent in another lifetime and would let her leave.

She knew there was virtually no chance of that, but she hoped anyway. She held up her hands and pleaded, "I mean you no harm, do you understand? I am not a threat to you...please."

Hope soared inside of her as it lowered its sword and stared at her. *Yes,* she thought with renewed optimism. But it left as quickly as it had come, as the creature raised its sword again and started toward her. Instinctively, she went back into the castle and bolted the door. The creature battered its sword against it, smashing the window in the door. *No!* She slowly backed away, growing more and more terrified by the second. *Must get to Vladimir, must get to Vladimir,* she repeated in her head. How else could she get out of the castle? *Think,* she thought, and realized there was one last hope: the secret exit in the cellar.

Feeling as though she had no choice, she headed for the stairs. As she fled, she could hear banging, and knew that the door had finally given in. The creature was in the castle.

Faster! She cried out in her mind. She couldn't fail. Vladimir would need her. The thick black smoke was filling up the halls. She bumped into an end table, her leg throbbing, and bit her lip. *A little further.*

She swerved around the many crates that littered the rooms filled with decorations for the upcoming dance. She reached the end of the long corridor, bursting open the closet doors and pushing the back wall. Stealthily, she snuck in and closed the door behind her. She raced down the narrow steps, the candles lighting up as she climbed down and into the tunnel. When she was first brought down here, she had asked how the candles lit up on their own, and Vlad had mumbled something. The tunnel led deep into the maze. She crept through it silently, hoping that those creatures were still back in the castle.

She continued to run full tilt until the end. She stopped for a moment to catch her breath, wiping the sweat from her brow. She needed to keep going; she wouldn't stop until her son was safely in her arms.

Reaching up to the metal hatch, she screamed in pain, and recoiled. It had burned her skin on contact. The maze fire had spread quicker than she imagined. She couldn't get out this way either.

Noooo! She screamed in her mind. She stood there for a moment, unmoving, as tears ran down her face. How would she ever be able to get to her son with no way out? The creatures were in the castle. She would have to take her chances. Dying down here was not an option.

She raced back to the closet door. *If* she could get to the roof, she would have a better vantage point. There might be another way to get into the Dark Woods. She got to the closet, and burst through the door, then sprinted for dear life to the mahogany staircase, all the way up four flights, skipping a step here and there to quicken the pace. One more flight…

BANG. She glanced behind her. There were three creatures two flights behind her. She turned and grabbed a heavy candleholder off the wall and threw it down at her attacker. It struck the first one in the head, making it fall back into the other one. *Yes!* She continued to race up the stairs not looking back. She ran up the last flight, down the narrow, darkened hallway to the wooden ladder, and climbed it as quickly as she could. At the top, she pushed the hatch up and climbed through, locking it behind her.

She was safe for now. Hurrying to the edge of the rooftop, she gasped at the sight when she got to it. The creatures had swarmed the village like locusts, demolishing everything that they touched. She was terrified for the life of her husband and their children. With every passing second, her life went up in flames, one cackling ember at a time.

The Dark Woods had to be safer than the village at this point. She needed a way to get to Vladimir. She felt a familiar chill go down her spine, even with all the heat surrounding the castle.

A cloud of smoke hit her face, and she turned away coughing. As she looked down, four more creatures looked back up at her. She would not be safe here for long. She ran along the roof's ledge, looking for a bush or something that might break her fall, out of the attackers' sight, but all she spotted was a wagon, packed full of bags of grain. Perhaps if she ran and jumped, she could make the distance. It was a fair distance, but from her altitude, she might be able to jump far enough to cover the distance. A loud splintering of wood caught her attention. They had broken through the latch to the roof!

She backed up, almost to the edge of the opposite end of the roof, bracing herself for the jump. She closed her eyes. *You can do it.* She opened them to start running, but stopped in her tracks, for she was facing a dressing-wrapped creature, whose red eyes burned into hers.

Was this the same one as before? She couldn't tell, as they all looked alike. She glanced at the sword it carried. It was the one she had seen earlier, covered in blood. She didn't move, and neither did the creature. It was like they were studying each other, both unsure of what to do. Slowly, she took out her sword, never taking her eyes off the creature. It wasn't as big as the creature's, but the blade was sharp. She had no doubt that it could slice through it.

She slowly moved to her right, holding her sword up. The creature mirrored her motions, then lifted its sword higher, to attack in a downwards motion. It lunged at her, bringing its sword down, but she moved her sword up to block. Their blades clashed violently, and swiftly, she spun and partially sliced through the creature's arm from behind.

The sword fell to the rooftop, and the creature stood there, looking down at its sword. There was no blood—only brownish ooze, gushing out violently. It didn't scream in pain, nor crumble to the ground. She continued to look at it in amazement, as it looked from its sword then back to her.

Suddenly it reached down with its remaining good arm and hand and picked up its weapon, then slowly started to approach her. She couldn't believe it. *What were these creatures? Who would create creatures like this?* These creatures were beyond anything from any nightmare she could remember.

If she could cut off its head, it wouldn't be able to attack her anymore—she hoped. She waited until it got a little closer, and then attacked with everything that she had. The creature lifted its sword in a defensive stance, but she struck high and fast. As she drove it back hard, she realized they were getting near the edge of the roof; she swung low, making it step onto the ledge. It lost its balance for a second and she seized the opportunity: she jumped up and drop kicked it backwards. She silently thanked Sentinel Master Astrivk for showing off the move during a Sentinel training practice that she had attended.

It tumbled off the roof. Crawling to the ledge, she saw it land in a flaming bush. She swelled with pride. They *could* be killed. She got to her feet and took a deep breath, noticing a bush that had not caught on fire yet. *Yes!* She backed up, preparing herself for the jump.

And then the loudest scream she had ever heard rang out. *Vlad.* Had it been Vlad's scream? Was he hurt? *No!* That wasn't the sound of physical pain—that was the scream of anguish. She was sure something bad had happened, and Vlad had not been able to stop it. Her heart told her that she was right. She let out a sob, fighting back tears.

From the corner of her eye, she caught someone jumping from rooftop to rooftop…Vlad! *What was he doing?* She had never seen him move that fast. He was increasing speed as he got closer to the harbour. She saw him leap through the air, toward the black vessels on the lake. Where were Micrea and Radu? There was a reason why it was only Vlad that she saw! That was why Vlad screamed. Pain shot through her heart, and she couldn't breathe. She clutched her chest tightly. *Was she going to lose all her boys and husband tonight?* She needed to get to Vladimir.

Just as Vasilisa turned around, she was staring into the faces of four more creatures. She was trapped.

She quickly spun around, peering downwards toward her escape route. The bush was now engulfed in flames. There was nothing but raging fires surrounding the castle. She turned back and lifted her sword up for the fight when she saw two more appear behind the other four. There were six now.

She had nowhere to run.

She gripped her sword tighter. She needed to clear a path somehow. Vasilisa knew of the stories of captured women. She instantly promised herself that that was not going to happen to her—even if it meant taking her own life.

Slowly, they began to approach, raising their swords to attack. She stood there and waited, knowing that she had no choice but to fight. She thought of Vladimir, how she would not fail to protect him. How he was too young to be all alone in the madness that had overtaken the land. How if she died, she would never see him grow older, know his children. Never be able to hold him in her arms again…never see his face again. *No.*

When they were mere feet away, she raised her sword and cracked a smile. "Do your worst!"

She charged the one closest to her, using all the fear, rage and sorrow inside of her as she swung her blade across its neck, removing its head from its body, which she kicked off the rooftop. She charged another, but this time the creature parried her blow, attacking her relentlessly. She blocked attack after attack, with no choice to go on the defensive.

Gasping for breath, she found herself slowly being forced back to the edge of the rooftop. "Die!" she screamed as she dodged another attack, slicing off one of her attacker's legs with all her strength. She smiled again as it fell forward. Using its own momentum against it, she thrust her sword into the attacker's body, lifting it off the ground and heaving it off the roof.

As she watched her former attacker catch fire and burn, her stomach felt hot and wet. She turned around and came face to face with another. Her gaze lowered to her torso, where a blade had gone through. She moved her hands downwards and grabbed it, slowly pulling it out. She had felt the metal slice through her skin, but her mind wasn't fully comprehending what was happening to her. Searing pain shot through her stomach, agony now consuming her. Her visions blurred as tears blinded her eyes. *NOOO!* This would not be her fate.

She viciously head-butted the creature, which drove it back in surprise. "I refuse to die!" she screamed with her rage, adrenaline fueled strength. *A life worth fighting for!* She charged the closest one, dropping to her knees, slid and sliced its leg off at the knee. It tumbled forward, falling heavy. Scrambling back to her feet, she brought her sword down and sliced off its head in one stroke. *Another one down.*

She twirled around, blocking a strike. Her attacker struck hard. Her arms were getting weaker, but she couldn't surrender…her son needed her. She could feel her strength leaving her. She clutched her stomach and her hand came back covered in blood.

Suddenly, the surface beneath her shook, nearly throwing her off balance. It shook again. What was happening now? It was only a matter of time before the castle collapsed in on itself. She heard shuffling behind her. She spun around, bringing up her sword and blocked another attack. All three of the creatures had closed in on her. She had nowhere to escape. She quickly glanced down below.

There were two more bandaged creatures accompanied the larger clay one. What had her husband taught her? The best defence is an even better offence. Screaming, she charged the nearest creature and managed to slice off its sword arm. She swung again and took off one of its legs. As she moved to attack another, her ankle got caught on something—the creature she had crippled had grabbed onto her and was not letting go. She hacked the other arm off and removed it from her ankle. As she got back up, she failed to notice the fist coming toward her, and she was struck straight in the face, bringing her down to one knee. The rooftop spun. Movement brought her back to reality. A creature attacked her. She tried to block it but was too slow. Her arm was cut open, and she dropped her sword. She screamed out in agony, clutching her arm. Her blood flowed out of her like a gushing stream.

"Damn you!" she screamed. The creature merely stood there, silent. "Why are you doing this?" she screamed again and rushed towards it. The creature stepped back in surprise, and she leapt at it and started punching it in the face as hard as she could. She didn't know how long she had been punching before she collapsed on top of it. She cried as she slid off. She looked up at the moons.

The rain was still pouring down on her. What had been warm rain had turned cold to her.

Without warning, the castle crumbled underneath her. She fell hard and bounced until, finally, she was lying on the rubble. Coughing through smoke, dust, and her own blood, she almost choked.

She gazed up at the moons, there were eight moons all jumbled together. There shouldn't be that many. Pain overtook her again and the moons seemed to vibrate. *How odd!* Hot and cold flashes overtook her. Her eyes were open, but she couldn't see anything clearly. Everything was fuzzy. She knew her rage had bought her a precious few minutes, but it was almost spent. She looked around, and there, standing above her, the monstrous clay like creature looked down at her. She blindly felt around for a weapon but was unable to find one. Her eyes were incredibly heavy. She closed them for the final time.

Vlad, Micrea, Radu, and Vladimir, how I love each of you. You are the lights in my sky. Thank you each for being...

She never finished the thought. Slowly and painfully, she reached for the crystal around her neck that Vlad had given her, imagining him in her mind one last time before darkness consumed her.

***

Sam walked over to Jessica, seeing the raging inferno that was at one time a quiet village. "Quite the busy night." He looked around at the buildings on fire. So much death inside of them, and around them. He could barely see the Soul Moon Convergence due to all the smoke. He wiped the rain from his eyes. He hated rain. It always rained on Tuesdays.

She smiled. "Job security at its finest. We need to head to the castle." He wondered about her sometimes. Their duty was sacred, but it seemed to him that it went beyond that for her, that she enjoyed it on some level. He nodded and they walked in silence up to the inferno that had been a happy family home.

He put on the best smile he could, looking down at Vasilisa as she lay there, dying. "Won't be much longer now."

Jessica nodded. "That was quite the fight she put up. It is a shame she lost. Her son needs her."

Sam nodded, looking over at the Dark Woods. "Yes. Yes, he will. Though, his father would be the best one to explain what will happen to him."

"That is also true. I almost feel bad for his first victim. It will not be pleasant, for either of them."

Sam agreed. Jessica touched his arm as he watched Vasilisa's last breath leave her body. He sighed heavily. Life was precious, and even though it was his duty to help those to move on, it was not one that he enjoyed. They waited. And waited.

He frowned. Something was wrong. He saw no life in her, yet her soul had not appeared for him to guide to the light.

"Sam. What's happening?"

He did not know. He walked over Vasilisa's dead body. Her eyes were open, with no light left in them, and yet...

"Is it possible she went to the Quintessence and is at the diner with Mother?" Jessica asked. It had been known to happen on more occasions than he would have liked. He viewed the diner as cheating death.

"No. We would have seen something happen even if that was the case. This is something else." An object glinting in Vasilisa's hand answered his question. "Damn. Why does everyone with the last name Drăculești have to be such a pain when it comes to death. Look at what's in her hand." He pointed to a crystal.

Jessica looked down beside him. "Ohhhhh! I have never encountered a crystal like that in this land. I thought they were strictly in Egyptia."

Sam nodded, "They are. Of course, the only one in this land would belong to a Drăculești." He sighed heavily. There was nothing left for them to do with Vasilisa. "Time to go. There are others that still need our services this night," he said as Jessica took his hand and steered him back into the village.

They walked past several Mummies. The sight of those unnatural abominations angered him greatly. Each one represented an affront to the natural order of life. If he had his way, he would destroy each one. But it was not up to him. It was up to the one that dwelled in the dark cloud in the night's sky. Sam often wished he could go up there and talk to the creator of these infernal crystals, but he knew he would never get the chance. The Sisterhood would stop him before he even got close enough to yell out what he wanted. Jessica gripped his arm. "I know. We have our duty. Let us focus on that. There are others that will deal with the Specter ...in time."

He knew she was right, but it didn't make him feel any better. He let out one last sigh. Time to go back to work.

Chapter 19

Tutankhamen II—Sighişoara

'Sinking Terror'

Captain Hekaib witnessed the obliteration of the village from the stern of his ship. Normally, Captains just ferried troops or supplies from one location to another. Being able to watch something like this from their cargo was a rare treat. Since the lands had been unified by the Pharaoh's ancestors, there was no longer any large-scale coastal battles. There were still skirmishes throughout the lands, of course, as not all the tribes got along all the time, but there was nothing like the former days of chaos. Any battles took place deep inland, far away from any views from rivers or lakes. He had next to no battle experience. He had his reservations about going through the curtain, but everything had gone according to General Pentu's grand plan so far. He had heard of the man's tactical genius, and tonight was a testament to it. The defenders had managed to sound the alarm, but to no avail. Their village crumbled like waves crashing down on a poor child's sand pyramid at the beach.

The Ushabti Warriors, with their incredible might, had made short work of the buildings faster than he anticipated. He had never seen one in action before. He had to admit they were very impressive. No wonder Tutankhamen's ancestors utilized these creatures to crush their competition. They were unstoppable.

People were screaming in terror as they fled their village. As much as he enjoyed watching the chaos, he was somewhat conflicted about what was happening. These people were not enemy soldiers that had tried to assassinate his Pharaoh. He doubted any of them even had knowledge of what had transpired. Their leaders had sealed their fates with their actions. Now, their people were paying with their lives. The lives of those who managed to escape would never be the same again.

The archers let their fire arrows loose. None of them had witnessed, nor partaken in anything like this before in their lives, and probably would not again. Being the first to travel to another land had been exhilarating. The vengeance-fueled obliteration before him had been what everyone had wanted.

A loud primordial scream emanated from the village. He wondered what made it. The Mummies and Ushabti Warriors made no such sounds. The only sounds they caused were of buildings crashing or terrified screams from their victims.

He glanced over at Tutankhamen I. General Pentu, Captain Khaemweset, and Chione were sitting around a table, staring out at the village, as well. He wondered what they were speaking about, though he was not entirely sure he wanted to know, as they began to laugh. They genuinely seemed to be enjoying the show—and some refreshments. One day, he would be the Captain of that vessel, he thought, and wondered if the General would be as congenial with him as he was with its current Captain.

From the time they had unloaded their forces to this very moment, it had been less than an hour, and the damage was irreversible. The rain hadn't even slowed them down, nor the fires. How effective they truly were at their tasks was staggering. To leave them here, prevent anyone from rebuilding, keeping everyone in fear, it was a brilliant plan.

Another volley of fire arrows unleashed. Was there anything left in range to be destroyed? He blinked, glimpsing at what looked like a man hopping from ruin to ruin. For a second, he thought the smoke was playing tricks on him—no one could do that. The hairs on the back of his neck stood on end. Suddenly, he was very frightened.

He continued to stare unblinking as the man jumped from rooftop to rooftop, getting closer to the harbour. He was moving so fast that it was like he was gliding on the air itself. Why was he going to the harbour? Everything was destroyed, and there was no one left to save. An uneasiness built inside of him.

The man made his way to the top of the harbour bell, then leapt over the lake. It dawned on him what the man was doing—heading toward their vessels. He needed to do something quickly.

He ran forward on the deck and pointed at the man. "Prepare to defend yourselves!" The crew looked momentarily confused, surely wondering what they needed to defend themselves from. *Damn it.* With the vessel slowly drifting back while the oarsmen kept firing, they were not in any position to increase speed or change course quickly. He stared in awe as the man flew and toward his vessel, landed successfully, and in seconds killed one of the Oar Captains. Then the man snapped another's neck, ripping it from its body. He did the same to crew member after crew member. Hekaib was petrified with fear at the sight. Two archers threw down their bows and grabbed their swords, charging forward, but both were killed as the attacker ripped out each of their hearts.

Chills ran down his spine as he witnessed the madness unfolding in front of him. He yelled at the archers, "Shoot that man. Kill him now!" The Captains took out their whips in preparation to join in the fight. These men were unnatural; could they even be killed? He took out his own sword, just in case, though he feared that it would not do much good against this foe, who was killing everything in his path. This must be what it felt like to be in front of an Ushabti Warrior. To his horror, Hekaib was mesmerized by the attacker's speed and cunning. Whenever the attacker avoided an arrow, he moved fast enough not to be hit, but one of the crew was.

"Watch where you are shooting! Do not accidently kill your crewmates!" Hekaib screamed, watching more of his crew go down in the frenzied assault on his vessel. The man attacked faster than his eyes could follow, the dead bodies piling up. A realization struck him. They were all going to die. He watched the attacker methodically kill his crew, one by one.

They were slowly moving closer to the curtain. *How many were going to die before they made it? What happened if their attacker made it through the curtain, too?* He locked eyes with the man, who smiled crazily back. Before he could blink, the man was standing in front of him. Hekaib threw aside his sword and clasped his hands together, falling to his knees and pleaded. "Mercy." The man's look changed from wild and crazy to dark and sinister. Hekaib was lifted off the deck with one hand.

"Where was the mercy for my village?" the man spat.

Hekaib had no real answer for him. "I was following orders."

"Whose orders?" Hekaib knew he was going to die, but he was loyal to his Pharaoh and would sooner die before responding. In the distance, Hekaib saw that some of the oarsmen had switched back to arrows. He back looked into the man's black eyes and knew what he was about to do next was a huge gamble. "Shoot!" he yelled. He saw a half dozen arrows shoot toward them. The man spun him around as he started writhing, trying to escape. An arrow shot past his head, but he felt two sharp pains in his back. He had been used as a human shield.

The crewmen froze in horror upon the realization that they had shot their Captain, and their expressions suggested they didn't know what to do next. None of their arrows had hit their target; the man outsmarted them all.

"Attack! Avenge me!" Hekaib screamed. The archers threw down their bows and grabbed their swords, rushing in toward him. He hoped they tore the man apart, one piece of flesh at a time. Being used as a human shield had been the man's undoing, though the man didn't know it. He smiled weakly at the thought. He felt his strength slowly ebb out of him as he was tossed on the deck like the evening's garbage. Determined that he was not going down without a fight, he crawled to his sword that was sprawled on the deck.

The screams of men filled his ears, but he was solely focused on retrieving his sword. He was going to die like a man, not lying on the deck waiting to bleed out. He deserved a better end than that. He felt hands push him down and a familiar voice command him, "I am going to pull them out, brace yourself, Captain." Hekaib clenched his hands into fists, and he felt the arrowheads being pulled out. He screamed in agony, kicking the deck with his feet as the pain brought him to the edge of unconsciousness.

"Here, Captain," someone uttered—not sure who— and he was handed an open flask. Gingerly, he drank some of the Blood Cider; its familiar warmth ebbed the pain away slowly. He felt wrappings being placed on his back and knew it was one of the ship's healers, Akilia.

"Thank you," he moaned, trying to stay conscious. He rolled his head over to look at the battle being waged on his ship, and it was as he feared: the attacker continued to decimate his crew with ease, randomly biting into some of his crew's necks! Even outnumbered, the man did not cower in fear as his crew fought him; in fact, with each death, the attacker seemed to gain in strength. Every time a crew member fell it was further proof that the Drăculeşti were living death... How could they be defeated?

One oarsman howled and raised his sword, trying to rally his comrades, which filled him with pride. His crew would never give up.

The Drăculeşti merely smiled, then raised both his middle fingers at them, gesturing as if to mean "Come, I am waiting for you." Truly the man was fearless.

"Stop him!" Hekaib cried. "Avenge the attack on our glorious Pharaoh!" He fell into a fit of coughs, pain coursing through his body. Wishing he had more Blood Cider to drink, he moaned in pain. More of his crew fell to the man. His movements were lethal to everyone that faced him.

The ship was long but not overly wide, so the oarsmen tried to make a circle around the attacker. *Good,* Hekaib thought. His crew were adjusting and working as a team, no longer blindly rushing in and charging the attacker and dying in the process. If he lived through his injuries, he would be handsomely rewarded for the bravery he and his crew showed against the lone attacker. He watched six oarsmen rush in as a team, swinging and lunging at the man with their swords in two groups, but at the last possible second the attacker twirled like a dancer, dodging their attacks. Out of the six that rushed in to attack, he had killed two in one swing doing a kind of pirouette, and another was stabbed inadvertently as the Drăculeşti expertly dodged the strike, rolling onto the deck and picking up a sword.

Screaming in anger at what they saw, the remaining oarsmen decided to create a semi-circle around the madman. Hekaib wondered if this tactic would work any better, but at least his men were brave enough to keep fighting. Several of the oarsmen stepped forward, but this time didn't lunge; they made quick thrusts with their swords, thrashing whatever part of the body of the man they could. Brilliant move—*bee stings hurt,* he thought. Waves of unconsciousness rocked him, but he fought to keep his eyes open to keep watching, nonetheless feeling helpless at the sight of his crew facing this impossibly difficult foe. He felt lightheaded and weak, reaching for something to use as support and managed to grab onto a railing. His vision was becoming more blurred with every passing second.

Even though the man was surrounded, he never backed down. Wielding his sword, he sliced off limbs at every opportunity with such ferocity that the deck was strewn with chopped off arms and heads, awash in blood. Hekaib was amazed they continued to fight.

The rain had not ceased; he was thankful it was a cold rain. *How could they stop this man?* Even though he was outnumbered, some two hundred to one, he seemed to revel in the battle, killing anyone that got too close with ease. With every passing minute, Hekaib knew his crew's confidence was being shaken, especially when the man simply stood there, roaring with laughter. Someone screamed "Fire!" He looked around to see where the voice had come from, and suddenly fire arrows shot toward them, landing on deck. He glanced up, and more fire arrows rained down. Then it dawned on him what was happening.

The Tutankhamen I had started firing on them. Hekaib's crew stood stunned for a moment, watching them fly overhead. He heard a scream, and to his left was a crew member with a fire arrow sticking out of his chest, with a look of utter shock on his face before falling to the deck, dead. Several more screams rang out, and he saw the semi-circle around the attacker was no longer intact, as his crew was running for the lives, trying to dodge the arrows. During all the commotion, the man got hit, but he casually pulled it out of his upper back with no visible signs of damage. Dozens more fire arrows rained down; a pain shot across his leg—he had been hit. Reaching down, he pulled it out and screamed.

Some of the crew had abandoned the fight, trying to put out the small fires forming on the deck while doing their best to dodge. More arrows came with more screams from the crew as they got hit, if not by arrows than by the deadly swiftness of the attacker's sword.

The ship was suddenly rocked by an eruption, as the front of the vessel exploded, causing crew members to fly, screaming at the top of their lungs. The front half of the vessel was engulfed in flames; the smoke covered the deck, making it near impossible to see what was happening. The clay piping carrying the oil must have been compromised. His crew continued to let out yelps of pain.

Hekaib agonizingly rolled over and looked at the unconscious attacker lying on the deck. He needed to get the man to the other ship as quickly as possible. "Help me!" he cried and was thankful to see two crewmembers rushing toward him. "Load the attacker onto the catapult and get him to the other vessel now! Our Pharaoh commanded we take a prisoner back!" he screamed. On the back of every Royal Navy vessel, there was a catapult that was used to transfer supplies from one ship to another in case of emergencies. This was one of those times.

He watched them grab the man and drag his body to the catapult. It was a wonder that it wasn't on fire or destroyed. One of the men uncovered the black cloth tarp while the other threw the body onto the netting. Hekaib hoped this gambit would work. Even if the Medjays failed, they would still have captured a prize. The men turned the circular base, doing their best to guess the angle and distance. They cranked the handwheel three times and looked over at him.

Suddenly, the deck tilted downwards, and he fell on his back. The vessel was starting to go down. He frantically grabbed for anything to stop his body from sliding into the lake, but the deck was drenched with water and blood. He managed to get a hold of a piece of deck that was sticking up to stop his slide.

"Now!" he screamed and held his breath. But to his horror, the man's eyes blinked open. He leapt out of the catapult, striking down the crew members who seconds ago were ready to blast him off.

The fire arrows caused more clay pipes to erupt into flames. They had done their damage; soon, the crew were going to be put out of their misery. Hekaib tried to see through the smoke, but it was impossible.

There was a loud *crack,* and he was being flung through the air. The main oil reservoir had been hit. He was flying to his death.

As he fell toward the water, he looked over and saw the other vessel and its Captain staring up at him. They locked eyes, knowing this was his end. His chance to replace the man's position was never going to happen. Hekaib was either going to drown or die from the large broken clay piping protruding from his stomach.

The other vessel started to enter the curtain. He hit the water hard as he flailed his arms wildly in the water trying to tread and stay afloat. Panic set in, and he found himself sinking as he kicked his legs frantically, managing to break up through the surface. He screamed in more pain than he thought possible. For a moment, he thought he was hallucinating as he saw the attacker fly toward the Tutankhamen I. As he fought consciousness, he spotted Chione standing on the deck holding a bright crystal in her hand, and she was looking up at the attacker flying toward her. Was she smiling? He watched her wave and blow a kiss—did she have a death wish?

He could feel death looming, but he fought it. He did not want to die. He clung desperately to a floating piece of lumber. By the Gods, he did not want to die! He knew it would happen one day, but he had so much he wanted to accomplish still. It wasn't fair.

He felt his strength ebb and lunged to crawl on top of the lumber. Perhaps if he rested, he might be able to pull the tubing out of his body and bandage it. With all his remaining strength, he was able to climb part way up but slid back down in extreme pain. The tubing that was sticking out of him was blocking him from climbing further. *Now what?* Tired, so very tired. Deciding he just needed to rest his head for a moment, he closed his eyes. He did not know how long he had closed his eyes, but he felt a cold hand on his cheek.

He opened his eyes and saw the most beautiful, short-haired brunette with large purple eyes starting directly at him. *Was she there?* Hekaib reached out and touched her cold cheek. It was flesh. Yes…he was saved! "Please…help…me" he managed to stammer. He was very cold. He was not sure if he would ever be warm again.

The woman swam right up to him in the water and smiled sweetly. "Who are you?" she said.

He was confused at the question, but answered anyway, "I am Hekaib, Captain of the Tutankhamen II." The woman smiled and shook her head, then moved closer to him. "No," she whispered. "You are conductor of death. Whenever your crew fired their instruments of death, it created a symphony of suffering and pain." He tried to answer, but no words came out of his mouth. "You have destroyed that which I protect. I am Rusalka. It is my duty to nurture the fields, so the villagers have a full bounty. Those fields are now burning, with no one to put out the fires. Now that you have taken that purpose from me."

Throughout the time she spoke, the woman's hair was wrapping itself tightly around his neck. "Stop…stop…please…" he pleaded. Her hair lifted him straight out of the water and suspended him by his neck; he flailed around helplessly. *Please let me die quickly,* he thought to himself before screaming out in pain—she had the pipe out of his body.

"Ahhhhh!" he screamed. "Kill me…kill me…" he continued to plead. He looked at the tubing that was now in front of him. *That was in my body*!? He watched as more hair entwined itself around the tube. Now what?

Without warning, the tube struck his stomach. He cried out in pain again as he was struck again and again. "Stop…please…" He was rewarded with a hard blow to the face. Stars appeared in front of his eyes, and any energy that once remained was drained out of him. "Kill…me…" Hekaib sobbed aloud.

The woman rose out of the water until they were face to face. "Kill…" was the last word he spoke as the tube struck him square in the head, knocking him unconscious for the very last time.

Sam watched the events unfold from the shore as he held hands with Jessica. It was almost time to go out onto the lake. They had already done their duty, though with one noticeable exception that they would deal with later. He watched one of the massive black ships explode and knew many now needed their assistance. He could feel the presence of the lost, confused souls that now littered the lake. "It's time," he said.

Jessica nodded back in agreement, and they started walking across the lake. "What day is it today?"

"Tuesday." *Tuesday,* he thought. *Why does it always seem like it's Tuesday?* As they neared the fiery wreckage, he could see the souls of the now spectral crewman standing around on the water, unsure of what to do.

"So much death, Sam. When was the last time we saw anything like this?"

"I don't know… It's been quite a few Tuesdays ago, I think." He got a playful slap on the arm for his cheeky answer. He smiled. They would need all the humour they could get to get through tonight. As they approached the first of the crewmen, he held his hands up. "We are not here to hurt you. I am Sam, and this is Jessica. We are here to help you go beyond."

"What has happened to us?" One of the crewmen cried.

"Well…you died." Sam said. There was no use sugar-coating it. "Some of you from the explosion, others while fighting. But it will be okay, I promise you."

"We are dead, how will it be okay?" Another crewman shouted. "What kind of moron are you?" *Moron. Great.* Not all souls went quietly into the night. Some jerks remained jerks, even in death, unfortunately.

"I am not a moron…you died," he said simply.

"How do you know we died?" one of the crewmen said stubbornly.

"You're walking on the water… Do you think that's something you would normally do?" Jessica said. Sam could tell she was fighting not to roll her eyes. "If it is, we need to talk, as you are in the wrong place right now." Everyone finally fell silent. Sam took it as a good thing.

"Are you Osiris?" a third crewman asked.

Sam shook his head. "I am going to help take you to him. All you need to do is grab our hands, and you will see him. It's painless…I promise." No one moved toward him. He didn't blame them. It was a hard concept to grasp, that oneself was dead. Sam walked to them and held out his hands. Jessica did the same, standing beside him. The one that had called him a moron stepped forward and reached out for Jessica's hands. Sam smiled—it was a start.

In a flash, the man was gone. "See, it's painless, as I said."

One by one, they took Jessica's hand. It was often like that. Men went to Jessica while woman gravitated toward him. Neither one took it personally. They were there to do their job— it didn't matter who went to whom. He did not know how much time passed, but they were finally done.

"You were amazing. How do you feel?" he asked Jessica.

She smiled back. "Good." He hugged her tightly. He was thankful that they had remained together in death after what had happened. He looked up and saw that the Soul Moon Convergence was over. The moons were moving away from each other now. There was something else, as well—a large dark cloud that didn't belong there. "Look Jessica. Look who showed up to watch," he said, pointing up to the cloud.

"I could sense His presence when we first arrived. This is all His doing," Jessica said, scowling. Neither one of them liked who dwelled up in the clouds, nor His servants— the Sisterhood.

"I know," he said. One day, vengeance would be his for the loss of his sister, Daniella. He swore it.

"I'm tired."

He agreed. It had been a long night. He couldn't remember the last time they had to help guide these many souls in one night. "Yes. We need our strength after all this. Let's head back to the diner once we are done in the village. Perhaps Mother would be gracious enough to give us one last meal before we move on."

They would need to go to Thebes to catch their runaway soul.

Micrea Drăculești.

Chapter 20

Tutankhamen I—Sighişoara

'Dinner and a Show'

Captain Khaemweset stood beside General Pentu and Chione. They gathered together on the side deck after unloading their cargo of destruction. Their vessel was gently gliding back to the middle of the lake toward the curtain. He noticed Chione still looked a bit peaked from keeping it open for so long. It was a good thing he had prepared in advance; he wanted to make sure that his honoured guests had excellent seats for the carnage that would unfold before their eyes. He had prepared a surprise for them without their knowledge, hoping it would be to their satisfaction.

The Captain clapped his hands twice. Two deck attendants rushed forward to his side, awaiting his command. "Bring the table out with its covering, then the food and wine," he ordered. The attendants scrambled to carry out his commands, disappearing out of sight. He turned to his guests and said, "Even though this is a short trip, I believe in being comfortable. In the presence of such honoured guests, I would be remiss in my hospitality if I could not provide refreshments for this occasion. I ordered some...*special* provisions, which will be coming out momentarily."

Chione and General Pentu grinned at his words. *Excellent.* He watched several of the crew members scurry past and place wooden containers on the deck, stacking them in threes to act as steps. They then placed a large rectangular table down on pre-built risers that he had installed on the deck. He had outdone himself on this one, he knew. A large royal purple cloth was extended above the table to protect the table and guests from the rain.

The attendants hastily brought out chairs and wiped them down. His crew were well organized and diligent in their duties. He had made sure of that. He hadn't had much preparation time to get all this accomplished. He had stressed how important it was, and there was a veiled hint at death if anything went wrong, which helped everything move along smoothly. The food and drinks were quickly brought out and placed on the table. Smiling broadly, he motioned to his guests to sit and enjoy the refreshments. "Please, I would be honoured," Khaemweset said cheerfully.

"Nothing like a show and a meal," General Pentu said, his smile just as wide, and took his seat, waiting as a crew member filled his glass with Blood Cider. Leaning back in his char, he sipped it, his eyes closed in bliss. "Your foresight and thoughtfulness will be mentioned to our glorious Pharaoh," the General added, raising his glass to him.

Khaemweset beamed. This was exactly what we wanted. His assistants had selected excellent vintages, as he had never sampled anything so exquisite. He wondered how much Atria this had cost him, but quickly dismissed the thought. He had told his staff only the finest, and they had succeeded, so it was worth it. Chione sat down and was watching the carnage, as well.

"I am honoured," the Captain said, bowing his head in respect.

"Indeed," she responded, and reached for a piece of cheese. "You are full of surprises, and pleasant ones at that. I can see why you command the namesake of our Pharaoh's fleet. This is an excellent vintage of Blood Cider." She gulped down her glass and raised it for a refill. Khaemweset saw to it first and topped her off. He had learned that a personal touch was always more appreciated.

"I am pleased that you find my humble refreshments to your satisfaction. May I propose a toast?" He lifted his glass. "To our Pharaoh. May Pharaoh Tutankhamen rule for as many years as there are stars in the night sky."

Both General Pentu and Chione raised their glasses and drank with him.

"Secondly, I would like to propose a toast to the destruction of our glorious Pharaoh's enemies. Long may they regret the day that they tried to kill him." Again, they cheered and drank. This was going as well as he had envisioned. The planning of hospitality was just as complex and subtle as any battle plan that the General could dream up.

"The destruction is going more quickly than I anticipated," the General said, emptying his glass. "Where are their Sentinels? If this is their capital, why is it not more heavily fortified and defended? They should have rallied whatever forces to its defence. We heard their warning horns. Disgraceful."

Khaemweset agreed. The attack was going remarkably well. "Perhaps these people think themselves so superior in their abilities that no one would ever attack them," he mused. Chione raised her glass to this, and he took a sip of wine in return. He glanced over at the General—his mood had changed; the General no longer looked like he was enjoying himself. He was still focused on the attack.

"Other than the Spiriduş raids, there is no large centralized threat against the Drăculeşti," Chione said matter-of-factly. "Throughout their history, there have been *viskta* wars, where one family tried to gain control from the ruling family, though on a much smaller scale now than the large battles of old. There used to be so much destruction, but they came together and agreed that if there is a challenge, then it's *viskta* versus *viskta*, so the population could continue their ordinary work and keep everything flowing." He wondered how she knew all this.

No, Khaemweset thought. There had to be large grand battles; then the smartest clan would come out on top, as they proved they outwitted their enemies in the field of battle. "If they don't choose to challenge or make their own clan stronger, then they deserve whatever they get."

Chione tilted her head, as though contemplative. "It leaves the overall population open to attack from an outside source, like us, for example. Look at their lack of defence of their capital. I would be ashamed if I were their Sentinel Commander. I would have actually designed defences, regardless if I knew there were other lands or not."

General Pentu spat on the deck, looking utterly disgusted. Khaemweset felt the same—this was shameful. Other than the irritating sound of the horns, there was nothing.

"Our Pharaoh's family has ruled for several generations, yet the army is still kept strong," Khaemweset said proudly. "It makes sense, as who knows when someone may challenge, or an unknown force may attack. Granted, there is no recorded attack in quite some time, but our leaders, regardless, always kept the army strong."

"Chione nodded. "They do have the Sentinels, which protect the cities and roads, but they are spread out and have no single large force to speak of. They are effective fighters, from what I have been told, but they have never faced anything like our forces. I believe that is why they went down quite quickly, with virtually no resistance."

She did have a point. Khaemweset knew that once the buildings were out of shooting range, their forces would continue with their mission, and the villagers would not be safe anywhere.

"You do not think that the remaining population would rise together and hunt us? Try to take their village back?" Khaemweset asked, since Chione seemed to know so much. "I believe all the other *visktas* will start fighting each other until one emerges victorious, or the Spiriduş may move in and take control," Chione said confidently. "Either way, there will not be a ruler for quite some time. By the time one emerges as a contender, our Pharaoh will have already taken control as a saviour and they will look to our glorious Pharaoh to lead them."

Khaemweset had to admit that she spoke sense.

"Also, it's not their way," she continued. "If the ruling *viskta* fled, it would show weakness. They would be branded as cowards and be hunted down and killed. There are perks to be the ruling *viskta*, but there are some disadvantages, as well."

Khaemweset wondered what the other disadvantages were. "Would they truly accept our Pharaoh's rule, even though he is not of their kind?" the General asked.

Chione nodded. "Yes, as he would have an army and a fleet, and be the strongest force, which would mean the strongest *viskta*. I believe over time, challengers may arise. Even in our own history, various rulers one by one have fallen as challengers stepped forward. It is the cycle of rulers," Chione said nonchalantly.

The General's face darkened. "What about the Spiriduş you mentioned? Do they have the strength to take over all the lands and pose a threat to our Pharaoh when it's time to liberate the lands?" The General was pressing Chione, and Khaemweset was impressed at how well the woman was holding her ground.

"The Spiriduş raid and steal, but other than that, it's the Sentinels who pose the greatest threat now, as it stands. I could see the Sentinels joining the bandits, as there would be no ruling *viskta*, therefore no one paying for their services anymore. This will help with the downfall of the lands and keep everything in chaos." Chione said smoothly, her beautiful smile reaching her eyes. The General nodded. Chione polished her glass and raised it, indicating she had more to add. "Either way, if they attack the village, they will be weakened considerably. It will take quite a long time for them to recover, and our glorious Pharaoh will be ruler long before then."

Silence took over as they watched the destruction unfold, occasionally sipping Blood Cider and nibbling on cheese and fruit. Khaemweset noticed the General and Chione were content to simply sit back and watch as their forces did their work, razing the village to the ground.

"Oh look, the Mummies we instructed have already made it to the castle," Chione said excitedly, pointing at the figures in the distance. Khaemweset squinted to try to make out what she was talking about. Before their forces had disembarked, several Mummies were given orders to make their way up the castle as quickly as they could—to terminate everything and everyone they encountered within and around it.

Khaemweset scrutinized the General, who was still watching intently for any signs of trouble. The General was in charge, and any failure would not go unpunished. *Yes,* he thought, the Pharaoh would be incredibly happy indeed with the results. He doubted a single Mummy or Ushabti Warrior had been taken down so far. The villagers were extremely fast at running; perhaps they were used to running like cowards instead of staying to defend their homes. He would have died, if necessary.

A loud roar sounded in the distance. From the village? Could it be possible? Surely, they were far enough out into the harbour that any person's scream would be drowned out by the chaos. He wasn't even sure the sound was human.

He scanned the village, not knowing what he was looking for, but sensed that he would know if he saw it. "Did anyone hear that?" he asked the others.

"It sounded almost like a primal scream of some sort," the General said astutely. "What kind of creatures do they have here, Chione?"

"I'm sure it's just being in a strange place, and the Blood Cider we have drunk has your senses confused, gentlemen. Let us just relax and enjoy the show. Soon we will be back home, and you both can sleep off all the spirits you have drunk tonight."

Khaemweset didn't think it should be brushed off so easily. "Is the curtain staying open dependent on when the rain stops?"

"As this is the first occasion in many years since I have opened a curtain, time is limited. As I continue to use my powers, I will be able to keep curtains open much longer, and larger if required. Perhaps I may even create a permanent curtain if the Pharaoh desires it."

The thought boggled Khaemweset mind, but the General's eyes lit up. "Imagine having a gateway, we could move supplies and people between at will."

"Indeed, that would be most beneficial to our Pharaoh," Khaemweset said. "The resources and slaves, all at his disposal. No longer would our people have to do the hard labourer's jobs; they would become the taskmasters. Yes...all this wealth for our Pharaoh, this is truly remarkable." The possibilities were endless with the conquering of this land and what they could pillage. He knew being involved in the invasion assured him more wealth than he could have possibly dreamed of. How unexpected all this had been.

"Yes Captain, it could be," the General said. "I have found even the best-laid plans are always subject to unexpected events. This land holds resources and people that our Pharaoh could put to great use, but one step at a time. We have all the time required to plan this conquest thoroughly, and I recommend we use it to our advantage. Let our forces do their jobs properly and weaken any resistance."

"You are correct, General Pentu, but I think our Pharaoh is more ambitious than you think," Chione said, the knowing in her tone never faltering. "I think he will want to liberate these lands sooner rather than later."

"Yes, that may be true, too," the General conceded.

"The rain will be stopping shortly," Chione stated, and he looked over at her and nodded. Soon, he would order the vessel through the curtain. And after what they had heard, he was confident that it was better to leave sooner rather than later.

He watched Chione get up and walk to the bow of the ship, clutching the Nexus Crystal around her neck. "Look," the General called, pointing up toward the nearest buildings. A man was jumping from crumbled rooftop to crumbled rooftop. How?

Khaemweset continued to stare in amazement until the man landed on the harbour, hopped atop the post where the harbour bell hung and made one giant leap through the air toward them. *No, it's not possible...* There was no chance the man could make it to the ship. They were much too far away now.

And yet the man was flying. For what seemed an eternity, he watched, awestruck, until he landed on the Tutankhamen II. As soon as his feet touched the deck, he was killing the crewmembers. *By the Gods…the attacker is biting into the crew members necks…drinking their blood!* Khaemweset looked over worriedly at the General, who was also staring in utter disbelief. They watched in silence at what was happening as crewman after crewman were slaughtered in the attacker's path. If the man wasn't drinking their blood, he was pulling hearts out of their chests!

Khaemweset was transfixed by the horrific scene. Finally, the General got up beside him. "Left side archers, direct aim to the Tutankhamen II immediately! Use fire arrows only."

What? Khaemweset was going to protest. All the archers needed to resume their oaring duties and move back through the curtain immediately.

The General sneered at him. "Follow my orders!" He knew he had almost overstepped. What would that have meant for him when they returned to Thebes? He turned to watch the arrows rain down on their sister ship. "Port side archers, odd numbered only, fire arrows aimed for the hull of the Tutankhamen II. The rest on the deck of the ship—and do not stop firing until that vessel is sinking into the lake!" the General bellowed.

Khaemweset looked at Chione, who was holding the Nexus Crystal and watching the arrows fly with great interest.

Was it him, or was she finding the destruction of the other ship amusing? She was also not showing any regard for any of the crew members that had fallen victim to their attacker.

Flames spread across the Tutankhamen II, but not fast enough for his liking. None of the arrows had even touched the attacker, just striking the crew. Nothing was slowing the attacker down. More drastic action was needed. The gap between the two ships was slowly widening, but he knew that the man could make the jump. They needed to go through the curtain *now*. But they couldn't leave without their prize.

"Fire at the clay pipes on the deck!" The General shouted. Of course—the pipes were filled with oil—mystically enhanced oil, so an explosion would cause even greater damage.

The screams from the Tutankhamen II grew louder. It pained him that his crew was responsible for it. An explosion rocked the stern, thick smoke billowing across the deck. It was starting to sink. Khaemweset was torn; he wanted to order all the archers back to their oars, but there were signals from the shore—the Medjays had captured their prize.

Khaemweset called out to the General, "Look. The signal! Our prize is on the way!" He turned to the crewmembers nearest to him. "Prepare the staffs. We need to get the Medjays' watercraft aboard as quickly as possible." The crewmembers scrambled around for their long staffs. They were going to hoist up the Medjays' boat when returned from the shore. It was hard to see where it was, as their vision was clouded by the thick smoke, still emanating from the village.

"There!" a crewmember called out. He could barely make out the watercraft, but it was slowly becoming more visible as it neared.

Moments later, it arrived. His crew was ready. "Hook and lift our prize up!" he yelled.

"Don't drop it! Keep pulling it upward!" the General said, appearing at his side. They were so close. *Finally*! Now parallel to the deck, the Medjays' prize was brought onto the deck and the stretcher unhooked.

"Secure him! Bring him below deck! Five guards on him always!" Khaemweset screamed as the unconscious body was dragged below deck.

Khaemweset caught Chione's mouth curl into a smile. He yearned to know what was going on in her mind but doubted he ever would.

The stern was starting to go through the curtain. Good. What stories the crew was going to tell their wives and children tonight. This was undoubtedly the most exciting night of their lives. It was only the first of many, he knew. They were all going to be legends throughout the lands.

An enormous explosion brought him back to reality, and he watched Captain Hekaib flying in the air. "Goodbye," Khaemweset mouthed as his long-time friend splashed into the water. He would miss his fellow captain. They had spent many a night lamenting over the trials of being a Captain in the Royal Navy.

They were almost through. Something from the sinking ship was flying toward them. The attacker? He stood there in awe as the man soared toward his vessel. This one was tough to kill!

Chione blew the man a kiss, and the curtain closed, slicing his body in half as he leapt in attempt to go through. The man's face was frozen in shock seconds before the top half of his body fall into the water.

Khaemweset took a moment to absorb it all. The fear and chaos, the obliteration of the village, the unexpected destruction of the Tutankhamen II. He looked back at Chione, who began giggling and then laughing loudly, almost hysterically. Chills ran through his body. *What kind of woman was she,* he wondered, though was not sure if he wanted to know the answer.

***

Massika stood there completely drenched by the rain, but she did not care. Her husband had told her he would not be there more than an hour, and she intended to keep him to his word. She had not been completely bored. The lightening show had kept her attention. It was beautiful and terrifying at the same time. How much destructive potential did it have?

She glanced around and saw that she was still the only one on the pier, still. She could not imagine being there to see her beloved Pentu off to whatever mission their Pharaoh called upon him to complete.

A massive black shape snapped her attention back. They had returned! She watched anxiously for both vessels to appear.

There was only one.

Both vessels had been virtually identical and unmarked, so she could not determine which one it was. The massive black vessel emerged from under the lightening, becoming more clearly visible to her. The lightening disappeared, and the air was calm once again. The rain subsided, as well. Everything was at peace.

It had to be the Tutankhamen I! She did not know what to do if it wasn't. Her beloved Pentu was not allowed to leave her, ever. Of course, she knew one day he would of old age, but not before that. She had made him promise on their wedding night, and he had agreed.

As it got closer to the dock, she still couldn't figure out which one it was. What had happened to cause the loss of one of those behemoth vessels? They looked indestructible. She continued to watch as it glided toward the dock, stern first. Then she realized that it was heading to where the Tutankhamen I had originally been docked. Her husband was still alive! Relief rushed over her. She waited patiently as the ship backed up slowly to its pier. She had all the time in the world now. It slowly glided backwards, positioning itself. She marvelled at how skilled the oarsmen were at their duties.

As the vessel was almost alongside the pier, she could start to hear the commotion— commands being called out for the final docking preparations. Where was her husband? She spied him on deck as he walked to the edge of the vessel, and they locked eyes. She knew with only one vessel returning, something had gone horribly wrong. And the look in her husband's eyes was not of victory. It was of sadness. It would be an exceptionally long night tonight, but she did not care. She would provide whatever her husband required of her. It was her duty. Pentu looked tired. It was time for him to retire and spend his days and nights with her. His duty to the Kingdom surely would be over now.

The vessel came to a halt, and the walking planks were lowered to the pier. Pentu was always the first to disembark, but when she moved to go to the plank, he gestured for her not to. *What was happening?*

Several crewmen along with Royal Guards disembarked first, carrying something. *No...someone?* She watched as they scurried away with a strangely dressed unconscious man, and she wondered who they had captured. Pentu disembarked next, and he walked down towards her. They did well to conceal their emotions in public at times like this, as it would be undignified. She moved close enough to the plank so that when her husband walked by, their hands could touch. Just like when he had left.

A Royal Carriage arrived. The door was opened for her husband, and he entered. He looked at her as he pulled away, and she knew her husband was off to the Royal Pyramid. It was going to be a long night. She decided to go home and rest until his return. She would need all the strength she could muster, as the look in her husband's eyes showed that his energy had been drained from this mission.

Interlude 0.5

Sighişoara – Europea

Micrea slowly opened his eyes. He felt cold. The last thing he remembered was feeling intense pain and his head hurting from when he fell forward after being stabbed. Had he blacked out and that was why his head felt groggy? Why was he so cold? He blew on his hands to warm them, but he felt no heat from his breath. *Odd!* He managed to get to his feet, and his feet carried him to the corpses of Kazia and her father. He cringed at the state of them—part of Kazia's neck had been…eaten? There was only one person that could have done that—Radu. Mr. Hindrick's neck, too. Blood flowed from it like lava spilling from a volcano. Father had done that…

Father must have been truly desperate to have done something as horrible as this. He hated that part of who he was. Though he had been born the way he was and passed the Rite of Manhood, he was never supremely comfortable with what he really was. Looking down at the corpses, he sighed heavily. *Poor Vladimir.* His brother really liked her. He hoped Vladimir never found out about this.

"Father!" his voice echoed. He spotted him, but he leapt away. "Father!" he screamed again, but still nothing.

"They can't hear you," a friendly voice said softly to him. He knew that voice; he turned to face Tomas. He was a friend of Vladimir's, though looked much paler than he remembered.

"Why couldn't father hear me? I was only several feet away… Radu!" Perhaps his brother would hear him. He ran to him, before he could follow their father, and reached out to grasp his shoulder, but was unable to. "Radu!" he yelled in his ear, but his brother couldn't see or hear him. It was like he was invisible.

A strange small wooden cylinder object struck his brother's neck, and he turned to see where it came from. Three strangely dressed men were partly visible behind a collapsed wall.

Micrea watched his brother rush to attack the strangers but was taken down by several more darts. Damnit! He went to charge the nearest attacker, but when he went for a punch, his fist was not able to hit the man. It stopped inches away from his target's face. It was as if he hit some sort of barrier. *What was happening?*

"I think we are dead," Erik whispered to him. Micrea spun around in shock. How did Vladimir's friend just suddenly appear?

Dead... dead? The thought was incomprehensible to him; he was a Drăculești. His own screams reverberated in his head. *Nooooo! I am too young to die!* This was all just a bad dream. A waking nightmare. That had to be it. Soon he would wake up in his bed, hoping he remembered none of this.

Marku, Kazia's betrothed, was staggering towards him. There was blood all over his clothes from multiple wounds. The boy was dying. "Marku!" Micrea yelled, then reached his arms out to catch his fall, but Marku went right through him, falling to the ground.

"It's true!" Tomas shouted. Around Micrea, more and more dead people started to show up. Tomas, Erik, a couple of Sentinels, whose names he couldn't remember. Micrea looked back down at Marku, who was crawling on his stomach toward Kazia. They were supposed to be married. It was fitting that they were going to die together. Marku pulled himself toward Kazia and covered Kazia's hand with his own. Micrea watched the light leave his eyes. Beside him, Tomas let out an anguished cry.

"We are all dead," Micrea said quietly. They all stared at one another, not knowing what to do. Detecting movement nearby, Micrea turned around. Two Sentinel Patrolmen were slowly walking toward them. What were their names? Olaf and Sven? Were they dead, too? The newcomers stood there looking around silently, confusion in their eyes.

"Everything will be alright," a smooth female voice said to him. A few feet away appeared a beautiful blonde woman standing next to a lanky, dark haired man.

"Are you dead too?" Micrea asked.

"No," the man replied. "My name is Sam. This is Jessica. We are here to take you beyond."

Beyond? What did he mean? "Beyond what?" Micrea demanded.

"Beyond where you are now," the woman named Jessica said. "To the next stage in your journey. Take my hand, I promise it will not hurt." She held out her hands to him. He stared at them; all this was too much for him to take in. This whole night had been some twisted nightmare, with no signs of ending.

Tomas stepped forward.

"No!" Micrea shouted, but it was too late. Upon touching Jessica's hand, he disappeared before everyone's eyes. Olaf and Sven stepped forward next. Before he could call out to them, they, too, disappeared in a flash.

"Micrea, it's perfectly fine to be scared," Sam said, taking a step toward him. "You saw, nothing bad happened. He went to a place with no pain or suffering. You can join them—just take Jessica's hand."

He didn't want to go on. He was not ready. His family still needed him. "No."

"Micrea, if you force us to take you, it will not be pleasant," Jessica cautioned, and started to approach him. *No!* He needed to get out of here with Radu. He turned to pick up Radu's body, but it was gone. It was being carried off by unknown men! Jessica moved towards him.

"No," he said again. He turned on his heel and bolted toward the harbour, hoping to catch up to where the strangers were taking his brother. In his path stood a broken wall, and he decided to test a theory. He ran right through it, unhindered. *Yes,* he thought to himself as he dashed down the street to the harbour as fast as he could, running right through any obstacle that lay before him. Every bone in his body told him he needed to get to his brother.

He turned a corner, and there Jessica was, holding out her hand, legs apart in a defiant stance. He dove headfirst between her legs and got back to his feet, continuing his sprint to the harbour. He may be dead, but he was determined to do whatever it took not to leave.

Where were they taking Radu? As he sensed Jessica's presence behind him, he rolled forward to escape the hand of doom that would take him beyond. Spotting his brother, he sprinted toward him. They had loaded Radu onto a small watercraft which was now moving deeper into the lake. He decided to put death to the test—he carried his sprint over on water. He was doing it. *Yes!*

He ran so fast he was able to catch up to the watercraft and jump onto it. "Don't worry Radu, I got you," he said as he looked ahead at their destination—a massive black vessel.

"Help us!" Micrea heard, and he turned to where the voices had come from. People were standing on the water. *What the…?* Some were holding their heads in their hands. Others were wandering around, their limbs missing—but all not knowing what was happening. Then it dawned on him…they were all dead, too.

More voices caught his attention, and he looked up. The crew of the large vessel were lowering long wooden hooks down to their watercraft. What were they doing? He looked around at Radu and noticed he was laying on a wooden stretcher with holes in the corners; they were going to lift him onto their ship. He watched as the three men hooked Radu's stretcher and used hand signals for his brother to be pulled up. "I won't leave you," he vowed. Micrea didn't know what was going to happen, but whatever it was, Radu would not have to face it alone. He would never leave his brother's side. He only had two problems besides being dead: Sam and Jessica. He spotted them watching him from the shoreline.

They did not look happy.

Chapter 21

Dark Woods—Europea

'Soul Moon Draw'

Vladimir Drăculeşti stared unblinking into the reflection on the water. *That's not my face!* Or was it? Did drinking the rainbow-coloured water change him into a strange, exotic-looking girl? He quickly looked at his hands and at his clothes to make sure they were still the same. They were. It must have been some sort of water creature trying to trick him. He yelled defiantly, "Begone, you foul water creature, or whatever you are! You are not welcome here!" He hoped that would do the trick.

The reflection staring back was of bewilderment. Perhaps he was wrong. He wasn't sure what to do next.

"I'm not a water creature, I'm a princess. I should like for you to treat me with more respect."

He laughed, replying smugly, "There are no princesses. I knew it—you are a trickster." He was proud of himself to see through the ruse. Though, the face staring back at him did pull him in. Her long black hair…and her eyes were different. They were not oval like his; hers were almond shaped. How odd, he thought. He was about to ask her about them, but she interrupted.

"I am Princess Pingyang of the Clan Tang. My father is Emperor Gaozu of Tang, ruler of all the lands, so you need to apologize. I demand to be treated with the respect I am owed."

How could one make such an incredible story up? This made no sense. He had never heard of any emperor or knew of any clans, or whatever Tang was. "What the frack is a Clan Tang? Is that a kind of seafood that you eat?" The nerve of tricksters; he was smarter than that. The 'Princess' gave him a look of utter disgust. Serves her right for whatever trick she was trying to play on him.

"Ta le me!"

What did that mean?

"What uncouth barbarian are you? Were you not taught proper etiquette when speaking to royalty? Are you always this brusque?"

"Listen, *'Princess'*…I don't even know what 'brusque' even means. All I know is there must have been something in the rainwater that I drank to be having this bizarre waking dream. At least I think I am awake." For a moment he thought he might be asleep in his bed. He was starting to get freaked out.

"You are so rude! I have properly introduced myself, and you have not. You are without a doubt the most frustrating takin goat herder that I have ever come across," the Princess scolded him.

"Hey! I am Vladimir of the *viskta* Drăculeşti. My father is Vlad Drăculeşti, ruler of Sighişoara and all the lands far and wide. I ain't no *'herder,'* Princess," he fired back.

He watched her face carefully, glistening on the water's surface. He could tell she was as confused and angry as he was. As he continued to gaze at her, realization set in at just how beautiful she was. She appeared exotic. Her fawn-coloured eyes were striking, along with her olive skin. The combination was truly breathtaking. He wiped the rain off his face so he could take another look at her. The more he looked at her, the more in awe he was of her features. What was happening to him? Where was she?

"Where are your lands located, as I have never heard of them," she said, asking the very thing he wondered. "Are they by Mount Hiromashi? You know, the biggest mountain in all the land?"

"No, I have not heard of this mountain before. Sighişoara is the capital of our lands, and it rests beside the lake that leads out to the ocean. Mount Hiro—sorry, I can't pronounce it—is unknown to me." He could tell by her expression that his answer saddened her. He felt dejected, as well, though he wasn't quite sure why.

"I have never heard of Sighişoara, either. The name is baffling. I knew from Xifeng that the Soul Moon Convergence was powerful; but to show me someone from a strange place is absolutely fantastic."

Xifeng? What kind of bizarre name was that? "I'm sorry, Princess, I don't know what to tell you. The Soul Moon Convergence? Wait…my mother talked to me about that earlier today. She asked me if I thought I had a soulmate." Okay, this was starting to make sense to him.

"You do have a soulmate. We are talking are we not? I know I believe I have a soulmate, though I must admit, I was not expecting…you."

He could tell she was as tentative about all this as he was. They both had no idea what to expect or what to do. *She had been expecting someone else?*

He stared blankly into the water. This was not possible. Kazia was his soulmate. "No!" he said much louder than he meant to.

The look of shock on her face must have rivaled his own. "What do you mean 'no'? Hello, we are somehow able to communicate, and we from places neither one of us has heard of before. Are you…simple?"

Simple! Frack me. "Listen here, Princess…Kazia is the one that I want." As soon as he said the words, he instantly regretted them. The look on the Princess's face unexpectedly pained him. But it was true. All he wanted was Kazia. The look of shock of Pingyang's face unexpectedly shook him to the core. He felt a twinge of pain in his heart. What was happening?

"H-how… This is not right! I was told I would meet my soulmate. Xifeng told me I would. I-I believed her!" Pingyang stammered.

"I'm sorry, Princess" he said, hoping the words did not sound empty to her.

"This should not be happening. My soulmate is supposed to want me as much as I want them. We are to live happily ever after. Instead I got…you!"

He stood over the stone, not knowing what to say back. She was his soulmate? He wanted Kazia. She was everything to him. He came here to find a way to impress her father, not…this! He stood there, letting the idea that this stranger could be meant for him sink in, and he noticed that she was looking up at something. "What are you looking at?"

"Do you see the lightening in the sky, too?"

He looked up past the surrounding trees to see lightening in the distance though it was barely visible. "Yes, I have never seen anything like that before. Wait, how can you see it, as well? Are you sure you don't live in some banished land because of *viskta*'s crimes?" He could tell she had no idea what he was talking about.

"What is a *viskta*? Sounds like a strange…disease. You are not diseased, are you?"

He chuckled. "No, that's cute."

She smiled back. "There are no banished lands. Criminals are executed or sent to prison for justice. It's possible there are places I haven't heard of, but nothing about banished families that I know of."

He continued to gaze into the water. Her eyes were so alluring. This Princess was beautiful. More so than Kazia. Even though she was as soaking wet as he was. At her next question, he was jolted out of his thoughts.

"What's wrong? Why are you staring at me? I know I must look hideous to you with the rain ruining my hair and face paint—are you listening to me?"

He quickly stammered a reply. "S-sorry, Princess. I was just...just…" He wasn't sure what to say; thankfully, she cut him off before he could say something "simple".

"Just what?" The Princess demanded. He was probably making her feel self-conscious.

"I was just looking at you...and…I think you are very...beautiful," he managed to get out. He hoped the darkness concealed the redness on his face.

The way her eyes widened, and cheeks flushed told him his response was not what she expected. He stood there, not knowing whether to apologize or not. To his surprise, she smiled. He smiled back, his stomach feeling as toasty as a fresh baked roll right out of the oven.

"Prettier than your precious Kazia?" And just like that, her smile dissipated. The warm feeling went ice cold inside of him.

He was such an asshat. His mind went blank.

"I thought so! You just said that to pretend to be nice. You are a false soulmate! Where is my real one? What have you done with him?"

"No, Princess, you are beautiful! Even though you look like a drowned rat—"

"Drowned rat?! Who are you to talk? You look like drowned takin herder!"

"What is a frackin' takin herder?"

They both fell silent, neither of them knowing what to say or do. After a few more awkward minutes, the Princess finally asked, "How did you find your Soul Rock?"

"What's a Soul Rock?"

Wrinkling her brow, and with a slight roll of her eyes, she said slowly, like she was explaining math to a child, "It's the rock you are standing at. What were you doing before you started talking to me?"

"I was out trying to find a hellsteed, as no one has ever captured one before. When I found one, I heard your voice from this rock. So, I came over…and the hellsteed left." He let out a big sigh.

"I'm sorry. What is a hellsteed? I have never heard of one before."

He looked over to where it had been and then back into the water. "It's the fastest and strongest horse of all. Its mane and tail are made of fire, and its eyes glow like red embers. It's said if you catch one, it will never leave your side. There are other special ones, like those that can even run on water. Part of me hoped they were real, and part of me thought it was a just dumb story, but I went out anyway tonight, and I found one. Now talking to you, I am beginning to think anything is possible. Like finding another one," he said, cracking a grin. Beaming, Pingyang nodded. Perhaps they could be civil to each other after all.

He felt the warm water on his face and noticed the rain was not hitting the small pool; he could see her face clearly. Where was she? None of the places she mentioned were familiar to him, and he had been forced to study all the lands that were known. Was is it possible that the maps were incomplete? He thought back to the map of the lands in the castle; some of them were unnamed if he remembered correctly. He decided to ask: "Are you on an island somewhere, perhaps off the coast of Zingarish?"

The blank look in her eyes was a definite no. *Hmm*. So, not any lands that he knew of, and not any islands either. Was it possible that she lived in the sky? No. He dismissed the idea; that was too weird. The only other place was the ocean, but no expeditions had ever returned, so everyone knew that if you ventured too far, you fell off and died.

Perhaps not. Perhaps no one had died, just captured. "Have you ever seen or heard of any vessels from unknown places entering your land unexpectedly? Anyone strange-looking, like me, with a lighter complexion?" It was a shot in the dark.

She shook her head. That didn't mean that it wasn't possible; after all, she was a girl—lots happened that she didn't know about. "I guess it's possible, but no one has ever mentioned anything to me. I do know that every expedition that has left our lands has never returned."

That startled him. Surely, with the Princess living in some faraway land, meant something. There had to be a way to get to her.

"Really? All the expeditions we have sent out have never come back either." He sensed she was starting to grow frustrated at the situation. They were both someplace that the other knew nothing about. How were they ever going to meet? Even though Kazia was the one he wanted, there was something about the Princess; he wanted to meet her. It seemed there was no point of reference between their respective locations, so he did not know how to even make a meeting possible.

He realized she had been rather quiet. "What's wrong, Princess?"

She looked worried. "Where are you right now?"

"In the Dark Woods, outside my village of Sighişoara. Where are you?"

"In the inner courtyard of the Imperial Palace of Chang'an, where I live. I can tell you have never heard of any of the places I have mentioned...so how are we ever to meet? If you even wanted to meet. You have your Kazia after all," she said sadly.

He sensed she feared the answer. Meeting her...the thought was becoming rather appealing. In fact, the more he thought about it, the more his insides heated. Though his father would hunt him down if he just disappeared. "I don't know, but I think we can find a way. I mean if this is possible...anything's possible."

She smiled up at him. "What's it like where you live?"

"It's nice. Sighişoara is on the shores of Lake Sfanta Ana, which goes out to the ocean. Sighişoara is also the capital, and it's surrounded to the left by rolling hills and on the right by farmland. There are various roads that lead out to the other smaller villages in the lands. The Sentinels do their best to guards against the Spiriduş, but they seem to be getting bolder lately.

"The Spiriduş are a gang of criminals that loot and plunder—and need to be destroyed. Father and my two older brothers are leaving in the morning to visit the last raid that the Spiriduş carried out. Father is finally going to do something about them, I have no doubt that he will end them once and for all. I must stay with Mother and make sure she is safe," he said. He felt at ease taking to Pingyang. Even though it had started rocky, it was becoming natural. Like he had always known her. "The village has bakers and smithies and carpenters and all sorts of tradecraft. There is always lots of bustling going on, and our castle sits higher than the rest of the village. Father says it's so we can see those that we are to protect better, and I admit the view is quite nice."

"What about your family, what are they like?"

"I am named after my father, Vlad, as he is the ruler of all the lands. Our family won the *viskta* wars and emerged the strongest, so we rule until we are challenged and defeated. Though, I do not think that will ever happen, as no one is stronger than Father. He is firm yet fair—he despises killing. But I have heard rumours that he once slaughtered an entire Spiriduş camp by himself. I'm not supposed to know, but once the Drăculeşti hit a certain age, they go through a rite of passage of sorts. Father has not sat with me and told me everything, but I do know, if we fail at the ritual, we die. But if we can adapt, we grow stronger—stronger than anyone else. It begins when we are in our late teen years, but it's different for everyone. I do have a question, Princess: You said earlier that I was not who you were expecting. Who were you expecting?" Vladimir hoped this would give him a breather. He could not remember speaking to a girl for so long at one time.

Pingyang looked away awkwardly as he looked at her in the water. The Princess had her sights on someone else, as well? "There is Duizhu Chao. Leader of the Dragon Squadron. He likes me…quite a bit, I think. Yes, I thought I might see him in the reflection. Though he does have attributes I appreciate, I do not gush over him, like you do with your Kazia."

"I think I understand, Princess. I am sorry I am not Chao." Vladimir wished he hadn't asked the question and was not sure what to say next.

"Tell me about this rite that you spoke of."

He breathed a small sigh of relief. The subject was changed. "I know Father will be there, so that will help when my time comes. As for the rite itself, I do not know anything about it. What I do know is that both my brothers came back different. Not in a good way either. They are still my brothers, but they're not, really. If that makes sense." He hoped it did.

"Is being a Drăculeşti special? Do all young men where you live go through this?"

He shook his head, "No. I don't know what makes us so special. All I know is soon it will be my turn. I hope I am up to whatever this rite of passage is."

She flashed a radiant smile. "I know you will be."

Vladimir's insides once again heated up. Her smile lit his whole world. "What about you, Princess. What's your father like?" he asked, wondering if the life of a princess was similar to his life at all.

"My father is Emperor Gaozu of Tang. He is the undisputed ruler of all the land. He is wise and very smart. He can have a sense of humour, though it has been some time since I have heard it. I can barely remember the last time he laughed. I don't get to spend a lot of time with him. I used to cherish it, not anymore. From what I have heard through whispers, he can be cruel."

"I am sorry, Princess, that your father is such an…asshat." He hoped he wasn't offending her with the comment.

She screwed up her face. "What is…asshat?"

He chuckled. "Umm…someone that acts in a way they shouldn't," he said, and she smiled back.

"I like asshat," she said. *Cool*. "He has grown more distant—his eyes have become darker and colder because of what happened to my mother. Her name is Duchess Dou. She was the most beautiful woman in the land. She has an illness. They do not know how to make her better, so she lays in bed all day, not moving. I want to go visit her, but I was told that I might catch what she has, so I am forbidden to see her anymore. Sometimes I sneak a peek through the door to see her...just lying there. It makes me sad. I know that Father tried everything to cure her, but nothing worked. I hope one day she gets better...I remember what it feels like to be in her arms...and I miss that."

"I am sorry, Pingyang." He thought he had it rough sometimes. Her parents were a mess.

"I have no brothers or sisters," she continued, "as my mom was young when she married my father and shortly after that, she became sick. I have lots of cousins and nieces and nephews that I can play with when they visit the castle, which is not often. Most of the time I'm with the masters, learning about stuff I don't know that I'll ever need; all I have ever been told is, 'when you get older, you will marry a husband and have lots of kids.' I cannot rule as a woman, so I need to be married off to keep the Tang line going."

"Oh, I'm sorry you are being forced to marry someone. Sometimes here that happens, as well, though generally we can choose, if both families agree to the marriage. If there is a blood feud between two *viskta*, however, then they are not allowed to marry." He thought about Kazia. She, too, was being forced to marry someone—unless he could stop it. "Kazia…she…is being forced to marry someone else. I thought…I don't know. Maybe it's best I don't interfere. I am conflicted about so many things. I need to wrap my head around all this. And I am sorry about your mother...I wish I could help in some way. I would not want to be without my mother either."

Pingyang smiled. "Thank you. I am sorry about Kazia. If you are meant to be together, you will find a way."

They fell silent for a few beats and stared at each other, almost as if trying to memorize each other's appearance.

And then Vladimir felt his whole body stop. He couldn't breathe. He was surrounded by white light for a flash as his world began to move in slow motion. He raised his hand and it left a rainbow streak in the air as he did, He exclaimed, "You're west of me!"

"What?"

"I-I don't know how I know that…if that makes any sense. It's like I can sense...your general direction. It's odd, it's like something just hit me."

Pingyang's eye lit up. "Yes...I know what you mean. It was like my whole body stopped working. It was just for a minute. Since this happened to you, I think that there may be some way. Maybe...I don't know. Like we have direction-sense to each other. It's romantic."

Romantic? At first, he was taken aback, but he thought about it for a second, and smirked. "Yeah, I guess so." He laughed, and they both fell into a fit of giggles. "I am glad I met you, Princess. I don't even mind getting completely drenched. Mother is going to be cross, but I don't care."

"Me either, meeting my soulmate is worth it," she said, continuing to laugh. He was still conflicted. He had been so focused on Kazia, the thought of liking another girl was foreign to him. Yet, here he was talking to one, and liking her more with every passing second. He didn't know why it felt so good to talk to her; what he did know was that talking to a girl never felt this easy. The more he spoke to her, the more his chest filled with warmth. He should have been tired and cold and miserable, but he wasn't. He continued to gaze down into her eyes, and as they gazed back up at him, time stood still. Neither he nor the Princess uttered a word; it was like they were trying to stay in the moment. The world melted away.

He was going to speak, but he caught a scent in the wind. It was smoke.

He looked over by the lightening that still danced in the sky. There was a large orangish green glow coming off the top of the trees not far off from the lightening. He started to panic that the forest might be on fire. He listened intently, but he heard no crackling. What was causing that glow? "There's something off happening in the sky Princess, and smoke in the air...a lot. It stretches out quite a bit, and it's in the direction...of...." He stopped, unable to speak.

"Vladimir...Vladimir...!" he heard from below, but he couldn't move. He was petrified in place. He now understood where the glow was coming from.

"Vladimir!" he heard again; slowly, he turned his gaze downwards. "My village...it's on fire...I have to go...my family...I have to go...my family." The Princess looked distressed that he had to leave, but he tore himself from the Soul Rock and raced toward the massive glow in the sky, his heart feeling more painful with each step. He tore through the forest as fast as he could, hoping his family was still alive, and that the Princess would forgive him for leaving her. The last thing he had heard the Princess say was to come find her. But he had taken off before he could respond. Guilt came over him as he realized that she did not know if he had heard her or not, nor whether he was going to go look for her. He wanted to run back and tell her he would, but he needed to make sure his family was safe.

Chapter 22

Imperial Palace—Chang'an

'Blind Love'

Inside the inner courtyard, Princess Pingyang stared down at the fountain in disbelief. This wasn't supposed to be happening. Tonight was supposed to be the best night of her life.

It was and wasn't. It never dawned on her that her soulmate might like another girl. Kazia. *What is so special about Kazia? Why Kazia? Kazia is being forced to marry someone she doesn't love? Does Kazia love Vladimir?*

She continued to stare into the reflection-less water, saddened by the sudden turn of events. At first, he was frustrating, but then it was…nice. And now it was over because his village was on fire, in some strange land that she had never heard of. The look on his face...he had been truly terrified at what he saw. She hoped that his family was alright. From what she understood, his family was powerful, so they should be okay.

She looked up. The Soul Moon Convergence hung in the night's sky, as majestic as ever. She was still being rained on, but she welcomed it.

Without warning, a powerful hand gripped her shoulder, and she spun around to face two Imperial Palace guards.

"You know the curfew, Princess," the brawnier of the two said. "You have broken it. We are taking you to your father in the Imperial Throne room, where you can explain your actions." *What if the guards overheard everything?*

They grabbed her by her arms and led her out of the inner courtyard and into the palace, where they dragged her down the halls all the way to the Imperial Throne room. She tried to squirm her arms out of their grasp, but they only squeezed tighter. "I'm going to tell my father about this cruel treatment! You will be sorry you ever laid a hand on me—I will tell him to cut both your hands off. Now, let me go!" But they ignored her, hauling her to the throne room. When she entered, her father was seated around a large square table with several advisors that she recognized, but whose names were lost on her. Xifeng was there, as well. They were all looking down at a large parchment that looked to be a map.

Tearing his gaze away from the map, he got off his chair, and walked around the table to her. "What is the meaning of this? Why is my daughter here, and why is she completely drenched?" her father shouted, his booming voice echoing across the room.

The brawnier guard that had grabbed her stepped forward. "We were on patrol in the inner courtyard, and we heard a noise. We found the Princess speaking to…no one. She was standing there in the rain, alone. Being out past curfew, talking to herself in the middle of the night during a downpour, is highly unusual behaviour." Her father stood unspeaking for ages. She could tell he was not sure what to make of this; she never broke curfew before.

He looked at her crossly. She was nervous as to what was going to happen. For the first time in her life, she had been treated harshly because she had broken a palace rule. She felt her body rocking back and forth like a metronome. She had to physically force herself to stop the motion. Those that broke palace rules were made an example of. His stare bore directly into her soul, uttering a single word. "Explain."

She stared at the floor, unsure of how to explain. The annoyed expression on his face told her she wasn't going to be able to cry her way out of this one. She took a deep breath. "Tonight is the night of the Soul Moon Convergence. I saw the moon in the night sky, so I went out into the rain. I looked around the inner courtyard and saw this strange rock, so I went to it. I said 'Hello' repeatedly into the water that was on top of it, until Vladimir showed up and—"

Her father raised his hand. "Stop. Who is Vladimir?" He took two steps closer to her, and repeated, "Who is Vladimir?"

The dark look in his eyes made her frightened even more. "V-Vladimir is the son of the ruler of Sighişoara. It's to the East I think...he s-said we were West of him."

He stared blankly back. "Sighişoara. Have any of you heard of this place before?" He bellowed, turning to his military advisors, who shook their heads.

Her spirits sunk lower, if that was possible. She had hoped that at least one person might have heard of the place Vladimir was from. Her father turned to Xifeng. "You say you have seen and heard of many places we have not—have you heard of this place that my daughter speaks of?"

Xifeng held her chin up, tapping it with one of her fingers. "No, I have not, my Emperor, but that does not mean that it does not exist. As you can see by this map, there are places unknown to you." Xifeng's response gave Pingyang a glimmer of hope. She looked back at her father, whose dark expression continued to terrify her.

"Indeed, the map that you have provided does open up a lot of possibilities, but that is for another time. Right now, I have to deal with a daughter that uses rocks to talk to boys that live in a land that no one has heard of before… What am I to do?" he said, throwing his hands up in the air, then stroking his beard.

This was going as bad as she thought. She was doomed. She wished she knew what to say to make this all better. No one dared say anything when he was in one of his moods; those that did often found their head detached from their body shortly afterwards.

Everyone stood there silently while her father continued to pace around, his fingers never leaving his beard, until at last he stopped in front of her. "You are my daughter, and I love you. I look at you and see much of your mother in you. It both warms and saddens my heart. I ask you—did someone put you up to all this? Have you been secretly ill? Has your mother's affliction come to you, as well? You can tell me," he said softly. "I will do whatever I can to help you, in any case. Just tell me the truth, and my guards will find the person responsible, or get the best healers in the land. Why were you out in the rain on this night? Please tell me."

She stood there and realized that her father did not believe her. She had never lied to him in her life, and she was not now—why did not he understand? Was he afraid of something?

"Father, I am telling you the truth. I would never lie to you, you know this. Even when I have gotten into trouble in the past, I have never lied to you... Why do you not believe me now? This is no different." She looked into her father's eyes and saw something—sadness?

"How can I marry off a daughter who lies? How can someone so dishonest continue our clan's legacy?"

Everyone in the room looked uncomfortable except for Xifeng, who merely stood idly by, like she was watching a play at the Imperial Theatre. Why she was not worried about his anger? Everyone else was. It was like Xifeng was almost oblivious to the tension, or simply didn't care. Xifeng had befriended her, given her Slithers as a present—why couldn't she defend her now? "Why should I believe you, daughter?" he continued, shaking his head. "You have broken curfew; you have broken my rules... Why should I believe someone that has no respect for her Emperor or her father?"

Tears rolled down her cheek, and she shot back, "Like I said, I have never lied to you, Father. Did you see the moons tonight? They converged. When was the last time that happened? The legend states when it happens, soulmates will be pulled to one another—that's how I know where Vladimir is. Do you remember the legend, Father? It's true...all of it. Does the Soul Moon Convergence not prove that to you, Father?" she pleaded.

She could tell by the look on his face that he finally understood. She watched as he ambled toward the windows and looked up at the moons. "What happens next?" he asked her, turning back toward his throne. He sat down, waiting for her to speak.

She dreaded what she was about to say. "Next, I do not know... I know that I can sense his whereabouts, but I do not know where Sighişoara is or how to get there. But I can feel that I have to go, that I *need* to go. It's like I am being pulled there, and...I need your help, Father. I need the company of guards while I look for Vladimir; and I believe he will be looking for me, as well. If we can meet, we could bring our lands together—would that not be incredible, Father? Think about it...we would know more of the world. I would be with my soulmate, and we could..." she trailed off, for her father's face remained unchanged.

"It sounds wonderful, my daughter. Let me ask you something: who would rule both lands? Never has there been two rulers over two sets of lands. What if they invade us once they learn of us, or make demands of us that we do not want to give? Your soulmate could very well lead to our destruction, and that is something I cannot allow. There will be no guards to accompany you anywhere, my daughter, as you are not going to find him. You are going to remain here. As long as you are here, you will never mention Vladimir's name—to anyone. You will forget tonight. Is that understood?"

She stood frozen. Forced to stay at the castle, and in time, forced to marry a man she did not know, or possibly did not ever want to know. Forced to have his children, to carry on the clan bloodline so they could continue to rule.

She knew she had to leave, to run away—and she had to do it as soon as possible. The longer she remained, the more difficult it would be to find Vladimir.

"My Emperor, if you may permit me to speak for a minute," Xifeng said, breaking Pingyang's thoughts. *Finally—would she speak up for her?* She hoped she could convince her father to change his mind. He gave her a curt nod. "I have heard of the legend, as well, and I believe your daughter speaks the truth. I can see it in her eyes that she truly believes what she says. We met in the inner courtyard earlier today, and we spoke about the Soul Moon's possibilities. I am afraid that the legend of the Soul Moon Convergence is true— that she is will feel a pull to this Vladimir. She will seek to find a way to get to him. If you keep her here, she will attempt to escape every chance she will get. She will be miserable and cause you no end of suffering and stress."

Pingyang's mouth dropped open at Xifeng's words. This didn't seem very helpful. She decided to remain silent.

"What am I supposed to do then, just let her go and wander the lands by herself? No. She needs to stay here and do her duty to the kingdom and her clan. There is no doubt, and no question. She is not allowed to leave to find her soulmate. I forbid it!" At his last words, he shot up from his chair and dashed toward her, then grabbed her by the arms. "Do you understand? You will remain here until you can look me in the eyes and say you no longer believe that this Vladimir exists, and you apologize for causing me so much distress." He shook her roughly as she sobbed. "Answer me! What say you?"

He had never acted this way before. He wasn't supposed to act this way; he is supposed to love and support her, not hurt her and make her live a life of misery.

Pingyang had hoped when the time came to marry whoever he had picked, Father would not make her go through with it if she chose not to. But now she knew she would be forced. All her worst fears were being realized. She didn't know what to do or say, so she said the only thing that she could think of. "Father, I love you. But I have to leave. I understand my duty, but this...this is beyond duty. This is my very essence...my soul. I have to follow it. Can you please understand and support me?" she asked, already knowing the answer.

"No."

She pushed away from him as hard as she could, falling to her knees, sobbing. Was her chance of happiness lost forever? *Is this what happened to her mother?* Had her mother secretly loved someone, was forced to marry her father, and couldn't take it anymore? Was this what caused her to become ill? Was that to be her fate, as well?

She brought her hands up to her face and wiped away her tears, not caring who was watching and what they thought. As far as she was concerned, her life was over unless she could escape the castle. Face whatever was out there. It couldn't be worse than the fate that awaited her here. Vladimir had not answered her when she asked him to find her. Would he come? Would he even try? Did he love Kazia so much as to forsake her?

No. She had to believe. She didn't know what she would do if she stopped believing. She had one small solace. Slithers.

"As you can see, my Emperor, the legend is true," Xifeng said, stepping in front of him. "She is lost to you and will be lost to any husband that you make her marry. Will she marry him? Of course. Will she have children? Yes. Will she be happy with her life? No, she will not. She will resent you *and* her husband and her children if things stay as they are now. While the legend may be true, it does not mean it is a happy legend. I believe the Soul Moon Convergence is a curse to those that become inflicted with it. Doomed to go off to find someone with little chance of success. To let her, even with guards, would only result in their deaths in a futile gesture. Something does need to be done, my Emperor, and I leave it in your capable hands to find a solution." Xifeng bowed, then rested her eyes on Pingyang. A strange silence hung between them. *Was Xifeng really a friend, or someone else entirely? Why was Xifeng not being more supportive?*

He father looked around the room, looking like he was at a loss for what to do next.

"Father, please...I need to do this. I beg of you to let me go!" An eternity passed before another word was uttered. As he turned away, she wondered what was going through his mind. He must know she would live a life of misery here in the castle and would always resent him; did he want that?

Her father turned to look at her. She could see how hard he was thinking. "What happens if I don't let you leave, what I am supposed to do?" he said quietly.

She thought carefully about her response before she spoke it. "I know you never imagined being in this position. That there had to be a solution to all this. Father, I must leave, I am being drawn to my soulmate. We must go to each other. Father, please trust me." Tears filled her eyes once more. She watched as he turned to the guard and commanded, "Go get the Black Witch. Tell her to bring her powders."

Her mind reeled at the thought of the Black Witch. Very few people had seen her, but everyone had heard of her. It was said she had abilities that were unnatural. She lived in a small hut just off the back of the palace grounds, covered by high shrubs. Off to the left of the hut, there was a small pond, where *things* lived...things that shouldn't still be alive or look the way they did. Pingyang had heard that the Black Witch had sold her soul to gain abilities, such as creating potions that brought loved ones back from the dead or communicating with the dead. She had also heard whispers about what she looked like underneath the black hood—an old and hideous woman. To look into her eyes was to look into the eyes of death itself.

No one spoke for quite some time—just uncomfortable glances, shuffling feet, and anxious pacing.

She heard a shuffling noise coming from the hallway, and she turned her head. The guards had returned with a black-robed woman, her face covered by a strange red and black mask that instantly terrified her. As the Black Witch's neck turned in Pingyang's direction, a terrifying thought went through her mind: did the Black Witch know it was she who attacked her with the rock earlier tonight? If the Black Witch told her father, then she would be in more trouble.

She glanced over at Xifeng, who brought her finger to her lips, mouthing "Shhh". What was Xifeng up to, she thought. She decided to keep quiet about the events earlier and hoped for the best.

She couldn't escape the horrible feeling that something very bad was going to happen to her. She tried to squirm out of the guard's grasp, but it was pointless.

"You sent for me, my Emperor?" the Black Witch said, her gravelly voice had an unpleasant rasp, like sandpaper. It scraped against Pingyang's soul. She tried to make out the woman's face, but it was hidden behind her black mask and hood.

She could tell her father was extremely uncomfortable in her presence, but he met her gaze. "Yes, we have a most peculiar problem. The Soul Moon's convergence has captured my daughter's soul, and she claims to have spoken to someone of another land. Now she is trapped by its power, and I need you to free her from it," he said flatly. She wished she could see the Black Witch's reaction, but there was no way to see through that mask.

The Black Witch walked up to her, lifted a set of old, shrivelled black hands, and grabbed her face to peer into her eyes. The eyes that stared into her were blacker than any coal she had ever seen. It was like the woman had no soul.

"My Emperor, the Soul Moon's draw, it is far too powerful to simply break. As you may know, the Soul Moon Convergence is an event that happens once every one hundred and twelve years, and during that time, all powers of the sky converge for one night. The power collected cannot be undone by a spell; even the most powerful one conceived would fail. Presently, I cannot undo it. It would take many years to gather the necessary power and harness it into one spell to break the hold of the moons.

"However, I have thought of a solution. It's not elegant, per say, but I think it will suffice, if you permit it. I am willing to do this by your command as it would be a challenge unlike any other I have ever faced. But as for now, your daughter will seek to leave the castle and venture into the world to find her soulmate. I fear for her safety. Confining her would not be enough, as she will search endlessly for an escape route—and therein lies the answer. Until she no longer believes, or until I create the spell to break the magic, I can take away her ability to seek out her soulmate by taking away her sight."

Her words pierced Pingyang's heart. "No, Father…you cannot! I beg of you…I do not want to be blind for the rest of my life! Kill me…kill me…I would prefer death to a life of not being able to see the sun or the moon! Please, do not do this father...I beg of you…!" Pinyang pleaded, knowing she had been right—something awfully bad was indeed happening. She couldn't image a worse fate right now than blindness. She wouldn't be able to escape if she was blind! She tried to squirm, twisting violently, but the guard's grasps were steel vices around her arms. She was helpless.

She watched her father look from the Black Witch to her, sigh loudly, and begin pacing around the room. She suspected he was thinking about his options. With her death, his bloodline would end. He could not permit that. Would he lock her up in her room until she was married? Was her fate to be the same as her mother's?

He eyed Pingyang for a moment, then nodded to the Black Witch. *No…*

The Black Witch retrieved some small vials from the pockets of her robe, strode over to the map table and grabbed a cup, and began to mix them inside the cup. She stared in horror, wondering what was happening. *How could her father do this to her?*

After a few minutes, a pile of purple dust appeared in a small metallic cup. The Black Witch picked up the flask, and with her other hand, made some gestures over the cup. Purple smoke started to rise out of it. Inhaling the smoke, the witch nodded her head in approval and walked toward Pingyang.

"NO! Father...I beg of you...please do not do this...please...I am sorry for everything...please...have mercy...I promise I will try to forget Vladimir...please, just give me a chance!" Pingyang said desperately, struggling to throw her weight back and forth in a desperate, pathetic attempt to free herself.

The Black Witch stood in front of her. For a moment, she thought she saw the mask move. As Pingyang started at the mask, she thought she saw small red eyes moves around the mask. Did a small creature live on the mask?

The Black Witch stepped back from her, raising her voice into a booming crescendo. *"Remove the light from her human eyes,*

Make her world dark forevermore,

Until the time she deems the Soul Moon lies,

Or until this spell I unbind"

Pingyang felt the dust hit her face, and instinctively she closed her eyes, but it was too late. Her eyes felt like they were on fire from the powder! Tears streamed down her face. Her cheeks felt like they were on fire as the tears felt like liquid fire going down them. She hoped the tears would wash away the magic in her eyes, but when she opened them, the world was black. She continued to sob uncontrollably.

"The magic has worked, my Emperor. Until she stops believing in the Soul Moon Convergence, or I can break the magic of the convergence, she will be ever blind, as she stands now. Does this meet with your approval, my Emperor?"

She heard her Father's reply, "Yes, you have once again proved your worth to the Empire. You are free to go to your hut. There will be a bonus tomorrow that should be sufficient for the request you made some time ago." She heard the Black Witch shuffle out of the room, and her father's footsteps approach. "I have decided that even though you are blind, you are still my daughter, and I cannot have you wandering clumsily about the castle; so until such time that a suitable husband can be found who will marry you with your...conditions, I have decided that you are to be sent away. Somewhere where there is no escape, and where you can forget about Vladimir and all this nonsense and regain your sight, as well as your honour, and carry out the duty for which you were born. You will be escorted and ferried to Justice Island." She was too stunned to reply. "Jin and Chi," he continued, his commanding voice projecting in front of her, "both of you will leave at once by carriage and escort my daughter to the prison, and then return. Leave as quickly as possible."

"Yes, my Emperor," Jin and Chi said in unison. She felt rough hands seize hers and was dragged toward the doorway. In one last desperate attempt to change her Father's mind, she cried: "Please, please I will do what you ask. Don't make me leave...I'm your daughter, your blood, please..." But all she received in return was dead silence.

She heard footsteps enter the room, followed by a familiar voice. "My Emperor, we have received a message from the skies. 'Beware the people that wear horns, welcome the people that wear gold.' It was a dragon that appeared and told me this, my Emperor, and then it just disappeared right before my eyes." It was Chang the Monk. What was he doing here?

She was being led away before she could hear any more. She sensed something else was about to happen, something not good.

"Let me grab our stuff, then we can leave and take the Princess to Justice Island," Pingyang heard one guard say to the other. The second guard grunted in reply.

She heard the guard leave and felt herself being led out of the room into the hallway. Desperation was taking hold of her. Why had her father not been more supportive? Why had Xifeng not done more to try to protect her? Her trust had been shattered in those that she believed in. Where was she? She knew the castle inside out, but without her sight she felt disorientated—and even more helpless. Smelling the air, she knew she was near the kitchen. The cooked jellyfish with cinnamon made her tummy rumble in hunger. She decided to remain silent; her life was horrible enough right now. She didn't know how long she had been standing there motionless before she heard one of the guards talk.

"What's wrong?" the closest guard asked.

"Nothing," said the other. "We've got a long trip—let's go."

They steered her out through the castle doors and to the carriage. She winced at the sound of a whip cracking and the horses neighing. They started to trot forward. It would take days to get to their destination. She had not been to Justice Island before, but she had heard about it—it was used to hold female prisoners.

She curled up on the seat and closed her eyes, crying silently, knowing everything about her life would never be the same again. As her mind began to drift toward darkness, her last thought was of Vladimir. She needed to hold onto him, or she would lose her mind forever.

***

Duchess Doa watched as the carriage left the Imperial Castle. She had heard everything that unfolded in the throne room, and her heart was in pain for her daughter. Even though she could not do anything to stop it, she hoped the letter she hastily scribbled would make her daughter's stay more bearable, provided that the guard, Jin, did what he said he would do. He would be paid handsomely for his troubles.

As she watched the carriage leave the Imperial Castle, she was proud of her daughter. Pingyang had been chosen to lead a life no other could even dream. Closing her eyes, she silently said some words of protection for her daughter. When she opened them, the carriage was out of sight. She needed to get back to her bed in case someone happened to check on her. She could never leave her bed for any length of time.

She scurried back underneath her bed covers. *Be safe, my precious Pingyang,* she prayed silently, and hoped whoever Vladimir was, he had the ability to find and rescue her daughter. And would love her forever.

Chapter 23

Dark Woods—Europea

'Running to Destruction'

Vladimir Drăculeşti raced frantically through the forest, using the orangish green glow in the distance as a beacon. His mind was frazzled with a sea of horrible images: what if the grain storage building had caught fire? He dismissed the thought, as it was too well protected. Were the Spiriduş attacking? It didn't seem likely; they would never attack with Father here. Was his family okay? Kazia! Had the bakery caught fire? Was Father helping fight the fire?

He knew he was making a boatload of noise, but he did not care if everything in the forest was watching him. As he got to a small clearing among the trees, he tripped over a large root, falling face-first onto the muddy ground.

He was dazed from the impact and struggled to breathe for a few seconds. A low growl emitted from the surrounding trees. He reached for his sword, momentarily forgetting he had left it at home, and grabbed air for his effort. An enormous wolf emerged from behind a tree. Vladimir slowly got up. The bright moons gleamed in the wolf's eyes. It growled at him, its mouth full of large teeth drooling heavily as it approached him.

Frack me!

He felt his heart pounding in his chest. He rose to his feet as he slowly backed up away from the savage creature. As terrified as he was, he was more determined to get past this creature and make it to his village. He had to finish this quickly. He slowly started to back up, scanning the ground for some sort of weapon, but he couldn't see anything other than a small rock. The wolf started to circle him, its ice blue eyes never leaving his. Another growl.

He had never been this close to a wolf before; he steeled himself to face it. The wolf lunged, and Vladimir dove out of the way, but was not quite fast enough. Its razor-sharp claws scratched his arm, leaving an excruciating burning sensation. Blood gushed from where the claws had sliced open his skin. Holding his injured arm, he stared into the wolf's eyes, and only saw death. He remembered something his father told him: if he was ever facing down death, no matter what form it took, to remember two words: *not today*.

The wolf jumped at him, but he dropped to the ground and rolled, the wolf flying over him. He got back up to his feet, pain searing through his arm; he fought back a scream. The wolf whirled around to face him. It was getting angry. He knew he was in trouble.

Scanning the ground again, he spotted a medium sized stick laying on the ground. He slowly moved toward it, reached down and picked it up with his good arm, and began twirling it. The broken end of the stick was sharp, hopefully sharp enough to go through the wolf's hide and pierce its heart.

The wolf crouched low; he crouched low, too, the branch still spinning between his fingers, at the ready. Suddenly, the wolf rushed and leapt at him. Timing was everything— before it landed, Vladimir jumped toward it, his hand outstretched. The wolf tried to twist away mid-jump, but it wasn't fast enough. He drove the jagged branch with all his might into the belly of the beast. A loud yelp escaped the creature as it twitched violently before falling to the ground, dead. But Vladimir did not come out of this fight unscathed; the wolf had raked his face with its claws. Blood dropped all over the ground around him, but he didn't care. *It was dead! He had won... He was alive!*

He ran his fingers across his face wiping off more blood. The vision on his left eye was skewed; he tried to open it, but his eyelid refused to cooperate. His fingers were wet with blood from the wounds on his face, and he was feeling weak. But he had to go on.

Forcing himself, he bolted through the trees toward the village. As he ran, he thought of his family and hoped that they were okay—and that he was able to make it back in time. Another terrifying thought entered his mind: Father would know he was not in his bed. He would be facing his Father's wrath once all this was done.

It was worth it, seeing that hellsteeds did exist and meeting Princess Pingyang. She was the most beautiful girl that he had ever seen. Even Kazia paled in comparison to her. He longed to meet her in person and felt terrible for not saying a proper goodbye. He had no choice in the matter, though.

He glanced over the trees—the greenish-orange light from the fire had gotten bigger. *Was the entire village on fire?* He knew that was not possible, as the Sentinels would have put it out. Also, it had been raining, though it seemed to have stopped; the moons were slowly moving apart. The convergence was over, but that did not matter right now, as he sensed he was nearing the end of the Dark Woods.

A noise to his left caught his attention. He stopped in his tracks; not much was visible through all the smoke. Perhaps it was just his imagination. He started to make his way through the trees again, fighting with the thick branches in his path, getting closer to the edge of the forest. He stopped for a second to catch his breath and gather enough strength for what he was about to face.

His left eye still sealed shut, he made to break into a run again—until a swarm of silver mist appeared. *What was happening?* It surrounded the area around him on all sides. This must have been the forest's magic—he didn't have time for this. He stepped forward.

As soon as he touched the mist, he recoiled in pain—it had scorched him. He backed up several more paces, holding onto a tree for support, but it, too, was suffering from the mist; he could feel pain coming from it when he touched it. A realization struck: the mist was not being created by the Dark Woods. It was something else entirely, and it was hurting the forest.

Insidious laughter rang out from all sides. The mist in front of him began swirling, and a figure emerged from it. It wore a long crimson cloak with a hood shielding its face, its hands covered in oversized red gloves encrusted with a rainbow of jewels. He tried to get a look at the person's face, but the hood completely covered it.

"Good evening, Vladimir Drăculeşti. I can see you had quite the adventurous night. Good for you." How did this person know his name? The man's voice grated on him like the sound of a fork accidentally scraping against his teeth.

"Who are you?" Vladimir demanded.

The stranger laughed. "I am the Alpha and the Omega—I am the Specter."

Vladimir stood there blankly. *Who?*

"You are running to a dead village, to your dead family. You are injured and half-blinded. Your soulmate lives beyond your reach. But you are fortunate, young Drăculeşti: I am going to relieve you of all that will ail you."

"How?"

The Specter stared back, and finally hissed, "Death."

Vladimir had no idea what the Specter was referring to. "What do you mean? Whose?"

The Specter rushed up to him, grabbing hold of him and bringing his mouth to Vladimir's ear. "Yours."

Vladimir moved his head away. "Why?"

The Specter glided over to his left. "Because, young Drăculeşti. I am finally free of my shackles. I made an error in my approach last time, and this time I mean to correct it. I will still have fun playing this game. It will be a new game, and you are my greatest threat. Not now, of course. You are pathetic. In time, though, you will have...potential. I am going to squash that now, before it has a chance to begin."

Blood boiling inside him, Vladimir charged forward, but was swatted away like an insect—he flew until he bounced off a tree, landing hard on the wet ground. The pain in his arm and eye was beyond anything he had ever felt. He screamed out in pain. He fought not to lose conscious. As he struggled to get back to his feet, he was hoisted up into the air, and investigated the face of the Specter.

But Vladimir did not see one. It was like staring into a starless night sky. *Frack me.*

He felt himself being tossed aside, back again against a tree. He lay sprawled on the ground, the Specter moving toward him. He felt weak and helpless. A loud *bang* startled him, and the Specter stepped backwards. Another *bang*.

A small violet mist formed inside the confines of the silver mist, and like the Specter, a figure stepped out of it. It was a man, one unlike any other Vladimir had seen. He was dressed strangely, with a yellow scarf around his neck and sporting a bright red shirt and dark blue pants. In each of his hands was a metallic object, smoke protruding from it. Vladimir had never seen the type of wide-brimmed hat that the man was wearing either. "This ends now," the man said, his low, brassy voice reverberating through the trees.

Vladimir couldn't agree more.

The metallic objects were pointed directly at the Specter. Vladimir had no idea what was going to happen next. It was as if there was a stalemate, or an unspoken agreement between the two strangers. The Specter blurred slightly, and Vladimir felt himself being lifted off the ground again. The Specter moved quicker than his one good eye could keep track of.

"You are still pathetic," the Specter spat. "We will meet again soon!" Again, he was tossed, and this time when he hit the ground hard, he lay there.

The silver mist slowly dissipated all around him. He was left alone with the stranger who had saved him. Rolling on his side, he tried to pull himself up. The stranger offered a hand, helping him get to his feet. "Thank you," Vladimir murmured.

The stranger smiled. "You're welcome, pard. You look like fire and lightening has run roughshod all over you. Sit a spell and regain your strength."

Vladimir looked up at the man. His eyes were black and piercing—there was something behind them, something powerful.

"Who are you?" Vladimir assumed pard meant acquaintance.

"Well, pard, I am like you. I, too, have a long journey to get to the one I love. No matter what happens, never give up. Even if you're walking through hellfire, you don't stop. She is worth it. No matter how much you may sometimes doubt it, she is worth it. I know this. My beloved…I would do anything for her. In fact, I did."

Vladimir believed the man's conviction. "If you don't mind me asking, what did you do?" He watched dumbfounded as the man leaned back against a tree and took out a small rolled up piece of paper. He then retrieved a small piece of wood from his pocket, a red tip on the end, and swept it quickly across a small rock; the red tip caught fire, then he brought it to the rolled-up paper between his lips, lit it and then…inhaled? The man then blew smoke out of his mouth. *How bizarre!*

"It's quite the tale, pard. My brother got caught up with some real bad hombres without knowing it. One of those hombres took a real shine to the woman I loved. Their leader, in fact. I made a deal with the lawman that I would bring down this thieving band of rustlers, but if anything should happen to me that my name be cleared. The lawmen agreed, and I went and sought out the thieves. I happened to know some, so it was not hard to infiltrate their gang. Those that knew me from before I joined the lawmen knew how lethal I was. So, I lied, cheated, killed all in my path to help my brother. I knew the ends justified the means, and they did. I plum shot out one of their leader's pretty eyes. The gang folded, and I was reunited with my brother and my soon-to-be-wife," the stranger said.

Vladimir's eyes dropped to the metallic objects that the man had used earlier that was now in some kind of large exterior pocket. He knew they could be useful. "Do you mind sparing one? I believe I could find use for it."

The stranger guffawed at him. "They won't work outside of the mist. Even if they did, they don't belong here. You have all the weapons you need," and the stranger tapped Vladimir on the head, then on his heart. He knew the man was right. Still, with everything that had just happened, too much protection was better than not enough.

"Thank you again for saving me. I thought for sure I was going to die."

Smiling, the stranger held out his hand, and he grasped it. "I wish I could help you, but know this: your journey will be long and hard. Be patient. I believe your soulmate is worth it. I heard his talk when I was going through, whatever it was. Ignore his feeble words. The look on your face tells me you are wondering how I know about her. I just do. I can't explain it."

The only journey Vladimir was concerned about was the one to his village. "I need to go."

The stranger nodded. "Yes, you do. It was a pleasure to meet you, Vladimir Drăculești. You have a good heart—remember that. My name is Jim Lacy, but my pards call me Nevada."

"It was an honour to meet you and thank you again."

Nevada tipped his hat and walked into the silver mist, which dissipated moments later. *Amazing!* His heart told him he had just met a legend.

Vladimir sprinted through the forest, now troubled with why the Specter wanted him dead. He burst into the opening and saw his world on fire. He was rooted to the spot, unable to process the horror before him. Past the burning fields, his entire village was up in flames. He stared, dumbfounded at the waking nightmare in front of him.

There was no one attempting to put out the fires, which made no sense to him. Snapping back to his senses, his head turned in the direction of the castle—it was engulfed in flames, too.

No…

He began to run, afraid that he was too late. As he made his way through the blazing cornfields, weaving his way through, he wondered what could have caused this. *Who* could have caused this? He was so focused on the castle that he tripped and fell over something bulky. Pain shot through him, and as he raised his head, he found himself looking into the dead eyes of Farmer Frankesen. He rolled away from the dead farmer, staring in horror at the fear that was frozen on the man's face.

His body was not burnt from the fire. Who would kill Farmer Frankesen out here, on the outskirts of the village?

A noise from behind caught his attention, and he whipped his head around to face something truly bizarre: a person that looked like they were wrapped in medical wrappings, wielding a sword. Was a person trapped underneath? He had never seen anything like this before. He spotted the blood dripping from the blade; he had found the case of Frankesen's death.

He looked into its eyes, as red as the blood on its sword. The creature swung it, but Vladimir dodged its attack, turned and made a run for it. He hoped the creature was as slow as it looked.

He glanced back—the thing was just standing there, watching him. He sighed in relief and continued to run until he got to the houses on the edge of the village, all of which were on fire. He thought he heard a woman's screams, but he could not see past the tall flames or smoke. The Smithy's was half knocked over and on fire. Burned bodies lay on the ground. He knew there would not be many survivors.

He looked up to the castle, let out a long breath, and sprinted toward it. As he turned the corner, he came face-to-face with another bandaged creature. It veered its head and bore his gaze into him, then lifted its sword and brought it down. Vladimir ducked under the swing and managed to grab its wrist, twisting its arm, and yanked the sword out of its hands. It fell to the ground. Vladimir dove, picking it up and jamming it deep into its stomach. To his shock, no blood spilled. Brownish ooze flowed out of its stomach instead.

The creature grabbed the sword and pulled it out of his torso and moved to strike him, but Vladimir twisted the sword out of its hands, grabbed it, and swung the sword at the creature's head—it came off as easily as a Blood Cider cap. Finally, the creature stopped moving.

Not tonight, death, he thought. *Not tonight.*

It would be he and his family that survived this night. He started to run up the path through the village, turned another corner, and ran into two more creatures. How many were there? They were everywhere—he couldn't fight them all by himself. And he needed to get to the castle.

He started to back up as the two creatures approached him. Perhaps if he went for the legs, it would buy him some time. As he raised his sword to attack, the wall to the left of him exploded, and a large clay-looking creature emerged, standing between him and the other creatures. *What the...?*

Without thinking, he spun around and quickly ran between destroyed houses, trying to find a different way up to the castle and avoid the raging flames reaching out to touch him, the heat scorching his face as he ran.

As he neared another building, the wall exploded in front of him. Losing his balance, he fell on his back, crashing heavy onto a pile of broken bricks. His back writhed in pain at the impact. His body protested at his attempt to move. He did not know how much more agony his body could take. He slowly got to his feet and sprinted as fast as his battered body would take him.

He passed dead villagers and Sentinels lying on the ground, dead from an assortment of fatal wounds, and he had to keep himself from stopping to check whether, by a slim chance, one was still alive. He glanced back and was relieved to see nothing chasing after him. He turned a corner of a building and ran into a badly injured Sasha, the weaponsmith. The man's arms were blackened, and his clothes stained with blood.

"Sasha! You are alive! What happened?"

"Vladimir! They came from the shore! Village...destroyed...help me." Blood spilled from gashes that covered nearly every inch of him. Vladimir was sure Sasha felt like he looked. He decided to take Sasha to the castle with him.

As he made to grab and support Sasha, he caught the scent of the man's blood. His heartbeat quickened and a hunger swelled inside of him. *What was happening to him?*

"Vladimir, what's wrong? We need to leave...help me please."

Vladimir was not listening. His breathing got heavier; he grabbed his stomach as it twisted in pain.

"Vladimir! Are you okay?"

Vladimir couldn't speak. He leaned forward and sniffed Sasha's blood. It smelled sweeter than any Blood Cider he had ever tasted.

"Vladimir…"

Pain shot through his mouth. He wanted to scream but couldn't. He touched his teeth. They were different, larger and thicker.

"Vladimir!" Sasha called out for the last time as he jumped on top of the man and ripped into his throat, tasting the sweetest nectar. He couldn't stop. He felt Sasha fight back until, at last, he stopped moving.

Vladimir screamed out into the night. He felt…power! And he stopped hurting. He could hear everything. He could see even farther than before. Even his injured eye worked again!

This was the Drăculeşti secret. There was nothing he could not do. He feared nothing.

He ran toward the castle, practically leaping with every step, coming across bodies of Sentinels everywhere. This was where they must have made a stand and lost miserably. He was getting closer to the castle, but more creatures—both clay-like and bandaged ones— lay ahead. It looked like the paths and castle grounds were heavily patrolled by them.

Flames spewed from every window of the castle, but he refused to believe his family was dead, even though it looked utterly hopeless. His father would have never allowed such destruction if he was still alive, nor his brothers.

He scanned his surroundings for a way to make it to the castle without being seen. It was impossible. *The best defence was an even better offence.* There were about seven creatures that he could count between him and the castle. If he ran fast enough, perhaps he would only have to fight one or two, and then lose the rest inside the castle. Even with his newly acquired strength, it was a long shot to go toe to toe with each of them.

He gripped the sword tight and took a deep breath, then bolted toward the castle, heading in the direction with the least number of creatures. He ran to the first one, coming up swinging and slicing through its right leg; he rushed to the next one, not waiting for the first one to fall, then jumped up and tore off the second one's head; he then dove under another's swing and continued to run, without looking back.

He flung the castle doors open, and flames burst out. The flames burned his clothes and the heat from the flames made his skin boil. It didn't hurt him. He could feel his skin repair itself. *He was invincible!* He ran into the castle, down the hallway to the closet with the secret back door that lead down the ramp to the hidden entrance that lead out into the maze behind the castle. Mother would be there—he was sure of it. *Where was his father and brothers?*

He plowed through the smoke and jumped through fires until he reached the large hallway, where the closet was. It was completely engulfed in flames, and so was everywhere else he looked. Even some of the walls had been pushed in from the outside. The air was thick in smoke, but he could still see clearly. Deciding that the roof was the best option, he turned and ran up the stairs to go to the roof; he noticed the hatch was ajar. Someone had made it up! There was still hope after all. As he burst through the opening, he climbed up and looked around frantically. "Mother! Mother, it is Vladimir…I am here to save you. Mother…Mother!" he cried, circling the rooftop.

He turned the corner of a chimney and came face to face with another bandaged creature. He froze. A sword swinging at him snapped him out of his daze, and he rolled out of the way. Back on his feet, he charged and when he was close enough, dropped to his knees and sliced off the creatures left leg. It fell over forward. He swung his sword back and took off its head, then continued to run around the roof looking around the chimneys.

His mother was not up here; he did not know what to do next. He walked to the edge and looked over the village. There was nothing but fire and destruction. The only area untouched was the harbour.

Where was his family? He was scared…he was alone. He had never been alone before, and he did not know what to do. His life as he knew it was over. He was in a dead village filled with strange creatures that would not hesitate to kill him.

He heard a noise behind him. Two more. He raised his sword and charged, but the nearest creature sidestepped him, and the second one smashed its fist into his face. His forward momentum was instantly halted. Standing there dazed, he didn't see that the one that had dodged his attack was lunging its sword at him, and he felt his shoulder go cold. He looked down and saw a sword sticking inside his shoulder.

Not today. He pulled the sword out from his shoulder and roared in anger. He watched the fist coming toward his face again, and his world exploded into colors; he was sent several paces backwards. His right leg stepped on air, and he felt himself falling backwards.

He stared at the creatures' faces as he fell, silently cursing them for what they had done. Then all at once, he felt numb. His head rolled to his left and he found himself looking into the eyes of his dead mother. Disbelief and horror shot through his body at the sight, and he crawled over to her.

Noooooo! Not you, Mother. He grabbed her cold, lifeless hand. Tears of pains flowed down his cheeks as raging rivers of remorse as he had not been there to protect her. "Mother come back to me. Even as a shadow, please come back to me. I don't know where father and my brothers are. Please don't leave me. I need you." She could not be dead. A massive shadow fell over him—a clay monstrosity was standing over him. "Get away from my mother!" Vladimir raged, and picked up a sword and hacked away mindlessly at it.

Something was burning inside of him, something he had not felt before. He took another massive swing at it, and the sword he was holding shattered into dozens of pieces. *Frack!* He could not leave his mother's corpse here, in the presence of these things. As he stared into the creature's eyes, he failed to see its massive rounded fist come toward his face, and his world erupted into overwhelming pain. He staggered back, dazed, then went down to one knee, fighting to stay conscious. Looking over at his mother's corpse, another intense fire lit inside of him; roaring, he got back up to his feet and lunged at the creature, then twisted its arm as hard as he could, and ripped it off the creature's body. He stood there holding it, flipped the arm so he was gripping it by its wrist and charged. The creature lost its balance, falling to the ground.

He leapt on top of it and smashed its face with its own severed arm until its head was rubble. Howling at the top of his lungs in fury, he glowered at the remaining creatures and they did not move to attack him. He threw down the arm, reached down, and picked up his mother's corpse, and absently started walking in the direction of the Dark Woods. He did not know why, but no creature attacked him as he passed them.

As he walked, he felt that he was dying. His wounds had taken its toll on his body. The power he had felt from drinking Sasha's blood had been spent. He felt cold blood leaking from his wounds down his body, but it didn't matter. He got to one of the farmers' fields that wasn't on fire near the Dark Woods. There was a small clearing in the field. He laid his mother's corpse on the ground tenderly. He leaned to kiss her forehead, tears streaming down his face. "I love you," he said one last time.

He had nothing left inside of him. All his strength was gone. He knew he was never going to see his family or Princess Pingyang again. He fell heavily to his knees. "Father, Radu, Micrea…Be safe wherever you are. Mother…I…failed you." lamented Vladimir.

He whispered out loud to Pingyang, "Please forgive me," and his world went black.

***

Vasilisa Drăculești opened her eyes as a hot licking sensation brought her back to reality. She looked up and saw a familiar furry face whose black eyes had been replaced with glowing red ones: Lacey, The Sentinel mascot. She tried to get up, but she was in too much pain; she stopped and took a deep breath. *Where was she? How had she been brought here?* She forced herself to stand. "How did we get here, Lacey? Wherever this is…" She tried to walk, but her legs wouldn't budge, making her fall forward. Her legs went straight through the ground.

What was happening? She tried to lift her leg again, and still nothing. What was wrong with her?

Anger built up inside her, and she didn't know why. The adrenaline must have been enough to move her legs, until she was able to get back to her feet and start walking. Her legs slid forward in the ground. "Ahhhh!" She looked at her hands, and they were covered in dirt and small rocks. She brushed her hands together to clean them, but nothing happened. The dirt remained, even though some was dropping to the ground. What madness was this?

She heard rustling behind her, and she tried to turn to face it, but she fell flat on her face. She screamed again, then peered behind her shoulders at the creatures coming toward her.

They were short and doll-like, with tattered clothes on. Beside her, Lacey let out a loud growl. She did not fear them though; she sensed a kindred spirit in them. Patting Lacey, she said, "It's okay, girl. I think they are here to help." With slightly less struggle, she got to her feet again. The tallest one stopped short just a few feet from her and pointed. "Drăculești."

Was she a Drăculești? What did that even mean? The name was foreign to her, but it meant something, she felt it.

The tall one held out its hand. Without hesitation, she took it. "Help, we will." She nodded as they began to walk deeper into the forest, oblivious to the destruction that was consuming her former home.

Chapter 24

Imperial Palace—Thebes

'Beaten Defiance'

"Radu, wake up," Micreas voice whispered into Radu's ear. Radu slowly opened his eyes, but his vision was blurred. His entire body felt like it was on fire from the pain.

"Micrea?" he mumbled and received a painful kick to the back.

"Be quiet, dog!" a strange male voice said to him. Radu turned to try to get up, but a stomp to his chest forced him down. Where was he? Who was kicking him? He was still groggy and tired. He could barely move.

"Where…?" He started to ask again and received another kick to his stomach.

"Quiet!" the voice hissed. He decided to oblige, as his whole body seared in agony. "The prisoner is awake."

Prisoner?

"Bring him."

Radu felt two rough pairs of hands grab his arms and begin to drag him. He blinked, his vision slowly returning to normal, and made out the shape of an unfamiliar hallway lined with cages. He heard clanking against metal and voices calling out, "Treacherous leech, you got what you deserved!" He did not need eyes to feel the hate directed towards him, though he did not know why.

Just when he thought the dragging would never stop, finally, they let him go. His arms were in more pain than he ever imagined possible. He laid there for a moment to let the pain subside.

"Get him up," a different male voice said. More hands took hold of him and yanked him up to his feet. He blinked open his eyes enough to see two men standing next to the most beautiful, exotic woman he had ever seen. Her eyes radiated with the glow of the sun. He had never seen a bald woman before. He felt his insides stir. Her golden headpiece matched her eyes, along with her gold trimmed outfit. A man caught his eye, sitting high up on a large chair. He knew that had to be their leader.

"Bring him closer…to the bottom of my stairs," their leader commanded as he was pushed closer to the steps. He looked up at the man. He thought they might be the same age. How did someone so young get so much power?

"One of my vessels was destroyed, and many of my men have died to get you here. Your people have paid for your family's treachery. What do you have to say for yourself, Drăculești?"

At a loss, he said the first thing that popped into his head. "How's the weather up there?" And he began chuckling uncontrollably.

"What?" Seeing the important man's face turn red brought him full-on laughter. "Enough!" The man said in a rage. He felt a sharp stinging sensation on his back, no doubt the thick leather whip he spotted in the man's hands. Hot blood ran down his spine. He was no longer laughing. Anger seethed inside him.

"My Pharaoh, this young man has no idea where he is or who he is in the presence of," the woman said, walking up to him. He looked directly into her golden eyes, and there, the truth about her was revealed: there was no life in them, just a void. There was something unnatural about this woman.

"You are quite correct," the leader said. "These men before you are my closest advisors, General Pentu and Royal Sorcerer Haphestus. I am the leader of Egyptia, Pharaoh Tutankhamen. You will show me the respect I am due, Drăculești."

The only thing he wanted to show the Pharaoh was his teeth. The Sorcerer walked over to him and scrutinized him. The silence hanging in the air was grating on his nerves.

"Hey, Pharaoh!" he called out, taunting the leader. "Do all men here dress and smell like women, including yourself? You will make someone a pretty wife someday." He started laughing uncontrollably again.

"Silence!" The Pharaoh cried, and his body was treated to a fist massage from behind. He fought not to whimper—he would not give these strangers the satisfaction.

"Amazing. Even in the face of death, he makes jokes," said the General. Radu glanced at him and winked, giving him the craziest grin, he could muster.

"Yes, these Drăculeşti are either more stupid than we imagined or simply foolish," the Sorcerer said. "Perhaps it is due to the nature of their abilities. Drinking the blood does something to their minds, and I would like to know for sure." The Sorcerer gave Radu a look of a child who was given a new toy to play with. How did these strangers know what he was capable of? They knew a lot more about him than most people did in the village.

"Why don't you all go *knott* yourself!" Radu yelled, receiving a brutal punch to his back from one of the guards that hauled him there.

"I can forgive an outburst only once—that is the extent of my mercy. You should be begging for forgiveness, Drăculeşti!" the Pharaoh bellowed. *Forgiveness for what?* Radu wondered.

"These people believe father ordered an attack on their Pharaoh's life. That is why they attacked our village," Micrea whispered to him from behind. Radu couldn't believe it. His father would never order an attack—he would do it himself. "That makes no sense, Micrea. Father is strong enough to—"

A punch to his face sent his senses reeling. "Who are you talking to? Who is…Micrea?" the leader said impatiently. Could they not see his brother? He had been so pre-occupied with everything going on, he had failed to notice Micrea had been in the room the entire time.

"If I might suggest, my Pharaoh, the apothecary would be an excellent place to teach this impudent dog some manners," the Sorcerer said gleefully. "With your permission, of course, I shall remove him from your sight and take him with me to begin." Reaching out, the Sorcerer stroked his face tenderly. *What kind of freaks lived in this place?*

"No," the Pharaoh said. Radu gave a sigh of relief; he did not want to go through whatever this strangely dressed man wanted to put him through. "I know you want to run your tests, Sorcerer. First, this dog needs to be made an example of, to show what happens when you try to kill a living God. There will still be enough left for you to do whatever you so desire." The Pharaoh glowered at Radu. The latter could see the Sorcerer was visibly disappointed.

"I am Chione," the woman suddenly said, approaching him. Radu looked into her eyes, still they were empty. How disappointing. "I can sense your power inside of you, perhaps one day you will be able to show it to me. Someplace more discreet," she whispered, giving him a quick wink.

"Not likely," he retorted. She smiled at him and kissed him hard, making his mouth bleed. "Yummy." She licked his blood off her lips, winking as she walked away from him.

"I will admit, the Drăculeşti are most impressive. If we had an army of them, there is nothing we could not accomplish," the General said. He sensed the General was not evil per se, but merely took his duty seriously. He could see into the man's eyes; there was pain from a life of duty.

The Sorcerer nodded. "I concur." Radu sensed the man was more of a threat than the Pharaoh. Whatever the Sorcerer had in store for him was beyond torture or pain. He needed to end all their lives and escape this place, wherever it was.

Micrea's voice was in his ear again. "I promise, Brother, we will make it back home."

Yes, we will, Brother, Radu silently agreed. "Why do you think my family tried to kill you?"

"What do you mean *why?*" the Pharaoh shouted back. "Your family sent assassins to try to kill me. Do not play innocent with me. I already told you this!"

Radu could see by the rage in the man's eyes that he was telling the truth. Chione's slight smile caught his attention. She knew more than she was letting on, he was sure of it.

"If my Father wanted you dead, he would do it himself!" he roared back, instantly receiving more blows by the guards. The room spun around him, but he managed to keep his wits about him.

"Your father was a coward! Look at my face—it was his Sentinels that did this too me!" The Pharaoh shot back. Sentinels…here? Radu couldn't believe it. His father feared no man nor beast. He would not have sent Sentinels here. There had to be something else going on. It was too bizarre not to have some truth in all this.

"My Pharaoh, he seems to have misplaced his tongue," the Sorcerer said, and the whole room burst out laughing, except for him.

"Where is your sense of humour now?" The Pharaoh said mockingly.

"The same place it's always been, little man. Let's see how tough a living God is without his attack dogs," Radu fired back, and paid a heavy price for it—the guards struck his back again, and again. As the room spun once more, his eyes fell on five ladies off to the side of the throne on their knees, scrubbing the floor. They were wearing small white dresses in gold trim with matching sleeveless top. He had never seen bald women before entering this room; he had to admit, he found it…arousing.

He caught the gaze of one of the girls who had the most striking emerald eyes he had ever come across. He moved his hand slightly as to say 'Hi', but she quickly turned away. He continued to gaze at her; she was quite pretty. She glanced back at him, and as he smiled back her eyes darted away again.

"What are you smiling at, boy?" the Sorcerer said. Radu turned his head toward the man and caught a whiff of his overly strong lily-scented perfume. The man must have bathed in it!

"I'm laughing because I figured out why you wear a skirt and smell like a woman. Because you have no balls." He roared with laughter again.

"How dare you!" the Sorcerer said, then spat at his feet. "When you are mine, you are going to suffer more than you have ever suffered before in your life."

"Wait—worse than right now, having to smell the overwhelming amount of perfume you are wearing?"

"Clearly, the Drăculeşti are utterly fearless," the General stated. Radu gave the man a thumbs up.

"Enough, get him up!" the Pharaoh yelled, and two sets of hands seized his shoulders, pulling him back to his feet.

"You are lucky my pet is not here, Radu, he would have lots of fun with you," Chione teased, making him wonder what kind of pet she had. With such a sweet smile, how was she able to make everything sound like a threat? "In fact, my pet would toss you in the air like a toy until he decided to eat your limbs, if I wanted. I believe you would make a delicious meal for him."

What is her game?

"What kind of pet do you speak of?" the Pharaoh said, leaning forward. She winked and gave Radu a wicked smile before turning to face her leader. "No pet. I was just teasing the prisoner. As we can tell, even in the face of danger, he has no fear. He fears no man, nor pain. But perhaps the thought of being ripped apart will make him rethink his actions. The longer this image lingers, the more terrified he will become. Like a wound that never closes."

Unable to control it, Radu was chuckling again.

"I am glad I was able to amuse you as much as you are going to amuse me," Chione said as she strode over and stroked his hair. He threw his head back and replied, "Get off me, woman. I don't know where those hands have been."

Chione's eyes wide and her mouth dropped open in disbelief at his comment. *Excellent!* Radu grinned. "Now, maybe if you wash them and slip into something more befitting to a woman—not that cheap dress and perfume you are wearing—then maybe, if you are lucky…" He winked.

A sudden, sharp slap rocked his face. Every muscle on his face stung, but he kept silent.

The General cleared his throat. "Excuse me, my Pharaoh, with your permission, I would like to return to the dock and check on the vessel for damage, as well as have a word with the Captain, see how his crew is holding up—they have had a most unusual night. And also to begin the preparations we discussed before our guest arrived."

Radu glanced up at the Pharaoh, who was clearly bored at his request but motioned for the General to leave. The General approached him and stared coldly into his eyes. "From what I saw tonight, your kind need to be exterminated. No man should have the abilities you do, except for a living God, like our Pharaoh." He watched the General walk away and leave the room, and he found himself respecting the man. It was too bad his Pharaoh was not of the same calibre; perhaps tonight would not have happened, and he would be back home.

The Pharaoh leaned back in his chair. "You will be cleaned up and put on display for my people to bear witness to. You will be a living testament to my greatness. There is no force more powerful than me. I am a living God!"

"Living God, you say? The way you are dressed, you look more like a cheap sex worker to me. You should take lessons from Deidra," Radu retorted, smiling. "Three…two…one," he counted aloud as fists contacted his body again, and he fell down to his knees. *Why did he not learn?*

"Who is Deidra? Enough. I am bored with your insolence. Soon though, *very* soon, your insolence shall be replaced with terror."

Radu slowly got back up to his feet. "I don't even know what 'terror' means, so I am going to say no to that. Now, this is your first and only warning, Pharaoh. Let me go, and I will forgive everything that happened here and return home, never to see or speak of any of you again. I don't want to have to kill any of you, but if you push me, I will." He wanted to slaughter them all and feast on their blood as soon as the first opportunity arose.

"Are you threatening me, dog?"

"Damn straight. When I get through with all of you, none of you will be left standing. I will revel as I feast on all your hearts. I shall bathe myself in all your blood. If you were half a man, you would come down here and face me. Coward!"

The room went dead silent, and he wondered if he had gone too far this time. He could tell the Pharaoh was silently fuming. He glanced around—no one dared move. Even the Sorcerer had his head down in submission. He did not know how long it had been, but the Pharaoh was thinking through something. Finally, the latter slowly got up and walked down the stairs to him. He felt the guards' grip on his arms tighten. He knew that they knew he would try to attack the Pharaoh. He watched the man closely as he neared. They were in breathing distance of each other. "Well, you are shorter than I expected," Radu snarked, and he was glad. Shorter men were generally timid around larger people.

The Pharaoh's eyes widened in anger. "Silence!" Radu chuckled at how his tiny eyebrows narrowed.

Before the punch to his spine he knew was coming, he harnessed his remaining strength and lunged forward, head-butting the man's nose. He heard a satisfying *crack*, knowing he had succeeded in breaking the Pharaoh's nose.

"Argh!" the Pharaoh screamed, and he started laughing again. Multiple blows stuck his body hard and fast; he went down in a heap, barely able to stay conscious. He was lifted again, supported by the guards, but this time there was a sword at his throat.

"Hey, Pharaoh, your nose never looked better. You should be thanking me."

"Take him away!"

"Hey, Tut!" Radu shouted as the guards pulled him away. "I'll be seeing you soon!" And he winked as he was taken down the hallway.

"Wait!" the Pharaoh yelled, and the guards halted. *Now what,* Radu thought. "Tomorrow, take this dog down to the pit. He will remain there until it is time for him to perform. He shall be put into the Crucible of Cages for all to see—this will be glorious. I shall enjoy your death, Drăculești. You can visit him in his cage, Sorcerer. But make sure he puts on a show at the proper time."

Radu smiled back, "Not if I enjoy your death first." The Pharaoh's face turned ghostly white. *Living God—no. A juicy meal—yes.* When he had first drunk human blood, he was traumatized by it. Now he longed for it…from each of them, except for the servant girl he saw. He wanted her the way a man wanted a woman. As he was dragged away, he looked around: everything was stone. What kind of building was this? The hallways seemed to last forever in this place. At the sight of bars, he knew that he was going back to his cell. He was tossed into it like a wild animal and fell hard onto the stone floor. As the guards turned to leave, he called out, "Smell you later!" and watched them until they were out of sight.

Radu lay there, unmoving for a few moments, and lowered his head onto the floor, closing his eyes. He had paid a heavy price for his humour, but it was worth it. The Pharaoh bled. If he bleeds, he can sink his teeth into him and kill him. The thought brought a broad smile to his face.

He thought of the servant girl. He could tell she liked him. If he could use that to his advantage, then he might be able to escape before the Sorcerer had his way with him after the Crucible of…whatever. "What are you thinking, Radu?" Micrea said, who appeared laying on the ground facing him. Radu looked around the cell. He could see his brother, but no one else could. What was happening?

He was rocked by immense pain—not physical. *His father, mother, brothers…all gone.* Tears welled in his eyes, and he couldn't stop the tears from flowing. How quickly his life had been irrevocably changed. He needed to get back home somehow. "I am sorry, Micrea," he added quietly, hoping his brother heard him.

"We will survive this, Radu. I swear we will somehow," Micrea vowed, but he was only half paying attention; he had never felt such despair. He had always counted on Father. Father, the brave. Powerful. Fearless. Unstoppable. Unkillable.

Gone.

Micrea was here, but not physically; there was no end to his grief. He couldn't even mourn his brother, as he was not truly gone. "Micrea. How did this happen? What did we do to deserve this?" Radu asked wearily.

"I don't know." Then, there was silence. What more was there to say? He was locked in a cell somewhere with his dead brother, surrounded by people that were going to have fun torturing him. Was this punishment for being a Drăculeşti? For drinking human blood? For enjoying flesh? "You will get out of here, Brother. I will do everything I can…I swear to you. We will be reunited with our family." Radu nodded silently. "What happened to Father?" Micrea asked. "I remember fighting alongside you, and then there was darkness. There are chunks of time missing from my memory."

Father? Father had made it to the black vessels in the harbour, with Radu following closely behind, but he was captured instead. "Father went to attack the black vessels in the harbour. I fear the worst. If Father was still alive, I would not be here. I am sure of it," Radu said sadly. He punched the jail floor hard. He didn't care about the pain. There would be enough time to grieve once he escaped. One of the lessons his father had taught them is never let them see you bleed. He would not let them break him. There had to be a way to escape…the Crucible of…whatever.

The girl with emerald eyes had looked at him. Perhaps if he could see her again and talk to her, then he could convince her to let him escape. A half-baked plan was better than no plan.

He had paid a heavy price for his comments, but it was worth every punch. As he felt sleep washing over him, he asked, "What is it like to be dead?" He lay on the floor, waiting, until at last his brother spoke. "I am not sure. I do not feel hunger or pain. I do not feel anything at all. I wonder if that is normal when you are dead. Be warned, Brother. There is a man and woman—I do not know what they are, specifically, but they are unnatural. They take people beyond this life. I do know they will come for me." Radu thought about it for a second, and his last words to his brother were: "Let them. Let them all come. We are Drăculeşti. If they think they have seen horror before…wait until they get a load of us."

As far as he knew, his mother and youngest brother were still alive. He had to keep holding onto that. That was his purpose now, to get to them and help them. Radu closed his eyes and whispered, "I'll save you, Mother, and Vladimir. I swear it on my life. I'm coming home as soon as I can." His thoughts drifted back to the emerald-eyed girl, and something tingled inside of him. There was something he saw in her eyes…but he was too exhausted to put much more thought into it. He rolled onto his side and curled into a ball, which racked him with pain, but he did not care. Every position he tried put him in extreme pain. He vowed he would have his vengeance…on all of them. Every second he lay in his cell was a second of regaining his strength. One last thought came to his mind. *What if Micrea isn't here, and I'm just losing my mind?*

At least if he went insane, he wouldn't be alone.

***

Kintiarra stopped scrubbing the floor to look up at the commotion around the throne. She had seen violence before, but nothing like the brutality that she was witnessing. The prisoner was being beaten beyond belief. At first, she had enjoyed it—no one tried to kill her Pharaoh. But the sheer defiance of the prisoner was truly remarkable. He feared nothing, not even death. What kind of man was like that? How was such a man possible? All the men she knew cowered in fear. They had been broken by violence. But this man revelled in it. Perhaps he was the one she had longed for.

In her nineteen years of life, she had never stepped outside of the Royal Pyramid. She was born inside its walls and had remained since. The only time she had stepped outside the walls of these rooms and corridors was on her birthday. On birthdays, the servants could go out onto the lower balconies and spend some time basking in the glow of the sun. She still remembered the stories that her mother told her when she was young. How her parents met along the banks of the Nile River, the long walks they would take along the beach.

She longed for that. The feel of the sand between her toes, to be with someone that wanted to be with her as much as she wanted to be with him. The only physical contact she had with a man was with the Pharaoh, whenever she was summoned to his bed chambers. The best part was that when she was there, she ate the best food and could drink as much Blood Cider that she wanted—the Blood Cider was what made the experience bearable. By the time it came to her turn, she was usually so drunk she could barely remember anything the next day, which she was immensely grateful for. She hated being summoned to his chambers. To resist would mean punishment. She had seen other girls after their punishment. That was her only incentive to go without resisting.

She had never tried to escape the Royal Pyramid. She had heard stories of other girls that had tried—not one was successful. They had paid a price worse than death: being sent to the Royal Apothecary. No one ever returned from there whole. Supposedly, the things that went on there were unnatural.

The prisoner showed no fear. Even being beaten, he was more defiant than all the men in the Royal Pyramid. It excited her. She needed to get to the prisoner and talk to him somehow. The male servants were the ones that brought the meals to the prisoners. She would never be allowed to do that. The only time females were allowed near the cells was once a week for cleaning. That would be her only chance to leave a note in his cell. She needed to find out which cell he was in. What would she put in the note? And how to tell him that it was from her?

He had looked directly at her several times. Into her eyes. *Yes!* She would sign the note 'Emerald Eyes'. That would tell him that it was her. With her knowledge of the Royal Pyramid and the prisoner's fearlessness, perhaps there was a chance they both could work together and escape.

It was more than the reckless bravery of the man that she was drawn to. In his eyes…there was…power. She could sense it. Together, she was confident they could escape these walls. And then she would do whatever it took to stay as close as possible to that power. It was her salvation.

Chapter 25

Yantze Trail—Zhongguolia

'Trail of Misfortune'

How many days had they been travelling, Princess Pingyang thought to herself as the carriage bumped along the path. She had no more tears to cry, and she did not know where she was. The two guards refused to answer her questions. She had never felt more alone and scared, blind, quite literally, to whatever life has in store for her. Her father abandoned her, exiling her for wanting to be with her soulmate. Her soulmate, Vladimir.

What had happened to his village? Was his family okay? Was he okay? Would he try to find her? That was the only hope that she clung to. Would he want to be with someone who was blind? Would he look into her eyes and see nothing looking back at him and be disappointed? Would he still think she was beautiful, or would Kazia still be the obstacle that stands in the way? Part of her hoped that if Vladimir's village was in trouble, Kazia did not make it. Did that make her a bad person? Perhaps Kazia would be married soon, so Vladimir could focus on her.

A hard bump brought her back to the present. Whenever the carriage came to a stop, she tried speaking to the guards, asking where they were and how much longer it was to the prison, but they ignored her. It was like she was not even there, for the most part, unless it was time to eat or sleep. At least they fed her. She knew they watched over her at night. Even though she was banished, she was still a princess. Also, if the guards did not deliver her safely, they would be punished harshly. She had heard of her father's punishments. She was living proof of how little he cared about anyone, even family.

She referred to them as Guard One and Two. She had heard their names at the palace, but neither called each other by their first names, so she did not know which one was which. Guard One was much rougher-sounding and was not very gentle when taking her out of the carriage or putting her back, and only grunted when she asked a question. Guard Two was not much better, though he was not quite as rough. Whenever she asked a question, at least she got an answer: "None of your concern." *Is this how I am going to live the rest of my life? Ignored and mistreated,* she thought.

She tried to remember where the island was from the maps she had seen, but she could not...she had not paid much attention to the maps; it had bored her. Now, she wished she had. She realized even if she had memorized all the land, she would not know where to go or what direction she was walking. She could walk over a cliff and fall to her death. She shivered at the thought.

Suddenly, she did not want the ride to end. She was safe, she had protection, she had food, and she was not alone. She curled up into a ball and hugged herself and started to weep again. She felt like she cried enough tears in the past days to fill an ocean, and yet here she was again, crying to herself silently in the dark. Why had her father not shown more compassion? Why was her mother always sick and lying in bed? While she was hugging herself, she remembered Slithers.

"Slithers...are you still there?" she said quietly. She waited a beat, and then she felt something sliding up her neck. A small forked tongue flicked her ear, and she giggled quietly. "Stop, Slithers...that tickles." He flicked his tongue again. As she giggled, she suddenly realized that through all that she had been through, she could still giggle. Perhaps, she could survive this with Slithers' help.

Slithers was a special snake, so perhaps it was possible. Could she communicate with him? She knew she had to try. "Slithers, if you can understand me, hiss three times." She hoped that it worked. If it did, it meant that perhaps she was not truly alone.

Hissss hissss hissss. Her heart leapt. *Yes!* Slithers was truly an extraordinary snake. She whispered, "Thank you for being here." She silently thanked Xifeng for the gift; she appreciated that she was not alone. "Okay, Slithers, you need to be my eyes, do you understand?" As he hissed three times again, she began to feel excited.

She felt the carriage stop. She heard the guards come around. "Quick, back to your hiding spot!" She felt Slithers return to his designated spot. She heard the door open.

"We are here, Princess," Guard Two said. "Time for the ferry trip to Justice Island." His rough hands seized her and removed her from the carriage. "The boat is here to take you and I to the island, while Chi watches the carriage." He steered her by the shoulders, and the smell of the sea water tickled her nose. She could taste the salt air on her tongue. She imaged the sapphire blues waves roaring down on the tidemark.

"Greetings, Quan, how are you today?" She recognized the booming voice from when the man had visited the Imperial Castle a couple of years ago. Her father had complained the man spoke much too loud for his liking. That was because Quan was used to yelling over the sounds of the ocean, so he had only one voice—loud. She had seen him in passing once at the Imperial Castle. She tried to remember his appearance: Quan was a younger man in his mid-twenties, with short black hair—that was all she remembered. He had inherited his job from his father; for generations his family served as the ferrymen to the island and back. Even though it did not seem like a prestigious job, it was important. There were dangerous creatures in the water that sometimes rose to the surface, attempting to tip the boat. Quan's family had never lost a passenger, and she hoped Quan was not about to break that tradition today.

"Hello, Jin. I am doing well, thank you for asking. I am honoured to meet you, Princess Pingyang, though I wish it were under happier circumstances," Quan said. She smiled at his kindness.

"Thank you, Quan. I wish the same. I have heard of your family; they have served with honour for many generations. The Empire is lucky to have such dedication."

Even though she was blind, she remembered all the proper etiquette she had been taught all her life. She felt a cold, wet hand touching her. She recoiled. "My apologies, Princess." Quan said quickly. "I meant to take your hand to lead you to the ferry. It is not a long trip, only about twenty-five minutes or so, and as you can feel, there is no breeze today, so it should be smooth crossings. May I please have the honour of taking your hand?"

"Yes, you may, and thank you for asking, Mr. Quan. It is most appreciated." She felt him take her hand as they began to walk.

"Take a step up, Princess." She felt her balance shift as she stepped onto the boat. "Three steps, stop and turn to your right, then sit down, Princess."

She did as instructed, sitting down on the hard, wooden bench along the side of the boat. The ocean breeze whipped her hair around her face. For a moment, it took her back to riding on Guang. She missed the dragon very much. "What is the boat like, Mr. Quan?"

"It holds ten people and has a triple long oar system, so one person can do the work of three people. It also has a harpoon shooter to deal with anything that may be lurking below and looking to cause trouble. Do not worry, Princess," he added, likely sensing her uneasiness. "It is very rare."

"Enough of the small talk, we need to go," Jin grumbled. "Chi gets impatient quickly, and we have a long journey back to the castle." She could tell in his voice he was tired. It had been a long trip for everyone. She smelled the air; it was filled with brine and seaweed. It reminded her of home. The saltwater smell gave a bit of comfort as well. For a moment, she imagined she was strolling along the beach alongside her father, like they did when she was younger. How she longed for those times now.

She felt the boat begin to move, the oars splashing hard against the water, and they slowly started picking up speed. She had never been on the water before; she found it relaxing. A splash of water hit her front, and she realized it had been three days since she had taken a bath; she instantly longed for one. She wondered if she was ever going to have a bath again. Who would fill the tub with hot water? How would she ever get hot water or even find it? Were prisoners allowed to bathe, or where they condemned to live in filth for the rest of their lives? She was a princess—surely, she would be allowed to have a bath...

She listened to the stroking of the oars. Each splash brought her closer to her destination. She wished she could see her new home. All her life, she had only known one home, and now that home was lost to her, forever. Her new home was to be all that she would ever know until she was married. Or Vladimir found her.

Suddenly, she was propelled forward, hard. She lurched off her seat onto the deck. Had they already reached shore? No. It was too sudden. She was dazed, fumbling around until she was able to sit again. Something was wrong.

"What was that?" She heard Jin yell out.

"Load the harpoon gun just in case!" Quan shouted back. "I didn't see what it was, but something that would cause this vessel to come to a complete stop would have to be...large."

She could tell he was worried by the tone of his voice. She felt the ferry start to pick up speed. Quan wanted to get to shore as quickly as possible, and so did she.

She was thrown forward again, falling face first on the deck of the ferry, her stomach hitting hard. She clung onto the rail and slowly pulled herself back up to her seat, gasping for air. She touched her cheek—it still stung from being thrown forward. On her fingers, she felt thick, warm liquid. Blood.

"What is happening?"

"Keep your eyes open, Jin—shoot at any sign of movement!" She hoped Jin was an excellent shot.

"Row faster!" Jin shouted. "Princess, stay low on the deck until we are safe!"

She felt for something to sit on and began wiping the blood off her face. Her stomach still ached from being thrown forward. She wished she could see what was happening.

"The water will start to shallow out shortly! We just need to hold out until then!" Quan yelled out. "Stay where you are, Princess! Do not present yourself as a potential target." Something hit the boat twice now, she felt it, and was still out there. She heard Quan grunting and panting heavily. She knew he was using all his strength to row as fast as he could.

The boat lurched upwards, and she was jerked off her seat, sliding backwards along the deck until her spine hit a rail. Her back stung. She let out a small scream. She wished she could look around herself.

"Jin! To your right!" Quan scream. *What was to the right?* She wondered in fear.

"I see it...*tiān nǎ!*" Jin cried.

"What is it?" she called out desperately. "Describe it!"

"It's...it's a Shuǐlóng!" Quan screamed out to her. A water dragon? She thought they were just a myth.

"Brace yourself, Princess!" Jin yelled as the vessel rocked violently. She thought back to her teachings in Imperial Real-World Deviant Creatures and remembered that they were monstrous creatures. The Shuǐlóng bodies consisted of ocean water held together by magic. What type of magic, no one knew—no one had ever captured one.

"Shoot!" Quan shouted, and moments later she heard a *whizzz* go by her head.

"The harpoon went right through it!" Jin yelled. Her hopes fell.

"How?" she thought aloud. She desperately tried to remember something, anything about them that might help them out of this. Then it struck her. "Aim for one of its eyes!" It was their only weakness, one of her master's had taught her.

"We are almost there! Keep shooting, Jin! Princess—remain low!"

"C'mon...get over here..." The Guard was incredibly brave, Pingyang thought.

"I see it! It's under the boat—get ready to shoot when it comes up!"

She closed her eyes—as though that would make a difference—and once again hoped for Jin's aim to be true. She clung to the rail as the ferry rocked again, tilting upwards, then landing hard. She heard a loud *crack*.   That couldn't be good.

"There!" A *whizzing* noise flew over her head, followed by a loud primal scream, then a loud splash. The boat rocked heavily side to side.

"Well done, Jin!" Quan whooped and she cheered.

"Princess! Are you badly injured? Let me help you up." Quan helped her off the deck and onto her seat.

"You're bleeding!" Jin panted heavily as he came to her side.

"I will be fine. Are we almost there?" This was her first time on any kind of vessel, and after this experience, her last.

"Yes, Princess. We are in the shallow water now. The tide will let us glide onto the shore," Quan said. She was immensely grateful for that.

"Here, let me wipe your face, Princess." She felt Jin clean her off, but her face still felt sticky. It would have to do for now. "When we get to the prison, I will demand of the High Warden that they allow you to bathe and clean up." She was happy to hear that. Going this long without bathing made her feel filthier than she had ever felt before, especially with all the dried blood.

"Well done, Quan, for saving our lives. I did not think it was possible for this boat to go so fast, but you did it. The Emperor will hear of your heroic effort, you have my word." Jin sounded giddier than ever.

"I am honoured. I will not forget that it was your aim that drove the Shuǐlóng back into the ocean either. Truly a team effort." She wished she could tell her father about both their acts of bravery. They deserved great rewards.

Minutes passed in silence, and then she felt the ferry gently slow to a stop. They had reached their destination, Justice Island. The woman's prison. She felt a cold shiver run up her spine. She had heard of this place, where women go, never to be seen again. She assumed that her father would have sent word ahead of their arrival via Dragon Messenger. In any case, she would find out very soon.

"Good luck, Princess. When you are cured of your...affliction, I would be honoured to give you a ride back to the side that leads home," Quan said, and reached over and took her hand, giving it a gently squeeze.

"Thank you, Quan, for saving my life and being an honourable man. I will always remember your kindness and hope to meet you again one day." She liked Quan and wished she could stay with him, but she knew she could not.

"Take my hand, Princess. We have many steps until we are at the top of prison, where the High Warden is waiting for us. Thank you again, Quan, for getting us here safely. I shall be back in a bit." She held out her hand and felt Jin grab it, and they disembarked the ferry together.

She felt the water hit her ankles. It was cold, but she did not mind. It felt good. She did not know what was going to happen next, so every second that was not inside the prison was to be cherished. She took in the ocean's smell and stopped walking.

"Princess, what is wrong?"

She did not answer. She twirled around with her arms flying in the air. "Princess?" Jin said again. At this moment, she felt freer than she had ever been in her life. She knew she looked crazy, but she did not care. When she was starting to feel a little dizzy, she stopped. The moment had past, as wonderous as it was.

She held out her arm. Jin took it, and they continued walking. She would not let her circumstances lower her spirit any longer. She would rise above. She had a destiny far greater than any other could imagine. As they walked up the stairs, she tripped forwards a few times, but Jim always managed to catch her fall.

"What does this place look like? If I am to spend the rest of my life here, I would like to have an image of it." She hoped Jin would understand her need to feel more acquainted with her surroundings. They had other prisons throughout the lands—why did her father not send her to one of those places? Was he so ashamed of her that he sent her to the farthest prison in the land from him?

"The prison sits on an island, as you know. It was built during Emperor Hitorachai's rule many generations ago for women who had originally committed crimes against the Empire or where born...*unnatural*. I guess it does not really matter, I guess. No one has ever left this place once they entered it. Yet I have faith you will, Princess. There is an...aura of sorts around you. Now, walk to your right, Princess. As I was saying, the current High Warden has run this place for the past thirty years. It is a tradition that is passed down from generation to generation; they know the place better than anyone else, as the family has been here since its creation. The High Warden can answer these questions far better than I can, if he chooses to, of course. What most people know is that the prison can hold up to a hundred prisoners, though it has never held that many at once, from what I am told. The worst offenders are kept in their cells in the lower part of the jail and are not allowed to speak to anyone. You get your meals through a slot in the door. I have heard that the Chief Chef is quite excellent, so there is that. I will admit that I would not want to be a... guest here." *Who would?* She did not want to be here. Why was he telling her these things? "I have heard that the criminals do chores around the prison, such as cleaning, laundry, and emptying out the buckets," Jin said as they came to a stop.

"I am Jin, personal guard to Emperor Gaozu and escort of his daughter, Princess Pingyang. We are here to see the High Warden." She wondered who Jin was taking to, until she heard a female voice reply, "You may enter. The High Warden is expecting you." She felt her arm being gently pulled, and they started to walk in silence. She heard a loud knock in front of her and a male voice call out, "Enter." At the sound of the door opening, she held her breath.

"I am Jin," Jin repeated. "Personal guard to Emperor Gaozu. I present his daughter to you, Princess Pingyang. She is to remain as your ward until such a time as you can determine that she no longer has her affliction, or you receive a summons from Emperor Gaozu stating that a husband has been found for her. Then she is to be released and sent back to the Emperor immediately. Do you have any questions about this, High Warden?"

The High Warden replied in his penetrating tone, "No questions, Personal Imperial Guard Jin. I witnessed the attack from the window. Thank you for bringing her safely to me."

"I take my leave of you, High Warden, but I do have two requests: first, that the Princess be allowed to bathe and be checked for injuries. Second, I confess I have always wanted to see what the prison looked like on the inside. May I take a few moments to look around? I will not be long, as Chi is waiting for me on the other side to return to the Imperial Palace."

There was a moment of silence, and she heard the High Warden's reluctant agreeance. "Of course. Please give Emperor Gaozu my best wishes, that his reign be as many years long as there are lights in the night sky." *The High Warden is a smooth talker.*

"Thank you, High Warden, I shall gladly pass your message along to our Emperor." Jin gave her hand a slight squeeze before he let go. She heard his footsteps slowly vanish, leaving her all alone with the High Warden. She stood in silence, waiting for him to say something but heard only his loud breathing. And she instinctively knew she did not like him—at all.

"Welcome to your new home, Princess Pingyang. There are some rules that you should be aware of that will make your life more bearable, until such time you are to be married...or no longer afflicted by your...condition. Your father sent an incredibly detailed letter about what happened. I admit, I saw the Soul Moon Convergence myself, but I do not have the same belief as you do and perhaps that is why I do not have a soulmate. I must admit part of me envies you, while on the flip side, pities you. That is my own opinion, however, which has no bearing on anything." She tried to keep her facial expression neutral, not speaking. *The man loves the sound of his own voice.*

"The first rule is whatever is asked of you, you do, no question asked. The second rule is to not create any trouble with any of the other prisoners. Though, I suspect you will not cause very much trouble, as you cannot see. You will be confined to your area of the prison, which is for the older prisoners. Your primary task will be to sweep and wash the floors; the current cleaner has not been performing as well as she has in the past. Perhaps her old age has affected her ability. You will learn everything about your tasks from her—her name is Mulan. Even though you are the Emperor's daughter, you will still be held to a certain standard, and if you fail to meet that standard, there will be consequences. I understand your blindness is a hindrance. Once you memorize every nook and cranny in this place, you will be as efficient as if you had working eyes. Do you understand?"

"Yes."

The High Warden pressed her. "If you have any questions, now is the time to ask them, as once you leave this office, we will likely not speak again. Here is your chance."

"Do you think it is right that I was sent here? I have committed no crimes." Silence fell again, and she wondered what was going through the High Warden's mind.

"No one here has committed any crimes, Princess. Women are sent here because the Empire has determined that they learned something they should not have. Or been in the wrong place at the wrong time, nothing to straight up murder them yet need to be disappeared. All the hardened, real criminals are in other prisons scattered throughout the lands. If you had done something truly terrible, you would be there."

She gasped, stunned at the revelation. "Everyone here is innocent?"

"Yes, Princess. The prisoners here are the ones the Empire is ashamed of."

She stood there, not sure what to think. Her heart sank; her father had no compassion after all. "I have one more question, High Warden. Why are you telling me this?"

"Because you will learn it in time anyway. I would never tell a common prisoner this. As you are not common, you deserve the truth." Pingyang stood there still shocked at what was revealed to her. She was lost for words and stood there immobilized by the truth.

"Goodbye, Princess." She heard him snap his fingers and the sound of footsteps rush forward. She realized they had not been alone.

"Mulan. Take her and train her to sweep and mop the floors. If the Princess does not meet my expectations, there will be consequences for both of you. But first, make sure she is cleaned up. A Princess should not be so filthy."

"Yes, High Warden." Her tight voice was rougher than most women. Pingyang felt a calloused hand grab her shoulder, then steer her away. She nearly tumbled down the stairs as she was brought to whatever fate was in store for her. She wished that Vladimir was here to rescue her, she thought just before walking straight into a wall. She cried out in pain.

"Quit your crying, we have work to do," Mulan snapped.

She swallowed the tears that fell to her lips as she was led away to her new life of suffering and misery.

***

Jin left the room feeling horrible for the Princess. She deserved a better father than this. Though, it was not his place to speak ill of matters that were not his own.

He scurried down the stairs. He did not have much time to complete his secondary mission. He had been fortunate that the High Warden had agreed; it certainly would have looked suspicious if he had not. He was, after all, a personal Imperial Guard that reported directly to the Emperor. He did not know specifically where he was going, as he had been given vague directions. Just that he needed to go the isolated cells, which were in the left wing of the prison, where someone awaited him.

For most of the trip, all he had thought about was this mission. He could not be caught. The Princess's life was at stake. Not to mention, the mountain of atria that had been promised to him. From what he was told, the Princess would need certain abilities that were unnatural to find her soulmate. *Soulmate.* All this had been truly remarkable, and a part of him was thankful he was involved.

Turning a corner, the corridor broke left, leading straight down to the person who awaited him. He had heard whispers of this woman, but never imagined he would meet her, yet here he was, walking toward her cell—Zing-Ho's cell—to complete his mission.

He truly hoped Duchess Dou knew what she was doing.

Chapter 26

The Quintessence

'Soul Food'

Vladimir Drăculeşti felt wet sandpaper rubbing against his cheek. He slowly opened his eyes, wondering if he was still alive. A large, brownish cat was looking down at him, licking his face. Surprisingly, his body did not hurt. Getting onto his elbows, he looked around to see he was in a bedroom. It was a teal color, with weird paintings on the walls of horses with a horn on their foreheads. *Odd, horses don't have horns.*

He was laying on a bed and covered in wool blankets. He felt his face, still expecting it to be in pain, but it felt fine. He felt fine. *Why was he fine?* He moved to sit up and ran his fingers through his hair. Had everything just been a wild, crazy dream? He glanced over at the cat. Not a dream after all. Whose bedroom was he in? The last thing he remembered was...

His mother. Anguish washed over him over, as the image of carrying her dead body flooded his memory. All he felt was grief and guilt. He had not been there to protect her. If only he had listened to his father, he never would have talked to Pingyang. Thinking of this past day's events, he was utterly conflicted in his emotions. Did Kazia escape the carnage?

"Meow." The cat was now seated on the bed, gazing at him. It was the largest cat he had ever seen. Something in its eyes warned him, "Don't mess with me." And he did not want to. He needed to find his mother for a proper burial. He slipped out of bed and got dressed, spotting his clothes neatly folded and smelling fresh. He felt his shoulder where the sword had pierced it, and it felt completely fine. There wasn't even a wound? He felt his face and it seemed...fine. Why was he not dead? Someone had taken pity on him. Of course, he was happy that he was alive. He decided to leave the room and thank whoever had saved him.

He grabbed the small piece of rope and pulled the wooden door back slowly and peeked through: it was a room filled with wooden tables of all shapes and size, with large, cushiony chairs placed around them; at the centre of the back wall was a bulky black fireplace, a fire roaring inside. No one else was in the room. Something brushed his leg; the cat *meowed* loudly as it pranced by him and ran across the floor and through a door.

Something caught his nose's attention—something delicious. His tummy rumbled in hunger as he walked into the room, peering around, wondering if he should sit down. He walked over to the immense three-paneled window to scan his surroundings, but only saw a white light in the distance. He felt it beckoning him. He took a step toward the door, but a female voice in a strange accent startled him. "If you go outside and head toward the light, you won't get a chance to taste some of my chicken soup. That would be a shame, indeed."

He turned around and saw an older woman behind a counter. She had plump, freckled face and had her red hair in a bun. She looked about the same age as his mother. She wore a plain green apron over a teal top that matched her unusual teal eyes, which pierced his soul.

Appearing as though out of nowhere, the cat jumped up on the counter and purred loudly, rubbing its face against the woman's arm. She laughed and said, "Get outta my kitchen, Hunter, mangy old cat." The cat let out another *meow* as he stubbornly stretched out onto the counter, his blue-violet eyes on him.

"What is that?" he asked, pointing at the furry creature.

The woman gave a chuckle. "That's Hunter, my cat. He goes out and does all the hunting for me. He always catches what he sets his keen eyes on, so remember that if you ever find yourself running from him."

Looking at Hunter, he got the feeling that she was not joking, and the cat was more deadly than it let on. He decided it would be best if he did not find himself in its sights.

"Where am I?" The woman smiled as she stirred whatever was cooking up in the large metal pot. He sniffed the air; the marjoram and onions smelled tantalizing. Better than his mother's, and that was saying something.

"Where are you? That seems to be the question. First, I am going to let you answer your question, and then we will compare. So, where do you think you are?" The smile on her face lingered, and Vladimir noticed just how mysterious it was. He wondered why and looked over at the window. There was a path going from the brown wooden door to the light; where had it come from?

He remembered the pain he felt from the sword that had pierced him, as well as the punch to the face that nearly killed him. Yet he had no visible wounds, and his clothes were clean, which made about as much sense as being here, in this place.

As he stood there, a terrifying thought hit him. He was dead, and this is where one stops before moving on. That was the only explanation.

The woman was still stirring her pot, looking at him curiously. He knew he was going to die one day but did not expect death to be a cook in a kitchen. "Am I…dead?" he asked, dreading the answer. Perhaps it was better that he was dead. His family was surely gone, and all he had was Princess Pingyang, who he had no idea how to find. He hoped he would see his dad and brothers in the afterlife, especially his mother, so he could spend an eternity begging for her forgiveness. He remembered carrying her body and tears streamed down his cheeks like raging rivers of sorrow. "Where is my mother?" he asked. He needed to know. He needed her forgiveness.

"No. You are not dead, but if you wanted, you could open the door and follow the path to the light. As for your mother, she will not come here. Her path is…different," she said, lifting her wooden spoon to her mouth. "Little more pepper, I think."

"What do you mean, my mother's path is different? I need to bury her!"

"Your mother's path I cannot describe other than unnatural. Just think, though—no more pain if you choose the light. But if you go back, you will suffer; what you feel inside of you, the guilt and loss. Not to mention the bodily pain from your injuries. You sure you really want to go back to that?"

The thought was not appealing to him. The woman took another taste. "Perfecto. If you want some, I suggest you grab a seat, and I promise it will put some hair on your chest and make you feel a thousand times better." His tummy rumbled at the fragrant chicken soup. He sat down and watched as the woman grabbed a bowl and filled it up with chicken soup and added a large wheat bun on the side. She placed it in front of him, along with a tall glass of water, and sat down across from him.

"My diner is the Quintessence. In extraordinary situations, someone caught between life and death might come here. They are presented with a choice to go either way. Often, they choose the path to the light, as it is the easier way. Some of their lives are so horrible that death is the only relief for them. If they choose to go on, I offer them a good last meal. It varies from person to person—for you, I made a hearty bowl of chicken soup. It's good for the soul," she said, giving him a wink.

He had to admit, with every sip, he felt his spirits lift and his strength returning. He could not remember the last time he tasted anything this good.

He felt incredibly thirsty for some reason. As he gulped down his glass, the woman got up to bring over a large wooden jug of water. "You have lost a lot of blood, that's why you're parched."

Blood. He was here but not *here*; his body was lying on the ground somewhere, bleeding next to his dead mother. His mind struggled to comprehend everything that had happened to him in such a short period of time. "Who are you?" he asked, realizing he did not know her name. He wanted to thank her for the soup properly, especially if she was also going to save his life—if he wanted saving. The thought of death also had its appeal.

She smiled at him. "I was beginning to wonder about you Drăculeşti men. When your father was here many moons ago, he was the exact same way. Did not properly ask who I was until he was here for quite a while. He, too, had been gravely injured. I am Ksenia." Absently, she scratched the cat's chin, who was making a kind of purring noise but not quite.

"What happened to my father?" Vladimir did not know much about his father's battles. Any story about his father would be welcome. Especially now. He could tell she was choosing her words.

"Ah yes," she said after a long pause. "There was an ambush by the Spiriduș on a caravan that your father was with. He managed to take most of them down, but was attacked from behind, viciously. But you know how tough a Drăculești is. His attacker was the leader of the Spiriduș at the time, and I believe he still is... Preslav." The Spiriduș. They were a scourge on the land. They were masters of ambushing. They needed to pay for everything that they had done and needed to be stopped before more innocent lives were destroyed. But it was more than that now. There was a mysterious threat that needed to be dealt with first.

"I see you have made your choice. It did not take your father long either," Ksenia said, getting up to refill his soup bowl and water.

He nodded. "It was never really a choice. This unexpected attack by those...abominations. They need to be destroyed. There is also someone that I need to find who is especially important to me." He took another bite of the scrumptious bun.

"Quite the tasks you got there for someone so young. But I know who you are and where you come from, so I understand." She got up to clear his place setting.

"Thank you, Ksenia, for the soup and the water, you have been most kind. I do not think I would still be alive if not for you." As Ksenia flashed him one last smile, he slid out of the booth and walked over to the front door.

It swung open just as a man and a woman were entering the diner. *Who were these people? Were they almost dead too?* The man, who was extremely tall, looked down at him with a grim look. "Look, Jessica—another Drăculești. They just don't seem to know how to die like everyone else. Darndest thing. You see, it's stuff like this that makes me hate coming to this land." *They didn't act like people that were on the verge of death,* he thought.

His companion rolled her eyes. "Please excuse Sam. He gets grumpy when things do not go his way, which is like every time we deal with a Drăculești. Your *viskta* just doesn't die like everyone else…for the most part. My name is Jessica, by the way. And yes, we know who you are, Vladimir Drăculești."

How did they know who he was? "Don't mind them, Vladimir." Ksenia said, appearing beside him. "They are Reapers. They find the souls of those that have died and help them move on to the next stage of their journey. Whether to the light, or the darkness."

Reapers? Vladimir had never heard of such a thing before. "What do you mean, the Drăculești don't die like everyone else?" *Was it possible his family was still alive somehow?*

Jessica smiled and patted his shoulder, which nearly turned to ice at her touch. "It doesn't matter. What is done is done. I am guessing you made your choice, haven't you Vladimir? Good for you." He shivered. His shoulder was still cold.

Ksenia rubbed it soothingly. "That is 'death's touch' that you are feeling. It is a good thing that you are not quite alive, or else you would not be here anymore." Vladimir glanced outside the window and saw the light. Was that where he would have gone after what he had just done to Sasha? He had attacked him and drank his blood. *Drank his blood!* Nausea came over him. He covered his mouth with his hand as he tried to swallow the bile that was rising in his throat. Choking it back down, he took two long strides to the water jug on the table and drank straight from it. He let out a few drawn-out breaths. He felt a little better.

"That did not look pleasant," Sam said. Vladimir shook his head.

"What happened?" Ksenia asked, concern in her voice.

They had just met—he was not comfortable divulging his dark thoughts to strangers. "Maybe gas or something." Gauging the disbelief on everyone's faces, he knew no one believed him.

"It is okay. You owe us no explanation," Jessica said. He was thankful he did not have to go into detail. He was not sure he could. Would anyone even believe him?

A realization struck him. He was sitting in a diner on the brink of death, talking to Reapers, and just had the most delicious bowl of chicken soup. Perhaps he really was dead. All this was just some sort of crazy…? Words could not explain what he was thinking. "I need to go," he finally said, and headed back towards the door.

"Bye," Sam said to him in a rather nasty tone.

"It was a pleasure to meet you, Vladimir," Jessica said kindly, unlike her rude counterpart. "I hope you manage to do everything you need to do." To Vladimir's surprised, she reached over and gave him a quick hug. He felt his face go red. Jessica was quite…gorgeous. Even though his body was nearly frozen from her hug, his insides warmed himself quite nicely.

"Now look what you did, he is going to leave here with that stupid grin on his face. Who knows how long it will be frozen on his face."

Vladimir wished he could chomp on Sam's neck. But if Jessica's touch was any indication of what she was capable of, he knew that would be a bad idea.

Ksenia linked her arms with his and steered him to the door. She stopped and gave him a big hug, then whispered in his ear, "When you wake up, your physical injuries will remain. You will still be on the brink of death. Remember that there is still hope. You have tasted human blood." He started to pull away when he heard what she said. *How did she know?* "It's okay, Vladimir. It is part of who you are. By drinking blood, you have activated the Drăculeşti part inside of you. Which means you will heal, slowly. If you want to heal faster, you will need more of it. A lot more—from any man or creature. The blood of the living will render you stronger, faster than you can imagine. The blood from the dead will sustain you until you can get living blood. You have a great many things you need to accomplish. Remember, there are allies everywhere. Even in places where you least expect. Good luck, Vladimir Drăculeşti. Go find your Princess."

How did she know everything? He nodded and opened the door, staring ahead at the dirt path that split in two different directions: one that led to the light, and one that twisted away from it, leading to what looked like the entrance of the maze at the back of their castle. *Odd.* "Will I ever see you again?"

"No matter how special someone is, no one ever comes back here twice." He let that sink in for a moment. This had been his bonus chance—there would not be another.

"Thank you, Ksenia. For everything" And he stepped through the door, making his way down the path toward the maze.

Instantly, his body was bombarded with pain. He wanted to cry out, but his face refused to cooperate. He attempted to move; none of his muscles flinched. He thought he had been in pain before. This was something beyond pain. An excruciating stench overwhelmed him. He covered his nose and tried to get up but lost his grip, tumbling over dead bodies. His body rocked with wave after wave of pain with every contact he made as he rolled. Thankfully, he eventually stopped, landing on his stomach. He did not know how long he lay there. He attempted to open his eyes several times, but it hurt too much.

"Please…give me strength to go on." He laid there for what seemed an eternity trying to block out the image of the dead bodies, gradually regaining his strength. When his mind finally begun to clear, the stench returned, too overpowering to ignore, and he nearly vomited. He needed to get up. At a snail's pace, he got to his elbows, then up on his knees. His body still screamed in protest—but he had to get up and move. He looked around. He could barely see out of one of his eyes still. He was afraid to touch the area and didn't want to know how badly it was damaged.

Finally, he was on his feet. He stood there gingerly, not fully comprehending what he was seeing. When he had been tumbling over the bodies it had been terrible, but the amount of dead bodies had not dawned on him until standing there! The sheer horror struck him as he collapsed back to his knees, retching at the sight: the bodies of dead villagers were piled up like items ready for shipment. He couldn't look anymore. He stumbled backwards and took off, wanting nothing more than to get away from the nightmare before him.

Ksenia's words came back to him: *dead blood could sustain him.* He stopped in his tracks and turned around, forcing himself to look at the pile of dead bodies. There was a lot of blood there—blood that could keep him going. There were large pools of dirty blood all over. Blood of the villagers blended. Could Tomas and Erik's blood be in there? He didn't want to take the chance of drinking a friend's blood. It would haunt him forever if he knew that he had. He looked around; he was near the edge of the Dark Woods. There were living creatures in there. Perhaps he could kill one instead. He started walking, and movement caught his attention. There was a rabbit hopping at the edge of the woods.

He took a deep breath and darted toward the rabbit—he found himself flat on his face. He couldn't catch a slow-moving donkey if his life depended on it…and it did. He felt his stomach get warm, and he reached down to feel it up. His hand came up with wet blood. *Ta la me.*

He didn't have the strength to get up, so he rolled over and started crawling back toward the corpses. The stench intensified as he neared, but he no longer cared. He needed to live. It felt like it had taken a lifetime to get there, but at last, he made it. There were a lot of familiar faces that he saw. His heart broke at the sight of seeing the kids he had grown up with.

Why? Why had this happened?

He spotted large puddles on the ground around the pile-up. Their collective blood. He closed his eyes, pounding the ground, consumed by anger. None of this was fair.

Still on his hands and knees, he inched toward the largest pool of blood. He reached down and scooped up blood into his hand. He stared at it. It was slightly brown—it was not clean. Glancing over at the corpses, he decided this was the better of the two options. He threw it into his mouth, though most of it landed on his face. As the blood dripped down into his body, he felt a small surge inside of him. This would work.

He scooped more handfuls and proceeded to drink as much as he could. When he felt satiated, he lay there for a few minutes; he was beginning to feel better. It *was* working. He felt his strength return and vision clear in his bad eye, though not entirely. He touched it, the skin was still bruised and tender. He had stopped bleeding, at least. He knew he still needed something fresh…living blood.

He was still exhausted, but he was able to move now; gradually, he got up to his feet and looked out to what was once his village. There were no flames from where he could see, but smoke still rose from it. How devastating; he was sure there were dozens of smaller fires still going throughout the village. He looked up at the castle, his home. Most of the grey stone had been charred black from the fires that raged out of it. It was also partially collapsed. His family…gone forever. His village…destroyed beyond belief.

He spied movement in the distance. He focused in and he saw a massive, thick clay creature. Instinctively, he touched the spot where the creature's fist had hit him. "Ow," he murmured, remembering what the impact felt like. The area was swarming with creatures. Too many for him to take on by himself. He would need help.

The Sentinels. If he could rally them, he stood a chance in reclaiming the village. Hope rose inside of him. Yes—he would lead the charge. As he walked closer to the edge of the burnt farmer's field, he stopped at the sight of a face that was much, much too familiar. *Kazia.*

Her body was near the bottom of the pile. He walked over to it and dropped to his knees. He ran his fingers through her dirtied, bloodied hair. His heart felt as if it had been shattered into a million pieces. He wept so profusely, he almost failed to notice that half her neck was ripped off.

There were bite marks on it—human bite marks. She had not been killed by the attackers, but viciously by one of his own family members! He saw Mr. Hendrick's body in the distance and laid Kazia's head back to rest and moved toward her father. He looked at the man's neck, and he too had bite marks; these were large and much deeper. His father had killed this man, which meant one of his brothers killed Kazia.

Why Kazia and her father? They knew how much he had liked her. There had to have been another person they could have killed to spare them. He pounded the ground hard with his fists in anger and sadness. He looked at Kazia again and saw above her Sasha's dead face. *He had killed Sasha!* He hadn't planned on it – it just happened. He couldn't control it. If he couldn't control the urge, then he doubted they could too. Anger was replaced with frustration. It hadn't been their fault as killing Sasha's wasn't his. It was just their nature.

He wanted to bury all the victims, but he did not have any tools. Nor could he go into the village and search for any, for fear of being caught. He could not stay here, either— he needed to go find the Sentinels. Where might they be gathering for a counterattack? They would have to follow him—he was the last surviving member of the ruling *vistka*. His father's words came to him, how he feared that the Sentinels and the Spiriduş were working together. Suddenly, the idea of finding a group of Sentinels did not appeal to him so much. Since he was the last ruling member of his household, that meant if he died, it would be open game for the leadership of the land.

Just because his village was destroyed did not mean that the rest of the villages were. They could still come together. Nevertheless, the best fighters were the Sentinels. Even if he could convince people to follow him, they did not have weapons, nor know how to fight. Neither did he, really. Though, if he could get his hands on a spear, it would be a different story. He remembered hearing a story of a legendary spear, Gáe Dearg, meaning Red Death.

If the Sentinels were out of the question, what other option did he have left? He remembered what Nevada had done. The lengths he went through to save those that he loved. He didn't have any brothers left. Kazia was dead. The villagers were all dead.

He looked back over at the village. He had to do something before another village was taken. There had to be another way. His mind jumped to Pingyang. She was…he had no idea where she was, other than a vague general direction. His eye started throbbing again. The effects of the blood were wearing off, though he was not hurting as much.

The only other solution he could think of lay with the Spiriduş. *Infiltrate them and do what?* He remembered his father saying they must have camps somewhere, from which they were operating. If he could find one of the camps and join them, perhaps there was a chance after all. If he could challenge for leadership of the camp and win…

A wide smile spread across his face, and he started laughing. He couldn't stop laughing at the sheer madness of it all. The effort hurt him, but he didn't care. He started walking around in small circles, trying to figure out the order of things he needed to do. Find his families' bodies and bury them properly. Infiltrate the nearest Spiriduş camp, find a legendary spear, challenge for leadership of said camp, free his village…and that was the easy stuff.

He also needed to find Pingyang. There, he was at a complete loss for where to begin. But there was one thing that concerned him even more.

Who was the Specter, and why was he such a threat to him?